THROUGH BLOOD AND DRAGONS

THE FORGED AND THE FALLEN - BOOK 1

R.M. SCHULTZ

SKY SEA AND SWORD PUBLISHING

CONTENTS

To all those who still dare to read and tread the worlds of imagination.

BY R.M. SCHULTZ

The Forged and The Fallen

Novels
Through Blood and Dragons
Through Fire and Shadow

Novella
The Taming and The Betrayal

NORTH CIMEREN

SOUTH CIMEREN

LAKE ON FIRE

N

THE SPIRES

EVENMERES

ANGOIRS

MARCHLANDS

NEVERGRACE

CASTLE SCYNE

HORMOON

BRANSHEER

THE OLD OAK

SCYNE

BEACON TOWER

SCYTHERIN WETTERMORES

SERFELL

KINGSWOOD SILVERSTONE

THE STRETCH

VELEN

ETTEL THE CONSTEELS

ISLE OF WOLVES

WESTORN SOMERREN

BELVENGUARD

FOLISARN KEEP

SILWOOD RVLEEN

SCONE RIVER

BROKENTORR ORVLLON

ARROW LAKE

REPUNTER BAY

THE VEE

SOUTHROAD

LAKE DISTREL

TRASTEN

SILVERBOW SILVERROAD

CITADEL OF THE MOONS

LYNDEN

STORMARK BAY

FROGTOWN

KISTENGROVE

STORMWATCH

MOUNTAIN OF TITANS

BARSTEL FOOTHILLS

TABLU

EVENTIDE SEA

SARZUTH

CRUE ROAD

WESTERN ERDLANDS

RORENLANDS

EASTERN ERDLANDS

SOUTHERN ISLES

JARDOOR

WESTERN RUN

LIGHTNING MOUNTRIN CISARN

EMERALD TOWER

PROLOGUE

Turin Bolenmane

TURIN CLENCHED HIS MOUNTED CROSSBOW AS THE DRAGON beneath him swooped over the peaks. The frigid wind of the north blasted his face and clawed at his blond hair and beard before streaming his cloak out behind him.

Sir Mirell, the dragonguard seated just behind the rose dragon's head, released a cry of alarm. The newly appointed dragonmage behind Mirell peeked around the guard's massive armor and shield and angled their flying mount closer to the scene. Their dragon screamed over the slopes, skimming just above rock and ice.

"There!" Mirell pointed.

Below, on the pass, the Murgare king—with his gold and platinum crown—hurried along beside his queen. Several dragons lay dead around them, as did a field of armored men.

The king's massive ice dragon shrieked, an echoing blast that rang the surrounding peaks and rolled away into the north. The dragon flapped wings like curtains of frozen leather as the king and queen rushed for their saddles.

Distant calls sounded, those of man and dragon.

"Another of their legions will be arriving soon," Sir Mirell shouted back as their dragon wheeled over a ravine. "Make sure the king does not escape."

Turin pivoted his crossbow around in its frame atop their dragon's back, the harness anchoring him to the quarterdeck biting into his legs and waist. Their rose dragon's wings lifted and then fell, leaving Turin with an unobstructed view of the ice dragon.

After swiveling his crossbow by subtler degrees and slighter angles than before, he sighted down the steel shaft of the dragonbolt. He squeezed the trigger handle toward the tiller. The crossbow's rope snapped forward, and the bolt launched and whistled as it knifed through the air.

A thud sounded as the bolt impaled the pure white scales of the ice dragon's chest. The dragon roared and threw its head back, spewing its frozen breath into the sky as Turin's dragon sailed nearer.

"One bolt is not enough to stop such a beast," Turin muttered to himself. "Unless it was a perfect shot."

Their rose dragon shielded its riders from the blast of icy breath, and they whipped around for another pass. The force of the turn threw Turin outward toward the open sky, but his harness and anchored bootstraps pulled him back to the quarterdeck.

Distant shouting from dragons and men grew louder. And closer.

"Hurry, now!" Sir Mirell shouted.

Turin retrieved another dragonbolt and wound the windlass, which drew the crossbow's rope back. The metal arms of the crossbow creaked with tension as he glanced in the direction of the tumult and approaching legion. Still nothing but sky and clouds showed above the peaks.

The rose dragon's wings lifted again and obscured Turin's view of most of the world. Then their mount seemed to drop out from underneath him, and they plunged downward. Turin's stomach catapulted up into his throat as his harnesses yanked him down with the plummeting beast.

The crossbow cocked, its rope locking into place, and the windlass lever in Turin's hand stopped turning. Ahead, Sir Mirell angled his dragonlance as they plunged toward the pass.

The Murgare king held his queen by the arm, and they raced along, almost to their dragon's side now. The ice dragon whipped its head about and roared, exposing the back of its neck. A dragonmage was not seated on the king's beast.

Without their mage, the royals won't be able to guide their mount. "We may yet be able to capture both the Murgare king and queen." Turin grinned ruefully as he angled his crossbow downward and pivoted to track his target points on the writhing ice dragon.

Except for the loss of far more dragons and men than they had hoped for, this day could still work out as planned. As long as they could take the king and queen and flee this pass before whatever legion was coming sailed over the eastern peaks.

Instead, a sun dragon wheeled out of the west and swung down toward the pass.

"Sir Paltere will carry the royals back to Galvenstone." Sir Mirell pointed to the approaching sun dragon. "But we'll have to buy him more time."

The rose dragon dived and barreled downward toward the king's ice beast with escalating momentum. Far too much momentum.

Turin strained to the side, fighting to see around the broad

Sir Mirell and his massive shield as the dragonguard realigned his lance.

With their trajectory, the guard would impale the ice dragon and leave the king and queen utterly stranded, at least for the moment. But they didn't need to continue increasing their speed, as the ice dragon was weakened and still earthbound. Also, the king's mage didn't appear to be nearby and was likely one of the many victims littering the pass. The ice dragon would remain nothing more than a wild beast.

Turin pivoted around in his circular frame, but he couldn't find a clear shot without potentially hitting his dragonmage or Mirell or Mirell's shield.

The king raced in a mad dash for his dragon, probably the only salvation he could imagine amidst the death surrounding him. But Turin and Mirell were going to beat the king to his destination.

Their rose dragon roared and lowered its head. Sir Mirell angled his lance in its mount, aiming along their dragon's path. All too quickly, the frost-covered pass and the blurring ice dragon swept up toward them. Turin braced for impact.

But at the last second, their dragon careened right. Sir Mirell's lance veered with the burst of movement.

As the king ran, Mirell's lance skewered the king through his torso. His body was wrenched up off the ground and onto the lance as the rose dragon twisted and turned, its feet and talons clomping on ice, its wings flapping wildly in an attempt to brace against the wind. The dragon ran in huge sweeping strides, as it had come in far too fast for a proper landing.

"No!" Mirell yelled.

Turin's heart sent a rush of cold blood spewing through his chest. *That was* not *how this was supposed to go.*

The frost dust of the pass engulfed them in a cloud and took a moment to settle. The Murgare king's body lay limp on the lance, his head hanging over his shoulder. Blood lacquered the dragonsteel of Sir Mirell's weapon.

The queen screamed as she stopped and stood still, her fists clenching. The ice dragon roared and faced them.

Turin wheeled his crossbow about and squeezed its trigger. Another dragonbolt tore away and struck the ice dragon in the rear leg.

The beast roared in pain and hobbled away, thrashing its wings. Sir Mirell gasped as he clambered out of his saddle.

"The king is dead," the dragonmage said evenly, now able to see directly ahead without Mirell's bulk in his way.

"I... I." Mirell stepped onto the ground and looked up at the king's body, lifting his visor. The guard's face was pale and drawn. "I was aiming for the king's mount."

But they had veered aside at the last moment. Turin studied the dragonmage, someone he did not know before today. Sir Paltere's sun dragon thumped onto the pass behind them.

The queen slowly backed away, but she did not turn to flee. Whether that was because of terror or grief or rage, Turin could only speculate.

"What have you done?" Sir Paltere said as he hurried toward them and the Murgare queen, his voice cracking, his words riddled with disbelief. "There will be hell to pay for this. After all we have already suffered this day. Belvenguard has now lost its paramount bargaining chip."

Sir Paltere grabbed the Murgare queen by the arm, the pale skin of her cheeks appearing like snow, her bronze eyes shadowed but smoldering. "You must come with me, Queen." Sir Paltere tugged her along. "Or I will have to force you."

"Very well," the queen said in a quiet tone ripe with animosity. "But my legion is coming, and you will not escape this. The death of our king will mark the beginning of the end for all of Cimeren."

Sir Paltere grunted, and two of his dragonarchers ran over and helped him escort the queen to their sun dragon.

The roars of dragons sounded just beyond the peaks.

"Ride!" Sir Paltere helped seat the queen in the empty mage saddle behind him, and his archers took their posts upon the quarterdeck on the dragon's back. The sun dragon beat its massive wings, its scales glistening gold within a storm of swirling white frost.

"We will give you as long as we can." Sir Mirell's tone turned hollow and lifeless. He raised his visor and saluted Paltere by pulling his dragonsteel sword from its sheath. He angled the glowing rose blade downward, the back of his hand pressed to his forehead.

Sir Paltere slowly nodded, a last salute for bravery and regret for whatever ill luck had struck them in the end. "Until we meet again."

A moment drew out until the roar of dragons sounded, and dark shapes appeared along the horizon. Sir Paltere whirled his mount around, and they rose into the air.

Mirell angled his lance downward to discard the impaled king's body, but the corpse's limbs only waved in response.

"We need to get into the air," their dragonmage said. "Or the coming legion will simply smother us and chase after Paltere and their queen."

Mirell dismounted quickly and paced just past the rose dragon's snout. He gingerly tested the king's body by pushing on a boot hovering overhead. The body sagged to its left.

"I cannot touch the body of a king," Mirell said. "Even if it is one from Murgare. We also cannot fly toward the coming legion with their king's corpse dangling before us. It will enrage all the north."

"Then we are already dead." Turin unclasped his bootstraps and ripped his harness free from his waist. "And so is Sir Paltere."

Turin leapt down from the rose dragon's back instead of taking the rope ladder. His legs jarred when he landed on the frozen ground, and he stumbled to his knees, scraping them. He grunted and pushed himself up before marching toward their dragon's head. Once he stood beside the king's body, he grabbed it by the legs and dragged the body down the long length of the dragonlance. It slipped free and dropped onto the pass with a smack and a crunch.

The face of the Murgare king, his black beard salted with gray, stared blankly into the heavens and the sky sea, his eyes cloudy and dull.

Turin winced. "It had to be done."

"I can only imagine the rumormongering that would spread if they witnessed us coming at them with their king's body on our lance." The dragonmage shook his head.

Sir Mirell swung onto his saddle and took up his shield. Turin limped back to the rope ladder and hurriedly ascended its rungs. Once on the quarterdeck, he quickly hauled the ladder up and slipped it over its holding hooks. The rose dragon stretched its wings, roared, and lifted into the air.

"We will distract the coming legion by flying in the opposite direction as Sir Paltere," the dragonmage said. "Then we'll swing about and fly to somewhere in eastern Belvenguard. Nevergrace may be the closest outpost that can offer us protection."

"We will give Sir Paltere as much time as we possibly can." Sir Mirell swiveled his lance around in its mount, testing its mobility after the recent impact. "We owe him that. We owe all of Belvenguard that and much more. And we may end up owing every kingdom in Cimeren."

"I am not losing my life to buy them another minute or two," the dragonmage said. "That was not part of the deal when I was sent with you."

Even under his fur cloak and chainmail, Turin's skin rippled with cold. *This mage was sent here for a purpose. And* he *controls the dragon.* Visions of the dragon's late change in course stormed through his mind.

Sir Mirell whipped around and grabbed the mage by the throat. "We will fly directly at and then fight our way through this legion."

The mage swallowed and sneered.

"And if by the grace of the Dragon god we survive, then and only then may we think about returning." The dark look in Mirell's eyes made it obvious he did not ever intend to return to Galvenstone or anywhere in Belvenguard. He did not wish to live with the disgrace of what'd happened. Mirell pulled a dagger from his saddle and pressed its tip against the mage's chest.

"As you wish." The mage snarled.

Turin's mouth went as dry as a frosted tundra. *We will not return home.*

The rose dragon spiraled up higher into the sky as the roar of a dozen dragons blasted over the pass. Frost and fire and mist and storm dragons sailed toward them on sheets of leathery wings, the deafening shriek of the mist dragon ringing Turin's ears and causing his head to throb. Turin flinched and covered an ear with one hand as he worked at fastening his bootstraps. The harness about his waist was loose but would probably hold him to the archer's quarterdeck.

"A harness and bootstraps will no longer even matter," Turin muttered as he stood straight. He plucked another dragonbolt from a bundled stack on the quarterdeck and cranked the windlass until the steel arms of the crossbow creaked and its rope clicked into a locked position.

The rose dragon flapped higher and hovered in the air as the north's legion flew toward them but split apart like water around rock and surrounded them.

"Charge the one in the front," Mirell said, having discarded his shield for his dagger, which he lifted in a threatening manner for the mage to see. "Against this legion, may you die swiftly and without pain. But if I have to kill you, it will be the slow death of a dagger in the belly."

The mage tapped their dragon with his staff, and the rose dragon shrieked, flapped its massive wings, and raced toward the frost dragon before them. Sir Mirell angled his lance, the weapon still enameled with the blood of a dead king.

The dragonmage whimpered.

"Let's make them angrier at us." Turin swung about in the frame of his pivoting crossbow. "Directing their anger at us will give Paltere more time." When the rose dragon's pale red wings fell like a curtain, he was ready, and he launched his bolt directly into the head of a mist dragon.

The bolt sank into the beast's flared nostril, and the dragon squealed, threw its head back, and roared. A dozen dragons came at them all at once, their enemies' lances angled for them and their mount.

At least two dozen bolts tore through the air, impaling their dragon's rose scales as well as Sir Mirell's shoulder. The bolt that struck Sir Mirell punched its way through the dragonguard's armor and erupted from the front of his breastplate.

Sharp pain, and something akin to fire, struck Turin's foot and ankle. A bolt as long as he was tall impaled his limb and nailed it to the quarterdeck. Turin bellowed as he attempted to wind his windlass and reload his crossbow. But the rose dragon fell out from underneath him, and more bolts rained around them and pierced their dragon's hide as they plummeted.

The side of a cliff rose up and hit them with a deafening crash.

Or maybe the sound was the cracking of bones in Turin's ears, or the cracking of Turin's skull.

1

CYRAN ORENDAIN

CYRAN ORENDAIN WIPED ALONG THE SHAFT OF A DRAGONBOLT with an oiled cloth, polishing and rubbing a speckling of rust from the metal. The wooden stands supporting the bolt and a dragonlance by their ends creaked. He mopped sweat from his forehead with the back of his hand and brushed his dark locks from his face.

"And what does the letter say?" Brelle asked Dage as she worked beside Cyran on the windlass and thick metal arms of a crossbow. Brelle leaned over to peek at Dage's parchment, but Dage angled the message away from her as he read, his eyes rolling across whatever words lay under a broken seal. A seal of red wax. The color of Galvenstone—the city of the king.

Cyran stopped polishing and straightened. Such a message was not merely idle conversation.

Dage's grip tightened on the parchment, his knuckles whitening, the cords of muscle in his arms leaping out through a layer of fine hair. His eyes wandered as he read.

"You finally being summoned to become one of the guard?" Brelle brushed her curled sandy hair behind her ears and settled a hand on one of her prominent hips. She tapped her foot. After another few seconds without a response from Dage, Brelle snatched at the letter, but she only managed to tear a chunk from its edge as Dage ripped it from her grip.

"These words are for my eyes only." Dage's long blond hair waved over his shoulders.

"Easy, you two," Cyran said. "We cannot start fighting yet. After we get through the weapons, we still need to oil all the harnesses."

"It better be an offer to go and be inducted into the dragonguard," Brelle said. "You're the biggest and strongest of all us poor miserable squires at the once mighty Nevergrace. If any one of us would be asked to join the guard, I always said it would be you. And you don't make enough coin here to have more than a few drinks at summer's end. Not much reason to stay."

Cyran studied Dage—a much larger and more hulking young man then he was. Cyran scrubbed harder at the rust on the old lance, and images of himself taking up the weapon of the dragonguard stormed through his mind. If he were ever chosen, he would have the opportunity to spear their great enemies in the north from the back of a dragon. He would be clad in armor, wielding a great shield, a dragonsteel sword strapped to his waist. But he would gladly settle with eventually becoming a dragonarcher—the people of Cimeren considered all crossbowmen archers, and the mounted crossbows on a dragon could deal far more damage than any longbow wielded by a man.

One day... soon.

"Come." Laren, another dragonsquire of Sir Kayom's, strode out from behind a stone wall. He held two hand crossbows. "It's time."

"We're supposed to finish up here first," Cyran said.

"Then we won't have enough time for a hunt," Laren replied.

Cyran shrugged. "We're almost done with the weapons, but there's still all the harnesses to tend to."

"Oh, Cyran," Brelle said. "The soldiers and knights and guard are all still in the keep for the lord's passing. They will be in there till nightfall. So no one will notice if we're gone for a few hours."

"We can always finish our work tomorrow," Laren said. Even though he was a young man, he still carried a boyish face and grin, which now promised excitement. "It's not like there's war coming before then."

Cyran hesitated and stopped wiping the lance. He glanced at the bolt—as long as a guard's spear but with a shaft four times as big around. Three-pronged blades protruded from its head, all steel.

Dage folded up his message and tucked it into his belt.

"I brought the dogs." Laren whistled.

Three canines that were more wolf than dog came loping up from behind the wall, their tongues lolling, their breaths rasping.

The darkest and smallest one sighted Cyran, wagged his tail, and ran up to him. The wolf's eyes lit up as it licked his hand.

"Smoke," Cyran whispered as his heart softened, and he pet the head of the littlest and most tender of the bunch.

Brelle and Dage strode over to Laren, and the three all turned and headed north for the woods. The other two wolves followed them.

"We're going to miss you on this one." Brelle waved over her shoulder to Cyran as she hefted one of the crossbows.

Smoke bounded around, hopping on his fore and then rear legs as his green wolf eyes twinkled with excitement. Something turned over inside of Cyran, and he sighed as he lifted the dragonbolt off the twin stands. He moved to set the bolt down in its leather-strapped bundle with a dozen others, but he stopped.

Someone behind him whistled an old tune as they approached. The song sounded familiar, but Cyran could not quite place it. And he couldn't decide if he'd actually even heard it before. The melody was both light and joyous but carried foreboding undertones that were almost lost amidst the deeper notes.

"Where are you going, Cyran?" A man's voice sounded behind him.

Cyran glanced over his shoulder at his older brother, Tamar, a young man of twenty and four years. Their younger sister, Jaslin, stood at his side, the wind—known as the breath of the Evenmeres—stirring tangles of her auburn hair.

"You aren't going into the forest, are you, Brother?" Tamar carried buckets heavy enough to bow his broad shoulders, but he smirked.

Cyran shrugged.

"You have a duty to Nevergrace and your lord and king," Tamar continued, his tone growing more and more facetious. "You cannot just shirk your duties whenever you feel like it. Not like we used to. We're men now. We"—he motioned to himself and Jaslin—"lowly servants of the outpost aren't allowed to skip over any of our work."

"And no one is supposed to go into the Evenmeres without the lord's permission, anyway." Jaslin set down the end of a cart she was pulling behind her and folded her adolescent arms over her chest. She cast Cyran a teasing grin. "Not even my mighty dragonsquire brother. And with the lord's recent death, such permission would be very hard to come by. If someone asks me where you've gone, I'm not sure my unblemished morals will allow me to lie to them."

Cyran sighed and motioned to the other squires. "We never

venture into the old woods, and there's probably nothing more dangerous than wolves in its other regions. At least not so close to Nevergrace or even beyond the angoias. We don't do this often anymore, but it's summer's end."

Jaslin cocked her head as she studied him. "I know you can take care of yourself. I just don't want to see you get tangled up in some brambles or get lost out there and for Sir Kayom to have to send a search party for you. Emellefer may hear about that, and your status in her eyes could plummet."

Warmth flowed through Cyran, and he chuckled and shook his head. He couldn't help but grin despite Jaslin's words and the reminder of the recent event of their lord's passing. The spark inside his sister, Cyran likened more to a conflagration. Such was Jaslin's typical jesting manner with him, although she always seemed to be kind to everyone else. After their childhood of many shared disagreements, his little sister never failed to overfill some cup of emotion inside him, no matter how sarcastic or authoritative she was trying to be.

Jaslin grabbed the handles of her cart. "Now that you're a dragonsquire, Tamar and I cannot take on any of your duties. We don't have the authority. And we're all supposed to carry on as we did before the lord died. Nevergrace has to be well kept when our new lord arrives. And there *is* plenty of danger in the woods. Everyone tells me I should never go near the place. But if I must, they tell me I should never leave the path."

Tamar turned and toted his buckets away. "I trust you'll commit to your duties."

Cyran hesitated for a minute until Jaslin followed their brother. A wolf yipped, and Cyran turned to see Smoke still bounding around, waiting for Cyran to follow the others. The squires and larger wolves had already disappeared around the outer stone wall of the keep.

After glancing back to make sure Jaslin had lost interest in him and wasn't watching over her shoulder, Cyran hurried after the wolf and around the keep. Smoke raced away, and his brother and sister disappeared behind the walls before he realized he was still carrying the dragonbolt. He groaned in frustration. In his haste, he hadn't even thought to set the bolt down. But if he went back now, Jaslin might try to stop him again. If he simply laid the weapon against the keep here and someone came along, there would be inquiries as to who had so carelessly left a decades- or even centuries-old bolt made of coveted dragonsteel lying around unattended. The punishment would be harsh, likely including several lashings. On the other hand, if he simply carried the bolt out of Nevergrace's boundaries and never left it unattended, the punishment would not be as brutal, and it would also be less likely that someone other than his friends would ever find out.

Cyran's stomach clenched as he strode on past the keep, carrying the bolt against his shoulder. The eastern and western twin towers of the Never stood in silent, untiring watch over the Evenmeres and the lone path to the northern kingdoms. The outpost's gates were wide open, and no soldiers were present. A late summer breeze swept through the grasses outside, exposing their silver underbellies.

The other dragonsquires were already half the distance to the woods—a line of primarily pines, maples, and oaks that ran like a battlement along Belvenguard's northern border. Towering walls of angoias, with their reddish bark and pale leaves that stretched to the sky, dominated the farther reaches of the forest, their crowns buried in a matting of clouds. Those trees stretched so far beyond the heights of the pines and oaks that they nearly reached the sky sea, which lay just above the clouds.

As always, a pair of sentries stood at attention on either side of the path that passed through the forest. Horns dangled from their necks, to be used to call out the soldiers and knights and perhaps even the dragonguard of Nevergrace if anything appeared amiss. Thankfully, their focus remained on the woods.

Cyran hunched low as he hurried through the grasses and kept to the west of the path, pursuing the other squires.

2

SIRRA BRACKENGLAVE

SIRRA'S MUSCLES TENSED AS HARD AS STONE AS SHE STOOD, forcing herself to control her breathing and her anger. *Murgare cannot respond fast enough to what has happened.*

A member of the onyx guard clasped on her armor. The blackened dragonsteel and the spikes protruding at her elbows and shoulders, in addition to those running along her back, felt as if they pulsed with a rage all their own. Torchlight wavered around her and fell across her armor, creating a dance of shadow and orange light.

"Strike a swift blow," Sir Trothen said as he stroked his gray beard and paced about, watching the onyx guard prepare Sirra for battle. "Free the king's unavenged soul and reclaim the queen, but—"

"The war will come later," Sirra finished for him. "Do not worry yourself, Sir Trothen. I will not attempt to destroy all of Belvenguard simply to gut their king in retaliation. At least not yet. I will save some of that for you."

Trothen, the genturion of the dragonguard at Northsheeren, nodded. His hand ran down over his own dragonguard armor—

plates of steel forged with dragon scales. "I fear for the queen's safety."

"I promise you that she will not have to remain with her captors long."

"And which route shall you take?" Sir Trothen handed Sirra her longsword, sheathed in its black metal casing.

An unsettling sensation recurred in the back of Sirra's mind. Someone had informed Belvenguard where her king would be on Breather's Pass, and when. They must have. This person probably also passed along information about how many dragons and onyx guard would be escorting him.

"The legions can cross the Lake on Fire when the time comes, but I will not fly that way," Sirra replied. "Galvenstone will long see us coming. And our dragons will not find adequate rest on the water." Sirra grasped her sword's hilt, and heat flowed through the dragonsteel and her gauntlet. She strapped the blade across her back.

"But you would not fly so far west as to pass through the spires," Sir Trothen said. "Even if the mountains offer a place for rest, the route will not keep you hidden once you sweep east to Galvenstone."

Sirra grabbed her barbed helm with its black visor from the guard and settled it over her head. Only her long brown hair would show beyond her armor, but no one needed that to recognize her, the Dragon Queen of Murgare.

"And passing over the marshes would hardly conceal you either," Trothen continued.

Sirra turned and paced down a winding tunnel inside Northsheeren Castle. Torches guttered as she passed, and Trothen's slapping footfalls trailed her.

"The spires and the marshes would be foolish routes for even the onyx guard, once they are assembled," Sirra said. "It would either take months to bring war upon King Igare, or our legions would eventually become fossilized in the bogs."

"Igare will be expecting retaliation. And swiftly. Belvenguard must already be preparing for war."

"Then let them prepare. Nothing will stop my coming now. Nor the coming of the north. And they will not expect any of us so soon."

Moonlight stole in through a crater of an opening in the mountain ahead and created a pool of silver light where others had gathered. A group of armored men and women and four dragons waited silently. But another beast lay hidden in the darkness, and that beast was almost too large to fit inside the cavern.

A man adorned in a silver robe hurried up to Sirra, holding out a hand for her to stop. "Dragon Queen, you must slow your—"

"*Vördelth mrac ell duenvíe!*" Sirra roared, using the voice of the dragon. A surge of power catapulted through her and streamed past her lips. Her words blasted through the cavern and hammered against its stone walls.

The man in silver fell onto his side and twitched, clutching his head and whimpering. Everyone else in the chamber clutched their ears and stumbled, wobbling about or leaning against the nearest object for support.

A scaled head shifted in the shadows, and a red eye nearly the size of a man flicked open to regard Sirra.

"Take this man to his quarters and revive him." Sirra gestured to the man in silver. "Now is not the time for discussion. Nor the time to attempt to change my mind."

Two onyx guards tentatively approached, their steps unsteady as they scooped up the man and dragged his limp body away.

Sir Vladden—his face hidden behind his black visor and

only his ranking of three ice dragon scales on his left breast narrowing down the possibilities of whom he could be— nodded as he cautiously approached Sirra from the assembled dragonguard. His steps were slow, and he could only manage to shuffle along, a result of Sirra having to use the dragon voice in this chamber.

"Shadowmar is nearly ready," Sir Vladden said.

"She is quiet." Sirra approached the shadows along the side of the cavern.

The titanic dragon concealed itself there in the darkness, and Sirra ran a hand along her glistening black scales. Sirra's palm tingled, and the feeling crept up her arm. She felt the beast's soul nudge hers. Energy and knowledge and wisdom bloomed inside her. The dragon's web within its nearly lost realm, the way these magnificent creatures saw the mortal world and how they interacted with it, crystalized in Sirra's mind. All people other than the dragonmages and the dragonknights— who were only a rare few—considered such things magic. The vibrations of her speaking with the dragon voice still reverberated in the other realm.

"We fly this night," Sirra said in her mind to Shadowmar.

The dragon did not reply. Only the sensation of seething rage answered Sirra.

"She is eager," Sirra said to those around her. "Shadowmar knows what we seek."

The colossal black dragon blew out a slow breath that rattled the air all around the chamber, and she lifted her head, one of her eyelids slipping open to reveal a blood-red eye with a slitted pupil. Shadowmar shifted her weight, and her scales rippled and rolled over muscle and around the base of ebony spikes that protruded near all the joints on her rear legs and wings as well as along the base of her head and back.

"Your steeds and archers are ready?" Sirra asked Vladden.

"Yes, Dragon Queen."

"Have them mount up."

Sirra tugged at the underside of Shadowmar's harnesses, the ones that held the upper archer's quarterdeck to her back, and she checked all its straps. Everything was bound tightly to Shadowmar's torso. Three archers already stood behind their mounted crossbows on the dragon's back—one crossbow on each side and one to the rear—all belted in and waiting. Yenthor, Sirra's hulking archer, nodded to her and held a fist aloft, his black armor almost making him appear as another spine protruding from Shadowmar's back.

Sirra strode past the frames of the lower turrets, which had not yet been belted into place. Zaldica and another archer waited beside their poled turrets, both armored in black, their excitement and yearning for revenge sheeting off them and threading into the dragon realm.

"We will avenge the king," Zaldica said as Sirra passed. "And his soul will escape torment."

Sirra examined the turrets and reached up and placed a palm on Shadowmar's underbelly. "It is time to rise, my beast," she said only to her mount.

Shadowmar shifted again, and a taloned foot snapped out from beneath her bulk and slapped onto the stone floor. The dragon groaned and heaved as her belly rose. The spines on her back jabbed into the ceiling.

"That is far enough," Sirra said to Shadowmar. Then to Zaldica, she said, "Secure the turrets."

Zaldica nodded, and she and the archer beside her quickly but smoothly passed several belts through loops in the harness for the upper quarterdeck. When they cinched everything down, the turrets were lifted off the ground and hung suspended from Shadowmar's underbelly. The archers climbed inside the poled frames and strapped themselves in behind their mounted crossbows.

Sirra approached her saddle, which was positioned and fastened behind Shadowmar's head. Her lance of shimmering black dragonsteel waited in its mount, the steel plate at the lance's base flaring before the handle she'd held so many times.

"It has been too long," Sirra whispered as she ran her fingers over the weapon's shaft. "And yet not long enough."

Sir Vladden mounted his ice dragon, whose scales shone as white as fresh snow under the torchlight. A hunched woman in a cloak climbed up the ice dragon's neck and sat in the saddle behind the dragonguard. All of the woman, including her black cloak, disappeared behind Vladden's shield, the crest of two rampant shadow dragons emblazoned on the shield's face. Only the dragonmage's twisted staff remained partially visible.

"But Dragon Queen, you cannot hope to fly through the Evenmeres." Sir Trothen finally caught up with Sirra after her use of the dragon voice, his armor rattling in his wake. "There is no safe route through the cursed woods. And no path is wide enough to allow your dragons to safely pass through."

Sirra remained silent as she considered her options. Much of the trees of the Evenmeres rose half a league into the sky, into the clouds, and their crowns neared the sky sea. Attempting to pass over them would force their dragons into too high of an altitude, where the air was too thin for most dragons. It would also be an unduly long journey. That forest was the size of an entire kingdom. There would be no safe place to rest during the crossing or before initiating their attack. This had all happened suddenly, which did not allow adequate time for planning, and Galvenstone was well fortified. Belvenguard's capital city would be prepared by the time the Dragon Queen's small legion arrived.

Sirra dismissed her doubts. She would discover her path as

she went, as always. "I will return with the queen." Sirra climbed into her saddle and settled into her seat.

The four dragonguard and their four mages waited silently for her command.

"Then you must go over the lake," Trothen said. "Once you reach our shores, if you wait and depart at nightfall and fly swiftly, you may cross much of the distance before daybreak. Then, during the light hours, you can skim low over the waters or rest upon them for as many days as you need while you time your assault."

"The watchtowers at Galvenstone will still be able to spot dragons as large as these filling the moonlit skies," a voice said, and a man in a mauve cloak strode forward, using his staff to aid him. His face was hidden within the shadows of his draping hood. A cone of purple flame rose from his palm and lit the caverns in a deep shade hardly brighter than the darkness.

Luminsteir. The conjuror and sorcerer of Northsheeren. His power was not from the dragon realm. His bone and earth magic flowed from somewhere else. Another man walked behind the conjuror, a man as tall as Restebarge, the former king. Oomaren, the king's brother.

"She means to go by way none would expect." Oomaren folded his arms across his chest. His scarred cheek and eye formed a permanent snarl on his face.

"But even flying farther out over the Eventide Sea and sweeping back inland would provide no more benefit than taking the spires," Trothen said as he scrutinized Sirra.

"I meant she will travel by way everyone assumes would be too obvious of a route to actually take," Oomaren said. "She will have to pass many sentinels and soldiers."

Trothen ran a hand over his gray beard, and the hairs rasped against his gauntlet. He studied Oomaren.

Sirra remained silent as she glanced about. The feeling that someone who shouldn't be listening but was rattled the bars of some cage in the back of her mind. She'd assumed it had been Astenor, the king's orator and man in the silver robes, but now she doubted her prior suspicions. Either way, this traitor would be found, and the onyx guard would have their way with them. Her attention settled on the cavern opening.

"Avenge my brother," Oomaren said to Sirra.

"I will," Sirra replied. "For you as well as for your niece, who shall become the new Queen of Murgare if anything should befall our current queen before I am able to save her."

The unscarred half of Oomaren's lips lifted in a grin.

I have never failed Murgare or the throne, and I will not fail them now. Sirra commanded Shadowmar to stride forward, and the beast heeded her call, the dragon's massive feet pounding and rumbling the roots of the mountain with each footfall.

"But the rest of the legion must know where you mean to travel and how your assault fares." Trothen paced beside her, his tone demanding authority and respect. "Elsewise we will gain little advantage from this... incursion."

"Then send a storm dragon." Sirra nodded to the genturion of the dragonguard of Northsheeren and nudged Shadowmar forward to the lip of the cavern.

The shadow dragon roared, belting out a deep and sonorous cry that rolled away over the surrounding cliffs and mountains. Her wings snapped out but collided with both walls before having extended even half their length.

"Travel well, Dragon Queen," Luminsteir said before muttering an incantation behind Sirra. Purple light flared.

"Fly," Sirra said to Shadowmar.

Her dragon lunged out from the cavern, leaping into the air as her wings unfurled like all the sails upon the mainmast of a galley. The massive weight of the beast sent them plummeting downward along the cliff faces. But within a moment, Shadowmar's leathery wings snapped and billowed with air. The shadow dragon flapped once and then twice, and they rose into the night. Four dragons swooped out of the cavern behind her.

They soared out over snowcapped mountains and valleys and forests far, far below, headed south. To Belvenguard.

3

CYRAN ORENDAIN

ONCE CYRAN ENTERED THE FOREST BETWEEN THE TRUNKS OF A gnarled oak and a straight pine, he spotted the other squires nearby, waiting for him. He stepped farther away from where the one path wound into the forest as he walked through the underbrush. Smoke loped over, panting as he joined the other two wolves before sniffing the plants and forest floor. Smoke stood only about half their height at the shoulders, and the realization of how small the littler wolf was opened a tender spot of emotion in Cyran's heart.

"What are you going to do with that?" Laren asked with a beaming boyish smile as he eyed the bolt in Cyran's hand.

"He wants to skewer a few wild boar at once or bring something *really* big back home." Brelle laughed and slapped Dage on his burly arm. "Something he can sell for plenty of coin. Like a dragon's hide. Then he can have more than those few drinks at summer's end. *If* he doesn't get a back full of lashings for having that bolt out here. And if any game he takes isn't rightfully handed over to the guard and the archers for hunting it with their weapon."

I am the fool this day.

"You won't be able to kill anything with that bolt." Dage scratched at a patch of blond hair protruding from the neck of his leather tunic. "Not unless something charges straight at you. Dragonbolts are as heavy as stones, and even I cannot throw one farther than a horse length."

Cyran hefted the bolt. Surely, he couldn't even throw it that far. "I'd take a crossbow, but I don't think I'll be able to carry both."

Laren shook his head. "No, you won't."

"Best just protect us from the charge of a wild hare." Brelle chuckled as she doubled over in feigned humor and slapped at her thick backside.

"Come," Garmeen—another dragonsquire standing in the shadows of a pine—said as he stepped closer. Garmeen hefted a longbow, which complemented his tall and wiry frame that was swallowed by his cloak. His face and head were also long and slender. He turned and led them on. "The day grows late, and you all gossip like old men."

Laren grinned and winked at the rest of them before following Garmeen.

"Oh, I'm Garmeen," Brelle said quietly but with an impertinent tone as she huffed and shoved her sandy hair from her face. "I've decided I'm akin to one of the lost rangers, and so I'll lead all you foolish little squires whenever we venture into the Evenmeres."

Dage chuckled, but he suddenly crouched and raised his crossbow, taking aim. Two squirrels tore around a trunk nearby, circling its length and scampering up into the canopy. Two birds flew away.

Brelle bellowed with laughter.

"If you wanted to hunt squirrels, we could have stayed inside Nevergrace," Laren said.

"I'm simply prepared and ready to take my kill before Cyran gets his," Dage said, casting Cyran a side glance.

Why only before me? Cyran brushed the comment aside. For some reason or another, the largest of the squires felt he always had to try to outdo all the others, even when cleaning and oiling weapons and harnesses. Dage had always done so before today, but now that he'd received a message from Galvenstone, things should have changed or, at a minimum, should be changing. Dage should no longer harbor the slightest worry that Cyran or another might best him or be invited into the guard before him. Unless the message was not such a summons.

The squires fanned out and crept through the brush in a moving line, keeping the main trail to their right and its general area in view. Cyran took the position farthest from the trail. The wolves trotted along in silence with them, repeatedly appearing and vanishing in the undergrowth and trees.

The ground beneath Dage crunched with each step as he walked along beside Cyran, the hulking squire making more noise than any of the others. Cyran studied his movements and manner. If Cyran were to truly compete with Dage in the hunt, Cyran would study his opponent's weaknesses, which primarily seemed to be his inability to move quietly. Dage never avoided the dead grass and vegetation and, in the past, he typically created even more noise when he was upset or anxious. Those emotions often revealed themselves in the midst of his meaning-less competitions. If Cyran had to, he could take advantage of the squire's weaknesses by distancing himself from Dage and then circling around in front of him, using the larger man's noise to push startled game in his direction.

"I don't understand why so many people are scared of this place," Brelle said as she picked her way through a patch of ferns, unconcerned about scaring off game, or finding it difficult to keep from speaking for too long. "It's just another forest."

"A forest larger than most kingdoms." Laren tugged at his leather tunic to unstick it from his back where sweat stains started to soak through. "And a forest where merchants and travelers are never seen or heard from again if they stray from the main path when passing through the angoia copses."

"That's all a bunch of myth conjured up by the great minds of our parents and their parents to keep us from wandering too far," Brelle said. "And some believe it because the north has sent brigands along the trails a few times in years past. If anything of real danger lived in here, certainly some of the people living at Nevergrace would have been witness to its evil doings. Nothing ever happens at Nevergrace. Nothing. And, therefore, the forest is safe."

No one answered for a moment.

"Nothing has ever happened at Nevergrace in the past decade." Cyran slipped quietly around a bush. "But—"

"Nor during our entire lifetimes," Brelle added.

Cyran shrugged. "But if the north were to attack again, like in past ages, it is possible that Nevergrace would be the first to feel their wrath. We could be the first line of defense for all of Belvenguard and the southern kingdoms."

"That's the reason why those vile bastards planted these woods and the angoias in the first place," Laren said. "They cultivated it all—the forest and those ancient trees—utilizing dark magic so almost none could pass through. At least nothing larger than a merchant caravan. Their wish to separate us permanently, so the people of Belvenguard could not witness the evils Murgare was conjuring and then try to stop them, only became reality after this forest grew up in the past age."

"That's similar to how my father tells it." Dage held his crossbow's butt against his shoulder, the loaded bolt pointed at the sky. "After this forest was allowed to grow, Nevergrace was no longer an outpost along an open border as it once was. We became less important to Belvenguard and the kings, and we have nearly been forgotten. And all those damn children's songs we still sing that tell us about our valiant ancestors will never be replaced with any new heroic deeds."

"But what if the magic of the north's mages allows their side to pass through the Evenmeres when they command it?" Cyran asked.

Dage and Brelle laughed.

"If they haven't used that opportunity against us—their despised enemy—in these past centuries, I think it's safe to assume they don't have the option." Brelle tied her sweaty hair back behind her head. "They'd as soon kill us as live on the other side of a forest from us. Even a forest nearly as big as the larger kingdoms."

Dage faced Cyran. "Even you must realize that the Murgare king's deepest desire is to destroy us and rule all the kingdoms south of these woods. As well as the kingdoms of the north."

Cyran nodded.

"Cyran understands," Laren said. "He just hasn't heard it as often as we have. Since his mother and father..."

The others fell into an uncomfortable silence.

Laren's boyish cheeks flushed under his short brown hair. "Sorry, Cyran."

"It's quite all right." Cyran waved away his friend's concern. "It's not like I just lost them, and I'd rather speak of them and try to remember them as best I can than have everyone around me terrified of uttering their names."

The squires trudged on through the brush and bracken, watching their surroundings for game. Birds trilled in the distance, but in the immediate vicinity, all lay silent. The wolves had vanished into the undergrowth and did not make a sound.

A quiet half hour or so later, something emerged as it stood up from the undergrowth far out to Cyran's left. A pig with black-speckled skin. Cyran lowered the bolt from where he'd leaned it against his shoulder and angled its barbed tip at the animal. Maybe it had been fortunate he'd brought the bolt along. He opened his mouth to shout for the others' attention, but he paused. The pig flicked its tail. A few piglets huddled beside it, trying to hide under its belly. He watched the sow for a moment, and his arm relaxed.

"And so you all believe that because of the Evenmeres, the north is no longer a real threat to Nevergrace?" Cyran asked, hoping to create enough noise as they passed by the wild sow that Dage would not hear the animal. Cyran casually placed the bolt against his other shoulder, as if he'd only intended to switch which arm he carried it with. "And that the legends of evil things lurking in the deeper woods is myth that harkens back to the north's attacks as well?"

Laren shook his head, his thick hair flopping about. "More people of the Never than just my father say dark things lurk under the canopy of the Evenmeres. And far too many merchants tell such tales to simply dismiss them all."

"I'm certain there are still wild forest dragons living in the old woods." Brelle swept her crossbow around in an arc to emphasize north and the direction of the angoias. "Maybe even a couple other breeds of dragons. But from what I've heard, they all avoid people and travelers of all types as much as they can. The same as all wild dragons have done for centuries. But our area of the woods is as unremarkable as any other forest in Belvenguard."

"All I ask is that when I'm summoned to the dragonguard, they don't place me at Nevergrace to watch the Evenmeres," Dage said. "I see myself accomplishing great feats and vanquishing wicked dragons and barbarian hordes from the north. If the north ever does come during our lifetime, they will fly over the lake like they did—"

A tune with a light and joyful melody flowed between shadowed trunks in the distance, a song with a foreboding undertone. It was no louder than a whisper.

Cyran strained to listen. A flash of light raced behind a tree, followed by a shifting shadow. The leaves in the area waved and then fell still.

"Someone's coming." Garmeen turned in the opposite direction of the music and the light and raised his bow with an arrow nocked.

Women's voices became recognizable and grew louder, pulling Cyran's attention away from the song he'd been listening for. That tune faded and died.

"Did you all hear that?" Cyran asked as he crouched and peered deeper into the woods.

The women's rising chanting approached along the path.

"How can we not?" Laren sighted down the length of the bolt on his crossbow.

"No, not the women, the... other sound," Cyran said, but none of the others paid him any mind.

A line of people cloaked in white seemed to float along the path to the east. They carried a litter on their shoulders, and a cone of flame rose from the litter and a body entwined in white cloth. The flames breathed plumes of pale smoke.

"It's the ladies in mourning." Brelle crouched down behind the foliage and lowered her crossbow. "We're not supposed to witness this."

Cyran knelt behind the blades of a bristling fern and hid the dragonbolt as well as he hid himself. The others found similar cover. Cyran glanced behind them in the direction he'd heard the other music. All lay still in those shadows and streaks of sunlight.

The line of mourners approached, singing an old tune, one

filled with words of the Cimeren tongue in addition to the language of the ancient world.

Till the end of days we soar
  Till the end of nights we reign
  For last of dark and first of light they hail
  The Never stands when blood flows in the lord's veins

Mörenth toi boménth bi droth su llith
  Mörenth toi boménth bi nomth su praëm

The entourage passed like specters, dropping blue petals in their wake.

A single tear rolled down Brelle's cheek. "I want to see what they do with a dead lord." Brelle crept after them.

"Brelle." Cyran tried to grab her, but she'd slipped too far away.

Laren silently followed Brelle, as did Dage, although Dage came close to creating as much noise as the singers. Garmeen kept his distance from Dage but moved in the same direction.

Cyran groaned. If they were caught witnessing this ceremony, they would face more severe consequences than he would for carrying a dragonsteel bolt out into the Evenmeres. He considered leaving the bolt where it was and returning later to retrieve it, but if they ventured too far away in this forest, it would be difficult to locate the exact same fern in a patch of undergrowth.

Cyran's gut cramped as he looked south and weighed returning to Nevergrace versus following the other squires. His friends kept far away from the trail as they moved. Cyran inhaled and hesitantly followed, picking his way along as silently as he could manage.

After a few minutes of trailing the procession, the cloaked woman in the lead stepped away from the pyre of a litter and threw a blue-petalled flower onto the path before them.

"The glacial rose," Brelle whispered.

The procession lowered their litter onto the path and backed away as they continued to sing in unison, with one high-pitched voice rising above the others, all their heads bowed in reverence. Nearly ten minutes of chanting and singing followed before the procession turned and appeared to glide away in silence.

The few memories Cyran had of the deceased lord surfaced from some recess in his mind. Cyran had not spent much time around the lord, but whenever he'd seen the man interact with anyone, it had been with kindness. The lord had been known as humble and considerate, someone who placed the needs of the Never and its people above his own. A sense of loss and regret flooded Cyran as he wondered who would be sent to replace this man. The Never would likely change, and given the reputation of the past lord, such changes might not be for the better.

A quiet settled over the forest like a blanket.

"Damn, I've never seen anything like that before," Brelle said.

"Why the glacial rose if it only grows in spilt blood?" One of Dage's eyebrows arched onto his forehead.

"It only grows in areas that have been watered by blood *and* that have also been burned by fire," Laren corrected him. "Namely dragon fire."

"The old stories my gaffer tells," Garmeen said, his voice airy, the red stubble on his cheeks and chin now visible under his hood, "say the angoias are simply glacial roses that have grown up over centuries without man there to intervene. Those roses never stop growing, and in here, they have become the deep woods."

Brelle chuckled. "Angoias and glacial roses don't even look the same. Red bark and white leaves versus a green stem and pale blue petals."

Garmeen's jaw tensed, and his cheeks hardened. "My gaffer says the petals lose their color to the sky and the green stem matures into bark over many, many years. Over centuries."

Brelle shrugged. "I don't know about any of that, but I doubt we'll be finding any game around after that little performance. Not to mention with the smoke they brought with them."

"They just leave the lord's body to burn, then?" Dage asked. "Out here in the Evenmeres?"

"Same as they'd do with you, if you're lucky," Laren replied.

"But what becomes of his bones?" Dage scratched his bare chin and pushed his hair behind a muscular shoulder. "I doubt glacial roses or angoia roots, even if they are the same, break down and take up bones before the scavengers come."

Cyran glanced back toward where he'd heard the song and seen the light. Still quiet and empty. But when he looked back to the others, he jolted. Someone hooded in a white cloak waited at the edge of the path, facing in their direction.

"The Blacksmith smite us," Cyran cursed under his breath.

The others picked their way toward the path, unaware of the woman watching them.

Brelle suddenly froze. "The Siren riding a shadow dragon," she snapped as she stared at the cloaked woman. "Shit."

The others stopped in their tracks.

"Come out of the forest and step onto the path, squires of the dragonguard," the woman said, her voice sounding young but carrying an air of authority and demanding to be obeyed.

Cyran's eyes fell shut like portcullis gates. He considered dropping the bolt into the brush, but if she'd somehow noticed them prior, she would likely notice him dropping the bolt now. And their punishment for having seen the lord's ceremony would supersede anything else. Garmeen glanced over his shoulder into the woods as if he was considering disappearing into the shadows.

"Come out, my friends," the young woman said again.

Cyran stepped forward, unconcerned with keeping quiet and crunching through the undergrowth before reaching the path. The others followed. The woman pushed back her hood as she strode closer. Her blond hair spilled out and shone under beams of sunlight sifting through the canopy. She was the young lady of Nevergrace, Menoria.

Cyran swallowed. He'd barely shared two words with the young woman, who was probably a couple years younger than he and somewhere around ten and eight.

"I am very sorry for your loss." Cyran bowed his head. The others hovered behind him and muttered their agreements.

Menoria stared at them, surprise showing in her eyes before she absently glanced at the bolt in Cyran's hands. "That is kind for you all to say, but we know it was not unexpected. My father was already an old man when I was born. This day has been coming for many long months. I believe his passing is even a blessing upon him. To ease the suffering he endured this past year."

Tense silence followed and seemed to wrap around the squires and the lady, weighing thick under the boughs.

"And do you know which of your relatives is to be named the new lord of the Never?" Brelle shuffled closer and stood beside Cyran as she attempted to straighten her curled locks.

"My uncle, from out near the Weltermores," Menoria answered.

"Bransheer?" Laren asked with an affable pitch clinging to his words.

"In the vicinity of Bransheer," Menoria replied.

"Then Nevergrace will be strong again." Dage strode up and stood at an angle just ahead of Cyran. "There is vigor in the blood of your family."

Menoria forced a smile.

"A-and you will be able to marry a lord soon," Dage stuttered.

"Yes." Her head drooped so that her chin rested on her dress. "I will have to leave Nevergrace, the only home I've ever known."

"Then the troubles of Cimeren will never touch you." Dage grinned, his expression forced and awkward. "It will be everything a young lady could hope for."

Cyran cringed.

"If you believe being forced to leave my home to serve and obey some man I do not know well is everything I've hoped for, you are mistaken," the lady replied in an even tone. "And it will probably be a man far too old for me. I often used to wish that I'd find friends my own age. Companions. But I hoped to find them long before reaching ten and eight. My fate seems certain now. I will be passed about like a family jewel, cared for and even nurtured before being traded away in return for strengthening the bond between lords."

Cyran's heart twinged with sympathy.

"But we all make sacrifices for duty, do we not?" Menoria forced a grin as she focused on each of them in turn. "Some of us just make more sacrifices than others."

Her last words struck Cyran in the heart like the blade of a dagger, and he winced, although in the moment, he wasn't entirely sure why. It simply reminded him of what his brother and sister had last said to him.

"You should all return to the Never before someone else sees you out here," Menoria continued. "It grows late, and I believe there are squires who still have chores to perform before summer's end. Squires who are also not supposed to witness the ladies in mourning." She glanced at the dragonbolt again. "Squires who should not be caught carrying a weapon of their guard-master's into the woods."

Cyran clenched his jaw and nodded. The sunlight slipping through the thinner canopy over the path had faded to twilight and threw long shadows out from the surrounding trunks.

A howl rang in the distance of the deeper forest, and it echoed around in the trees before slowly dying out. A second howl rose from somewhere much farther east than the first.

The hair on the back of Cyran's neck prickled. *Smoke.*

"It sounds like your wolves may have picked up the scent of whatever you were hunting," Menoria said.

Brelle glanced around, her sandy curls leaping like coiled snakes. "I don't think any game we'd want to eat would come this close to a burning body." Her cheeks reddened as she looked at Menoria. "Begging your pardon, milady. I meant this close to your father. Or at least his body... while it burns." She groaned and stopped talking.

Menoria dismissed her concerns with a wave.

"It's gone." Garmeen's voice was stretched thin with surprise.

Cyran looked up the path. The packed trail was empty, the lord's corpse missing entirely—no wrappings, no pyre, no litter. Only a lingering fog from the smoke choked the air.

"Maybe one of the wolves dragged it off." Laren's face paled.

"We all best return to the Never at once," Menoria said. "If you all had to hear the tales I was forced to learn—those pertaining the history of these woods—you'd fear ever stepping foot out here."

She whipped around and hurried along the path.

4

CYRAN ORENDAIN

Fires burned in the courtyard. Flames flashed about the faces of the stone walls.

Dage swung a wooden sword in a wide arc of a blow, and Cyran raised his training blade to parry it aside. Wood clattered against wood. Cyran's hand vibrated and stung from the impact. Dage pressed him back.

"Keep him on the retreat, Dage," someone shouted from the circle of squires and soldiers around them.

Music drifted out of the keep's windows. Dage's nostrils flared as he huffed—the sign he was growing frustrated and angry. When he did that, he'd rely on his strength to try to win the sparring, sure as sunset.

Use an opponent's weaknesses against them.

Dage stalked closer, and Cyran circled around. Dage raised his sword, rearing back before he would lunge in and swipe, utilizing all his might in one attack.

Cyran raised his blade as if preparing to block the attack, but he would wait a split second longer and perform a technique that in the elder tongue meant to *follow the force*, instead of

parrying, whose word in the elder tongue meant to *meet the force.*
He did not intend for his weapon to clash with Dage's. Even steel
weapons, unless they were forged of dragonsteel, would chip
and crack after too many blows. It was always better to practice
as if the fight were against a real enemy and the outcome of such
a battle was either life or death. The best course of action was to
not have to accept the full force of any of Dage's attacks.

Dage growled as he lunged forward and swung.

Cyran leaned away as Dage's weapon descended, and Cyran
flicked his sword back and then around his opponent's swiping
blade, catching the sword on the back side and adding to its
momentum. The motion threw his opponent's blade in nearly
the same direction it was already traveling but with even greater
force.

Dage grunted in surprise and stumbled forward, landing off
balance with his lunging foot and careening toward Cyran.
Cyran sidestepped him and let Dage's arms flail as the squire ran
a few choppy steps and crashed face-first into the dirt.

Some in the crowd groaned in frustration while a few
cheered and applauded. Cyran stood over Dage's back with his
blade poised for a killing stab.

"You are dead, Dage." Sir Ymar approached, his green and
gray dragonsteel armor discarded for the time being and his
brigandine sparkling in the firelight. "You gave your opponent
the opportunity to use the *omercón* on you. Same as he did last
time."

Dage growled and pushed himself up. His tunic and the
knees of his leggings were smeared with mud.

Sir Kayom—Cyran's guard-master—stood in the shadows
along the periphery of the circle but remained silent, his arms
folded across his chest as he chewed at his lip.

"You need to remember who you spar with." Sir Ymar

stroked his white beard and continued addressing Dage. "And use your head as well as your strength when you fight. Then you may become a force to be reckoned with."

Dage brushed himself off. "But in a real battle, I won't know my opponent. That's why I prefer to fight pretending I don't know what they will do."

"Then you will never make the guard. Even someone you meet on the field of battle will give certain tells about their abilities and plans of attack, be it in their stance, their weapons, their grips, or where they are looking."

Brelle snickered.

"And you." Sir Ymar approached Cyran, his pale eyes alight with the reflections of flame, his white beard thick like wool. "You anticipated your opponent's attack well, but as Dage said, you will not be as familiar with a true enemy. You cannot always rely on what you know about your comrades and what you've learned from past experiences with them. You still must be able to adapt. Or they will catch you off guard, and you will be dead."

Cyran nodded as Sir Ymar looked him over.

"You are tall, but you are not nearly broad enough to be in the guard," Sir Ymar added as if wanting to note all of Cyran's unfavorable qualities and lay them out in the open for the other squires. "Unless you pack on at least half of Dage's bulk, you'll never be able to adequately protect your mage."

Cyran gritted his teeth. *And what can I do about that?*

"Now it is time for some crossbow work." Sir Ymar gestured to the dozen squires around them. "And you can all thank certain squire friends of yours who did not finish oiling the saddles and harnesses for this late-night treat."

More than a few of the squires grumbled, but they all picked up crossbows from a rack. Cyran found one with a bolt crank, his preferred style, instead of a windlass. He wrenched the bolt forward, and the rope stretched backward and clicked into place. After loading a bolt, he lay on his stomach in the mud. Across the courtyard, the targets—straw men in tunics suspended by poles—waited.

"Take aim." Sir Ymar paced behind them.

Cyran sighted down the shaft of the bolt. He gripped the trigger handle and exhaled slowly.

"Loose."

Cyran squeezed the trigger toward the tiller. His rope snapped forward and twanged, and his bolt screamed over the courtyard, impaling one of the dummies in an area that would have been right between its eyes. A dozen other bolts thumped into the targets a split second later, most striking areas around their chests, one other in the face. Two bolts missed the straw men completely and clattered against the stone wall behind them before dropping.

Cyran cranked the hand lever, and his rope once again clicked into its loaded position.

Sir Ymar eyed Cyran but quickly averted his gaze and studied the others. "Dismal at best. Reload."

The sound of a dozen cocking crossbows pinged through the courtyard.

"And... ah!" Sir Ymar wobbled as a deep vibration rumbled all around them. The ground started to quake. The dragonguard trainer stumbled and nearly fell.

Nevergrace's stone walls grated and thrummed, and the earth beneath Cyran trembled. The music inside the keep screeched to a halt. Gasps of surprise erupted amid shouts of fear sounding within the keep.

A few heartbeats later, the deep rumble that came from the roots of the earth faded. The ground fell still again, and the castle and its stone walls returned to their quiet slumber.

"Another damn angoia tree has fallen," Sir Ymar said. "That's the third one in less than a year."

"Maybe too many forest dragons are roaming the old woods and knocking over its trees," Laren said. "My old man says that, anyway."

"Maybe so," Sir Ymar replied, his usually ruddy face nearly as pale as his beard. A sheen of sweat enameled his bald head. "If there are enough of them. But even a dozen forest dragons leaping about an angoia wouldn't carry sufficient force to bring one of those trees down." He swallowed and rubbed his damp scalp. "We'd send you all to try to trap a few of the hatchlings or younglings—or have the wolves sniff out a clutch of eggs— except a few of the men we've sent into the copses over the past year have yet to return."

"I told you," Laren said to Brelle, who rolled her eyes. "And those who have ventured close to the angoias and managed to return insist they saw some of the trees catch fire. For no reason at all."

"That will be all for your training this night." Sir Ymar wiped his palm on the boiled leather of his tunic. "You may join the celebrations of summer's end. And may we all forget about these quakes for the time being."

A few of the squires cheered as they stood and returned their crossbows to the rack. Sir Kayom departed for the keep, and Ymar stalked after him. Music returned from the confines of the keep, at the point where the song had left off. Cyran stood and pulled off his muddy tunic before hurrying away for a clean replacement from the squires' quarters, which was nestled within the inner curtain. Most of the other squires did likewise. Brelle headed for a waiting barrel with a stack of tankards sitting on top.

After Cyran exited the squires' quarters with a fresh tunic of boiled leather, the keep's doors opened, and people began filtering outside. Most carried tankards or goblets and wobbled as they walked—hand in hand, alone, in large groups. A few children burst out and tore across the inner bailey. An older woman shuffled toward the dragonsquires, toting a steaming pot, a much younger woman carrying the pot by its other handle. A little redheaded girl darted about behind them, holding a lute by its neck and occasionally dragging it through the dirt.

Cyran hurried over to assist the two women, forcing himself to look at and acknowledge the older one at least as much as the younger, but he feared in at least two instances during his approach, he stared at the younger, Emellefer, for too long. "Another of your finest stews?"

"Same crap you always get," Ulba, the old woman, said without even a subtle smirk. She brushed thinning white hair back into her coif as her stocky legs hobbled along. "But today I hope you earned it."

Cyran took hold of Ulba's end of the pot, and the older woman stepped aside. He helped Emellefer carry it toward the squire house while trying not to stare at her.

She's beautiful. "It's a fine night for summer's end." Cyran immediately lidded his eyes. *Even during a celebration, all I can think to mention to her is the weather?*

"Yes." Emellefer's long legs only made short strides. "In an hour, I'm certain all you squires will be as drunk as the old blacksmith gets every night."

"Well, I better take it slow, then." Cyran motioned to the little redheaded girl and the lute she carried. "I'd like to play a song or two first."

"Then you best do so *before* you start on the ale and mulled wine." Emellefer set the pot down outside the squires' quarters and smoothed her tunic before tucking her dark hair behind an ear. "For you, the lute is enough of a struggle when you're sober."

Cyran winced because he worried it was true.

Emellefer laughed and touched his arm. "I'm only jesting. You play beautifully." She winked.

Heat rose in Cyran's cheeks.

"Here you are, sir squire." Renily, the little redhead, bowed and offered Cyran the lute.

Cyran bowed in return and accepted the instrument. "When I play, it will be for you, milady."

Renily grinned and looked down as she sheepishly kicked at the dirt. "The nyren said you can borrow the lute for the evening. As long as you don't damage it."

Cyran wiped a crusting of dirt from the bottom of the instrument where Renily had dragged it, and he cringed at the sight. He sat and strummed the strings before tuning each one to match the pitch in his mind.

"Oh no, I fear we're in for a song." Brelle's smile encompassed her cheeks and made her eyes squint as she plopped down in front of Cyran and brushed her curly hair aside. She took Emellefer's hand and pulled the serving girl down beside her. "Cannot listen to this alone. My ears would probably end up bleeding."

Emellefer settled in beside Brelle as Renily skipped and danced around them. Ulba dished up bowls of stew brimming with summer squash, dark chunks of meat, and carrots.

The old nyren of Nevergrace sauntered through the bailey in his red robe, his chain belt jingling, his long white beard waving as he neared the squires' quarters. He eyed the lute in Cyran's hand with longing, but he did not utter a word before moving on.

Ulba watched the nyren warily until he passed out of earshot. "I don't feel at ease when that old river rat is around."

Laren exited the squires' house. "He's a healer and a scholar."

"Well, he makes me uncomfortable," Ulba replied.

"You probably only get that sense, Ulba, because he's trying to win your affection." Brelle sipped from her tankard, her cheeks already ruddy.

Ulba grimaced. "Not at my age, he isn't. Even if my husband died long ago."

"He doesn't mind when I play some of the Never's lutes." Cyran wound a string too tight, and it creaked, making him worry it might snap. He released it a quarter turn. "And the vast majority of the time you see me playing, he even allowed for it."

"But he only lets you tinker with the shoddier instruments." Brelle arched an eyebrow as she indicated the creaking string. She downed her mulled wine before looking in the direction the old man had gone. "I bet that old nyren has wizard nipples."

"*Wizard* nipples?" Emellefer's gaping eyes expressed her horror.

"Of course." Brelle's face turned even and somber.

"What do wizards do to their nipples?" Emellefer asked.

"I don't desire to know the answer to that question," Brelle replied, "but those old men you hear about in stories cannot only have long scraggly white hair dangling from their eyebrows and chins."

The image Brelle instilled in Cyran's mind caused him to groan. Ulba snorted and started coughing before hacking and spitting as she nearly tripped over the pot.

Dage stalked out of the squire house and strode straight away without a word. The letter he'd received from Galvenstone had affected his mood, and he still hadn't let any of the other squires know what it said. Garmeen emerged from their quarters and leaned against the outer curtain wall near Cyran and Laren. Garmeen's hood was pushed back and revealed his long and slender nose and jaw in addition to his red stubble and wavy hair. Another dozen dragonsquires picked up bowls of stew and mingled about the inner bailey as they ate and drank.

Cyran sipped his wine as he tuned the last two gut strings on the lute. He kept an eye out for his brother and sister, as he didn't want to start playing until they arrived. His music was usually more for them than for anyone else. But they were not in sight. *Probably still finishing up with all their duties.*

Smoke curled up against the wall near Cyran and laid his head down on his paws before closing his green eyes. Brelle went to fetch another drink.

"How'd you learn to play the lute?" Renily asked Cyran, and she stopped skipping around. "That's not part of being a squire."

"I learned when I was a boy." Cyran brushed his dark hair out of his face and rubbed at the sparse scruff on his chin. "My mother taught me the basics when I was a child."

"Your mother?" Renily twirled in a circle. "Then my mother should teach me."

"Are you ever going to play?" Brelle returned from the barrel with another full tankard.

Cyran cast her a tight-lipped grin. He cleared his throat and hummed for a minute first. Then he opened with the song of Nevergrace, a ballad that rose and fell from a high resonate pride to a deep and sorrowful loss. He sang of the Scyne River to the east and Galvenstone with Castle Dashtok and the Summerswept Keep to the west. The song told the story of how the dragons of the north came and destroyed all the lands around them, but Nevergrace held firm. He missed a few strings and struck the wrong ones a couple times, but he sang with all the emotion he could muster as pride and sadness twined within him. A nostalgia for Nevergrace's past welled up inside him, as it always did when he sang. It was the reason why he continued to play even after he'd grown into a man. He sang boldly and with as much resonance as he could rally, attempting to sound like the traveling bard that had passed through in midsummer.

When Cyran finished the song of the Never, everyone around him had fallen silent, and he was almost afraid to look at them.

"Well, do you want to be a bard or a dragonguard?" Brelle asked.

Cyran laughed, and his gaze strayed to Emellefer, who stared back at him with bleary eyes as he said, "I don't know. How bad was it?"

Brelle wobbled her hand but wiped at her eyes. "You don't quite have the skill and perfection of a bard, but I bet if you started honing your voice and practicing with the lute as much as you do with your weapons, you could probably make the switch."

Two people broke out into applause—Tamar and Jaslin, who stood off to the side of the crowd.

"My brother, everyone." Tamar stepped forward and made a sweeping gesture at Cyran as he beamed with pride. "The brother who inherited all the skills I should have gotten. And I believe he may have the best voice in the Never, including all those who have been thrown in the dungeons."

People laughed. Jaslin smiled and applauded again. She carried a book in the crook of her arm, as she often did. Her idea of celebrating summer's end would come with a good story.

"Ah, it's just for fun." Cyran grinned and sipped his wine. "And I wouldn't have honed any skills or been able to become a dragonsquire or have learned to play the lute without all the sacrifices Tamar has made for me. I owe him all... He... I wasn't always the hardest-working woodsman or farmhand when I was a boy."

"Isn't that the truth," Tamar muttered.

Brelle guffawed. "Same as he is now."

Many around them laughed.

"I am content with simple work and accomplishing as much as I can every day." Tamar's tone carried a hint of melancholy but also pride as he stepped closer and wrapped Cyran in an embrace, thumping his back.

Several people jeered. "I used to share fists with my brother," one young woodsman said, and another agreed.

"I must also express my gratitude for Jaslin's encouragement." Cyran stepped back from Tamar and gestured to his sister, but when all the attention settled on her, she took a step back into the crowd to hide.

"And why do you play music when your duty is with the blade and shield?" Renily hopped in place, facing Cyran.

"To lift the spirits," Cyran said. "I realize I do not have a grand enough voice to perform before lords and kings." He didn't wish for the best voice in all the kingdom or for the most impressive skills with the lute. He simply wished to be good enough to stir the emotions of others and make them feel an inkling of what he did when he sang his songs, to help them release whatever pent-up emotion needed to be released. And he wanted to be able to reach and bestow that cathartic feeling that settled people and made them content for a time. The dragonguard called to him with more intensity than his music did, but he still yearned for that emotional connection at times. The other squires and guard needed it as well. All people needed it.

Renily gazed off, as if brooding on his words, although she could have been distracted by a wolf for all Cyran knew.

"And I do not want to have only one means of defending Nevergrace, that by which I have to harm others," Cyran continued, in case Renily was truly pondering learning to play and sing. "I also want to be able to touch people in the heart and stave off whatever demons are lurking in there at the moment."

Renily did not move or respond.

Someone gasped, and Cyran glanced up. Sir Kayom—the guard-master of Cyran's group of squires—marched through the crowd and stopped outside their circle. His green and gray dragonsteel armor flickered with firelight.

"Cyran, fetch Eidelmere." The look in the dragonguard's eyes was as firm as his posture. The rigid set of his chin made his salted beard protrude more than normal. "The rest of you, come with me. I must ride this night."

A heartbeat of silence settled over their circle, but the music in the keep played on.

"What has happened?" Cyran climbed to his feet and set the lute against the curtain wall.

Smoke rose and shook out his coat before blinking repeatedly, as if he'd been woken from a dream.

"Something of great importance." Sir Kayom's visage didn't break, his hands clasped behind his back. "I must ride for Galvenstone and Castle Dashtok."

"Is the capital in danger?" Garmeen stepped from the shadows. "The king?"

"No, but I cannot speak openly of the events." Sir Kayom's forehead wrinkled as he looked at Ulba and then Renily, Emellefer, and Jaslin. "But all the genturions of the guard in all the cities of Belvenguard have been summoned."

Sir Kayom's tone and demeanor strummed Cyran's nerves. "Are the other guard or any knights or soldiers traveling with you?"

"Sir Ymar will be, but no knights or soldiers. Sir Ilion and the others are to stay and watch over Nevergrace. But I must depart at once. You and the rest of my squires are to travel by caravan along the Scyne Road at dawn. Ride hard and meet me at the castle in Galvenstone in as few days as possible." He faced and addressed the other squires. "The rest of you, find my mage and my archers. And gather and prepare my arms that you left scattered about the Never." Sir Kayom wheeled about and marched for the keep, the layered plates of his armor clanking, sounding reminiscent of swords banging against shields.

5

CYRAN ORENDAIN

THE STEEL GATE AT THE ENTRANCE TO THE DEN WAS CLOSED AND bolted. No soldiers stood on either side of the gate this night. Not on summer's end. Smoke sat on his haunches and whined as he watched from a distance. The wolf would never follow Cyran down there.

Cyran grabbed a torch burning beside the entrance and used one of the keys on his ring to unlatch the lock. He swung the gate outward, and it creaked and groaned. A chill scampered up his back, as if little sprites used his ribs like a ladder.

The darkness inside the den spewed out of its maw-like entrance in fading tendrils, making the night appear blacker just outside. The torch guttered and nearly died before slowly returning in twining orange flames.

Cyran swallowed and held his torch aloft. After shutting and locking the gate behind him, he strode under the archway and followed a ramp down into the earth. The air grew heavier and denser. Hotter. A warmth sheeting off massive bodies stirred the air.

A low rumble carried out, but this sound was deeper and throatier than the quake caused by the falling angoia tree. Cyran steeled his nerves. He hadn't ventured down here more than a few times, and only since becoming a squire, which hadn't happened until recently. The environment and aura of the place still unsettled him. It would unsettle any man. Another long and resonate exhale of a breath echoed in the chamber below.

As he walked, his firelight lunged about the stone walls and across the ceiling, chasing shadows into the corners. But the shadows immediately swung back into place after he passed or when the flames crackled or guttered.

Cyran reached the lower landing, where passageways ran off into the darkness to his left and right. He turned right and continued past a towering pillar and wall before the chamber opened up. He paced along a walkway, and soon, a stall appeared in the firelight to his left. A bent steel grate hung from only two of its original dozen hinges. Gigantic chain links were anchored to the walls of the stall and dangled to the bare floor. Charred areas streaked the stone ceiling and walls.

Cyran shivered, although sweat beaded on his forehead. He stepped past the empty stall and stopped outside the next. This one was larger and filled with more shadows. He leaned closer and held his torch out to throw light over the area.

A deafening roar erupted and shook the walls.

Cyran's ears rang with a high-pitched whine, and the flash of green scales appeared in a flicker of light. It was a face, and its mouth opened, battlements of teeth reflecting flame. Its steaming breath spewed out.

Cyran's eyes clamped shut.

A deluge of water struck him, snuffing out his torch and hurling him backward. He landed on his side with a thump and slid across the walkway, only stopping after smacking his shoulder into the far wall. He lay still for a moment in a pool of water and total darkness, wondering if he was still alive.

A forest dragon does not breathe fire but rather what is said to be rain.

Cyran touched his shoulder and winced before wiping sheets of water from his face and sitting up. Darkness engulfed the entire chamber, and the rumble of a beast's breathing echoed all around, a rumble that drew closer. The air also grew hotter. This beast could still bite him in half or swallow him whole. He pressed himself against the far wall and used its stability to clamber to his feet.

The water on the floor rose past his ankles. His tunic and leggings were soaked through, and if he lived or not, no one would be able to tell if he'd urinated himself.

"You come and wake me with your bright flame," Eidelmere's voice throbbed against the plates of Cyran's skull. Cyran flinched and clamped his hands over his ears. "And without bringing me a meal."

Cyran trembled as he crouched against the wall. Not only had he barely visited Nevergrace's den since being sent back to the outpost as a dragonsquire, but he also had not spent much time around the dragons. He knew they could speak the language of men, but they rarely chose to do so. And this particular dragon was known to be the harshest and most bitter toward all the squires.

"I didn't have time to bring you a meal," Cyran said quietly, his voice shaking. "I was ordered to fetch and prepare you as swiftly as possible."

"And where is Morden?" Eidelmere's breath heated the water droplets clinging to Cyran's cheeks.

"The dragonmage? The sickly old man?"

"He is one of the *mëris*." The beast's fuming words and grumbles erupted around Cyran. "One of the dragon blessed. A soul who can view the threads of our realm. A place most humans cannot see, much less understand. They lack the wits."

Cyran pressed himself even tighter against the stone wall. "I am... a knight." *Or I was, for less than a minute.* "If that does not suffice for you, perhaps I can see if Sir Kayom will come and assist me. I know where he is."

"Kayom is no *mëris*. He is a simple rider. A passenger. Nothing more. The same as most all the other humans here."

Cyran slipped to the side, feeling his way along stones in the pitch blackness. "But Sir Kayom can save your life in battle."

"Ha! He cannot save me." The thunder of the dragon's breath came from all around, his voice pounding the walls. "He uses me to train himself. And when there is real battle, he uses me to help him slay his enemies. Nothing more."

Cyran slid farther away along the wall.

"I can smell where you are and where you attempt to hide," Eidelmere said.

"I will fetch you a meal if you agree to follow me out of your stall. Then you may eat as I harness you. But afterward, we must leave the den."

"Then release me, and I will come with you."

Cyran realized he was no longer holding his key ring. He fumbled around in the dark, feeling in the water and along the base of the wall, where that deluge of a breath would most likely have pushed something. Within a minute, his hand bumped against the key ring, but he couldn't tell by feel which key would release the dragon's bonds. He stepped forward with one hand out in front of him, imagining the beast chomping off his entire arm.

"I cannot see to unlatch you," Cyran said.

"Then hurry back and grab a torch. I will still be waiting. Fool."

Cyran's breathing slowed, and he nodded. He ran a hand along the wall as he shuffled through the darkness back up the rampway. When he approached the arch at the den's entrance, torchlight from the bailey lit up the area. He heaved a sigh of relief, unlocked the gate, and dashed directly for the nearby hanging house. The bailey was quiet. The music from the keep continued but sounded much farther away than he'd ever thought the keep to be. He grabbed a barrow and slipped inside the hanging house, where carcasses of pigs, sheep, and oxen dangled from the rafters. After passing between the carcasses meant for the people of Nevergrace, he located the section for the dragons. A haunch and half a sheep dangled before many other drying cuts. He unhooked the haunch and half carcass and loaded them onto his barrow.

After retrieving another torch, he reentered the den and paused at the lower landing. The dragon might just eat the meal and not follow him at all. It might try to make him look the fool. He turned left this time and approached a massive archway supported by twin pillars. Beyond the pillars lay a dark chamber. He entered, lighting torches along the walls as he went, which revealed an expansive chamber where saddles and wooden platforms were stored. All of the dragon tack in here was supported on metal stands or frames.

When he reached the middle of the chamber, he spun about to study the pillars ringing the margins of the domed ceiling. The name 'Eidelmere' was etched into the outer wall over one quartered-off area. He wheeled his barrow over and set it down before the tack. Then he exited the harnessing chamber and returned to the walkway and stalls.

Eidelmere stood waiting, his mass of green scales reflecting firelight, his neck raised. The spines atop the back of his head scraped against the ceiling. His yellow slitted eyes did not blink. An acrid tang of urine and the strong musk of feces filled the air, emanating from a hole in the stone floor.

Cyran tentatively approached the iron links binding the dragon's neck. "I cannot reach."

"You are as helpless as the others." Eidelmere groaned. "And where is my meal?"

"It is waiting for you in the harnessing chamber."

Eidelmere cocked his head and studied Cyran. "You had better not be lying to me, or you will feel my outrage. And my hunger."

"I am not lying. Now, please, lower your head." Cyran waited, and after a minute, the dragon dipped his neck. Cyran reached up to insert his key and popped the circular irons open. They swung away, carried by the chains anchored into the walls. When the irons struck stone, a clang rang out, deafening in the otherwise quiet of the den. Cyran cringed and held his breath.

Something else in the darkness snorted and huffed. Then it groaned, and the moist sound of it working its mouth during sleep followed.

"Will you follow me to the harnessing chamber?" Cyran whispered, afraid of waking another dragon.

Eidelmere exhaled and slapped a taloned foot forward outside his stall, and the screech of talons scraping against rock sounded. Cyran turned and forced himself to walk, although he was still probably moving far too fast to exude any sense of calmness or confidence. The dragon's pounding footfalls followed him to the lower landing and then past it to the harnessing chamber. Cyran headed straight for the loaded barrow. He picked it up and wheeled it around to display its contents to Eidelmere.

Once inside the vaulted chamber, the dragon stretched his neck upward and worked out some kink. His wings unfurled, but the bony limbs appeared stiff. And a few of the joints were swollen where the beast's long finger-like projections segmented off portions of his wings. The crevices in the scales around his jaw and eyes were deep, a sign of tremendous age.

"Here is the meal I promised you." Cyran nodded to the

barrow. "Eat, and I will get you saddled and your quarterdeck placed."

Eidelmere rubbed at his head with the clawed tip of his wing. "Make sure it is my quarterdeck, squire."

The dragon slowly approached, and Cyran rolled the barrow closer and set it down. Eidelmere eyed him and flicked his muzzle as if to indicate for Cyran to move aside. Cyran stepped away, and the dragon's jaws gaped. Eidelmere inhaled, his torso expanding like a bellows. When he exhaled, he released a torrent of water that gushed over the barrow and its contents, knocking the barrow over. The dragon reached out and gingerly plucked the haunch up with his teeth before swallowing it whole. Then he tore into the carcass.

Cyran fetched the mage's saddle and returned to the feasting dragon. He glanced toward the entrance. Sir Kayom's other squires should probably have arrived by now, and they needed to help him attach the quarterdeck, as he'd never done it by himself before. Or perhaps this was all a test, sending him in alone to face the oldest and bitterest of dragons to see if he could saddle and harness the beast by himself when he was slightly intoxicated.

Cyran's heartrate slowed a bit. Maybe there was no real threat to Belvenguard and Galvenstone.

Lumps of food slid down Eidelmere's serpentine neck, but he seemed to have to work at getting them all the way down.

He is getting very *old.* And forest dragons were said to be some of the shortest living of all dragons.

"I am tired," Eidelmere said offhandedly as he chewed and swallowed. "And I've lived far too many centuries inside this den. I miss the smell and touch of the angoia trees. I miss their bark against my scales. My bones have begun to ache, and yet the guard of Nevergrace and their young squires keep coming in unending lines."

"And you see me only as another nameless face in that line."

Eidelmere stopped chewing, his yellow eye and black pupil narrowing as he focused on Cyran. "I have gotten to know several humans only to see them pass in the blink of an eye. Many times, their deaths have occurred during a single bout of slumber. I've known Sir Kayom for longer than most, but after the long centuries I've seen, the majority of men run together. And the younger generations of your people grow softer and weaker. They not only lose sight of the true realm, but also of *this* world."

Eidelmere sounded a lot like the old men of Nevergrace. Those men often shook their heads when they saw the outpost's youth, and they wondered aloud how their kingdom was ever going to survive.

"But Morden, we are... joined," the dragon said. "Our souls see each other's."

"And that's how a dragonmage—I mean a *mëris*—commands you?"

"If you want to call it *commanding*. But that is such a strong word in your tongue." Eidelmere lowered his head, allowing Cyran to place Morden's saddle on his neck, behind the spikes of his skull.

Cyran buckled the crisscrossing cinches.

"I know what it is you desire, boy." Eidelmere crunched through a few dry bones. "The young men of the Never all seek the same—glory and valor. To prove their worth to this world. And you are not even content with knighthood, something you held for less than a minute."

Cyran bit his lip to control a look of astonishment. Had the dragon heard of the event? Or maybe he read Cyran's thoughts.

"Steeds of the hoofed kind no longer stir your blood like they used to." Eidelmere swallowed and finished off his meal. "You wish to sail the skies and joust upon a steed of scale and fire. To shatter shields and loose dragonsteel bolts at your enemies. To unseat your adversaries from their mounts. But if you pursue such a path, you will find yourself on a dark road amassing glory only to earn the right for people to tremble at the mention of your name."

Cyran retrieved the much heavier guard saddle and grunted as he shuffled closer and laid it in front of the mage's saddle. "Then do you claim to see the fates in this dragon realm of yours?"

A raspy bellow erupted from his jaws and bombarded the chamber. "There are no fates in this world of yours, child of a man. You are the unfated."

A shudder ran through Cyran.

"Your coming was not prophesied," Eidelmere continued. "Nor was anyone's around you, except perhaps one. The Dragon Queen. She has walked these lands and our realm for as long as even I have. And she is the enemy of Nevergrace. If you wish to follow a path of your choosing and not one you are shoved onto, you must forge such a path using blood as your fire, bone as your anvil, and sweat as your bellows. Your will must become your hammer."

Cyran swallowed, his blurring thoughts trying to keep up with all this dragon was saying. "I will do what I can. I try to do so every day."

The dragon's eyes settled closed, and he looked as if he'd fallen asleep. Cyran retrieved the quarterdeck and its holding rack, using its wheeled mount to roll it over to the dragon. He positioned the rack beside the dragon's back, having only watched the placement of the quarterdeck a few times before. Ropes ran through sets of pulleys in the frame before continuing downward to attach to hooks and shackles on the quarterdeck. He took all the ropes on one side in his hands and heaved on them. The wooden platform with mounted crossbows rose a handsbreadth off its stand. Cyran grunted and kept hauling each side of the quarterdeck up until it was as high as its frame allowed. He tied off the ropes to anchor the quarterdeck in its raised position and then climbed up a ladder in the frame and used a crank similar to a windlass to ratchet the upper bars out over the dragon. When the quarterdeck appeared to be hovering over its intended position on Eidelmere's back, Cyran gently lowered the ropes a little bit at a time.

The quarterdeck eventually settled into place, the leather and wood and padding—comparable to the tree of a horse's saddle—on its underside fitting snug with the contours of Eidelmere's back. Even the larger spines protruding from the dragon's topline had matching slots cut out of the platform. Cyran tossed the cinches and crisscrossing harnesses over the dragon's far side, climbed down from the frame, and shoved the frame away. Its wheels squeaked as it rolled only a short distance before stopping.

"Can you rise so that I may secure the quarterdeck?" Cyran asked.

Eidelmere's eyes remained closed as he grunted and slowly lifted his bulk. Cyran looped straps through harnesses and cinched everything down against the dragon's underbelly, across his back, and around the base of his wings.

"Men used to worship dragons." Eidelmere still did not crack his eyelids, but his eyes twitched beneath the thinner scales there, an alertness wafting from the dragon. "They worshipped them as gods. Primarily because of the power of the other realm and the fact that only dragons could access it. But now, such respect has faded and died. Only the Smoke Breathers of the far north still see us in the same light as men did in past ages."

"The Smoke Breathers? They are nothing more than barbarian hordes."

"As I've heard as well. But civilized men enslave dragons and

use them as chattel. And as weapons and engines for their wars
—the most powerful weapons man has ever been able to
design."

Cyran looped the leather straps meant to support the lower
turret into the upper harness. Footsteps echoed on the landing
and in the hall outside. Sir Kayom marched into the harnessing
chamber followed by Morden, a hunched old man. The entire
left side of the dragonmage's body was limp, and he dragged his
left foot while using the staff in his right hand to assist him.
Morden wobbled even more than normal, probably a result of
his love affair with drink and the fact that this was summer's
end. Eidelmere raised his head, and his mouth and lips curled
into a strange expression, either a grimace or perhaps even a
grin directed at the dragonmage. Cyran could not hear any
words, but he sensed that the two of them shared a conversation.

Morden pulled his brown cloak tighter about his chest as he
approached his saddle. "Forest dragons do not enjoy flying at
night. Especially elderly ones."

"We will fly high enough to avoid any obstacles." Sir Kayom
inspected his guard's saddle. "And soon enough, all the lights of
Galvenstone will guide us."

This was no test.

The mage struggled as he attempted to climb into his saddle,
but Eidelmere tilted his head, which made it easier for the mage
to step into a stirrup and slide onto his seat.

"Everything is secured?" Sir Kayom asked Cyran as the
guard shoved against and pulled on the saddles and harnesses,
testing them.

"As best as I could do alone," Cyran answered.

"It is all rightly done." Kayom turned for the weapons and
waved for Cyran to assist him. They wheeled over a frame
supporting his dragonlance and used ropes and pulleys to settle
the weapon into a mount and arret hook on his saddle.

After they locked the lance in position, Morden laid his staff against the side of Eidelmere's neck, and the dragon turned and lumbered out of the chamber. Sir Kayom and Cyran followed. Outside, a middle-aged man and woman, both wearing metal-plated brigandines, waited under firelight.

Kayom's dragonarchers.

The woman climbed a rope ladder up onto the quarterdeck before tossing a pair of ropes over and asking Cyran to tie their ends to a bundle of dragonbolts sitting on a cart. He quickly complied, and she hoisted the bundle up. The man hauled his bolts over on a barrow and entered the lower turret, and both archers strapped themselves in at the feet and waists.

Sir Kayom mounted his saddle using long stirrups with multiple steps made for climbing. He situated himself and angled his lance in a downward position as he addressed Cyran. "Ride for Galvenstone at first light. Sir Ymar will join me as soon as he is able."

Cyran nodded, and Eidelmere's wings stretched, the dragon's old limbs no longer hesitant and sluggish. When Eidelmere flapped his wings, a rush of wind spiraled around Cyran and the bailey. The gusts tore at Cyran's hair and tunic as the forest dragon and his guard and mage and archers rose up into the night, blotting out the veiled light of the moons.

6

PRAVON THE DRAGON THIEF

"You want to turn around?" Kridmore asked over his shoulder. Twilight blues and purples silhouetted his figure.

Pravon studied the man in the black cloak who marched along the road ahead of him and Aneen. Kridmore gave off the persona of a well-armed thief. He probably hid two dozen throwing knives under that cloak, and he kept his face shadowed, allowing only his black hair to show.

"Then we'd have the dread king's men *and* his assassins hunting us for the rest of our days," Aneen said in airy and sultry voice as she pulled the hood of her cloak lower over her face. Locks of vibrant red hair hung around her shoulders and stirred in the wind. "They'd track us to every corner of Cimeren and beyond. And even if that tyrant were to ever die—as I so often hear people wish—his orders wouldn't be abandoned immediately."

"I was not suggesting abandoning anything." Pravon paced with his head down. "I was merely mentioning it is not likely we will survive all he or his creepy conjuror will ask of us."

"But this way, at least we have a chance to live." Aneen cast Pravon a side glance. "And afterward, he will set us free."

"But we must realize that by fulfilling this contract, some of the gods may come after our souls in the next life," Pravon said. "If not all nine of the gods."

Aneen chuckled. "It wouldn't be all nine. And I'd prefer to have the Paladin pursue me rather than break a blood deal and endure the Thief's or the Assassin's torment."

Pravon shook his head and opened his mouth, about to mention the secretive skills he possessed. But he closed his lips fast. *No, I cannot tell them.* "I side with you on that. But I would fear it more if the Dragon took an interest in us."

"Worries for another day." Kridmore led them around a bend in the road, the area and terrain unfamiliar to Pravon. He could only recall the general location from the map he'd seen. "And you flatter yourselves if you believe our miserable souls would ever catch the interest of a god."

A spur road led east over a hill and away from the main road. Kridmore followed the alternate path.

"We're to follow the main road to the town." Pravon pointed along that path. Aneen paused at the fork.

"This way is quicker." Kridmore waved them on without slowing.

"But night is falling, and there was mention of bandits along the spur trail." Pravon stood his ground.

Kridmore stopped and faced him, his oily locks dangling around a shovel chin. "Do you know these lands?"

Pravon glanced at Aneen before shaking his head.

"I do." Kridmore's hands moved to two areas on his chest while remaining hidden beneath his cloak. He probably gripped daggers or throwing knives. "We will be safe if we take this path. And the sooner we arrive at our destination, the better it will be for everyone. I'd like to fulfill our contract—if you can call being forced into an agreement that may allow each of us to live a contract—and go our separate ways."

Pravon waited quietly for Aneen's input.

She raised an eyebrow at Pravon. "I do not know these lands either. If Kridmore is familiar with them, then perhaps we should listen to him."

Another few heartbeats passed, and Kridmore threw up his hands and paced away along his chosen path. "You can follow me if you wish, or you can try to meet up with me at our destination."

Aneen exhaled and shrugged before following him.

We only have to fulfill specific demands. The contract does not hold us to a route. Pravon hesitantly trailed behind them.

Darkness settled over the terrain, but swaths of moonlight from the thousand moons stole through the sky sea. All those celestial bodies suspended water in the heavens, and their pale beams sliced through banks of clouds and painted silvery patches upon the land. During the day, the sky sea and sunlight veiled so many moons as well as all their light.

Kridmore began to hum a tune with small intervals between pitches. An old tune. At first he did so quietly, but over the next half hour, the volume of his humming increased, as did the tempo.

"Can we at least keep it down and pretend we are thieves working secretively on a contract?" Pravon asked from the rear of their trio. "Or are you so confident this desolate path is safe that we may sing and celebrate to our heart's content?"

Kridmore paused his song for a moment before he took it up again, this time even louder while adding mumbled lyrics. Irritation brewed inside Pravon as he gritted his teeth and pushed his hood back so he could keep a better eye on his surroundings. His brown locks fell across his cheeks, and he gripped the hilts of his daggers.

At the top of the next rise, Kridmore froze and tensed, his hands creeping for items beneath his cloak. Pravon's blood spiked with fear and anxiety. Aneen drew a scimitar and slipped up behind Kridmore. Pravon unsheathed his daggers as he glanced behind them and to either side. Other than for brush and a few rocks, the rolling hillside appeared empty. But the scuff of boots on dirt sounded ahead, and an odor of unwashed men hung in the air. Pravon darted up the incline to take a defensive position just behind Aneen.

At least a half-dozen men stepped from behind boulders on either side of the path beyond Kridmore.

"The Assassin take the Maiden," Pravon cursed and bit his tongue.

The approaching bandits brandished weapons—axes, mauls, swords, a longbow.

"A fine night for a walk," the bandit in the lead, whose shoulders sloped like peaks, said as he approached Kridmore. "Unfortunately, you sing so loudly the dead can hear you. And there ain't many who still tread this path, especially not after nightfall."

"It is a fine night to run into you," Kridmore replied, and the bandit hesitated for a moment, studying the thief as if he were entertaining the notion that he should recognize Kridmore.

"I don't think you're in the position to try the friendly approach," Sloping Shoulders said. "I don't know you. And even if I did, I wouldn't let you keep any of your coin. Only a fool and his company wander this path at night."

Kridmore didn't move, and Sloping Shoulders stepped closer, clutching a maul in both hands.

"Get out your coin purses and all you carry." Sloping Shoulders gestured at their waists as his men fanned out and surrounded them. "Or get out your shovels and dig yourselves your own shallow graves."

"They have a woman with them," a squat bandit to Pravon's right said. "And she has pretty hair."

A couple of the men jeered. Aneen flashed her scimitar in the moonlight and sidled closer to Pravon.

"Ah, and she wants a fight," another bandit said. "I like my women feisty."

"Let us pass, and you will not die." Kridmore's hands were still hidden beneath his cloak.

Sloping Shoulders glanced at his men and laughed, the moonlight highlighting a few of his remaining teeth. "It's seven against three. We would rather do this the easy way, but if you wish to fight and die, we will oblige you."

Pravon groaned as he pressed his back against Aneen's. Sloping Shoulders raised his maul over his head and stepped closer to Kridmore. Kridmore casually reached a hand out from his cloak, his palm empty. He shrugged.

Sloping Shoulders hesitated. "You cannot convince me you carry no coin at all. We will search each of you. And we will flush out *every* hiding place on your bodies."

"I do carry plenty of coin," Kridmore said. "But you simply cannot see what it is I hold in my hand."

The bandit's eyes narrowed as he peered closer. Kridmore muttered something, and light flashed in his palm, a burst of violet and something even darker, a blackness deeper than the night. The ethereal darkness expanded and lengthened, growing into a blade and then longer. It became a lance of shadow.

Magic. Pravon's hackles spiked, and he stepped away from his companion. Aneen retreated with him.

Sloping Shoulders stumbled back as his men gasped and muttered. "What is this?" the lead bandit asked.

"He's a conjuror," another bandit said.

The remainder of the bandits retreated a few more paces, and Sloping Shoulders attempted to do so as well, but he appeared frozen, his eyes gaping. His lips worked, but no sound escaped from them.

"You wanted what I carry, remember?" Kridmore said to Sloping Shoulders. Kridmore's other hand shot out from beneath his cloak and made a come-hither motion with two fingers. Sloping Shoulders was dragged through the air toward Kridmore, the bandit's toes and feet scraping along the ground even though they were not moving.

The bandit's eyes gaped wider as he floated toward Kridmore's ethereal lance. Over what seemed like a full minute, the bandit was pulled up to the tip of the lance, and he screamed. Then he was spun around in the air and jerked backward. The lance impaled his spine, the shadowy weapon piercing flesh and bone, and the bandit howled. His cry sounded as if it came from something inhuman.

The tip of the lance erupted from Sloping Shoulder's belly as he continued to be dragged toward Kridmore. After the bandit was impaled up to about half the length of the lance, his head fell back, his eyes glassy and distant appearing before they turned black and shriveled. He groaned.

Is this bone and earth magic, or something else entirely?

The other bandits fled.

Kridmore uttered something under his breath, and his lance solidified. The thief—no, assassin. He had to be an assassin and a conjuror of some sort. The assassin lifted his lance and hefted the bandit up into the air. Sloping Shoulders bowed backward and hung in his impaled position. Kridmore planted the base of the lance into the ground, staking the bandit there as the bandit moaned.

Kridmore dusted off his gloved hands and walked down the path in the direction they had been headed. Aneen tugged at Pravon's cloak, her eyes wide as she motioned for the two of them to consider traveling back the way they had come.

"Come along now," Kridmore said. "I told you, all would be fine."

Pravon and Aneen shared a terrified glance.

Bolts of lightning arced around them, creating nimbuses that surrounded the fleeing bandits. The violet bolts flashed a few times, joining all the bandits in a sizzling circle before dying out. The bandits screamed and toppled, leaving behind only a speckling of embers in the night.

7

CYRAN ORENDAIN

A SONG CARRIED THROUGH THE FABRIC OF DREAMS. DRAGON voices rumbled in Cyran's head, and fire burned in the sky like orange clouds. Cyran crept through the woods, the massive trunk of an angoia tree rising before him. Its bark released a pungent scent reminiscent of cedar, and he remembered someone wishing to taste it.

Something watched him from between the blades of a sword fern, a dark face and a shadow. It lurked beneath the angoia. A flash of light followed, and a bang sounded, ringing his ears. He lurched in bed. His eyes fluttered in the predawn darkness as he shoved his hair from his face. Smoke whimpered in the shadows nearby.

"Cyran," a voice said from the doorway of the squire house. "Cyran?"

"I am here." Young men and a few women slept around him, their breathing and snores heavy from drink and deep sleep.

"Come. Something has happened."

Cyran's skin prickled along his arms. He flung his blanket aside, sat up, and grabbed his leggings and tunic as he headed for the doorway.

Emellefer stood near the entrance, her face pale under distant torchlight.

"What is it?" Cyran glanced out into the moonlight.

"There's been an accident."

"What kind of accident?" *It must somehow relate to me.*

"Come. I will take you to Ezul."

Ezul, the nyren... why?

Emellefer turned and rushed across the bailey to the keep. She passed the spear-toting soldiers stationed there, who did not question her, and stepped inside. Cyran trailed her, following her through the atrium and down a hallway, then up a few flights of stairs. The keep was quiet and dark except for the occasional flicker of torchlight.

"Please tell me what happened," Cyran said as he gripped her shoulder.

Emellefer's voice trembled. "I cannot say, but Ezul will explain everything."

A pit of dread opened in Cyran's stomach before clenching in on itself. Emellefer led him to a chamber at the end of the hall. The symbols of a staff, serpent, and eagle stood out in bronze over the doorway. When they entered, a man loomed over someone lying on a bed. Tapers burned in a candelabrum on a table, and other tapers were clustered around the chamber. Two other men stood in the shadows beside the bed.

Ezul looked up from where he leaned over the person in bed, a poultice in his hand, which he was using to dab at the person's forehead. "Ah, you have come," the nyren said.

Cyran stepped up to the bedside. The person Ezul was tending to was a young farmhand and woodsman named Rilar, one of Cyran's brother's closest friends. Rilar's eyes were closed, his skin pale, but there was no blood or bruising, and he had no visible wounds.

"Rilar." Cyran leaned closer. "What has happened to him?"

"There was an unfortunate event that transpired on summer's end," Ezul said. "Take a seat, dragonsquire."

Cyran's heart rattled in his chest, but he glanced around, finding a chair against the wall. He grabbed it and sat, his mouth feeling as dry as sunbaked leather.

"A few of the younger men ventured into the woods late last night, or early this morning, rather. And a tree fell."

"And Rilar was struck by it?" Cyran leapt up and looked over Rilar again, although a sheet covered the man from the waist down.

Ezul shook his head. "Rilar was with Tamar." The nyren swallowed as he gazed directly at Cyran. "Tamar was under the tree when they found him."

Cyran choked. "Where is Tamar?"

Ezul dabbed absently at Rilar's head. "He... his body was taken to a chamber."

Cyran stumbled back. "His body?"

Ezul nodded. "He was unfortunate enough to be in the area, and he was likely intoxicated. It was nothing more than a hapless accident."

Disbelief and twinges of anger swelled inside Cyran like the Scyne River under spring melt. "No. Tamar is *not* dead. I just saw him yesterday."

Emellefer settled a warm hand on Cyran's neck, but he shook it off and spun around.

"I need to see him," Cyran said.

"It is better if you do not," Ezul replied. "Once he is prepared for his ceremony, we may all pay our respects."

Cyran trembled and braced himself against the wall as his chest heaved, but he still could not catch his breath. This was only a nightmare. It had to be. "Where is Jaslin?"

"She already knows," Emellefer said. "She is in her quarters in the bailey."

"Why was she told before me?"

"She was waiting for Tamar to return from the woods." Ezul motioned to the two young men standing in the shadows. "Tamar and Rilar's companions could not hide it from her."

Cyran doubled over as his stomach clenched and released. He dry heaved a few times before swallowing and wiping at his lips. His mind spun wildly as disbelief faded a touch in favor of anger. "What was Tamar doing in the woods?"

Emellefer rubbed Cyran's back. "It doesn't matter."

"Why was he out there? And why at night?"

"I do not know."

Cyran glanced at Ezul, but the nyren only shrugged. The chain about Ezul's waist rattled as the nyren returned his attention to the unconscious man.

"And what happened to Rilar?" Cyran faced the two young men.

"His friends brought him back." Ezul wiped Rilar's scalp.

"He was lying near Tamar but not under the tree," a farmhand named Frain said. His words were haunted not only by remorse, but also by fear. "We found him nonresponsive and pale."

"But he wasn't struck by the tree?" Cyran lifted one of Rilar's eyelids. The pupil looked glassy, and red vessels streaked around the whites. Once he released the eyelid, it slowly slid closed.

"The only wound I could find on him was this." Ezul gingerly lifted Rilar's head and parted the hair at his crown.

A bloody wound had been concealed under the hair, and marks like teeth stood out along the wound's margins. But the gash or bite was small—far too small to have been caused by a human mouth. And some of the skin around the teeth marks was blackened, as if it had been seared. Cyran's intestines writhed like a nest of serpents.

"What type of animal or beast could have done that?" Cyran asked. "And why would it cause him to be in this state?"

"Mayhap it is only by chance that part of the laceration resembles teeth marks." Ezul shook his head. "In reality, Rilar may have been knocked over the head by the tree or one of its branches."

"A branch that was on fire?"

Ezul dabbed at the edges of the wound. "Fire was my first suspicion as well, but the dark areas may simply be dirt and debris driven deep into the skin."

Cyran stepped back, still shocked and shaking as he glanced at the two young men. They remained silent.

"If you will not allow me to see Tamar, then I must go to Jaslin," Cyran said.

Ezul nodded. "Please do. But make your visit as quick as you are able, given the situation. I do not know what is afflicting Rilar, and therefore I fear I do not possess the skills required to cure him. You still must travel to Galvenstone and Castle Dashtok within the hour. And so you will bring Rilar with you. The nyrens of King Igare are some of the most skilled in all of Cimeren, and they have specified training in medicine far exceeding mine." Ezul patted Cyran's shoulder. "You must remain strong despite what has happened. You may grieve with all of us soon."

"I cannot..." Cyran rubbed at his face. "I should not go to Galvenstone now. Jaslin..."

"There is a matter even more pressing than Rilar's and what has happened here at Nevergrace," Ezul said. "You may not believe it to be so, but the fate of everyone at Nevergrace may depend on the affairs at Galvenstone. If Sir Kayom was summoned to the city of the king, the situation may already be dire."

Cyran's heart twinged and ached. He slowly turned around

and shuffled for the doorway. "Can Ymar fly Rilar to Galvenstone?"

"Sir Ymar departed hours ago," Ezul replied.

Cyran swallowed a lump. "What about one of the other dragons and their guard?"

"We require all the others for defense, as it is written under the laws of the king and this outpost. I've already discussed the matter with the late lord's wife. We do not have enough dragons as it is, and without Sirs Kayom and Ymar, we at the Never are utterly vulnerable to an attack."

Cyran's eyes fell shut as he struggled for breath.

"We will have a litter prepared for you to bear Rilar," Ezul said. "You must leave at first light, and you must hurry, as the paleness of his skin and thready beat of his heart indicate an impending death."

Cyran stopped, and he glanced back at the nyren. "How long does he have?"

"Hard to say, but probably not as long as it will take you to reach Galvenstone."

Cyran opened a door and entered a small house along the outer curtain of Nevergrace. A single taper flickered behind the silhouette of a girl, a few open books scattered across her bed. She hummed a familiar tune that was both joyful and foreboding, one Cyran had heard too often lately.

"What is that song?" Cyran asked as he stepped inside and sat on the straw bed beside Jaslin. Tear tracks ran down her cheeks, and she stared absently at a crystal flagon in her hands, much of the flagon's bright surface stained.

"It's the song Tamar was singing the last few days." Her voice was choked with tears.

Cyran ran a hand down the back of her head and auburn hair before wrapping his arm around her.

"He wanted to go out to the woods at night because he never gets to celebrate and have fun during the day." She paused and hummed. "He always had too much work to do. And he just wanted to be able to do what you did."

A fist of angry fury and guilt struck Cyran in the gut, and he hunched over. "He wanted to go on a hunt? Because I'd gone?"

Jaslin nodded as she stared at the flagon without blinking and rotated it around on her palm. "Night was the only time when he felt he didn't have other more pressing duties. And he was acting a little off lately. Not going to bed as early as usual and always wanting to talk about the woods. Humming that song. It seemed he was happier at times, but also, he was often much more tired."

Cyran's eyes stung and then burned as tears brimmed and blurred his vision. Since he'd become a dragonsquire, he'd not even been around enough to notice any change in Tamar. He blinked, and images on the outer flagon became clearer amidst his tears—figures dancing hand in hand in addition to single men and women with raised arms who appeared to be chanting or singing and celebrating.

"They said something about a sinkhole," Jaslin said.

"Who?" Cyran wiped away a few tears as an angry curiosity surfaced inside him.

"His friends who made it out of the forest. They said a sinkhole opened up and caused the tree to fall."

Cyran's forehead furrowed. *A sinkhole?* He'd never seen such a thing anywhere around Nevergrace, and he hadn't even heard of anything similar happening in this region of Cimeren. The chances that such an event occurred at random, and at just the moment to cause a tree to fall on his brother, seemed miniscule.

"I was reading through all my old story books to see if there were any where a sinkhole opened up." She hummed absently. "I don't remember reading about anything like that, and so far, I haven't found mention of such a thing."

"Well, if anyone at the Never knows books and stories, it's you." Cyran almost tousled her hair like he often did, but this hardly felt like the time. He hugged her instead and wished he knew a good long story he could share with her to make her feel better. "The few stories I've read, I have told you about. And you've long finished them all. Stories about the original dragonguard, those soldiers who banded together some time before the Dragon Wars."

"Of Sir Bleedstrom, who united and led the first guard in a time of honor and for the greater good." Jaslin's tone was so soft and distant that her voice sounded a league away. "They stood against all injustice. And it was said that their greatest accomplishment was not riding their dragons and fighting but that they uncovered the truth of any controversial events. Even the events that initiated and preceded the Dragon Wars."

Cyran held her tighter.

"The first guard accomplished their feats by using what little facts they had gathered and assessing their suspects and their opponents." Jaslin did not seem to notice Cyran now, apparently lost in some other world. He would let her stay there for as long as possible. "With minimal knowledge, they gauged the strengths and weaknesses of others and eventually found the answers."

Cyran nodded, and he held her in silence for nearly half an hour. "I wish I could stay here with you for days and share stories until all our pain has passed, but I fear our pain will never be gone after..."

Jaslin's eyes remained glazed over.

The carved figures on the flagon drew Cyran's scrutiny again. Shadows loomed behind some of the people, as did a sphere that looked as if it was supposed to be made of light, and back-dropping all of this was the outline of a winged serpent exhaling fire. Another indistinct form was hidden beneath the dancers' feet.

"Where did you get that?" Cyran asked.

"Tamar gave me this decanter. He found it out in the woods."

Disbelief circled in Cyran's gut. "A decanter? How do you know that is what this is?"

"It looks like a decanter."

"It looks like a fancy flagon to me. Maybe a lord's flagon. And Tamar found it like that? So... old but intact? Then he must have gone out before this past night."

Jaslin nodded. "He went out a couple times during the past weeks."

"He did? Why did he never tell me?"

"You're always training and working with your squire friends now." Her lower lip stuck out a bit, reminiscent of when she was a decade younger and was pouting.

The fist of guilt in Cyran's gut twisted and grinded its knuckles against his intestines.

Jaslin's lip returned to its typical position. "He said something about following the lights, and he was always humming that song. And he said this"—she held up the decanter—"is an artifact from the past age."

A shout of warning echoed in the back of Cyran's mind. He snatched the decanter from Jaslin's hands.

"What are you doing?" Her voice cracked.

Cyran turned the crystal artifact over, scrutinizing it. Something about it felt off. He wanted to smash it, but if it was her last connection to Tamar...

Tears streamed from Jaslin's eyes as she reached out for the decanter. Cyran allowed her to take it. She clutched it to her chest and fell onto her side on the bed, sobbing.

"There's something wrong with the woods," Cyran said. "I am as broken over Tamar as you are, but I worry about that thing." He pointed at the decanter. "And something has ventured out beyond the angoias and is prowling closer to Nevergrace."

She continued sobbing.

Another vicious bite of shame sank its teeth into Cyran's heart, and his suspicions cooled. Perhaps she was only attached to the decanter because of Tamar. "I am truly sorry for our brother, Jaslin." He reached out to smooth her hair, but she shied away from him. His hand fell to the empty portion of the bed as a storm of emotion stewed inside him. "But something in the woods and that song could be linked to Tamar's... accident." He gently touched her leg, but she pulled it away. "I need you to stay far away from the Evenmeres, at least until I return. We can both try to look into this further then."

She didn't respond or look at him.

"I am beyond sorry I have to leave now, but—"

"I know." She hid her face, her words muffled. "You have a duty to the guard and the king, and they have summoned you."

Cyran sighed. "I wish it were not so, especially now. I will ask Emellefer to check in on you while I'm gone."

"You could run away, you know. Far away. Find a place where they cannot make you go to Galvenstone."

"Then I would be abandoning you and everything I love."

Jaslin slipped off the bed and huddled over the decanter.

"I will return as swiftly as I can." He clutched her arm. "I wish to be here for you during this time, but I should not be gone long. And I need *you* as well." She looked up at him then, and he forced a smile. "Promise me you won't go anywhere near the woods."

"I won't."

Cyran smoothed her hair. "I am sorry about everything."

8

CYRAN ORENDAIN

THE REMAINDER OF SIR KAYOM'S DRAGONSQUIRES WERE WAITING at the gates of Nevergrace, all of them on horseback. Two additional horses were bound together with a litter secured between them.

"What happened to you?" Dage asked, and Laren smacked him with the back of his hand before whispering something to the hulking squire. Dage's face paled.

"I am ready to ride for Galvenstone." Cyran led a chestnut destrier named Hammerhoof, a steed one of the knights of the Never allowed him to borrow. He glanced at the sun—just peeking over the eastern horizon—and he planted his foot in a stirrup and swung onto his saddle. He strapped his broadsword to the saddlebags. "Sorry for the delay. I had to speak with Jaslin, but we must make haste."

The others turned their mounts for the road.

"How is he?" Cyran nodded at the litter.

Brelle shrugged. "I'm no nyren, but he doesn't look good."

Garmeen led the party, remaining as silent as usual. The old oak—a sentinel of a tree with a trunk nearly as big around as one of Nevergrace's twin watchtowers—hunched over the field to the south of the outpost.

"We need to maintain a steady pace for as long as possible." Cyran urged his destrier into a league-eating trot. "Ezul feared that Rilar may not survive long enough to make it to Galvenstone."

As their horses' hoofs and shoes pounded the road and the morning light grew brighter, Cyran often attempted to peek between the curtains of the litter. In flashes of movement, all he could make out was Rilar's unmoving figure covered in blankets, a wrap over his face.

Hours dwindled away as they clopped along the Scyne Road. They passed a hamlet and sprawling farmlands, but there were not many people who lived this far in the northeast of Belvenguard. And there were few travelers.

Memories of Tamar and Jaslin flashed through Cyran's mind as not only sorrow and longing but also an unsettled feeling pulled at him.

"My father wanted to keep it a secret between us, but one time he told me that in the past age, Nevergrace was a slavery castle that held men and women," Laren said. His and Brelle's near constant banter usually faded into background noise, but this statement broke through Cyran's reverie. "It was the closest outpost to the elven city, and the elves kept human slaves."

Brelle bellowed with laughter. "There's not even such a thing as elves. And if there were, they were a just and honest folk. They wouldn't have kept slaves. It was the dwarves who kept slaves. Or maybe dwarves were the slaves of the north. I cannot remember it all."

"You two should ask a nyren and stop spreading fabrications and then arguing about them," Garmeen said. He hadn't spoken since they had left, but he still didn't bother turning around from his position in the front of their line to address them.

"Well, what do you believe?" Brelle faced Cyran. "We never hear you spouting off anything of interest about Nevergrace. Other than the songs you sing about it."

Thoughts tumbled around in Cyran's mind as he mulled over so many things he'd heard through the years, much of it based in song. "I remember my mother sharing all the Never's songs and a few stories with my brother and sister and me when we were young. The parts I can recall, and what I've always believed, is that the north initiated the Dragon Wars. They destroyed every city and castle that resided across mid Cimeren. Then they cursed and cultivated the Evenmeres so they could do whatever they wished without Belvenguard acting as a witness or being able to interfere. Murgare harbors dark magics, and their kings rule through fear, intimidation, torture, and never-ending wars. Over the centuries, the north has often used the paths in the forest to sneak assassins and thieves and warriors into Belvenguard simply to kill our people and instill fear. Their own cursed forest has helped and hindered them, as their king's deepest desire is to rule all of Cimeren."

"Simple enough of an explanation." Laren nodded. "But you're missing so many of the important details."

"You mean fabrications," Brelle said. "Like how you insist Sir Marenbore's dragonsteel sword is the same as Sir Kayom's—The Flame in the Forest. The sword Marenbore of Nevergrace used against Murgare's legions of onyx guard when they came over the seas and swept through the Weltermores at the turn of the age."

"That is true!" Laren said. "The Flame in the Forest has been passed down through the Never's guard since it was forged. It has always resided at our outpost, and so the fact that Sir Kayom now carries the same blade should not even be too difficult for *you* to accept."

"I believe Laren to be correct on that one," Garmeen added.

"Except that the blade was lost to the Weltermores at some point in its history and was wielded by an enemy for a time. Marenbore was from Nevergrace, and The Flame in the Forest is dragonsteel. There is no reason the blade cannot last centuries, if not longer."

Dage nodded. "I've heard the same, except that it was one of Murgare's vile guard who wielded the Flame for a span."

Laren laughed in Brelle's face, and the two fell into another argument about a time when Laren had been dead wrong.

Cyran lost track of their conversation, rode up beside the litter, and eased the pack horses to a stop. "I should give Rilar some more water."

Garmeen nodded and stopped as Cyran dismounted and pulled himself halfway up into the litter. Rilar's eyes were veiled behind a wrap, his mouth gaping open. He hadn't moved at all. Cyran turned his waterskin over and dribbled a few drops onto his lips and then into his mouth, waiting to make sure the farmhand didn't cough or choke before pouring in a steady trickle.

As Cyran continued watering the young man, possibilities about what could have befallen Rilar and Tamar out in the woods came scampering back into his thoughts. Why had Tamar suddenly started venturing out into the woods at night? Jaslin insisted he'd done so multiple times and she listed her reasons as to why, but Cyran suspected there had to be more to it. Tamar had been humming the same song Cyran heard when he and his squire friends went out for that hunt. Tamar had also been such a dedicated worker of the outpost, and he focused primarily on his duties. Something must have distracted or enticed him. Most likely something in the woods. Perhaps after he'd found that decanter, he wanted to unearth more artifacts. The hair on Cyran's arms prickled with the thought of Jaslin holding that thing.

Rilar coughed weakly. Cyran jerked and stopped dripping

water into Rilar's mouth. He mopped up what had dribbled around the farmhand's lips with a blanket, then tucked the blanket in tight around the man's neck and shoulders. The wrap around Rilar's eyes suddenly seemed to hide a dark secret. Cyran's skin chilled as he exhaled and slipped back out of the litter before climbing onto Hammerhoof and riding on, forcing himself to ignore a growing worry.

Cyran dismounted late in the night. All their horses were layered in white sweat, and their necks and flanks steamed. A light drizzle fell from the sky sea and muddied the earth around them.

"That's one," Laren said to Brelle as they argued about something. "Sir Useth was summoned to the Summerswept Keep and found his calling as a guard there."

"If that tale is even true." Dage uncinched his saddle and yanked it off his horse before dropping it on the ground. "And that would make *one* guard from Nevergrace who's been honored and invited into the royal guard of the king."

"And if you believe that, you probably also believe that Sir Useth climbed all the way into the canopy of an angoia tree and caught a dragon hiding there," Brelle added. "Then at the battle of the Red Scyne when the Weltermores became their own kingdom, the tales say Useth slayed a hundred knights after being unseated from his dragon. None of the legends about Useth are true. Every squire from Nevergrace who enters the guard stays at Nevergrace."

Laren swept a hand through the white foam on his horse's neck and flung it at Brelle. "Then maybe Dage will be the first. If he ever shares what that letter from Galvenstone said."

Dage shoved his blond hair away from his face but didn't

answer. Cyran unsaddled and unbridled Hammerhoof and led the gelding to a stream weltering beside the road. Rain dripped from the hood of Cyran's cloak in steady intervals. The horse drank deep, his flanks heaving as he swallowed. Once the destrier had taken his fill, he nibbled at the grasses along the banks. Cyran's companions watered their horses nearby.

Once again, in the growing quiet, thoughts of Tamar ran rampant through Cyran's head—their youth spent together, most of it without parents, growing up and taking separate paths, the idea that a sinkhole and a tree killed him.

"Call me cruel or uncaring, but I don't want to touch our wounded comrade." Brelle crouched over the stream beside her mount, cupping her hands and drinking. "I'm not the motherly or nyren type when it comes to death and disease."

"I'll take care of Rilar." Cyran knelt and splashed water on his face before standing and turning for the litter.

"You've been caring for him all day." Laren dug into his saddlebags and rustled through their contents. "Someone else can take a turn."

"I'll bring our wounded companion water." Garmeen walked toward the litter.

"At least we're covering a lot of road." Dage slipped the bridle over his destrier's head, and the bit banged on the horse's teeth with a hollow clunk as the animal tried to drop it. "We should reach Galvenstone in good time."

"If our mounts can keep up this pace," Brelle said. "The young lady of Nevergrace should have slipped us one of her dragons and a mage. Rilar isn't going to live for many days looking like that and only taking a squirt of water every hour or so."

"But everyone was on edge and worried about defending the outpost." Cyran emptied his waterskin into his mouth and refilled it in the stream. "Ever since Sir Kayom's hasty departure.

I asked Ezul, and he said the king's laws and those of the Never would not allow for another dragon to be taken from the outpost."

"And it's not Menoria's decision." Laren removed bread and cheese from his saddlebag and used a knife to carve into both. He ate chunks of white cheese straight off the blade. "Nevergrace is under her mother's authority till the new lord arrives."

Cyran withdrew an apple from his packs and bit into it, the fruit crisp and sweet this time of year.

"I wish we had enough coin to stay at the inn we passed a while back," Brelle said between bites of salted meat. "Rather than sleeping out here. I could piss in a chamber pot instead of beside the road with all you fools."

"None of us squires have enough coin to spare for an inn." Dage chewed on a hunk of dark bread. "And we don't deserve soft beds. The road will have to do for our lot. Only those in the guard have earned the right for such comforts. And when or if we become one of them, then the jingle of our coin purses will draw ears for—"

"He's gone!" Garmeen's voice carried more emotion than Cyran had ever heard the squire use.

"Who?" Cyran dropped his waterskin and rushed over to his comrade.

The blankets inside the litter had been thrown back, the pillow still indented where Rilar's head had lain.

Cyran glanced at Garmeen, whose face was ashen. After a moment of surprise dragged out, Cyran ran around the horses to the other side of the litter. Rilar wasn't lying on the ground there either.

"He couldn't have fallen out." Garmeen felt through the blankets, as if the small pile could have hidden a full-sized man. "He'd have to climb over the rail."

"And we would have seen or at least heard something."

Cyran grabbed a hooded oil lamp from outside the litter and walked back along the road, shining the firelight about.

"If it was indeed a wound to the head, he could have turned delusional and climbed out hours ago," Brelle said as she approached Cyran. "When was the last time you gave him water?"

"It must have been over an hour ago now." Cyran recalled all he could of the last time he'd stopped the packhorses and leaned into the litter. He'd dribbled water into Rilar's mouth, and the man's lips twitched but nothing more.

"Did he carry a fever?" Laren used their other lamp to look under the litter and along its tented roof.

"Not that I could tell," Cyran replied, "but I didn't feel his skin. I just gave him water."

"Mayhap he felt better and needed a walk after lying down for so long." Brelle's tone sounded skeptical of her own suggestion, not facetious, as typical for her.

Cyran glanced along the road and all around. "I will have to go back for him."

"We're supposed to hurry to Galvenstone," Dage grumbled.

The hair on the back of Cyran's neck prickled as he eyed the Evenmeres still running along the northern boundary of Belvenguard. "But we're also supposed to *bring* Rilar to a nyren in the city, and as quickly as possible."

The slap of scampering footsteps sounded off in the darkness. The squires shared a glance. A cold wash of blood rolled through Cyran's veins.

"Who's there?" Laren called out, holding his lamp aloft.

"Rilar?" Cyran said. "If you can hear me, please return at once. We need to keep moving, and you are in no shape to travel alone."

The only response was a chilling silence until the wind—the

breath of the Evenmeres—gusted, throwing a sheet of rain at them.

A shriek sounded somewhere between them and the woods, and a flash of firelight followed. The rain obscured Cyran's view, but what appeared to be a dark silhouette with tufts of purple flame rising from its body and cloak walked through the darkness.

Cyran ran for his saddle and ripped his broadsword from its sheath before returning to the others.

"You plan on attacking Rilar if he doesn't answer you?" Brelle asked over the drumming of the rain.

"No," Laren replied for Cyran. "You saw something, didn't you?"

Cyran nodded and stepped beyond Laren's sphere of light and out toward the woods. He held his lamp high overhead as the rain berated its glass.

"I don't like this one bit," Brelle said from behind Cyran. She was not following him.

"I thought you believed there was nothing to worry about with the forest," Laren said.

"We're not in the forest, you dragon's ass. And I started to worry once a dying man just vanished in..." Brelle's words faded in the rain between them as Cyran crept closer to the Evenmeres.

Then he saw it again, a silhouette with violet light or flame licking at its cloak. It had ventured closer to the road. And just behind the silhouette, a ball of white light darted about, winking. A familiar and joyful tune rose from the light. It gamboled about, as if trying to speak with Cyran, to entice him. The deeper undertones of its song vibrated the air.

Cyran froze, and he could no longer control his body. He walked toward the silhouette, his legs moving by some command not his own. He thought he should want to shriek with terror, but any dangers seemed distant, as if they belonged to another world. A clamor sounded behind him—the other squires yelling to get his attention—but Cyran marched on toward the lighted figure and the ball. The squires' voices turned frantic, morphing into screams. But Cyran was too far from them now, and the figure waved him closer and closer to the woods.

Another step, and another.

The dark figure hovered just ahead, and in the next moment Cyran stood before it. His sword hand fell to his side. The lamp was no longer in his other hand.

Someone grabbed Cyran's shoulder and shook him. Garmeen's voice erupted just behind him. "Cyran! What are you doing?"

Cyran blinked, and the roaring of the wind and stinging rain on the back of his neck returned. Some dark figure stood before him, violet flames writhing on its back. Cyran lurched and stabbed at the figure with his broadsword. But his blade merely passed through the apparition without resistance or any sound.

Terror surged through Cyran, and his sword turned to ice and shattered into a hundred fragments, leaving the hilt so cold in his gloved grip it felt as if it were burning his palm.

Garmeen yanked Cyran away and pulled him along as Cyran opened his fist but also had to peel the frozen hilt from his glove and fling it away. His legs and feet felt as heavy as boulders as he moved. The dark figure shrieked from near the tree line and floated after them. After a few more steps, Cyran's legs limbered up, and he and Garmeen ran faster. The flames of some burning thing crackled behind them.

The others had already started riding away when Garmeen shoved Cyran up onto his now saddled horse.

"We ride on this night," Garmeen said as he took Cyran's reins and kicked their horses into full gallops.

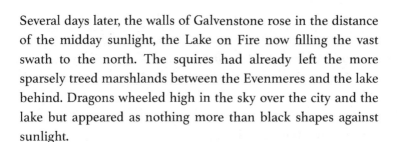

Several days later, the walls of Galvenstone rose in the distance of the midday sunlight, the Lake on Fire now filling the vast swath to the north. The squires had already left the more sparsely treed marshlands between the Evenmeres and the lake behind. Dragons wheeled high in the sky over the city and the lake but appeared as nothing more than black shapes against sunlight.

Cyran rubbed at his gritty eyes. They had ended up riding through much of the nights, and while they had slowed to a walk days ago, his destrier was dragging his hoofs along the road. The horses bearing the empty litter had also galloped along and kept pace with their company, as if they had sensed the terror and didn't want to leave the comfort of the group.

Visions of a man in a flaming black cloak accosted Cyran again but started to seem more and more imaginary. The fright of Rilar's missing body that night, which now seemed so long ago, had probably made his mind run wild. And the others still claimed they had not seen a thing, although Laren and Garmeen swore they had heard shrieks and the crackle of fire. Cyran glanced at his ungloved hand. A red mark still ran across his palm, but it didn't hurt. Was the mark truly from his sword's hilt freezing in his grip?

Cyran sighed and shook his head, but his thoughts would not wander far from the events of that night. It was Garmeen who had risked his life to stop Cyran from entering the woods and Garmeen who had broken whatever spell came over Cyran. It was also Garmeen who had forced him to gallop away from the area. Cyran studied his quiet companion, the silent leader of their group, the man who had been a squire longer than any of the others and who was approaching his third decade of life. Garmeen rode along, gazing up at the city on the hill. Cyran would have to be much more careful around that forest. He had no doubt that evil lurked in there, although he still wasn't convinced the apparition he thought he saw was real. His musings about the forest made him more anxious over Jaslin and of leaving her behind with only memories of Tamar and that decanter and song to comfort her.

"The lake's not actually burning." Brelle's shoulders and thick hips rocked with the moving of her steed. "I think about that every time someone mentions the Lake on Fire. And every time I've ever traveled this way."

"It's not burning *now*." Garmeen's thin figure hunched beneath his cloak. "The name harkens back to the past age and came about because of the Dragon Wars. That's what my gaffer says, anyway."

Laren nodded his agreement. "I've heard tales of the war upon the lake where dragons burned every ship in the king's armada. Made it look like the lake was on fire."

"That's not true," Brelle said. "It was a city by the lake that was burning."

No one spoke or argued for a few heartbeats.

"It's as big as the sea," Cyran muttered, unable to see any distant shore. He took in the approaching walls of Galvenstone, a tiered city with Castle Dashtok sprawling across the top of a central hill. The four hatchery towers surrounded the castle, one at each corner. Those were the only known hatcheries in the entire kingdom of Belvenguard. Cyran wondered if one day he would become the dragonguard of a creature reared there.

Laren yawned and stretched. "Nothing feels frightening now that there's daylight and Galvenstone is near."

"I still wonder what could have possibly happened to Rilar." Dage's voice was thick and grumbly.

No one said a word for another ten minutes.

A group of riders approached, headed away from Galvenstone. Four men and two women. The men wore leather armor, and broadswords were sheathed at their waists. They eyed the squires as they passed, two of the men's hands on the hilts of their swords. The litter drew the women's attention.

The group passed with nothing more than a sneer, and Cyran urged Hammerhoof to increase his pace. Thick lines of travelers were filing into the city, a sparser line headed away.

Once the squires arrived at the city, they joined the incoming line before passing through the massive gates and archway and entering the first tier of Galvenstone. Red flags with gilded borders and a golden dragon snapped overhead. Their horses' hoofs clopped on the cobbled streets as they wound around buildings and houses.

"We traveled much faster than anyone—including Sir Kayom—could have ever expected of us." Brelle's eyelids sagged under her curls. "I'd like to leave the horses at the squires' stables and find a place to sleep for an entire day."

Merchants selling bread and wares from their carts choked the streets, and haggling arose in punctuated crescendos. A church with a massive dome loomed over the next tier of the city, a golden statue of the Paladin standing proud under the sunlight on its peak.

So much wealth flows within these walls. Galvenstone could devote single churches to each of the nine gods.

Laren glanced around at the towering shops and buildings in wonder. "There it is." He pointed. "The Tavern of the Shield Maiden. Not more famous of a tavern there ever was." He stopped, and Hammerhoof bumped into the rear of his mount. "You can sleep as much as you'd like, Brelle, but the energy of this city has enlivened my heart. I will see the inside of that tavern before we leave."

"We're not here for socializing and drinking spirits."

Garmeen turned around in his saddle. "We are here to meet Sir Kayom."

"But we are *early*." Laren's eyes vibrated with energy. "And we no longer carry a farmhand whose life hangs in the balance."

No one answered him, and as Hammerhoof shoved past Laren's mount, Cyran caught the other horse's reins and guided both horses onward.

After winding their way up through the second tier, they left their horses and the empty litter with a few stable hands who waited just outside the entrance to the third tier—the gates of Castle Dashtok.

"We have come to meet with Sir Kayom of Nevergrace," Cyran said to one of a dozen soldiers standing before the gates. All the soldiers toted spears, their faces buried beneath steel helms.

"And this dragonguard is expecting you?" the soldier asked.

"Indeed. It was by his order that we traveled here."

The soldier called to a messenger boy in a bright yellow tunic and whispered an order before the boy ran off. Cyran and his friends were asked to move aside from the main entryway, and they waited out of the way for half an hour before the messenger returned and spoke with the soldier. The soldier waved them over.

"Sir Kayom has not yet arrived," the soldier said to Cyran as the squires approached.

"But he flew here by dragon." Cyran glanced back at the others in surprise. "Days ago."

Dage cursed under his breath.

"Maybe he made another stop during his travels," the soldier said. "Either way, squires, you are not allowed entrance into the castle without your guard." Cyran opened his mouth to protest, but the soldier cut him off. "That is all. Be on your way. When your Sir Kayom arrives, you may once again request entrance."

Laren tugged at Cyran's shoulder, and all five of the squires shuffled away toward the stables where they had left their steeds.

"Maybe we can find beds in the stable hands' quarters," Brelle said.

"No, we need to find Sir Kayom." Cyran glanced over his shoulder at the soldiers and the gap between their ranks. "Or find out what happened to him."

The soldier they had been speaking to retained a neutral expression, but his tone carried across the distance between them and made it clear he would find it annoying if they challenged his word. "You try to sneak inside the castle without permission and you'll find yourselves sleeping in the dungeons for a good long time."

"Come, my friends," Laren said. "I know the remedy for this predicament."

They continued on toward the stables, and Laren's steps lightened as he strode along.

9

SIRRA BRACKENGLAVE

THE WINDS IN THE UPPER REACHES OF THE SKY SCREAMED AND gusted, but their angry voices and breaths broke against the Dragon Queen's armor and her cloak of woven shadow. Rain pounded against Shadowmar's scales, and lightning flashed within a cloud to their right.

The Evenmeres forest loomed below and all around them. Sirra veered Shadowmar around a copse of angoias. The crowns of some of those monstrous trees reached up to the level where they were flying, and the air was already growing too thin. They would not be able to ascend any higher. Not that they would want to with the sky sea looming an uncomfortably close distance overhead.

Sirra headed more easterly than she'd wanted, to avoid a copse, and she flew over an area composed of clusters of conifers and maples. Those trees were so far below them that their greenery blended into each other's and made them appear like the surface of a sea.

"The others are falling behind," Yenthor shouted over the raging wind.

Sirra glanced back. Sir Vladden and his ice dragon led the

rest of their legion, but even they were a hundred dragon lengths behind her. The other ice dragon and the mist and fire dragons were farther behind. Sirra wheeled Shadowmar around in a wide arc and swooped in beside Vladden and his dragon with the snow-white scales.

Vladden glanced back at the woman behind him, her hunched frame almost completely hidden by his bulk. "Quarren pushes our mount as much as we dare, but we may have to stop and rest him soon. Or we won't be able to make the crossing."

Sirra glanced down at the Evenmeres. "We will find no repose in those woods."

Vladden's voice softened, and Sirra could barely make out his words over the beating of their dragons' wings in the wind. "I do not mean to question you, Dragon Queen. There was no better alternative than what we—"

"But you are beginning to question if we should have come this way at all." Her voice rumbled around inside her helm as Shadowmar glided along beside the much slower ice dragon.

Vladden hesitated before slowly nodding, his dark helm and its horns armored in ice and dripping rain. "Your shadow dragon may be able to fly this entire route without rest, but our mounts are weakening. Even if we could make it to the other side of these cursed woods, we would not be fit for an attack."

"Maybe you should have sent a legion of storm dragons instead," she chided him. "I left the decisions and details concerning who would accompany me up to you, Sir Vladden."

Vladden fell silent for a few heartbeats, and fear sheeted off him as his dragon struggled with each flap of its wings. "Even with a shadow dragon, four storm dragons would hardly create the ideal legion meant to launch an assault on any city or outpost."

Sirra nodded. "I agree with that reasoning, but four living

storm dragons would be superior to four dead dragons of any type."

Vladden slowed his mount further and allowed the other ice dragon, the red fire dragon, and the pale mist dragon with jet black wings to catch up.

"Perhaps we should fly west to the marshlands," Vladden said. "We could take our respite in that filth. At least for a day or so."

"And risk being spotted by the watchtowers of Galvenstone? Our vengeance would die before it began."

"Or we could fly to the Elmoor sea."

"That route could add weeks to our travels, heading east and then soaring back west. And it would not leave us much or any more rested."

"What would you have me do with the legion, Dragon Queen?"

Sirra studied the forest below in addition to some of the angoias they had managed to veer around before she took in the horizons all around them. "We are safe as long as we hover over Belvenguard's abominable woods, but if we are forced to go down into them, we risk everything."

"Maybe we could convince the dragons to sleep in the angoia trees." Vladden's words carried a heavy air of pessimism. "Surely whatever lurks in these woods would not be able to reach us way up there."

"It is probably true that we would not be in danger, but only forest dragons are able to adequately rest in trees. Your ice dragons and the fire and mist dragons would be forced to cling to the trunks, and they would tire themselves out as much as if they were flying."

"Then tell me your command." Sir Vladden waited, his monstrous armor barely visible behind his shield.

Sirra's mind churned. There was no clear answer to this

riddle, and there had not been one since the forest had grown over the region of a previous kingdom, back when she was young.

A screech radiated up from the pines, and a raptor larger than a man wheeled over the canopy below. Hundreds of smaller birds burst from the crowns of many oaks, twisting and turning in their attempts to avoid the raptor. The fire dragon dived toward the raptor, and when it eventually neared the bird, it released a cone of fiery breath. The raptor ignited in a blaze, its wings flaming as it continued to soar in a ball of fire. The dragon swooped down on the burning bird and devoured its charred remains.

"The flaming raptor." Quarren, the dragonmage behind Vladden, kept her face veiled by her cloak but stared in the direction of the spectacle. "I do not believe in portents, but I've only heard of such a thing happening once before on the eve of a great battle. And that battle turned into the Dragon Wars. Such imagery is hard to ignore."

Sirra did not answer. She would not bring attention to any supposed sign.

"Then we shall bring fire and death to Belvenguard." Vladden's posture stiffened.

A moment of silence passed as the wind gusted and cried through the angoias.

"That meal would hardly sustain any dragon." Sirra glanced about.

The other ice dragon veered toward the flock that had been fleeing the raptor. The dragon inhaled and expelled a gale of frost over the birds, freezing most of them instantly. The ice dragon scooped up about a dozen of the frozen birds in its jaws before the rest plummeted like stones. The beast barely chewed its prey before swallowing.

Vladden glanced at Sirra, as if curious or afraid of what else had just happened.

Sirra pondered their legion's situation trapped above the Evenmeres, ignoring any suggestion of omens or signs. Vladden might be unsettled either by fear of what could happen to them or fear of all the death they might cause, but Sirra considered neither the flaming nor frozen birds to be more than necessity, the work of tired and hungry dragons. The nine gods had forgotten or forsaken Cimeren. That was all there was to know.

"Follow Shadowmar." She angled her dragon downward, and her mount plunged like a diving eagle, angling around copses of angoias while drifting west.

She watched the woods closely, searching for an area to land —the main path or a clearing of any kind—but nothing presented itself. The trails were the only safe route through the Evenmeres, but they were narrow and wound about the woods, unable to be seen in their entirety from above. Not that any of her legion's dragons would fit on such paths.

A few trees below her shifted, moving slowly at first before picking up speed. It was not a group of trees clustered together, nor those in a line, but rather only a few scattered trees that crept about. And a deep rumble carried up from the woods. Something much more dangerous than giant raptors lurked down there.

And it is not the trees themselves that should be feared.

10

CYRAN ORENDAIN

THE INTERIOR OF THE TAVERN OF THE SHIELD MAIDEN WAS AS dark as any other tavern. Men and women crowded around tables, shouting and spilling drink. Foam lacquered tabletops and knuckles as well as dealt cards and those stacked between patrons. Dice rolled, and cleavage popped from corsets. Cyran rubbed his heavy eyelids. He'd tried to sleep, but his nerves were on edge and he couldn't. Maybe a few drinks would help ease his mind and his worries, not to mention his sorrow over Tamar. There could also be a small chance that some patron or barkeep knew of Sir Kayom or had heard word about his delayed arrival.

A man at a table nearby towered over every other patron in the place, and he watched Cyran and his friends while gulping straight from a flagon. A double-bladed axe was strapped to his back. A few women displaying their ample cleavage between their corsets and black or violet chokers wandered about, and two others hovered in a dark corner, watching the squires as well. After all Laren's talk of this place, Cyran had pictured something much different, not a riotous tavern full of drunk men and women in the afternoon. He'd started to imagine an establishment with a touch of elegance.

Laren and Dage stood near the counter in the middle of the chamber, laughing and drinking while three women vied for their attention. All three were as scantily clad as most of the other women in this tavern.

"I won't ever be one of the dragonguard anyway," Garmeen said, pulling Cyran's attention away from the questionable patrons.

"Oh, you'll make it." Brelle emptied her stein into her mouth and swallowed. "It's me you should all worry about. There are only a few women dragonguard in all the kingdoms."

"But there's the Dragon Queen." Garmeen thumbed through a stack of greasy cards on the table. Cyran had never heard the squire talk so much. "The most formidable dragonknight who has ever lived. And she rides the most powerful dragon in all the kingdoms."

"Yes, but there's only ever been one of her, and she's supposed to be hundreds of years old." Brelle dismissed his comments with a wave, but her eyes shimmered. "Not to mention, she's from Murgare."

"Well then, maybe the south will find her equal in Brelle of Nevergrace." Garmeen chuckled, and Brelle's wistful expression dropped. He shuffled the cards, many of them sticking to each other. "Maybe you're another dragonmage. One who's not crippled by whatever power the dragon realm bestows on those who can see it."

"And per the tales, there are other dragonknights in Cimeren," Cyran said. "There might even be some in Belvenguard. More than only Sir Paltere. It may just be that none of the others' achievements are as legendary as the Dragon Queen's, so we haven't heard of them."

Garmeen smiled and lifted his stein. "May our Brelle become one of them. And although Sir Paltere is unequaled in Belvenguard, may his skills not be enough to match hers." He drank, and Cyran and Brelle did as well, although Brelle shook her head afterward and Garmeen continued speaking. "It's been said that Sir Paltere single-handedly won the battle of Seafell after the north surprised and decimated most of the guard in one of our dragonguard legions."

Sir Paltere. Cyran's lips lifted into a grin. He remembered that man from a tournament he'd attended in Galvenstone not long ago. Sir Paltere was not nearly as large or imposing as most of the dragonguard, but he carried an air of authority and casual confidence. And everyone respected and listened to him.

"Then why did you join the squires?" Cyran asked Brelle as he sipped at a hearty ale brimming with earthy flavor. "If as a woman you don't believe you'll make it into the guard? You must have known being a dragonsquire would never allow you to make enough coin to live a decent life."

"If you die on the back of a dragon, you will be remembered. Forever." She grinned as she stared into the depths of her empty stein. "Because I've never wanted anything more than to ride a dragon. To soar over all the lands, commanding respect and inspiring awe in children who dream similar dreams to what I once did. To have scales surrounding me and wings beating at the wind behind me. To have clouds in my hair and a shield and lance in my hands. Or a crossbow. I'd be more than happy to be strapped onto the quarterdeck of a rose or sun dragon, shooting down our enemies of the north."

Cyran's vision blurred with her words as he imagined the sensations and excitement of becoming one of the few men to ever ride a dragon.

"I've come to accept that I'll never be called to the guard." Garmeen began dealing out the cards as patrons at the table nearby bet and cast coins onto a heaping pot. "I'm not accurate enough with the crossbow, and I'm not a big man. Not big enough to easily protect my mage."

Cyran swallowed a mouthful of ale and nearly choked before wiping a runnel from his chin. "I've been told that about my size as well." A deep sense of loss pulled at the hope that had burgeoned inside him. He tried to ignore the sensation and glanced at his cards—a knight and a thief thus far. "Several people have said I'm tall but not broad enough to provide the protection required from a guard."

Garmeen nodded and finished dealing out nine cards to each of them, one card for each of the gods. He broke the remaining stack into three smaller ones before placing two of them in the middle of the table and pushing the last stack aside. "With your skills, I always hoped you'd have been summoned to the guard long before now. And because you haven't, I've lost any hope for myself."

"We're all getting a touch too old to be squires anyway." Brelle lifted the corners of her cards while blocking Cyran's view of them with her other hand. "They will probably replace us soon with the quickest and biggest young fighters of Belvenguard. Those who still cling to the dream of what they could become and who are still shamelessly eager to impress their guard-masters."

"Maybe there aren't enough dragons to bring in more guard." Garmeen picked up his cards and started switching their positions. "And maybe they keep those of the old guard, like Kayom and Ymar, around instead of replacing them at a certain age because of the bond they already share with their mounts or their mages."

"Or maybe there's a scarcity of dragonmages." Cyran gulped down the contents of his stein. "Given the sizes of those massive hatcheries, it seems like there should always be dragons being raised in them."

"Unless it takes decades or longer to rear a single dragon." Brelle motioned for a serving woman to bring more ales.

"But we know there are plenty of squires who wish to become one of the guard." Garmeen's head wobbled as he studied his cards. "So the reason not many are being taken into the guard must be because there aren't enough dragons or there aren't enough mages." He furrowed his chin and nodded. "Dealer calls first attack. Mine will be"—he looked through his cards again—"the Shield Maiden's revenge."

Brelle groaned as she threw her cards on the table before picking them back up and choosing three. "Or there's not enough coin in the Summerswept Keep's coffers to support expanding the legion." Brelle belched, long and loud, without covering her mouth. "In the end, everything comes down to coin. Or power."

"Mark my words." Garmeen laid out a card of the Shield Maiden, the Paladin, and then the Dragon. "If another dragon and mage are ever sent to Nevergrace, they will be for Dage. He best fits everything the legion is looking for in a guard."

"Fuck you, Garmeen." Brelle threw out a nyren and two servant cards. "How are we supposed to beat that run? You can have my crappy hand." She grabbed for a set of dice and studied the signs on them—shield, sword, horse, arrow, staff, dragon, dagger, anvil, and ship. "I'm ready to play dice."

Garmeen grinned but shook his head.

Cyran wasn't going to beat Garmeen's play either. It would be best for him to get rid of the cards he'd be least likely to need in the future. He tossed out a blacksmith, a sailor, and a sea wolf. Garmeen gathered the nine played cards and stacked them into his taken pile that at the end of the game would be used to tally points based on each card's value.

As Brelle dealt out three more cards each, the serving woman returned and dropped a tray onto their table, her cleavage escaping as she leaned over. Cyran handed over the last of his halfpennies. He had only a few farthings left to his name.

Cyran reached for a drink, but he paused. Nestled between the steins on the tray was a wooden box with a slit of an opening.

Brelle and Garmeen hefted their steins and drank without even noticing the small box. Cyran snatched up the object and glanced around, trying to find the serving woman, but she'd vanished into the crowd.

"What's that?" Brelle asked.

Cyran held up the box and shrugged. He shook it, but nothing came out of the slit and no coins jingled inside it. "Maybe it's to encourage us to leave offerings for the servers."

"Not with an opening that size." Garmeen's head wobbled more as he tried to focus on the object Cyran held. "All the coin would fall out, and someone could easily pilfer from it. Not to mention just steal a box that small by slipping it into a pouch."

Cyran turned the box over, studying its smoothed surfaces.

Brelle's forehead pinched and wrinkled as she scrutinized it. "Stick your finger inside it."

Cyran considered that for only a second before shaking his head. With the look of the people in this place, he wouldn't trust anything other than the drink, and he didn't trust the drink all that much either. He angled the slit toward the torchlight.

"Something is in there." Cyran could only make out a dark lump.

"Are you afraid we're important enough that someone wants to assassinate us using a poisoned needle inside a box?" Brelle snatched the box from Cyran. "I'll do it."

She squinted as she peeked inside and slid a finger through the slit. Her eyes rolled about as she felt around. She screamed.

Cyran jolted and reached to tear her hand from the box, but Brelle burst out laughing.

The patrons closest to them, who had fallen silent for a

moment and stared at them, soon returned to their drinking, cards, and boisterous conversations.

"You two are far too wound up after whatever you thought you saw or heard the night Rilar deserted us," Brelle said.

"I am not sure what I saw." Garmeen grouped some of his cards together. "But I'll never forget the chill and overwhelming dread I felt."

"And not having slept much for so many days doesn't help." Cyran snatched the box from Brelle.

"Give it back," she said. "I was going to make sure there was nothing hidden inside. Right after I gave you both a good scare."

Cyran jammed his first finger into the box and felt around for the object he'd seen. Once he located it, he worked at it until it loosened and wobbled and then slid out. It was a small tile with a symbol—a strange marking resembling a letter but with too many arcing lines—etched onto its face.

"What is that supposed to represent?" Brelle asked.

"It is the *pallënsir*." Cyran spun the tile as he studied it, his vision blurring. "It means... to see or discover."

No one replied, and Cyran eventually realized that Brelle and Garmeen were staring at him.

"Is that a word from the elder tongue?" The stein in Brelle's hand tilted, and drink spilled over its lip and foamed over her cards. "What some call old Cimerian or Cithöshak?"

Cyran thought about what he'd just said. "I don't know."

"Then how do you know what it means?" Garmeen laid his cards face down on the table, his reddening eyes boring into Cyran.

"It just... sort of came to me." Cyran looked the box over, hoping to see or discover something else about it. It was plain and rectangular. Besides the slit, all its surfaces were smooth. "Why would a symbol meaning to discover something be hidden inside a box delivered to our table?" Cyran furtively glanced around at the patrons again, but no one was watching them any more closely than they had been. The towering man at the table nearby even appeared less interested in them. But his altered manner could be a deception.

Cyran ran the box between his fingers, and he found a groove that was almost invisible in the dim tavern. He pressed on the area, and a length of wood slid out from the opposite face of the box. On this little drawer lay a letter sealed with red wax. A rampant dragon was imprinted in the seal.

"A letter." Brelle's eyes widened. "Now this box is starting to worry me."

Cyran took the letter and placed his finger beneath the seal. He hesitated, but the surrounding patrons appeared lost in drunken conversation and gambling punctuated by gales of laughter.

He broke the seal and turned his back to the nearby table before unfolding the message.

Beware of one in the king's council, dragonsquires of Nevergrace. You are not wanted in the Summerswept Keep. Tell no one of this warning but take heed. Your lives may depend on it.

Cyran nearly dropped the letter as he whipped around. No one was watching him. He slowly slid the message across the table for the others to read.

"What in all the bloody holds?" Brelle asked.

Cyran folded the letter back up, shoved it into the box, and shut the drawer. He set the box back onto the tray and placed his stein beside it, pretending he hadn't even seen the box yet.

Brelle peered over her shoulder and watched Laren and

Dage laugh and drink while the same three women leaned against them.

"Dage recently received a letter with a red seal." Cyran picked up his cards to give the impression they were only interested in gambling.

"But he still hasn't told me what it said." Brelle took a long drink.

Ideas swirled in Cyran's mind as he prayed this message had nothing to do with Sir Kayom not being at Castle Dashtok. "If we liken ourselves to the dragonguard of old, we are supposed to use our heads as well as our might. They had to gauge and judge an opponent and their strengths and weaknesses with minimal knowledge."

"What can we piece together from that?" Fear stretched Garmeen's face tight. "Other than someone wants to warn us before we enter the castle."

"Someone could have done it simply to frighten us." Brelle picked three of her cards and, in a much louder voice, said, "We play the Thief's heist."

"We know whoever set this up has knowledge of the elder tongue, if I am correct in interpreting that symbol." Cyran's voice was a whisper as he laid out three random cards. "And we know they used a skilled craftsman to make a box for a simple letter."

"Maybe so no one else would easily find it," Brelle said.

"We can also assume that Dage's message was probably not a summons to the dragonguard," Cyran continued.

"And why do you say that?" Garmeen flung out three cards— a bandit, a conjuror, and a whore. "We all believed it was an invitation to the guard."

"Because if it was, Dage would have gladly told everyone within ten leagues of the Never," Cyran said. "Plus anyone else who would have listened. But he didn't tell anyone. Not that we know of."

"Then perhaps he received a similar letter of warning?" Garmeen took the hand and added the cards to his taken pile. In a much louder voice, he said, "You two play like drunken fools." Then quieter, he added, "But who would send us such letters? And why?"

A minute of silence passed.

"Well, we do know one other thing." Brelle downed her ale before continuing. "Dage's letter couldn't have arrived in a similar box. He never would have figured out how to open it."

Cyran almost chuckled, but he realized she was probably right.

"He might have broken the box open though." Garmeen passed the dealer cards to Cyran.

Brelle wavered her hand in a noncommittal manner. "Only if he suspected there might be something of value—"

"He can play a song of Nevergrace," Laren shouted over the crowd as he came stumbling up to their table. He pointed at Cyran. One of the women who had been pressing her skirts up against Laren approached, carrying a lute. The instrument's body was stripped clean of its finish where the player's hand would strum, but its strings were intact.

The woman giggled and placed the lute in Cyran's hands. She stepped back, and the patrons began clapping to create a beat, not a regular one but a beat more typical of drunken fools. Cyran cursed as he glanced from the box to the lute.

Another woman set a tankard down in front of him. "Please, play us a song from your valiant outpost near the Weltermores."

The crowd cheered and applauded. Cyran groaned as his head spun. He strummed the strings and began tuning them. Laren squeezed between Brelle and Garmeen and sat down.

"You know those women hanging on you are whores, right?" Brelle whispered to Laren.

Laren swayed in a drunken stupor. "No. They're ladies of Galvenstone."

"They are only trying to get your coin."

"Well, then Dage and I fooled them as they didn't get either of us up to a bedchamber."

"Did you spend all your coin?"

Laren grabbed his coin purse, which collapsed under his fingers. "Certainly did. But I spent it all on drink." He grinned.

"Drinks for those three women as well?" Brelle took three cards from Cyran, as he hadn't dealt any out.

Laren's eyes wandered over some foggy memory. "Of course I did. Did you see them?"

Brelle rolled her eyes. "When you buy women like that a drink, the innkeeper takes the coin and gives them a stein of water. Then they split your coin between them. So you did pay for their womanly companionship. You just made their part in the affair quite easy."

Laren's boyish grin fell so fast it seemed it could have dropped onto the floor. "They... they wanted to know all about us and Nevergrace. They laughed at every jape I..."

Brelle shook her head and scoffed.

The crowd roared with impatience, and Cyran strummed a few chords, opening with a song about the legendary king and dragon buried beneath the Never and the stars hidden above the sky sea.

11

CYRAN ORENDAIN

In Cyran's waking dream, memories of Tamar and Jaslin assaulted him. Even strong drink could not clear his mind and force him to pass out. At least not for long. He may have slept for a couple hours, but then he woke. He couldn't fall back asleep, no matter how hard he tried, and his head throbbed as if a hammer beat against the anvil of his temples.

Another memory surfaced. His brother and sister were children, and they were driving a plow horse out in the fields beyond Nevergrace. Cyran practiced with his wooden sword and crossbow, picking leaves off an alder.

"He cannot just play all the time when we have to work," Jaslin had said loud enough for Cyran to hear as they passed by, and she shoved against the plow.

"He's practicing to be a knight." Tamar wiped at his forehead with a rag and brushed aside locks of sweaty hair. "I don't know if he will make it, but he's actually quite good. Much better than I am." Tamar waved at Cyran, and Cyran's guilt and sheepishness faded like dew on sunny battlements. "I can take up some of his work, if it gives him a chance. A real shot at becoming a knight."

Cyran smiled. "Thank you, Brother." He placed his hand over his heart and then held out his fists, crossed at the wrists, as he'd seen some of the men in the dragonguard do.

Tamar returned a smile and laughed before making the same gesture.

"Well, I'd like to be reading my stories instead of pushing a plow." Jaslin huffed and folded her arms over her chest. "I'm really good at that."

Tamar chuckled and ruffled her hair. She knocked his hand away.

"And if he does get to be a knight, and I'm ever in trouble, it better be his duty to save me." Jaslin stomped about. "Like if old Ulba starts tracking me down again. She's always yelling at me about something."

Tamar bellowed before whispering something to her. Her pouty lips squirmed and almost formed a grin, but she fought it off. Tamar stepped up beside the horse and unstrapped the plow. He boosted Jaslin onto its back, took the lead lines, and hopped up behind her. The horse flicked its ears and snorted. Tamar nudged their steed into a trot, and they rode across the field while a man in the distance shouted for them to stop playing around.

Cyran gripped his crossbow and ran after them. His brother turned the horse and circled Cyran a couple times while raising a fist and shouting, "I am the greatest knight in Belvenguard! Hear me or feel my blade."

Jaslin howled with laughter before Tamar reined their mount in. "Jump on," Tamar said to Cyran.

Cyran glanced over at the nearest field where others were working or shouting at them. One man came rushing over.

"Hurry!" Jaslin said. "Let's all ride away together. The three Orendains!"

Tamar reached out a hand and hauled Cyran up behind

them. They wheeled around, and they all kicked at their steed's flanks until it galloped off into a field of grass and wildflowers. The man chasing them shook his fist and hollered. Jaslin threw her head back and laughed hysterically as she held her arms out to catch the wind. Tamar laughed with her and then hummed a tune, and Cyran tried to match his brother's melody. Tamar had always been better at remembering tunes and matching pitches. He just couldn't play the lute. And then Cyran cried. Or maybe it was only that he cried now. He didn't remember doing it then.

Someone shook Cyran as he lay in a cot, and he groaned. "Jaslin. Tamar."

"Cyran, wake."

Cyran's eyes unlidded, although he'd not been sleeping, and he wiped stinging tears away. He stared past dancing torchlight into Sir Kayom's salted beard.

"We have to go," Sir Kayom said, and Cyran bolted upright.

He sat on a cot in the stable hands' quarters, his skull feeling like it was pounding against his brain. His friends slept nearby, most of them snoring more than usual.

"We were charged with bringing an injured farmhand to Galvenstone's nyrens," Cyran said, "but the man disappeared and we cannot find him."

Sir Kayom's faced contorted with confusion as he grabbed Cyran's arm and assisted him with standing. "I've been looking all over the city for my squires, and I find you all passed out in here. Whatever this other issue is, it will have to be dealt with later."

"I..." Cyran studied Kayom—graying beard, strong jaw, dark eyes that scrutinized him. He wore the green and gray armor of Nevergrace. "Why weren't you at the castle yesterday?"

"I can attempt to explain that later, but we are already late. Very late. We must hurry." The dragonguard turned and strode straight away, waving for Cyran to follow him.

"What about the others?"

"Their breaths smell so strongly of drink I could probably light their snores with a torch."

Cyran was still fully dressed in his squire's leather tunic, leggings, and boots. He tried to ignore the throbbing in his head as he belted on Laren's broadsword—thinking his friend would be in no shape to use it. Then he followed his guard-master. They stepped outside into the morning sunlight and wound up the street to the castle's gates, where they marched under the archway without any of the soldiers there protesting. Sir Kayom's dragonsteel armor and sword probably told the soldiers everything they needed to know. The promenade to the castle was lined by red carpet with gold trim, and it drew them on. Soldiers were stationed across from each other at regular intervals.

"I ask you all to arrive as soon as possible and meet me, but then *I* have to hunt you down." Sir Kayom's tone bordered on outrage. "And when I finally find you, you are all passed out. Every one of you is so drunk you could have fallen asleep in the streets of Galvenstone. My trusted squires are unable to control themselves outside of their outpost."

Cyran swallowed as two great weights of regret and shame twined in his chest. If he explained, would Kayom think he was only trying to make poor excuses? "We arrived yesterday, much quicker than anticipated, as we had some strange things happen to us during our journey. We rode through the days and much of the nights. Then the Dashtok soldiers, through a messenger, told us you weren't at the castle and hadn't arrived yet. We believed we were early."

"We will discuss this later." Kayom led Cyran beyond the great doors and into the castle. They paced across a long atrium before turning left, following hallways, and winding down staircases. "Now, listen closely."

Cyran nodded but remained silent.

"We will be allowed into the conclave, but you are *only* there to serve as my squire." Kayom's tone had hardly improved. "The doors will be sealed, and no matter what you hear or see, you absolutely *cannot* speak of it to anyone. Not even in your prayers to your dead parents. And you will remain silent for the entire duration, no matter how long it takes. You will dishonor Nevergrace if you act otherwise."

Cyran swallowed. "I understand."

"I hope you do. And if you act the part of a drunken fool, I will have Ymar plant his sword so far up your arse, you'll taste dragonsteel."

Cyran cringed. Kayom had never been an open or warm man, but he'd never been this harsh before either.

He must have expected us to arrive as quickly as we did, or something of an even graver nature than anyone let on is about to unfold.

Sir Kayom strode up to twin doors that were barred with a heavy beam. Soldiers stood at both sides of the doorway.

"I apologize for our late arrival." Sir Kayom nodded to them.

Two soldiers unbarred the door but took extra care to silently swing it open. Kayom nodded his apologies again and slipped inside. Cyran hurried after him.

The chamber beyond was circular, and barred doors ran all around its perimeter. The outer portion of the chamber was similar to an arena, made up of tiers of stone benches that descended toward the center. People sat together under dim lighting and watched the lowest section—an inner circle. There, a few men and a couple women sat in tense silence at a table that bisected the lower chamber. But only one woman was seated far away from all the others.

Sir Kayom sat on the highest benches in the rear of the chamber beside Sir Ymar. Cyran silently took a seat beside his guard-master.

A man in gray robes stood and stalked around the table, stroking his gray goatee. Torches burned along the border of the inner circle, and a multi-tiered chandelier with hundreds of tapers hung over the center. The man spoke as he paced. "And in the matter of Murgare cultivating the Evermeres and cursing the woods with dark magic, you plead innocent for yourself, your king, and all the north?"

"I do," the woman at the far end of the table replied. She wore a velvet dress, and her gray-streaked hair was tied back from her face. She might have been fifty years old, with skin as pale as a winter sky.

This woman is from the north...

"But before the Evenmeres, there was only the Lake of Glass —as it was once called—and peace and prosperity flourished between the northern and southern kingdoms. Now the forest divides our world in two. It breeds distrust and creates a nearly impassible wall between us. It is also said to be the home of bandits and is responsible for many people going missing."

The woman did not answer.

The north must have cursed the Evenmeres, and if that is true, they are ultimately responsible for Tamar's death.

The man sitting at the opposite end of the table from the woman being questioned wore a crown. The king of Belvenguard—King Igare Dragonblade—a stocky man with a kind face and unruly blond locks streaked with gray.

Cyran's heart thumped against his ribs as he recalled the mysterious message in the box at the tavern. Did someone in the king's court truly not want the dragonsquires of Nevergrace inside the Summerswept Keep? Or did someone not want anyone from Nevergrace here?

"And the vast riches of the north," the orator—this man had to be King Igare's personal orator—continued, "have primarily been amassed by conquests of other kingdoms, the pilfering of riches obtained through raiding and war. Through death. There are also accusations against Murgare alleging that the kingdom overtaxes and impoverishes people who will not fight and die for the northern crown."

"The riches of Murgare are largely attributed to our past and our mines in the upper mountain valleys," the lady said. "And trade."

"And who currently works these mines?"

"Our people, who are paid laborers... in addition to dwarves from Darynbroad."

"Dwarven slaves?"

"No. Also paid miners. Dwarves work the mines of their own kingdom, but there are so many of their kind that some seek work elsewhere."

The orator's forehead wrinkled, and he lowered his head and rubbed his temple.

The woman being questioned jabbed her finger in the air, pointing at the orator and then the king. Her face contorted with rage. "Belvenguard and the south sowed the Evenmeres with dark magic and cursed the land between us. If there is indeed evil lurking in the woods, it is your people who are responsible for putting it there!"

The chamber fell silent as the woman's words echoed above the chandelier, and the woman regained her composure.

She attempts to display a cool exterior, but a hidden monster lurks beneath.

The orator cleared his throat and paced around the table. "Then we shall move on to more grievous matters." The orator stopped when he stood beside the king. "In these past years under the Murgare king, your late husband, the north no longer—"

"King Restebarge," she almost shouted before calming herself. "That was his name."

Cyran nearly fell off the bench as he jerked and looked to Sir Kayom. The dragonguard did not acknowledge him, but given the gaping look of Kayom's eyes, he was similarly shocked. Sir Ymar turned as pale as snow, and the other guard and squires in the chamber were not any more adept at hiding their surprise.

The Murgare king is dead! And his queen is a prisoner at Castle Dashtok.

"Remain quiet," Sir Kayom whispered to Cyran, and Cyran faced the inner circle again.

"And your people murdered him," the queen continued. "He has yet to be avenged, and thus his soul remains trapped in the sky sea, under torment."

The orator laid out a series of parchments before the king and then strode over and set down a similar number of parchments before the queen of Murgare. "Yes, the Murgare king's death was a tragedy, an accident caused by one of Galvenstone's dragonguard. King Igare deeply regrets the end result, but such undertakings carry a certain degree of risk. And given the Murgare king's predilection for deadly acts, we decided the dragonguard's venture to be worth that risk."

The queen did not answer.

The orator picked up another stack of parchments. "Also, during King Restebarge's reign, we discovered that it became law for the north to no longer hold captives of war for more than a day. Murgare performed torture and executed any prisoners. And King Restebarge and Queen Elra—you—oversaw all conflicts and all of your legions' actions, including those where prisoners were taken." He jabbed a finger onto the documents. "The skirmish of Wellingdore. The River of the Helm. The Valley of the Smoke Breathers."

The orator stood back and waited for an answer.

A dragonguard on one of the benches below Cyran leaned over and whispered something to the guard next to him. Cyran recognized the man, and a rush of memories followed. He'd spoken to this man before, at the tournament here in Galvenstone. Sir Paltere, a middle-aged man whose thin but strapping muscles stood out on his neck, his hair and stubble dark with hints of gray. He was not nearly as big as most of the dragonguard, and his gaunt face made it clear he carried less body fat than a hunting cat. But he was no dragonguard. He was a dragonknight of Galvenstone, a rare person who was a dragonmage but was not crippled by whatever magic afflicted those men and women. If this city had any others of his kind, Cyran had not heard of them by name. In fact, he hadn't specifically heard of any other dragonknights besides the dark Dragon Queen of the north.

"And on these matters, how do you plead, Queen Elra?" the orator asked.

"Innocent," the Murgare queen replied.

"Very well." The orator turned and whisked away to a bench overflowing with parchments.

The two other men and the other woman at the table whispered amongst themselves. One older man wore the red robes and chain of a nyren healer and scholar. A much younger man was adorned in the white robes of a priest of the nine, the woman dressed in a mauve cloak—one typical of conjurors.

"And how do you plead for Murgare in response to the accusations of genocide?" the orator asked. "For the genocide of the elves of old Cimerenden as well as the Smoke Breathers who you share your kingdom with."

"Innocent."

The orator sighed. "And now we move on to more recent matters concerning the murders of people in small towns across Belvenguard." He circled the table again and shuffled through parchments. "We have discovered that small groups of thieves and murderers were employed by the Murgare king. These men have admitted to working for King Restebarge for the simple purpose of killing and creating chaos in the southern kingdoms. Four small bands of brigands have already been tracked down and apprehended, but at least one more still prowls our lands."

"We do not employ thieves or bandits or the like, and we certainly never used such men against our enemies." The Murgare queen's expression was now devoid of emotion, but her bronze eyes smoldered with animosity and rage. "My husband was a good man who did whatever he could with what he had. He loved his kingdom and his people. And they loved him."

"Then you deny such accusations against him in addition to those against yourself? Other than admitting your husband did 'whatever he could with what he had'?"

Queen Elra scowled. "I deny *all* the accusations that have been brought against me and King Restebarge within this"—she glanced around—"chamber."

"Would you include the accusation that Murgare has additional men within Belvenguard who are in its coffers in that denial?"

The queen's pale skin flushed, and her eyes burned like metal in a forge. "They came to *us*! Any from the south who..." She leapt from her chair, but rings of purple light flashed in the air around her.

The woman in the mauve cloak stood and gestured, her long white hair spilling out of her cowl.

The lights tightened around Queen Elra, who cursed and struggled against their bonds, but they forced her back into her chair. "Damn Belvenguard and its wretched trickery." She twisted and turned until her face purpled, fighting to stand and pull at the magical ropes. Eventually, the Murgare queen panted for breath and fell still.

The chamber turned silent.

"Please continue, Queen Elra," the orator said. "I believe you were about to tell us of the people in Belvenguard who made contact with you. We'd like to know who they are. And when and how they approached you."

The Murgare queen glared at the orator, her mouth a tight-lipped smirk. Her bronze eyes blazed with hatred.

12

PRAVON THE DRAGON THIEF

KRIDMORE LEAPT OUT OF THE TREE AND LANDED ATOP A patrolling soldier, burying his dagger into the man's back and killing him instantly.

Pravon climbed down from the maple, studying the accuracy of the assassin's or conjuror's strike while attempting not to reveal fear or awe. Aneen followed Pravon but pushed around him and checked the dead soldier's coin purse before removing a few bits and farthings.

"We don't have to kill every person we come across," Pravon said.

Kridmore wiped his blade clean and studied the closed gates under moonlight.

"You also didn't have to kill all those bandits," Aneen said.

Pravon was not a decent man, but he nodded his assent. He'd done many terrible things in his life without remorse, but an unsettled discomfort had not left him since the encounter with the bandits. Kridmore could command magic unlike anything Pravon had ever seen. If the assassin's magic was bone and earth magic, it carried a different flare. But having such a dangerous man in their group was not what unsettled him the most. What left the worst taste in his mouth was the memory of watching those bandits flee followed by the image of Kridmore departing as the bandits' bodies smoked on the ground.

"You were more than happy to check them all over and rid them of their coin." Kridmore chuckled as he glanced at Aneen.

"We didn't have to take that route," Aneen replied. "In fact, we weren't supposed to. But given the results, it would have been a waste to leave good coin lying around."

Pravon's gnawing discomfort bloomed into something larger as a thought struck him and he addressed Kridmore. "You knew those bandits would attack us. That's why you took that road. Why you were making so much noise. You *wanted* them to come for us. So you could kill them."

"Why are you two so worried about a few bandits?" Kridmore pressed his shoulder against the gates of the village. They held firm, barred on the inside. "They were rapists and thieves and murderers."

"Well, those are our kind of people." Pravon watched their surroundings for any more patrolling sentries.

"No people are my kind of people." Kridmore's reply sounded uninterested and distant as he crouched and shut his eyes. "And you should want those men dead, perhaps even to kill them yourselves."

"I would have tried to kill them if they attacked me, but—"

"They did attack you."

Pravon stepped out from under the canopy of the maple and into the night. "But you drew them in. Tempted them, even. Almost forced them into the situation."

Kridmore's voice was a whisper. "And you believe that to be wrong?"

Pravon didn't answer. There seemed to be no point in arguing with this man, and they had their contracts to fulfill for the tyrant king, whom they had never met or even seen from afar. A man behind a man, probably behind many others. Who even knew if the king oversaw their orders? The king could die and certainly their contact wouldn't tell them about the event. But even then, if they didn't still honor their contract, their lives were forfeit.

"This village has two of *them* inside." Kridmore stood and opened his eyes, returning to awareness. Pravon imagined the conjuror's mind or soul had left his body and scouted about.

"Then there are two we *should* kill." Aneen clamped her fingertips around the iron frame of the gates and hoisted herself up for a moment before easing herself back down and turning around. "I will make this easy and pass over the walls using the maple."

"I wouldn't do that." Kridmore whispered a command and rubbed his fingers together. Purple flames sprouted from his palm, and sparks arced away into the night. He muttered something, and a patch of shadow seemed to crawl from beneath the tree and wrap around him like a curtain, veiling his fire.

"And why not?" Aneen planted her hands on her hips. "If you wish, we can take hostages and force our targets out instead, make this easier on ourselves. I have no problem with hostages, if they serve a purpose."

Kridmore touched the flames in his hand to the gates. A crackle sounded as the gates smoldered, and he continued to stalk around the walls and light them at regular intervals. Pravon and Aneen followed him, keeping their distance. Once they had traveled full circle and again stood before the gates, Kridmore whispered and made a quick motion. All the flames licking at the walls flared, their flickering teeth sawing and chewing into the logs of the wall, releasing black tendrils of smoke into the sky. In under a minute, voices of alarm sounded within the village. Screams followed.

Pravon's pulse turned thready, and cold sweat broke out on

his forehead. "There are only *two* dragonmages in the entire village. There are also women and children in there. Surely, you do not intend to kill everyone."

"Besides ridding the world of the mages, we are also supposed to create as much havoc and chaos and spread as much fear as possible."

That is part of the contract. But Pravon had never imagined such a situation.

The front gates rattled as people on the inside unbarred them. One of the gates cracked open, allowing more screams to rush out. Kridmore held up a hand, although he stood ten paces away. The gate slowly shuddered and would not open any farther. Then it slowly started to slide closed.

The screams turned more frantic, ringing in the night and buzzing in Pravon's ears.

Pravon heaved for breath as he turned away. Aneen trembled and dry heaved.

The shadowed form of a dragon landed near the maple, its dark blue scales reflecting the mounting flames. This dragon was small, relatively speaking, not even rising a quarter as tall as the tree. No quarterdeck or archers would fit on this beast. It carried only two riders—a mage with a staff and another who sat behind the mage. Both riders made the dragon appear even smaller.

The rider in the rear climbed down from the dragon, their cloak billowing in the fire's hot wind. The storm dragon shrieked and exhaled a bolt of lightning that struck the maple, lit it up, and caused it to smolder.

"Dragonmages?" the cloaked man asked, not revealing his face but gesturing at the village.

Kridmore nodded. "You've taken a great risk, coming up here with just a storm dragon. And besides knowing our general whereabouts, how did you ever manage to find us in the middle of the night?" The conjuror laughed.

The man stared at the burning cone of the village for a moment but did not answer. The last of the screams died out and faded. "But no dragons, I assume. Not in this miserable little place."

Kridmore shook his head.

"They have too many mages at their disposal." Their contact folded his arms and tucked his hands into his sleeves. "It is a danger with these people. But, if you are finished playing around with this trite little hamlet, I carry orders from the... from your new employer. A change of plans for you three."

Pravon glanced at Aneen, who raised an eyebrow. *New employer? What happened to the dread king?*

"Belvenguard prepares for war," the cloaked man said, only his voice familiar. Pravon would never recognize him for any other trait, not even in broad daylight. "And the north gathers its banners from across the vast tundras. From the dwarves of Darynbroad to the barbarians in the Valley of the Smoke Breathers. But an assault is coming sooner than the war Belvenguard is preparing for, and I have an inkling where this assault will occur."

The flames behind them crackled and popped, sending embers shooting high into the night sky. Kridmore suddenly held a glowing lance of deep violet light in his hand, and he planted it into the ground before the conflagration of the village. The lance solidified and stood erect, waiting like a silent omen, a harbinger of death.

"There is one new objective that *must* be attained." Their contact used two fingers to wipe at the corners of his lips. "What you decide to do with whatever else you encounter is up to each of you."

13

CYRAN ORENDAIN

THE SUNLIGHT WAS MORE VEILED THAN USUAL BEHIND THE SKY SEA and a nest of low clouds as Cyran stepped out of the Summerswept Keep and walked the promenade. He headed for the outer gates of the castle. Other squires hustled past him as they whispered amongst themselves.

The trial had concluded following a sustained silence by the Murgare queen, and she'd been escorted out of the chamber. Sir Kayom wished to stay behind and discuss matters with the other dragonguard, but he'd ordered Cyran to care for Eidelmere and then gather the remainder of his squires.

"I'll give you three full pennies if you feed our dragons and clean their stalls." Someone bordering between adolescence and manhood and maybe five years younger than Cyran hurried up to him with a friendly smile. The stranger held out a clenched fist.

Cyran paused and almost retreated a step as the stranger entered his personal space. The young man was dressed in a tunic and leggings, but they were boiled leathers, not the typical garb of most people. A broadsword was strapped to his waist. Two other young men in similar attire waited behind the first.

They were dressed in the same fashion as the squires at Nevergrace, although these men's attire appeared newer and fresher.

Cyran quickly glanced down and ran a hand over his leathers—what must have signaled to them that he was also a dragonsquire, those and his broadsword.

"What do you say, friend?" the young man asked.

Three pennies was more than Cyran was paid for a few days of work. "Why? What draws your interest more than tending to your duties and holding on to your coin?"

The closest squire scratched his head, and his brow furrowed as if he was bemused by Cyran's question. "We wish to watch the tourney. Like everyone else."

Cyran glanced around. "And where's this tourney taking place?"

The squire laughed. "In the sky. You're from a small town, aren't you?"

Cyran shrugged. "Not even a small town. I'm from an outpost. Nevergrace."

The squire frowned. "You probably would have cared for our dragons for a single penny, then."

Cyran curtailed a look of having taken offense. Were Nevergrace's workers really paid so much less than at other places? "How long is the tourney running for?"

"Oh, it'll last all day, but we want to watch the banners fly in for the opening ceremony."

"You only have three dragons to feed and care for?"

The young squire nodded, and his smile spread across his cheeks. "Two silvers and a sun. They are all easygoing. And their guard are not riding today."

Cyran held out his hand, consciously fighting off an expression of awe and wonder so he would not reveal that he had never actually seen a sun or a silver. The young man dropped three pennies onto his palm, quickly gave directions to the hanging house and the den, explained which dragons were theirs, and turned for his comrades.

"Rumors carry to our city, outpost squire," the young man said over his shoulder. "People say war is coming from the north, and everyone is preparing. All of Belvenguard. Just to let you know."

Cyran nodded, and the young man and his comrades cheered and dashed away.

Cyran found a barrow waiting outside the hanging house in the outer bailey. He took it and slipped through an arched doorway. Inside, he loaded up the hind quarters of an ox before wheeling the barrow down a long stone walk to the den—a gargantuan building larger than the rest of the entire castle. And most of the den's interior would be underground.

A cylindrical tower rising more than ten stories backdropped the den. Soldiers in helms, carrying shields and spears, patrolled each level of the tower.

One of the hatcheries.

Cyran had never seen a dragon egg, and to his knowledge, Nevergrace had never housed any eggs. Maybe if any of their dragons laid them, the eggs were immediately brought to Castle Dashtok to be placed under the protection of the king and the hatcheries.

Above and behind the hatchery, several dragons emerged and wheeled in the sky, turning about and racing straight for each other only to skim past one another. Gasps and cheers sounded somewhere off in the castle and beyond its walls. Banners waved on the dragons' tails and streamed behind them. Red and gold were by far the most prominent colors, but there were several others—silver and white, blue and gray, violet and emerald. Thin training bolts arced back and forth between the soaring dragons. The spectacle was far enough away that when some of the training bolts struck their targets of either dragon or shield, there was a delay before the metallic clang of their impact reached Cyran's ears.

The dragons then flew alongside each other. Rivers of fire bloomed in the sky, followed by breaths of water and ice and a few bolts of lightning, creating a spectacle of light and magic.

"It's quite something, isn't it?"

Cyran hefted his barrow and marched on, realizing he'd stopped to watch. Sir Paltere—in dragonsteel armor of red and gold with the sigil of a golden dragon on his breast—stood on the other side of the walk, gazing at the sky. His dark hair waved in the wind, making his face appear gaunter as he whistled a cheerful melody.

"Sir Paltere?" Cyran asked. "Are you not riding?"

The dragonknight laughed. "Why do you ask? Do you think I need the training?"

Cyran bit his lip. "That is not what I meant."

Paltere chuckled. "I remember you. From the past knight tourney. You were the clear winner and were sent back to Nevergrace, but as a dragonsquire."

Cyran grinned as a warm feeling bloomed inside him. He'd made an impression on the dragonknight of Belvenguard.

"An admirable outpost to train at." Paltere approached. "Most of our squires in Galvenstone are paid too well, and they have become... soft. And now some of them have paid you to care for their dragons, haven't they?"

Cyran slowly nodded.

Paltere shook his head and chuckled again. "Knowing your dragon is *the* most important factor if you become one of the guard. If you do not know your dragon, you are both as good as dead."

"Yes, sir."

"That is why I feed and care for mine every chance I get. But it is different for a knight. We also share a much deeper bond, one only a dragonmage can understand."

The sentiment his words carried almost made Cyran wish he were a crippled young man who could enter a dragon's mind and their world.

The deafening roar of a crowd erupted not far away, and it echoed off the castle and den around them.

The sound of massive wings beating and snapping in the wind followed. Cyran spun around. A dragon more golden than the sun and as massive as a tower swooped low and then soared over the battlements on the other side of the outer curtain. A dragon the color of a red rose dived from the sky and leveled out, flying in the opposite direction as the sun dragon, and both beasts sailed straight toward each other. Gargantuan wings blotted out the sunlight and cast shadows across the entire walkway around Cyran.

Cyran's heart raced as the dragons faced off. The dragonguard sitting just behind the head of each mount tilted and angled titanic lances that extended well beyond the mounts' snouts. Archers swiveled around their mounted crossbows on top of the dragons' backs and in the turrets below their bellies.

Wind surged and pummeled Cyran, tearing at his hair and tunic as the dragons flew closer and closer to each other.

"Here comes the tilt," Paltere whispered.

The guard on what must have been a sun dragon wielded a lance capped with a metal fist. The guard on the rose dragon bore a lance tipped by blunted prongs, resembling the crenellations of a tower.

"But do not fear," Paltere added. "It is only a training tilt."

A clash of metal sounded as lances struck shields. The rose's guard catapulted from his saddle and was launched away. His lance broke free from its mount with a crack, and the guard plummeted and disappeared behind the outer curtain. His lance tumbled after him. The impact bowed the other guard back at the waist, but he remained seated as the dragons angled their heads away from the attacking lances. The dragons veered past each other, their wings smashing against one another's with a sound similar to bony knuckles punching flesh. The beasts shrieked, and their raging voices shook the castle walls. The dragonmages on each mount did not stand out much more than another hump of scales, their forms low and blending with the dragons' necks.

The beasts whipped past each other in an instant, flapping enormous wings and ascending into the sky. The seated guard regained his posture.

The crowd erupted with applause and cheers.

"What happens to the guard who are unseated?" Cyran asked as Sir Paltere stood with his arms folded, still watching.

"I told you not to worry. Those who are jousted out of the sky are caught by storm dragons." When Cyran raised an eyebrow, the dragonknight continued, "Storm dragons are small but are by far the fastest and most nimble of their species. The guard who was unseated right out there landed in the street, which has been prepared. The squires layered it with a man's height of straw. That's why we did not hear his armor smash into the cobbles. He may have broken his arm or dislocated his shoulder during the joust, but he should still be alive."

Cyran imagined the guard digging himself out of a river of straw with a shattered arm.

"A training tilt it was." Paltere shrugged. "More for show than anything else. In true battle, the enemy comes at you from any number of directions, not straight on as you see in tourneys with horses and knights. And so in battle, a guard must account for unlimited changes and uncertainties by shifting angles while turning and ascending and descending in the wind."

"Then a dragonknight would hold a massive advantage over

a guard." In Cyran's head, dragon battles composed of the guard of Galvenstone and Nevergrace raged as they fought the beasts of the north, and Cyran's voice sounded distant even to his own ears. "Not just because of some title or ability to communicate with dragons, but because a guard would have to constantly adjust his position to compensate for his mount, who is following a mage's commands. But a knight, like you, controls his dragon and every motion it makes. You know where and how your mount will move, and you can make adjustments prior."

Sir Paltere grinned. "Well, I wouldn't say 'controls his dragon and every motion it makes,' as that sounds tyrannic, but you have the rest of it right. I am not some god among men as you may have heard. I am as slow as any other guard, but everything is much easier for me when I ride Hasminth. Rather than setting up and targeting the area where my opponent and I are currently headed, I simply adjust my aim for where I *will* be—which is almost always a different location than where I appear to be headed." He pointed at Cyran's chest. "So remember to always aim for where your opponent will be, not where they are."

Cyran visualized a scenario where Sir Paltere angled his lance downward while flying at an opponent, his opponent's lance pointing straight at him. Then at the last moment, Sir Paltere would command his dragon to swoop up, and he'd already have the correct alignment to strike his target while his opponent would be floundering around, trying to adjust, and would likely miss.

But something else kept niggling at the back of Cyran's mind. "And why don't the fire breathers use their breath to attack another? Instead of waiting for a lance to come at them?"

Paltere glanced down and studied Cyran. "Do they still only have forest dragons at Nevergrace?"

Cyran nodded.

Paltere pursed his lips, making his cheeks appear even more sunken beneath graying stubble. "Because the fire or ice or whatever breath each dragon wields cannot harm another dragon. And even if one beast attempted it, the defending dragon would simply raise its head or ascend and show its belly and shield its passengers by that means or with its wings. The breath could strike the defending dragon but then would do nothing to the guard and mage and archers. The use of breath rarely ever happens in a dragon-on-dragon battle, unless one dragon is dying and has lost its wits. Also, there is a law in the dragon realm that says dragons will not use their breaths against each other even for show, as it is deemed disrespectful and ignoble. When dragons fight each other, they use claws and teeth and fury. Their breaths are reserved for preparing their food as they like it, and to kill men and armies who are not dragon bound."

Paltere strode over and picked up a wooden lance for jousting on horseback in addition to a shield leaning against the outer wall. He tossed Cyran the shield, and Cyran caught it with two hands.

"Prepare yourself for a tilt," the dragonknight said.

Cyran raised the shield, bracing his arm against it as best he could manage.

Paltere angled the steel-capped tip of the lance at Cyran. "Now, if I came at you with the full force of a flying dragon, how would you want to defend against my strike?"

"I would want to strike you with my lance and avoid being hit altogether."

Paltere began a slow and steady march toward Cyran. "Even with all the nearly unbreakable steel and scale of a guard's shield, the impact of a joust at full speed can shatter every bone in your body."

The dragonknight started to jog at him, and Cyran planted

his feet and leaned into the shield, bracing with all his weight and strength.

Sir Paltere released a lighthearted cry and lunged forward. At the last moment, Cyran leapt to the side and angled his shield so the lance deflected off its face, causing minimal impact.

Sir Paltere sailed past and then turned to face him. The dragonknight slowly lowered his lance and applauded. "And so you understand what so many of the guard do not, even after I harp on it. What you just did would be considered unchivalrous if you were on horseback, and you would be disqualified from the tournament. Most of the guard have the same notion locked in their mind. They see their size and strength as what they are. As who they are. Their great size is even why they were chosen for the guard. A guard must be a big man in order to protect their mage, but growing up with and continuing to live their life bound to such beliefs does not allow many men to get over that image of themselves. And never can they do so in the densest seconds of battle when their instincts take control. But even the greatest human strength cannot save anyone when the might of dragons is at play. Take as little of the blow as possible while still defending your mage. That is the answer."

Cyran peered over the shield and nodded.

Paltere tossed the lance toward the wall and strode away, whistling.

"And why aren't mages and the guard strapped into harnesses if the archers are?" Cyran asked.

Paltere paused and turned as he furrowed his forehead. "Because the archers are moving about and would otherwise fall. Many of the guard prefer not to be strapped in because a lance strike with the full impact of a dragon behind it could then snap their back in two. They prefer to be unseated, as there is always the chance of being caught by another dragon, or surviving the landing. Others of the guard are... let's say fearful of falling to their deaths and would rather die in their saddles. So many of the guard are strapped in. Mages, on the other hand, say they feel like part of their dragon. They become one with their mounts. They would never fall off a dragon they were bound to without being struck."

Cyran pondered that for a moment but had another burning question, and this man was more willing to discuss theory than Sir Kayom ever was. He studied the tall and svelte man. "And why is it that you, out of all the dragonmages, are not crippled but hale and fit?"

Paltere's lighthearted expression fell and turned somber. "For two reasons. One, because I assume I was not born with my mind and thoughts already residing within the dragon realm, which is why most mages are crippled as babies. And two, because I still do not allow myself to spend too much mental time and effort in the other realm. Even though it is a constant temptation. A place of wonder and magic. The mages would say it is a much grander world than the real one around us. But you must sacrifice something—part of yourself, at least your body if not your soul—to walk among those threads."

14

CYRAN ORENDAIN

THE CEILING OF THE DEN ROSE HIGHER OVER CYRAN'S HEAD THAN any church dome. Torchlight danced and flickered across the walls.

Cyran pushed the barrow with the carcass inside along a stone walk. Its wheel squeaked, and down in these depths, the noise sounded so loud it hurt Cyran's ears and rattled his nerves. The dragons here would not be happy, especially those he was not going to feed.

At least there was torchlight in this den. He eased past the first stalls, this place having stalls on both his left and right around a central walkway. Loud sniffing sounded, and he turned to find a dragon with scales the color of a silver coin mashing its muzzle against the bars of its stall door.

"Sorry, my friend," Cyran whispered, "you are not the one I am supposed to feed."

A growl sounded on his far side, and he whipped about. A dragon with ruby scales glared at him, its nostrils smoking.

"I am hungry," the dragon said in a gravelly voice.

"I'm sure your squire will be down shortly." Cyran hurried along.

The dragon roared, and its cry shook the ceiling and blasted Cyran's ears. It breathed a plume of fire into the air, the flames snapping and smoldering and blackening the stones overhead.

Cyran's heart bucked and hammered against his lungs as he rushed on, heat bubbling around him and drawing beads of sweat from his forehead. This place was even more dangerous than the den at Nevergrace. Much more. No wonder the squires had to be paid well.

He passed a few more stalls, most of which were empty, although they appeared to have been recently occupied given the straw and water inside. Those dragons were probably participating in the tourney. Other stalls held sleeping dragons, which made Cyran breathe a sigh of relief. He passed a stall twice the size of most of the others. A dragon with blue-green scales the color of the sea slept with its head on its wings. Then he saw that this dragon had several heads and necks resting on its wings, but only one body.

Cyran never would have guessed there were so many different breeds of dragons, but then he remembered Smoke and their wolves. Many types of domestic and wild dogs existed. The same with horses. Why not dragons? Growing up in Nevergrace, he'd come to think of dragons only as green, the forest dragons of the Evenmeres.

He stopped outside the twenty-first stall on his left. A dragon as silver as steel armor sat on its haunches inside, and it watched him.

"Do I have to breathe fire in order to convince you to pass over my meal?" the dragon asked.

Cyran swallowed and shook his head before wheeling the barrow over to its stall door, where he dumped the carcass through a slot. The carcass slid through and plopped onto the floor.

The dragon sucked in a deep breath, and Cyran retreated.

Silver fire billowed from its gaping maw and charred the raw carcass. Then the beast began to gingerly peel off chunks with its teeth.

"Do you always watch a dragon when it eats?" the silver asked.

Cyran whipped his barrow around and hurried back along the walkway and out of the den.

After he'd loaded up the barrow for the third and final delivery and was pushing it back toward the den, he passed Sirs Kayom and Ymar, who were involved in a deep discussion. Six other guard members in an array of colored dragon armor, including Sir Paltere, spoke with them. A few shouts, sounding less enthusiastic than earlier, came from a crowd outside the castle, and dragons still swooped and dived across the skies.

Another man in red and gold dragonsteel armor burst from the castle's entrance and hurried over to the group, his face drawn and etched with worry. Cyran stopped as the new arrival began to speak, but Cyran couldn't hear exactly what was being said. However, everyone's postures stiffened, and their mannerisms revealed a shared chagrin. Cyran eased his barrow down and paced toward them, catching part of the arriving guard's words.

"And the king asks that we all convene in the audience chamber within the hour," the guard said.

"War is already upon us, whether we see it or not." Kayom's head drooped, and he rubbed at his forehead before looking around at his fellow guard and tugging at his ear.

"Murgare knows their king is dead, but we still have their queen." Ymar stroked his white beard. "We do not like to think of her as a hostage, but that is how the north will see her situation. They may not bring a full-scale assault knowing it could place her safety in jeopardy."

"They will still come." Sir Paltere's finger traced the curled dragon sigil on his breastplate. "Either for an attack or with their entire legion, hoping to drive all of Cimeren into war. We must expect them at any time. The death of their king will not go unavenged. The north still believes that the souls of the slain become trapped and tormented in the sky sea until vengeance has been served."

The newest arrival turned and motioned for the rest of the guard to follow him into the castle.

"Cyran," Sir Kayom called. "To me at once."

Cyran hurried over.

"Have you found the others?" he asked.

A sinking feeling pulled at Cyran's gut. "No... I was feeding dragons."

Sir Kayom's eyes narrowed, but one of his eyebrows arched into a bemused expression. "Come with me. We will find the others later."

They trailed the others through the castle, but this time they headed straight for an archway beyond towering double doors. A long chamber with a runner of red and gold carpet, a raised dais, and a throne composed of hulking bones and gold- and rose-scaled hides awaited them.

King Igare entered through a side door and sat upon the throne. He rubbed at a bony protrusion at the end of an armrest. The king's council stood on the lower steps of the dais, but no one spoke. Over the next ten minutes, a score of dragonguard from Galvenstone and other towns and cities, and a few of their squires, entered the audience chamber. Then the towering doors were sealed, and the king stood.

"I called a choice few from each region back to inform you of what has transpired." King Igare's voice was not booming, but it carried well, a contemplative and even gentle tone.

Whispers inside the chamber died out as fast as the wind had after being trapped by the sealed doors.

"What I am about to tell you, you must not share with anyone who is not currently in this chamber or who is not one of your fellow guard members," Igare continued. "Keeping it secret from the towns and cities of Belvenguard is not paramount, but we *must* not allow this information to pass to the north. Not yet. Not until we decide how to handle it and we have prepared. After the queen's trial and learning what we did, I worry there are still others in our kingdom who would betray us for coin." He glanced around, and everyone in the chamber stared, their breaths held in anticipation. He inhaled deeply and clapped his hands together before steepling his first fingers and pressing them into his chin. "The Murgare queen is dead."

The feeling of a stone falling through Cyran's chest and into his guts followed, and silence swelled inside the chamber. *Then war is a certainty.*

"We initially believed she killed herself immediately after being returned to her cell." The king paced along the front of the dais. "After the trauma of having to face up to her and her late husband's atrocities. And the scene was made to appear as if she'd hanged herself with her bedding."

A murmur rose within the chamber, the undertones ripe with apprehension.

"You said 'we initially believed,'" Sir Paltere said.

"Then we found her assassin." The king gestured at the side doorway to the right of the throne.

Four kingsknights in their typical gilded armor strode forth, a man in a cloak in their midst.

"It seems that someone sent an assassin to kill her," Igare said. "But we do not know why. The assassin will not speak. He cannot speak, as his tongue has been removed."

Kayom groaned. "And where was this assassin found? And how did you know it was his doing?"

"One of the kingsknights spotted him in a corner of the

chamber where the queen was being held." The king's orator spoke louder than the king, and this man in gray robes stepped up onto the dais beside Igare. "And by corner, I mean a corner of the ceiling. This assassin had somehow wedged himself up there among the rafters, attempting to go unnoticed."

"He simply scaled the walls of a cell?" a guard in the distance asked, incredulous. "The gaps between stones in a holding chamber should not be big enough for even thieves or assassins to do such a thing."

"No," the king's conjuror answered, her long white hair spilling out of her hood. "To have done so in that chamber, he must have wielded some of the arcane arts. But by the time I arrived, the kingsknights had already broken his attachment to the stones by using grappling hooks to pull him down."

A rush of whispers followed.

Assassins wielding magic. The queen was accused of utilizing similar types of people against Belvenguard's crown, and if such men could gain entrance to the Summerswept Keep, they could lurk anywhere.

"I have blessed the cell and much of the keep before the nine," a young clergyman in white said. "I will be able to detect any more conjuring tricks that occur in here."

The kingsknights marched the cloaked assassin before an archway towering over the dais. One threw a length of rope over the archway, and another fashioned a noose.

"We cannot count on keeping the queen's untimely passing secret for long." Igare sank back onto his throne and rubbed a hand over the rose scales on one armrest and the gold scales of the other. Then he held his forehead, as if having to support a great weight. "We are here now to discuss how to best deal with this development."

"But first we will hang the assassin." The orator's voice

echoed around the chamber as he stroked his gray goatee and gestured to the kingsknights.

One of the knights shoved the hood back from the assassin's face. The assassin was a gaunt man with a dirty complexion. Another kingsknight looped the noose over the assassin's head.

"Now, assassin," the orator began, "this is your final chance. If you can write and wish to tell us why you did what you did and who hired you, we will spare your life."

The assassin's blank stare didn't break.

The orator pointed, and the kingsknights hauled the assassin into the air. He didn't even struggle much, nothing more than attempting to grab at the rope about his neck as the taut fibers creaked. The assassin's mouth gaped as he struggled to breathe, revealing his absent tongue. In a few heartbeats, the deed was done, and his head lolled to one side, exposing a tattoo on his throat, a marking too small to make out from where Cyran stood.

"And now we must address the events that will spring forth with the queen's passing," the orator said.

"Why would the north want their own queen assassinated?" a guard behind Cyran asked.

The orator shrugged.

Possibilities swarmed around in Cyran's mind like trapped wasps. *Be like the dragonguard of old and use your head as well as your might. Use whatever knowledge you have to figure out the reasons, the motive.*

The king's nyren—in his red robe and chain belt—stepped up beside the orator. "The Murgare queen could have been assassinated for these reasons: because someone in the north wished to silence a royal who could have revealed many of their secrets to us, someone in the north wished to remove an obstacle in their way to the throne, or someone believed they would be saving Elra from the types of torture the north puts their prisoners through. Murgare may hold the assumption that we would have employed the same methods on their queen."

"A pity killing?" Kayom asked. "That seems unlikely for the north. And who of them would command enough power to have an assassin sent to kill their own queen?"

Everything comes down to coin or power.

"The Dragon Queen would be one of the few with that kind of authority," Paltere said. "And if the north sent the assassin, they will suspect the queen to be dead, whether the assassin returns or not. Keeping her death a secret may not matter."

"But in case the assassin was working for someone else, we will all still refrain from discussing her death after those doors are unsealed." The orator pointed to the towering twin doors at the entrance. "And the north could still want confirmation, even if it was their assassin. We at Galvenstone have been arming and readying our soldiers and knights and dragonguard since the day the Murgare king was killed, but we require more time. We must increase the number of our soldiers and dragonguard. And train them. We must craft more weapons and armor for these men. The dragons and mages of the vast north are said to outnumber ours almost two to one. We also wish to accomplish all this without alerting the masses and creating hysteria over a coming war."

"Then we must hope that the north believes their queen is still alive," Paltere said. "It is the only way to delay a war that will draw all the kingdoms into its grip."

"I had not finished listing all the options for Queen Elra's assassination." The nyren stroked his curly gray beard. "There is also the possibility that one of the nobles or lords—someone with enough coin to hire a conjuror who is also an assassin—currently at Belvenguard sought to avenge a death that Murgare was responsible for. Perhaps one of their family members was slain. The north *has* been linked to the killings of many of our people."

Everyone in the chamber fell into silent contemplation.

"Are there any more suggestions for why the queen would have been assassinated?" the orator asked.

"To start a war," Cyran blurted.

All eyes turned to regard him. A few glares carried animosity, probably hoping to belittle him for speaking out of station. Sir Kayom stepped before Cyran and held his hands behind his back in an authoritative pose, as if challenging any of the guard to admonish his squire.

"Have your squire explain his reasoning, dragonguard," the orator said.

Cyran nervously cleared his throat as he sidled around Kayom. "The nyren alluded to it being someone who sought to become the new king or queen of Murgare, but he didn't mention that it could be someone who wished to start a war between Murgare and Belvenguard."

The nyren tapped his chin and paced. "Then this someone would have to possess the knowledge that Belvenguard abducted Queen Elra and was holding her here."

"Indeed," Cyran added.

"And who would that most likely be?" The nyren quickly answered his own rhetorical question. "Someone in the north who is powerful and knew the results of the incursion meant to take the king... Although, I would also have to consider the possibility that one of Galvenstone's dragonguard, who was involved in the incursion, or one of us in the king's council, who helped plan it, could be involved in such a plot."

The chamber fell into a shocked silence.

The nyren paced before the king. "It could be any of those possibilities. I suspect the Dragon Queen, of course. But we cannot ignore the possibility that some relative of King Restebarge has their eye on the throne. In the north, a queen can rule alone, and thus someone may have desired to remove Elra as well. Or this someone may have wanted to initiate a war that could draw all of Cimeren into its clutches."

The slapping of the nyren's feet echoed through the chamber.

"We have already assembled a few regiments of knights and soldiers to question everyone about the castle and to pursue all leads in the queen's assassination," the orator said. "We shall begin at once. And King Igare has granted me the authority of overseeing the stationing of the dragonguard. Some of you or your comrades may have to be shifted from your current locations, given the escalating dangers. You are all dismissed for the moment, but do not yet depart Belvenguard."

The doors were unsealed, and the guard all turned and exited. Cyran moved to the back of the line, wandering closer to the hanging body as the kingsknights cut the assassin down. The body hit the steps leading up to the throne and sprawled out. The tattoo on the assassin's neck was that of a raven within a black triangle.

∼

Sir Kayom marched out of the keep, involved in a quiet discussion with Ymar, who raked fingers across his bare scalp. Cyran trailed behind them.

"Cyran," Kayom called over his shoulder after they crossed half the promenade. "Find my other squires and saddle Eidelmere." Then to Ymar, he said, "If the north attacks, everyone assumes they will come over the lake. Therefore, Murgare may finally decide to send its soldiers through the Evenmeres."

"We must return to Nevergrace as soon as possible." Ymar's dragonsteel boots pounded the flagstones.

"No army has or ever will be able to move through the Even-meres," a man said from behind them. Ten paces back, the king's orator walked beside Sir Paltere, and the orator continued speaking. "The forest's paths are far too narrow to advance a legion. Utilizing that route would be equivalent to an army using a narrow ravine to attack rather than to defend. And straying from the Evenmeres's paths is said to be dangerous, even for the north. Although other than for brigands, I believe any tales about the woods to be myth." The orator wove his fingers together and rested his hands against his thighs. "Also, dragons cannot cross those woods. Nothing other than weak storm drag-ons, anyway. There is no place for the other beasts to stop and rest."

"Nevergrace is a lone outpost along the border, Riscott," Kayom replied. "The *only* outpost defending the paths leading from those woods. If I thought as you do, and I was of the north, the Evenmeres would be the route I'd choose. For no other reason than my adversaries would not be prepared and would not see us coming from many leagues away, like with the lake and the spires. I would sacrifice spreading my legion out in a long line through the woods as we could still burst from cover and storm a solitary outpost."

"The old outpost is safe and has had a nearly uneventful if not unending watch." Riscott strode up to Kayom. "Galvenstone, on the other hand, has to watch over the lake at all times, and enemies have crossed it in many instances. Murgare's fleets could be coming day or night."

"Then may you send swift word to us at Nevergrace if they do." Kayom's tone was not confrontational but carried an abra-sive edge. "We will answer your call as soon as it arrives." Kayom turned to Cyran. "Now, go."

Cyran turned for the outer gates.

"No, Sir Kayom." Riscott pursed his lips and tapped them. "If the true danger lurks across the lake, I—and by 'I,' I mean by the king's authority—will require as many of the guard as possible to stay in Galvenstone."

Kayom's jaw tensed.

"You shall remain here per my kind request." Riscott's words and grin were affable but firm. "And you will assist with the watch and be ready for an impending assault. Ymar may return to Nevergrace."

Kayom's cheeks flushed, and Cyran thought he might admonish the orator. But the dragonguard turned to Cyran and said, "Cyran, tell my other squires we are to stay in Galvenstone for the time being."

Ymar leaned over and whispered to Kayom, "Three of my squires and your dragonmage are unaccounted for. Same as with your other four squires. They're all probably staggering drunk and still down at the whore houses. And from what we've heard, Nevergrace may be in more danger than we ever realized. You should send Cyran with me. We'll need all the help we can get."

Kayom studied Cyran for a moment as he folded his arms over his breastplate and the sigil of angoia trees behind a keep and twin watchtowers.

"We have plenty of dragonsquires in Galvenstone," Riscott said, also studying Cyran, and the letter of warning flooded Cyran's thoughts again. "Send however many squires you deem appropriate back to Nevergrace. We will supply you with more. It is the dragons and their riders we need to keep at the castle."

Sir Kayom's head drooped.

"I wish to stay here with Sir Kayom." Cyran strode closer to his guard-master.

"No," Kayom said. "You will return to Nevergrace and assist Ymar."

"I—" Cyran started.

"It is an order," Kayom barked.

Cyran's shoulders felt as if an enormous weight settled upon them. "Yes, sir."

15

SIRRA BRACKENGLAVE

THE TREES THINNED BENEATH SHADOWMAR AS THE BEATING OF the dragon's wings slowed. Sirra guided her mount to a halt, hovering just over the treetops, the remainder of her legion trailing behind her. Night had finally fallen over Cimeren. The marshlands lay just ahead. To the north and the west, the Lake on Fire extended to the horizon, its surface rippling with light— like a valley of silver painted by the thousand moons.

"The watchtowers of Galvenstone are near." Quarren lifted her head from behind Sir Vladden as the ice dragon arrived and hovered beside Sirra, the dragonmage's voice a sneer. The ice dragon's wings flapped slowly, its body riddled with fatigue. "We risk everything."

Sirra's visored gaze swept across the lake. Shadowed spires of watchtowers dappled the shoreline far to the south.

"Most nights in Cimeren are far too bright to allow a dragon to sneak out from the Evenmeres without being spotted." Vladden's helmed head whipped to the side to regard Sirra. "Much less five dragons."

"But most dragons are not veiled in fog." Sirra raised a hand and gestured around them in a silent command.

The mist dragon and its riders arrived, and the dragon expelled a breath. A gush of fog billowed out from its maw and rolled slowly outward. They waited for a few minutes, and Sirra waved for the beast to continue its work. Over the next hour, the fog thickened and clung to the trees before churning and creeping outward over the marshlands.

"The fog must look as natural as possible." Sirra oversaw the dragon's progress, but her nerves ate at her. Her king had been murdered, and his soul was currently being tormented because his death was still unavenged, the guiltiest killer or killers who ordered and orchestrated the attack unpunished. And the risk of her queen being harmed grew with every minute that passed. "Or it will not matter what we intend to do."

Once the mist had rolled out from the Evenmeres and wreathed the nearby trees and the marshlands, Sirra guided Shadowmar over the last of the forest's treetops and dropped into the less dense region beyond. Her legion quickly followed. Shadowmar's hindlimbs plunked down into the stagnant water between a spotting of pines, sending waves battering against trunks. The squelching of feet sinking into and pulling out of mud sounded.

"Will we find rest in the outskirts of the marshes?" Quarren rose in her saddle and shoved her hood back, her tawny hair shimmering under the muted moonlight within the fog. She rubbed at the hip of her misshapen leg as if it ached. "We have avoided the curse of the Evenmeres and hopefully Belvenguard's watch, but there are other things that lurk in the marshes."

"We will not find much of a respite here." Sirra studied the brackish water surrounding them. "But our options were slim, and our mounts must catch their breaths. Let them be."

The two ice dragons and the mist dragon slumped down into the mud and sprawled their wings out. Their eyes settled closed. The fire dragon soon followed their lead. Shadowmar's anger had cooled following her prolonged exertion, but she remained standing, on alert, for she knew what lived in the murk.

"Rest," Sirra said in her mind to Shadowmar, and the dragon grumbled and resisted before finally complying. *"You can do nothing else to abate your anger now."*

Minutes crawled by like hours as Sirra watched the waters around them. A few bubbles surfaced and popped several dragon lengths away. A burst of fire lit up in a spout beyond a few trees.

"The marsh dragons have taken notice." Quarren lay forward in her saddle, splaying out on her ice dragon's neck. "Even if Belvenguard has not seen us."

"Of course such beasts are aware of our presence." Sirra surveyed their surroundings. "Anything that moves in their waters draws attention, and we cannot hope to hide the movements of creatures as large as dragons."

"What do we plan to do when they surround us and then decide to strike?" Quarren's eyes settled closed as if she had no concerns about the possibility.

"We kill them or we die." Sirra's hand had not released her sword's hilt since she'd landed. "But they should not rush in for a kill when a legion of dragons has landed in the marsh. We should primarily concern ourselves with the breath of these creatures and if they will use it when our dragons are too tired to shield their riders."

"But the laws of the realm..."

"Swamp dragons do not adhere to the laws of other dragons."

Quarren did not respond, and half an hour crawled by while bubbles intermittently erupted on the surface of the marsh in several areas around them. Cones of fires also lit up atop the water and then died out, leaving only smoke amidst the fog.

Sirra released her sword's hilt and slowly pulled her lance

toward her, passing the weapon through its mount and arret hook until she could reach its tip. She uncapped the end, a plate of dragonsteel forged into the image of a shadow dragon's head. Beneath the cap, her lance narrowed to a point like a spearhead.

"How did Belvenguard know where Restebarge would be traveling?" Vladden sat poised for battle, his white glowing blade resting across his lap, his tight fist seeming to crush its hilt.

"It was his annual visit to the Valley of the Smoke Breathers," Sirra said. "Belvenguard must have caught wind of it then ambushed him and his legion on Breather's Pass."

"But he does not travel on the same day every year."

Sirra shook her head. "No. He does not."

"Further proof Belvenguard had preemptive knowledge of Restebarge's plans."

Sirra nodded.

"Then a traitor has worked their way close to Restebarge," Vladden said. "Someone within Murgare."

"It seems likely. Otherwise it would be difficult for such information to reach Igare's ears, especially if those as high ranking as yourself were not even supposed to know beforehand."

"He should have stopped traveling to the valley long ago." Vladden shook his head. "His entire royal legion even accompanied him, but there was no need for them to stop on Breather's Pass."

"He was paying tribute to the first taming and the brotherhood. Without them, our world would have been shaped much differently. Nothing would be as you or I know it now. You wouldn't even recognize the world I was born into."

A low roar rumbled somewhere in the distance, and water frothed and foamed between the rotting trunks of a partially submerged oak and maple.

Vladden's armor creaked as he raised his sword. "The predators of the area grow weary of waiting. And their hunger ripens."

"At least a legion of Belvenguard dragons have not sailed through the mist, hunting for us." Sirra remained calm and relaxed, although she noted the distance between her legion and all the nearing spouts of fire and surfacing bubbles.

Vladden didn't respond for a minute, and Sirra imagined his face paling.

A few minutes later, an ice dragon began to snore.

The archer in the mist dragon's turret struggled to free himself from the pole frame and plopped into the marsh.

"Where are you going?" Vladden asked.

"I need to piss." The archer took a few steps through the muck, slogging along. "And the turret's position isn't exactly keeping me dry either."

The archer turned away from them and reached to his groin.

A massive neck snaked up from the water a dragon's length from the archer and reared back, expelling a gush of brown liquid that splattered over the man and his armor. The archer screamed and stumbled as the mist dragon shrieked and flapped its wings, attempting to cover the man. But the archer was too far away, and the swamp dragon had surfaced too quickly.

The acidic froth of the swamp dragon's breath steamed as it seeped into and ate away at the archer's armor. His helm melted and sizzled. His scream faded into a gurgle as his skin and bones followed suit.

Shadowmar lunged forward through the muck, and the swamp dragon roared. Sirra drove her dragonsteel lance through its open mouth, and the weapon's tip erupted from the back of its skull. The beast's neck fell slack, and its head slid off the lance before plopping back into the swamp.

The raised and reflective eyes of a half-dozen other dragons surfaced and glided closer, barely creating ripples in the murk.

"We will no longer find rest here." Sirra whipped her head around, scrutinizing the marsh, the approaching eyes, and a few scaled nostrils. "There will be no more rest for any of you until we claim a castle in Belvenguard. Now, fly."

Shadowmar leapt into the air and beat her wings, and the ice and fire and mist dragons all quickly followed.

A set of enormous jaws erupted in a geyser of brackish water, breaking through the murk and lunging for an ice dragon's legs. The teeth snapped closed with a crunch but narrowly missed their target. Then a half-dozen swamp dragons roared, thrashed about in the water, and fell into feasting and ripping apart the body of the dragon Sirra had skewered.

Sirra veered Shadowmar through the mist, angling her mount so that as they flew back over the Evenmeres, they would pass around to the south side of the wall of angoias and closer to the lands of Belvenguard.

16

CYRAN ORENDAIN

THE BONFIRES INSIDE NEVERGRACE BURNED BRIGHT AND HAPPY AS Cyran sat outside the squire house with a lute in hand.

"To the new lord of the Never." Brelle raised a tankard and drained it in one long series of swallows as Cyran strummed a few chords. At least one of the strings was out of tune, but he was having trouble identifying which one was the culprit. "May Galvenstone's problems stay far away from here."

Laren flashed his boyish grin. "I thought you saw Nevergrace as a boring hole and you wanted something to happen here."

"I do not fancy an attack from the north." Brelle shuddered. "Now that that possibility is very real, I am hesitant to embrace it." She glanced about in search of another tankard.

"And you probably shouldn't be drinking quite so heavily," Laren said. "If one of the guard sees you, they will reprimand you. Or worse. We're supposed to be ready at a moment's notice."

A massive breath and shuffling rose from a distant corner of the bailey. A forest dragon rustled around on straw and lay her enormous bulk down, tucking her wings against her body, both saddles still cinched in place on her neck, the quarterdeck on her back. Her dragonmage sat beside her, ready to take his position on her if not also making sure the dragon did not try to flee to the forest.

Cyran glanced to the far end of the bailey. Soldiers remained on double duty along the battlements and in the watchtowers, and another forest dragon waited in the shadows packed into a corner of the outer wall, casting a pall over the celebrations for the new lord of the Never. The three other dragons of Nevergrace rested in the den but could be quickly harnessed and ready for battle. And the already prepared dragons and those resting more deeply in the den were switched daily.

Smoke lay down beside Cyran, and Cyran pet his dark fur. The wolf licked his own lips and then rested his head on his paws. Garmeen sat in his typical silence near the much taller wolves.

"I wish I were at Galvenstone." Dage paced about with a tankard in hand, and drink sloshed over the side and foamed on his knuckles. "To be sent back here and not have been inducted into the guard is humiliating. With everything that is happening, I was sure I'd be called up."

"So Cyran was right," Brelle said. "That letter you wouldn't show me *wasn't* any kind of summons from the guard."

Dage stopped. "What letter?" His eyes wandered about before flashing with recognition. He shook his head and continued pacing.

"Garmeen, Cyran, and I received a letter as well." Brelle spun her empty tankard around on her palm. "It also bore a dragon seal in red wax. So you can tell us what your letter said, and I'll share what ours said with you."

Garmeen tried to furtively kick at Brelle's foot as he said, "The message mentioned not telling anyone, remember? It said our lives may depend on it."

"We're no longer in Galvenstone." Brelle grinned, a runnel of ale slipping past her lips. "And the message was addressed to us squires. Who is to know that didn't mean Dage and Laren? Even if they weren't with us at the time because they were giving their coin to the whores."

Dage's eyes narrowed. "You really did receive a letter with a Galvenstone seal?"

Brelle nodded. "In the Tavern of the Shield Maiden."

Laren's jaw dropped open a finger's width.

"What did yours say?" Dage's voice rumbled in his throat. "None of *you* were called into the guard, were you?"

"If the message were meant for Dage, he probably wouldn't have received his own prior." Cyran plucked a few strings, and a dissonant chord rang. "So perhaps Garmeen is right—that he, Brelle, and I are not supposed to talk to anyone else about its contents." He turned and addressed Dage. "I'm guessing your message mentioned something similar, and that's why you haven't told us what it said."

"But the letter's warning feels fairly empty back here in Nevergrace," Brelle said. "I think we should tell what each other's said. It could help us determine who sent them."

Cyran considered her words for only a couple heartbeats and then nodded his assent. *More details could help us discover the truth.* Any risk would hopefully be worth the added information.

Dage's shoulders tensed. "But I received mine here. Before any of you did."

"Ours was anonymously delivered on our drink tray." Brelle stared into the empty depths of her tankard with longing. "As we feigned gambling. It told us to be wary of someone in the king's council."

Dage's face paled.

"Was yours different?" Brelle asked.

Dage nodded.

"Well, what did yours say?" Brelle's tone bordered on demanding and confrontational.

Dage's mouth opened, and his jaw worked a few times. But instead of speaking, he turned and strode away several paces.

"Damn that dragon's ass." Brelle slammed her tankard onto the ground.

"Are you ever going to play, Cyran?" Renily skipped out of the shadows of the squire house, her red hair rising and falling with each stride.

Cyran repeatedly plucked the string he believed was not harmonizing with the others. "It's out of tune."

"Doesn't matter," Renily said.

Cyran wound one of the tuning pegs tighter, but the tone still sounded off. He plucked the string, and it snapped, recoiling against the fingers of his chording hand. "Bloody hell. Even the lute and gut are on edge. Renily, can you fetch another length of gut from the nyren?"

Renily dashed off.

A drumbeat sounded, and Cyran lurched to his feet. On a balcony near the top of the keep, doors parted, and a man stepped out onto the landing. He was short with graying brown hair and a stocky frame. The new lord of the Never—Lord Dainen. He gripped a tankard and teetered as he walked. Menoria, the young lady of Nevergrace, and her mother accompanied him but remained two steps behind.

"My people of the Never." Dainen spread his short arms as wide as they would reach, attempting to address everyone in the baileys. "Including those who have just returned from Galvenstone. It is in a time of great sadness that I have arrived, and yet I feel a spark of joy and hope for our days to come. I will treat Nevergrace and its people as well as my uncle did."

Applause sounded all through the baileys.

"And may darkness never arrive at our door," Dainen continued. "But if it does, our enemies will find Nevergrace a formidable outpost that will break their legions like boulders upon the Scyne River. For we are stones with scales and teeth!"

More people hooted and hollered.

"We will keep our senses keen but our spirits light." The lord twirled himself in a circle. "The shadowy forces of the north will not wear down our resolve or our determination." He raised his drink and saluted everyone. Then he turned and pulled Menoria to him and kissed her on the lips before leading her back into the keep.

The burgeoning inspiration inside Cyran died as his stomach churned. Was that a lover's kiss? But Menoria was far too young for that man. Maybe it was only a family affection type of kiss with more enthusiasm, given the moment.

"He likes the Never because his young cousin is here," Brelle said.

"They were close when she was a child." Dage approached the other squires again and glared at Brelle. "It is nothing more than that."

Brelle shrugged.

Renily returned with gut string, and after Cyran attached and wound it, he strummed several chords. Jaslin stepped from the crowd around them and settled into the shadows beneath the nearest torch, watching the squires. Cyran's heart ached. He'd gone to look for her immediately upon his return, but she'd been away from her quarters and seemed to have been avoiding him over the past day. She must still be angry with him because he'd left the outpost, or maybe she blamed him for Tamar's death.

Cyran smiled and waved at his sister, whose expression remained blank as she stared back. He played for her.

. . .

Rain broke upon roofs of stone
  Rivers drained around their home
  In the Never they found their joy
  But times of darkness swelled and roamed

He continued with the story of Sir Marenbore, a dragonguard of Nevergrace, who remained vigilant and drove back the armies of the north as they poured down the River Scyne and marched on the outpost. Cyran sang with power, his voice ringing off the walls around him, a sense of boldness and perseverance welling up inside him as he closed his eyes so he could better feel and channel his emotions. And when he strummed the last chord and let it ring, he held the note with his voice and sounded the name of the Never.

When he opened his eyes, everyone around had fallen silent, gawking at him. Jaslin was gone.

A massive snore broke the spell he'd created and carried through the bailey.

Brelle bellowed and slapped her thigh. "Cyran's playing has put the dragons to sleep!"

People erupted with laughter.

"If the dragons of the north come at us, Cyran could be our secret weapon," Laren shouted.

More choruses of laughter followed.

Cyran shook his head but couldn't stop a grin from lifting his lips. At least he'd amused everyone. He placed the lute in Renily's hands. Her eyes widened as she held it and studied him. He kissed her on the head and said, "I have to find my sister."

He rushed away past the torch Jaslin had stood under, headed toward her chamber. Music played within the keep, and people began dancing through the bailey. Someone within the crowd grabbed his hand and said, "Were you looking for me?"

Emellefer smiled up at him and brushed her dark hair from her face.

"I... I, yes, but I was after Jaslin as well," he said. "I'd hoped for you to hear me play, but you were probably still serving suppers. I will return as soon as I speak with my sister."

A dull shimmer lurked behind Emellefer's eyes. She turned away.

"I left Jaslin just after... after Tamar," Cyran said. "She probably needs me. And I her."

"I've been checking up on her regularly. She is quiet and sad but is holding it together better than most her age would. She seems to take comfort in that crystal flagon she's always holding."

A painful bite sank into Cyran's gut. That decanter had felt off somehow, like it was trying to tempt her into the forest. Or maybe he'd had the presentiment that no one should ever lay eyes upon it. Hopefully she was only attached to it because Tamar had given it to her.

"She has been avoiding you," Emellefer said.

Cyran groaned. "I suspected as much. She probably wants to make me suffer for traveling to Galvenstone right after Tamar was..."

"I can help you find her. She likes me. But she won't be in her quarters now. Not during the festivities. So it will be difficult to track her down at the moment." Emellefer cast him a bashful look. "Will you ask me for a dance?"

Desire flooded Cyran, but he pressed it back. "I have to at least try to find her. But I'll return within the hour." He smiled at Emellefer, hoping she would understand, before he paced away.

When he neared Jaslin's chamber, the outline of someone sitting along the edge of the curtain came into view. This person had positioned themselves over Jaslin's roof and in the shadows just beyond a pocket of torchlight. They were swaying, but their movements didn't match the music being played in the distance.

Cyran found a ladder and climbed up the outer curtain wall, sidled over to his sister in the shadows, and sat down. She passed an object in her hands around to her far side, and the object glittered with reflected light. Her eyes were closed as she continued to move to a rhythm other than the music Cyran could hear. He gazed out over the castle's grounds, where spheres of torchlight lit up areas filled with people dancing and drinking.

"I thought you'd be reading a story." Cyran eased his arm around his sister's shoulders and pulled her head against his chest. "How have you been feeling?"

Jaslin alternated kicking each of her feet as they dangled over her roof. "It's beautiful, isn't it? All this joy filling the Never?"

"It is."

A song came and went, and neither of them spoke. They simply continued to lean against each other.

"At times, he is all I can think about." Cyran swallowed, his voice a harsh whisper that cracked. "And when that happens, a feeling of emptiness consumes me. But with everything I've been through recently, I haven't been able to spend enough time remembering him. Although not a day has gone by that I haven't thought of you and Tamar and of certain moments he and I, or all of us, shared."

Jaslin mumbled something, and a long stretch of silence settled between them as they watched the people of the Never celebrate. Then she said, "I like to go to the edge of the Evenmeres and stare into their depths. I feel him best there. Especially at night."

Cyran tensed. "You haven't gone into the woods since then, have you?"

"I've seen the lights he mentioned, and I've heard the song he was always humming. It's more beautiful than anything I could have imagined."

The hair on the back of Cyran's neck spiked. "Jaslin..."

She fell silent. "I know I shouldn't, but you did it as well."

Guilt pinched Cyran's heart.

"There's something beautiful in there." She held up the object she'd placed at her far side. Its crystal surface glittered with distant torchlight. An ominous feeling seemed to waft from the decanter, and the sensation lingered. "And as long as I have this, I feel safe."

A wave of fear and anger surged through Cyran with the thought of his sister venturing out into the woods at night, alone, heeding a call similar to what he may have experienced the night Rilar went missing. He snatched the decanter from her and, in one motion, smashed it against the stone of the curtain. It shattered into a hundred shards. Some skittered across the curtain's stones while others fell onto the roof of Jaslin's chamber.

"What are you doing?" Jaslin screamed as she snapped her head around to face Cyran.

He stood and stomped the shards around him into fragments. "The woods are no longer safe. I told you that."

"The decanter was the last thing Tamar gave me!" Jaslin's lower lip trembled as she leaned back in shock and braced herself with her arms extended behind her, her eyes gaping.

"I am sorry, but that thing felt evil." He placed a hand on her leg, and she scooted away. "I fear it was somehow influencing you. Something strange and yet similar happened to me when I was gone."

She sobbed as she crawled around him and huddled over the crystal fragments. She shifted through them, and a trickle of blood ran from one of her fingers as she plucked out a shard.

The head of a figure could still be made out on the piece, and she caressed the fragment and pressed it to her chest.

"Jaslin, I think you should—"

She whipped around and seemed to bite the air with her teeth as she spewed out the words, "Leave me alone."

Cyran lurched back, his arms snapping forward in defense, as if he needed to protect himself from her. His sister glared at him with reddened eyes as she cried and huddled against the nearest wall. Cyran reached out to her, but she jerked away.

"I am sorry." He stood.

"Just go!"

"I hope you feel better tomorrow. I think the decanter was affecting you."

Jaslin continued to sob, and after a minute, Cyran climbed down the ladder and sauntered along through the baileys toward the dragonsquires' quarters. Sensations of regret and guilt haunted his steps as he pressed through throngs of dancing drunken men and women.

A gentle hand clasped his arm. "Are you all right?" Emellefer's smile faded as she studied him.

Cyran forced a grin. "I am fine. It's just my sister. We…"

Emellefer nodded. "Family." She sighed. "My sister and I have had more than our fair share of quarrels. And your ears could have been permanently scarred if you'd ever heard them."

Cyran scoffed and shook his head, but his grin was no longer forced.

"I heard your song." Emellefer smiled again and pulled her hand back from his arm, as if she just noticed she'd still been holding on to him. Her bright eyes captured Cyran's attention, and she shifted her hips about, the music not allowing her to remain still.

"I looked for you but didn't see you before I played a song on the lute."

"I... I showed up in time."

"Did you like it?"

"If"—she hesitated and glanced away—"you want me to be completely honest with you, it may not have been the single best version of Sir Marenbore's Storm that I've ever heard, but it was nearly so. It made me cry."

Cyran's heart exploded with warmth and a rush of emotion. "I do not pretend to be as accomplished as the bards. I simply try to bestow upon others what I feel when I sing. Especially upon you and Jaslin."

She stood on her tiptoes and twirled in a circle. "Do you wish to become a singing minstrel? Or remain a dragonsquire?"

"I wish to become one of the guard."

Her eyes widened. "I thought so, but Ulba says you'll have to add a lot of muscle and girth to your bones to become a guard. Maybe I can help you with that." She chuckled and cast him a wry smile. "I work in the kitchens."

Cyran lidded his eyes, rolled his head back, and released a dry laugh. "I don't think girth across the midsection is what they are looking for."

"It does seem that Sir Kayom has taken a liking to you, but he didn't keep you with him in Galvenstone." She smiled but glanced away. "And I, for one, am fine with that."

Cyran shrugged as he studied her closer, the playful grin he'd never seen on her before. "Sir Kayom does sometimes look for me when he wants to give a squire a duty, but I'm not sure that's because he wants to make me into a guard. He wanted me to stay with him at Galvenstone, but we needed more people here. And the king's orator encouraged me to return."

A tingle of warning emerged in the back of Cyran's mind. *The orator, Riscott.* He could be the person in the king's council who did not want Nevergrace squires around. But if it was him, what would that mean? That the orator was a traitor? Cyran didn't even know who wrote or sent him that message, or if he could trust that person.

"No matter what happens, I am still proud of you, Cyran." Emellefer took his hand again, and her eyes sparkled. "For being a dragonsquire and taking care of those beasts. And for your skills with the blade and lance that got you there. You could always become a soldier if you ever wanted to. Maybe even a knight."

"I was a knight for less than a minute before the king took away my title and made me a dragonsquire instead. After the king's tourney. I don't think they give out second knighthoods once one has been revoked."

"I remember. I was there." She squeezed his hand, which made his skin tingle. "Then if you are not big enough to be a guard, you will be a dragonsquire for as long as you see fit. And then a soldier. The best soldier Nevergrace has ever seen. And if you ever ask me to dance, you will never have to worry about me. No lord or noble is seeking to take me as their wife and make me a lady. At least not yet." She winked at him.

Cyran couldn't tell if she was trying to make him jealous or ease his mind. He blinked to clear his confusion, something that often ensued when Emellefer was around. He glanced at the frolicking couples filling the bailey. "Very well, milady. Will you dance with me?"

Emellefer scooted closer before quickly stepping away, lifting the hem of her skirt, and smiling. She twisted her hips and then took a few mincing steps forward while kicking with her boots. Her long legs swiveled. Cyran tried to follow her lead but had only seen others perform the dance. He slid the toe of his boot against his opposite ankle and stepped after her. She glanced back at him and giggled. She was beautiful.

Cyran sighed. Jaslin had been angry with him plenty of times in the past, but soon she'd be over it. Then they could comfort each other and reminisce over Tamar. They had to. Jaslin was his only family now.

"Try to keep up." Emellefer's teasing smile broadened. She whipped her skirt side to side, lifted the front, and stomped her boots in a rapid rhythm of heels and toes before dancing on.

Cyran stepped after her.

17

CYRAN ORENDAIN

In Cyran's dream, the woods around him wavered. He called out for Tamar and Jaslin, both of whom were running deeper into the forest. Jaslin laughed as she skipped along, the crystal decanter in her hands bobbing with her movements.

"Drop the decanter," Cyran shouted, his voice sounding empty and hollow. "And don't go into the woods. You promised me."

His brother and sister ignored him as they talked to each other and chuckled while hurrying along.

"Watch out for the trees." Cyran ran after them, but his legs moved much slower than theirs.

A deep rumble sounded somewhere in the distance, and the ground fell out from underneath him. He dropped into a sinking crater, sliding atop the plummeting dirt. He grabbed at everything—branches, brush, roots—around him, trying to stop his fall, but he landed at the bottom of the sinkhole with a thud. A tree at the edge of the crater creaked. Then it slowly teetered before falling, swinging down toward him. He tried to roll out of the way, but he couldn't move. The trunk of a pine smashed down onto him. Pain erupted through his chest.

Cyran lay there under a tree, dying, watching the woods around him, unable to speak. Tamar's head peeked over the lip of the crater, and Jaslin's face emerged beside their brother's. Cyran's siblings spoke quietly to each other as they pointed at him.

"All I ever wanted to do was fly a dragon." Jaslin glared down at Cyran, as if scolding or blaming him for his predicament.

"Jaslin," Cyran said, "I wanted to comfort you. I truly did. I wanted to make sure you would be all right. But I couldn't ignore the summons of a king."

"All I ever wanted to do was join you for a hunt out in the woods, Brother," Tamar said.

Cyran swallowed a stone of guilt.

A flaming black figure with charred skin appeared behind them. The figure moved, and its skin cracked apart in patches, revealing violet fire beneath. Cyran attempted to yell, but no sound escaped his lips. The burning figure shoved both his siblings into the crater, and they tumbled and rolled down the incline, screaming.

A boom shook the walls of the squire house around Cyran, waking him. He sat up. The drunken murmur of other squires sounded in the dark. Someone outside shouted. They sounded far away. A high-pitched shriek echoed all around and knifed at Cyran's ears, ringing his skull and causing him to drop over the side of his cot and fall to his knees. Other squires stumbled and fell onto the ground before writhing about and clutching at their ears.

Cyran grabbed his broadsword and rushed out into the dim torchlight of the bailey.

Dragons.

Dragons swirled in the moonlit sky, and plumes of fire erupted over Nevergrace, painting the night in oranges and reds. Other dragons expelled windy breaths that hit the battlements with a crack and mantled them in ice. Another dragon with a ghostly body and whose black wings nearly camouflaged with the night soared overhead, blowing thick mist around the periphery, engulfing the outpost in fog.

To hide the fires they are creating from neighboring villages.

But how could dragons even arrive at Nevergrace without being spotted coming over the lake?

Smoke and the other wolves howled and barked in the distance. The mist-breathing beast screeched again, and Cyran covered his ears as fear lanced through him and forced him to double over. The soldiers on the battlements buckled and collapsed, many dropping their weapons.

Nevergrace's bells rang crisp and clear in the night.

"Ready the other dragons!" Ymar burst from the shadows, running, and he grabbed Cyran by the tunic and shook him. "Go!"

Cyran dashed for the den as a mage and guard mounted a forest dragon in the bailey. The beast unfurled and flapped mighty wings, slowly rising as the other dragons he'd seen swarmed the battlements. Cyran burst through the unlocked outer gate of the den and grabbed a ring of keys. After he raced down the rampway, he approached the first stall. The forest dragon inside craned its head about and eyed him.

"Yes, the north has come." Cyran inserted a key and unlatched one of the shackles around its massive neck. The shackle swung wide along the arc of its chain and struck the wall, cracking and rattling against stone. "And we must defend Nevergrace."

After freeing the dragon, Cyran led it out of its stall, but he paused. It would take too long to bring each dragon to the harnessing chamber.

"Stay here," Cyran commanded it, and he turned and freed a second dragon while watching the first. His anxiety surged as he recalled the unlocked gate above, and he imagined the dragon trying to flee the battle and the Never. Losing even one dragon could lead to the fall of the outpost.

The first dragon took a step forward along the walkway.

"Stay," Cyran said. "As I told you. Your mage will be here at any moment."

Cyran hurriedly freed the second dragon and ushered it from the stall. He ran up to the first and led them in single file to the harnessing chamber. After he guided them into their respective tack areas, two squires stumbled inside. Both of their faces were ashen, and their knees buckled as they walked.

Dage burst through the entrance and hurried to the saddling area, his hands trembling. Brelle, Garmeen, and Laren followed him, leading the last forest dragon that would have been inside the den. All six of the new arrivals and Cyran worked as quickly as their shaking limbs allowed, placing saddles and quarter-decks while other squires filtered in and assisted them. Two of those who entered most recently smelled of urine and worse but, in spite of everything, they had come. Most were still absent.

Once the rigging and tack were in place on the dragon Cyran and his comrades were working on, Garmeen grunted and motioned to a lance. He attempted to lift the weapon from the assisting frame, but he couldn't budge it. Cyran raced over, and together, they wheeled the frame closer. Cyran climbed the frame and cranked the lance out over its respective position on the saddle. They slid the lance onto its mount and arret hook, and Cyran buckled the shackle of the mount closed.

More squires entered and assisted with the preparations of the other dragons.

An old man in a cloak, a dragonmage, hobbled into the chamber, heading toward Cyran. "I see my dragon is ready, but where is my guard? And where are my archers?"

"Probably fighting with the soldiers." Another dragonmage, this one a woman, trailed the first. Her shuffling gait didn't allow her to move any faster.

Cyran led the dragon to the approaching mage, who climbed into the saddle behind the guard saddle. The mage tapped the dragon with his staff. The beast reared up toward the domed ceiling, and its feet moved quickly, pounding stone as it ran from the chamber. The woman mounted one of the other dragons and followed. The remaining dragon was soon saddled and harnessed, and another mage arrived and rode it from the chamber.

"What now?" Brelle's bloodshot eyes gaped. "We've never come this far before. What do we do after we've sent the dragons to battle?"

"Help the soldiers and the knights." Cyran tugged at her tunic and then raced toward the exit.

His comrades followed him, and they burst out into the night. More dragonsquires ran about the area, screaming and ducking for cover, only to get up and run again.

The forest dragons they had just harnessed still waited in the bailey nearby. Archers were strapping themselves into the quarterdecks or lower turrets or rushing toward their dragons with their guard.

Lines of dragon breath swept the battlements in regimented attacks as the north's dragons danced in the sky, alternating positions by twisting and looping around one another—a dance of haunting beauty. Their fires swept along the lengths of the eastern and western walls, ice blasting the northern and southern faces. The attacks formed a pattern, and the dragons followed one another with ease, with a discipline and choreography Cyran had not fathomed.

After the dragonguard near the den climbed into their saddles and two archers took their stations on each forest dragon, one above and one below, the dragons rose into the sky. Bolts flew from the archers' crossbows and streaked toward their attackers.

Cyran ran and grabbed a handheld crossbow from a training rack. He worried it would not be of much use against their enemies now, but he aimed as a dragon as pale as snow weaved overhead. The beast's dragonmage was not visible, and its dragonguard was too well armored. He loosed his bolt at the archer in the lower turret.

Cyran couldn't see if his bolt struck its target or not, but he cranked the hand lever on his crossbow back and fitted another bolt. Nevergrace's forest dragons appeared diminutive beside what must have been fire and ice and mist dragons. And there was a fifth attacking dragon. A dragon as massive as Nevergrace's keep.

Orange and black flames from dragon breath flared along most of the battlements, but forest dragons swooped past and doused the fires with their rain breaths. Cyran sprinted for the western watchtower and climbed its outer stairs. When he reached the top, he stood behind two of Nevergrace's soldiers who manned a dragoncrossbow. They tilted and angled their weapon, trying to track the soaring beasts.

Mounted knights and regiments of soldiers rode and marched out from the castle, flinging spears and loosing arrows whenever an adversary drew near. But the north's dragons blasted their ranks with fire and ice. Most of the knights' and soldiers' attacks were futile, as were all their swords and axes and pikes, why it was often said that a dragon with a guard and archers was worth a thousand soldiers and a hundred mounted knights.

Cyran cringed.

The two archers on the watchtower swiveled their gigantic crossbow, but the weapon moved too slowly to keep up with their twisting and diving targets. Their crossbow loosed with a thrum, and its enormous dragonbolt arced away, sailing harmlessly off into the night.

"I cannot get a clean shot," the aiming archer said to the other as they cranked their weapon's rope back into its cocked position. "And if we loose one of these beasts"—he hefted another dragonbolt—"we need it to count."

A whistling sounded, and almost immediately, three dragonbolts rained down on the watchtower. Two skewered the archers, and a third buried deep into solid stone, its end vibrating with a high-pitched whine.

Cyran nearly dropped his crossbow in shock, but an instant later, he ducked behind a merlon.

A fire flared in the distance, out in the fields southwest of Nevergrace, in the direction of Galvenstone.

One of the beacon towers.

The mist dragon shrieked and soared away after the signal, and within what might have been a minute, the north's beast surrounded the beacon with its fog breath.

The Never's best chance for victory rested in the possibility that the second tower along the Scyne Road had seen the brief light of the first.

Then the path of the beacons will follow, and Galvenstone will answer.

18

SIRRA BRACKENGLAVE

SHADOWMAR SWOOPED LOWER, ANGLING FOR THE TORCHLIGHT OF the outpost. A fire and ice dragon implemented a crisscrossing pattern below Sirra, nearly grazing each other, a move meant to distract and confuse their enemy's archers. It marked the opening of the *kiölen* attack. A dance of death.

Yenthor shouted from behind his mounted crossbow. The steel arms of his bow thrummed when he loosed a dragonbolt. The two other archers on Shadowmar's quarterdeck, and Zaldica and the other archer below, followed Yenthor's lead. Their bolts buried into soldiers on the watchtower or the stone around them.

Bells pealed in the night. More torchlight sprang up inside the bailey. Sirra dived and led the attack, and her mount twisted sideways and tore past the eastern watchtower, throwing a couple remaining soldiers off their feet. Shadowmar's jaws gaped, and she inhaled a mighty breath before expelling black flames, flames that sucked in the darkness of the night around them and swallowed light. The fiery breath struck the battlements with a roar and hiss, and soldiers screamed. The mist dragon shrieked as it darted about, weaving around the watchtowers, battlements, and keep. The soldiers and knights on the ground bellowed and ran as the dragon's voice decimated their resolve and flooded them with fear.

Shadowmar dipped to the right and whipped around the castle, grazing the keep and releasing another fiery breath. A line of soldiers appeared like demons, roasting and dancing in black fires.

Two forest dragons quickly rose from within the bailey and took to the skies, flying toward her guard's dragons without maintaining disciplined formation.

This outpost expected an attack.

One forest dragon wheeled about and swooped past Shadowmar, and the enemy archer on its quarterdeck launched a bolt. Sirra dipped Shadowmar, and the bolt whizzed just over her mount's wings.

Yenthor's bolt then screamed through the night. It thudded as it struck the forest dragon in the thigh. The dragon screeched and flapped wildly as its dragonguard wrenched their lance around, preparing for Sirra to charge them. The forest dragon bobbed up and down in the sky, and its guard had to readjust with every movement.

Sirra swiveled her lance in its mount.

Another forest dragon rushed toward her but stopped, its wings flapping slowly and steadily as it hovered in place before the keep.

"Please, stop your attack, Dragon Queen," a dragonguard in green and gray armor shouted, his white beard protruding beneath his visor. The wind tormented his beard's wooly bulk.

Sirra angled her lance and rolled Shadowmar forward, positioning herself to come down at this guard from above. Shadowmar's anger sheeted off her as she dived lower and closer, extending her feet and talons. Sirra's dragonlance was no longer poised and ready to skewer the man. But the old guard didn't even try to defend himself, at least not with his lance. He only crouched behind his shield.

Shadowmar roared as Sirra pulled her up short, and her bracing wings threw out a gale as they slowed. Then Shadowmar flapped steadily to keep them aloft, hovering just before and above the forest dragon.

Sirra's archers' lines of sight would be partially obstructed with their target directly in front of them, and they couldn't fire without risking striking Sirra or Shadowmar's head or neck. But because her archers were fanned out across Shadowmar's gigantic back, their sights would not be as inhibited as the archers who rode smaller dragons.

"You wish to parlay?" Sirra asked, her tone deadly calm. "Now that you are frightened? After you and your people arrived in the north for a secretive assault and killed many of our men and dragons, and our *king*? And then you went even further and abducted our queen."

The old guard swallowed and hesitated before nodding. "I was not involved in the events you mentioned. I am Sir Ymar, the master-at-arms of Nevergrace. And I invite you into our keep for an early breakfast. So we may discuss the unfortunate situation that has arisen on both sides."

"I would not enter your keep on such pretenses, not even if the entire onyx guard escorted me inside. My dragonguard and I would all be ambushed and killed. Just as our king was." Sirra reached out into the dragon realm, pulling and shifting through threads that ran within invisible windows. She stopped when she found *desirité*. Her mind opened and expanded, and she probed the outer portions of Ymar's consciousness, as if using her fingers to part curtains and search around, tossing aside unwanted things and inspecting others more closely. This guard was speaking honestly and was not attempting to deceive her, but even if she knew that, she would not play the credulous fool.

"We will not attack you if you come peacefully." Sir Ymar's voice was laced with fear. "I swear it on my honor."

Sirra laughed. "Do you believe I fear your attacks while we are in the sky? It is you who now begs for peace, and only to save your own skin. It was your king who ordered the attack on ours."

The much smaller forest dragon flapped its wings faster, and the guard rose higher in order to address Sirra from the same altitude. "I do not have the power to supersede orders from King Igare, but I will send a messenger to discuss any demands you may have."

"And what makes you believe my desire is not to simply wipe out all those at this outpost and then take Belvenguard?"

"You did not bring a large enough legion to attempt all that."

This man was no fool. "But if *you* sent a messenger to the king, Igare would then send an entire legion of dragonguard to destroy us. No. We will take Nevergrace by force. And then we will make our demands of Galvenstone, while keeping our location secret."

Ymar's stiff posture broke. "Igare's retribution will be swift."

"Not as swift as mine." She angled her lance at the guard. "Prepare yourself for death."

Ymar pressed his helm tighter on his head and raised his lance so it pointed at Sirra. Shadowmar shrieked and beat her wings. The shadow dragon tore forward. The forest dragon banked hard to the west, but Sirra's mind and soul were one with her dragon's—a monumental advantage a dragonknight held over a guard. All Sirra had to do was think where she wished to go. Shadowmar and her wings were part of Sirra, like Sirra's arms. Shadowmar dipped and wheeled after the forest dragon, coming down on it from above. Sirra's archers drew in sharp breaths as they held on and tried to man their weapons under the forces pulling at them. Only their straps kept them from flying away.

Sir Ymar's lance angled past his dragon's snout as he sought to reposition the weapon. His forest dragon's flapping grew more frantic before it dived. Sirra continued to pursue them, but after the forest dragon had put a little more distance between them, it circled around and soared back at her.

The two dragons came at each other with great speed and from diagonals with Shadowmar above the other.

The instant before Ymar's lance clashed with Sirra's shield, she angled her shield to the side and dipped Shadowmar. Ymar's lance grated against the face of her shield and skittered away, the impact on her and her shoulder minimal. But Sirra's lance smashed into Ymar with a thunderous crash, shattering his shield to splinters. A jarring force thumped against her weapon arm and shoulder, ringing her armor.

Ymar catapulted from his saddle and flew away into the night with a cry.

The forest dragon wailed and dived, and the mage hunkering down against its neck drew Sirra's attention.

19

CYRAN ORENDAIN

CYRAN CRANKED THE WINDLASS ON THE MOUNTED CROSSBOW ATOP the watchtower, bracing himself and heaving against its tension until the rope clicked into place. The intermittent whoosh of dragon wings beating the air sounded close by as he loaded a dragonbolt into the crossbow. But before he could return to the trigger, a dragon rose over the merlons, and its talons thumped on stone as it landed in front of him. Cyran lurched, and his hands shook as he lunged for the trigger handle. But this dragon's scales were deep green.

"Squire," Sir Ilion—the guard riding the dragon—said as he studied the dead bodies of the archers. "Are you adept at the turret bow?"

Cyran glanced at the turret beneath the dragon, which hung to the dragon's knees and was not in danger of being crushed during a typical landing. A man hung limp there, held in place by the harness at his waist and straps around his boots. A dragonbolt must have torn completely through his abdomen, given the gaping hole there.

"It is a terrible loss, but thank the Paladin the bolt did not hit its intended target—our dragon," Ilion said. "We still have a chance to defend the outpost. Move quickly, squire. Nevergrace is under attack!"

Cyran sprinted for the turret. "I am adept at the hand crossbow, but I have yet to fly."

Ilion groaned and glanced around while the archer on the quarterdeck shouted, "We do not have time to be choosy. And we need another archer. I cannot hope to shoot down all these dragons myself." The mage behind Ilion whispered something as well.

"Mount up, quickly," Ilion said, and Cyran climbed into the turret. He worked at the buckles and straps binding the dead man's boots as his hands shook. "Hurry, squire. There are five dragons attacking our outpost. We must shoot them down, or Nevergrace will fall."

Cyran jerked at a strap, and the harness around the dead archer's waist came free. The body toppled over, striking one of the three poles making up the frame and suspended basket of the turret before bouncing off and falling toward the watchtower. Cyran caught the dead archer by his tunic and eased him over the edge, setting him gently down on the stones. Then he worked to pull the harness off the body.

"At a minimum, you should also take his chainmail," Ilion shouted from above.

Cyran eyed the links of armor and the gaping hole in it. *Little good it did him against a dragonbolt.* He knelt and worked at the straps on the man's back.

Dragon shrieks rang in the distance.

"This is taking too long," the archer on the quarterdeck said.

"Just strap yourself in, squire," Ilion said, and the forest dragon's wings beat the air.

Cyran snatched the harness and leapt into the turret, working his boots into the straps of the rotating platform. A dragon shrieked, and beating wings sounded. The forest dragon lifted from the watchtower and dipped its wings, swinging out to the west. Cyran stumbled but held himself in place by gripping the handle of the crossbow, only one of his feet strapped in. Once they leveled out, he worked at the straps for his other foot. But they dipped and rose on air currents, the force of the movements pulling Cyran off balance and throwing him out flat along the lip of the platform. His head and back slipped over the edge. He hung there for a moment with one leg extended and wrenched beyond its normal range of motion, only that foot bound to the turret. He stared down at the torches burning in the bailey far, far below. Time stood still.

The rope and arms of the crossbow up on the quarterdeck snapped and thrummed, and a bolt screamed away.

"Where's your bolt, squire?" Ilion asked.

Cyran grabbed the knee of his strapped-in leg, prayed the straps would hold for what he had to do, and jerked his torso back over the edge of the turret. He grabbed the crossbow with one hand to steady himself as everything around him wheeled and turned.

"Our only hope is to shoot down all of the north's dragons," Ilion said loud enough so Cyran could hear over the beating of wings. "Or we will all die." Cyran buckled a strap over the top of his loose foot and another behind his heel. "But we have to avoid a direct confrontation with that shadow dragon at all costs." Cyran wrapped the loops of the harness around his upper thighs and waist. He cinched them down. "Even if that means we have to enter the forest. That colossal beast won't be able to follow us into the woods."

Cyran snapped the harness to a line wrapped around the crossbow's frame, completely anchoring himself in. He exhaled a stale breath. Dragons dropped and climbed in the fire- and moonlit skies around them. The white ice dragons stood out against the night more than any others, and they passed around the castle.

"We must concentrate on shooting them down," Ilion said. The dragonmage's response was muffled by the shrieks and beating of wings around them. "No. We will not engage in any attempt at jousting. Not even if coming directly at the shadow dragon protects us from all her archers. We will fly after each dragon and try to take them by surprise. With our bolts."

"But you watch out for those lances coming at us," the archer on the quarterdeck said. "If they take you out, we won't be alive for long."

"I will do my part as best I can," Ilion replied. "I'll protect you and spear a dragon's eye or heart if it comes too close. But you two need to shoot down five dragons."

They swooped around the watchtower in a tight arc, and Cyran's stomach slid up into his throat. Then they launched out into the night at the attacking dragons, one of which highlighted itself with firelight. Other icy and fiery breaths continued to bombard the castle.

Wind battered Cyran's cheeks and grasped at his hair with chill fingers as Nevergrace swirled and blurred beneath him. He was flying... on a dragon. His stomach settled, and his heart pounded with a renewed force.

He swiveled his crossbow around and tilted it upward, but the highlighted fire dragon moved too quickly. It created beautiful soaring patterns that filled Cyran with dread, and it never repeated its pattern or made its lines of flight predictable. The ice dragons darted and weaved about, often disappearing behind the watchtowers and keep. The mist dragon appeared only as a pale body, its wings blending with the night as it spewed fog around the periphery of the outpost. A vision of what this creature would look like in the daylight and against the sky sea and clouds suddenly struck Cyran. It would appear as only two black wings descending from above. Cyran shuddered as he continued searching for a target. A massive black beast glided overhead in the distance, visible only because of its size, its silhouette blotting out the light of the moons that was splattered across the sky sea.

Their forest dragon's wings dropped and obscured Cyran's view of everything to either side of them. He would have to be careful not to fire when the wings were descending, something he'd barely thought of before. He glanced to the dragon's legs. Those enormous limbs were tucked close to its body and should not come into his line of fire, not unless the dragon was tearing at soldiers or knights on the ground. And their dragon would find no such adversaries in this battle. Then there was also their dragon's tail. It moved more erratically than the wings but was comparatively small and thin.

The forest dragon rolled hard to the left and grazed the top of the battlements, chasing after an ice dragon that had just made its pass and was climbing away.

"Get ready to bring her down," Sir Ilion yelled. "Roll east in ten flaps."

The forest dragon ascended, and Cyran pivoted around, trying to find a line of sight. But the ice dragon was not only out in front but also above them. Taking a shot would risk hitting his own dragon's underbelly.

The mist dragon shrieked, curtailing its fog making, and it dived into a legion of crossbow-wielding soldiers and knights, raking through their lines with its feet and talons. The beast ripped some of the men and a horse up from the earth and crushed them before flinging their bodies into others. Some in Nevergrace's army screamed, and their ranks fell apart as many raced back toward the outer curtain.

Shock and anger bit into Cyran. He dipped his crossbow as he attempted to track the mist dragon, but it rolled back and forth over the fields below. Cyran squeezed the trigger handle, and the rope shot forward, the metal arms reverberating. His bolt tore straight through one of the three poles supporting his turret and sailed away, arcing well over its target. The turret pitched downward and to the side over the damaged portion of the frame as it hung by its two remaining poles. A strangling sensation pulled at the base of Cyran's tongue with cold fingers.

Shit. Another obstacle to watch out for.

The turret held but wobbled much more as their dragon sailed along, the rattle of the two severed portions of the pole jarring Cyran's skull. The outpost below appeared much farther away now, and its walls and buildings seemed to spin and blur more than they had just moments ago.

Such a far, far way to fall. Cold sweat broke out on Cyran's back and on his palms.

"Stop wasting bolts," Sir Ilion said. "We do not carry an unlimited supply. Only loose if you have a clean shot."

Cyran swallowed his fear and cranked the windlass until the rope clicked into place. He found the stack of dragonbolts hanging in their leather straps overhead, and he grabbed one just behind its barbed head. Its length slipped free, and its weight seemed to increase and press against him, bending his shoulders back as the forest dragon veered, throwing him off balance. The leaning turret pitched farther down toward its damaged side. Wood creaked and popped, and the bolt slipped from his hands and plummeted out into the night. Cyran gasped and stared, watching the length of steel twist and turn horizontally in the air before it disappeared.

"Prepare," Ilion said.

Cyran jerked and quickly pulled out another bolt, fitting it onto the crossbow.

Nearby, the red dragon dived and breathed fire upon the outer curtain where Nevergrace archers waited with mounted crossbows. The fire dragon's archers also released a volley of bolts at Cyran and their dragon, and Sir Ilion cried and pointed. They dived, and most of the bolts whizzed by just overhead. But one bolt tore through the thin flesh of their dragon's wing, and the beast wailed. On the wing's descent, Cyran could see a narrow view of the battle through the hole the weapon had punched in its leathery flap.

Cyran attempted to track the fire dragon's path, but the beast did not fly straight. And neither did their forest dragon. Their own movements of rising and falling and sweeping from side to side were just as unpredictable as their enemy's.

Cyran grunted in frustration. It was all so much different from taking careful and practiced aim with a crossbow on the ground or even on horseback. He wouldn't be able to hit anything up here.

The forest dragon rolled to the east. The ice dragon they pursued swooped away north, its flight path erratic as it tried to avoid potential projectiles.

"Now!" Sir Ilion bellowed, and the upper crossbow rope thwacked and buzzed. The bolt tore away.

Cyran sighted the ice dragon and squeezed the trigger handle. The bolt from the archer on the quarterdeck sailed off to the right of its target. Cyran's bolt streaked closer and closer, possibly on a trajectory that would hit the beast. Cyran held his breath. The ice dragon veered, and the bolt raked across the side of its tail and leg, the projectile's pronged head cutting a gash as it passed. Dark blood drained from the wound and stained its scales.

The ice dragon roared and glanced back before arching and diving.

"After it." Sir Ilion pointed with his lance.

The forest dragon plunged after it, and Cyran's stomach

leapt into his throat as the flimsy turret frame bowed and sagged under the force of the movement.

A scream rang out. To the west, the enormous shadow dragon nearly collided with a forest dragon, but the shadow dragon's lance smashed into their opponent's shield. The shield exploded, and what sounded like metallic thunder rolled through the night. The guard was launched out of his saddle. He plummeted through the sky as the dragons swooped past each other, grazing wings.

"Sir Ymar," Cyran yelled. "He's been unseated."

A moment passed. "It is too late to catch him," Ilion answered. "And the rider of the shadow dragon is likely the Dragon Queen. She would destroy us."

The person on the shadow dragon rode alone with her archers, without a mage. It had to be the Dragon Queen.

"Then bring us closer, and I will shoot her in her chest." Cyran wound the windlass.

"You cannot even target a dragon." Ilion scoffed. "It's nearly impossible to hit a rider or archer when flying. Whenever that happens, it's merely chance."

Like with the archer I removed from this turret? "What if you engaged her in a joust?"

"You won't find a clear shot when jousting. You'd be much more likely to hit me or our dragon. Engage the dragon we chase, damn it."

The injured ice dragon swooped over the woods, flying low. Their dragon tailed it.

But Cyran watched the shadow dragon over his shoulder. It spun around and came down on the forest dragon before the forest dragon had fully recovered. The enemy's black lance flashed. And the Dragon Queen speared the mage on the forest dragon as he attempted to hide and shield himself behind his saddle and the forest dragon's scales. He flew off the side of his mount, his cloak whipping in the wind, his body already limp.

The forest dragon humped its back and flapped wildly. It clawed at the harness for the quarterdeck. A sickening feeling rose in Cyran's guts, and any warmth drained from his face. The quarterdeck's cinches broke and snapped under its talons, and the beast tore the hanging turret free. The archer inside the turret screamed as its frame collapsed, and the dragon let it fall.

The dragon no longer has a mage commanding it.

The forest dragon shook itself off like a dog rising from sleep, and ripples carried from the scales of its neck down to its tail. It dipped, and the quarterdeck slowly slid and tilted. The dragon leaned farther to one side, and the quarterdeck wobbled and slipped and then came off completely, toppling over and swinging end over end as it plummeted downward. Another archer's scream faded as they plunged toward the castle below. A heartbeat later, a resounding thump rolled out over the land.

Cyran winced. The now free forest dragon flapped and angled northwest, flying as fast as it could as it fled toward the forest and the horizon. At best, Nevergrace was now down to four dragons—plus Eidelmere, who was far away in Galvenstone.

Cyran stared in bewilderment.

The pale mist dragon erupted from a cloud of fog to Cyran's right. It barreled straight for Sir Ilion, its guard's lance positioned to strike. Sir Ilion released a cry of alarm, and his lance's mount creaked as he repositioned.

A jarring impact blasted through the forest dragon with a crunch, and Sir Ilion sailed past Cyran, out into the night.

"*Fuck.*"

The whistling scream of bolts ended abruptly as two buried into the neck of Cyran's dragon, just above him. Their dragon shrieked and bobbed left and right as it squealed and wavered, trying to pick up speed and fly as fast as it could. Cyran was flung side to side as he fought to hang on to the crossbow. His turret creaked and swung about.

The shadow dragon—whose archers were responsible for impaling their dragon with bolts—swooped in closer, the archers already reloading. And the Dragon Queen sat poised, leaning forward with her lance directed at their forest dragon's neck.

She's targeting our mage.

Cyran raised his crossbow as she swooped in, but he couldn't find a clear shot. The Dragon Queen struck something above him. An ear-piercing crack rang out, and their mage was hurled from their dragon. He plummeted downward, and his cloak billowed like wings.

More bolts tore into their forest dragon, this time from the ice dragon's archers, as that beast had turned around and veered back toward them.

And their forest dragon's flapping slowed as the beast skimmed over the treetops, losing altitude and cracking and breaking branches before battering into trunks and crashing.

20

CYRAN ORENDAIN

BRANCHES GRABBED AT CYRAN AND THE TURRET AND SNAPPED ITS last two poles. He plummeted through a gauntlet of green needles and trunks and leaves, wood breaking and popping as he fell. The dragon he'd been attached to barreled away into the forest, pummeling and snapping trunks. Something got hung up, and the turret jerked to a halt, whipping Cyran's neck and wrenching his back. The thicker branches bowed up and down before slowly settling.

When the waving needles and trees stilled and came into focus, Cyran found himself hanging from the lower portion of a pine, his turret barely intact around him. The forest dragon was nowhere in sight. His neck ached, and a dull throbbing pain arced down his spine. His face and hands were covered in bleeding scratches.

After a minute, his senses returned. He gathered his wits and unstrapped his boots and waist from the frame. Then he climbed out of the turret and down the tree, using its branches as a ladder. Once his feet settled on the ground, he glanced up. The twisted turret was suspended by several branches, one pole

of its frame completely severed by Cyran's bolt, another pole
cracked and bent.

It was possible the only reason he'd survived the crash was
because he'd broken free from the dragon when his turret
collided with all the treetops. And maybe the turret had only
broken free because he'd shot out one of its poles.

Cyran shivered as he considered the possibility of being
crushed under a crashing dragon. He turned to take in his
surroundings. Dense woods. Early morning light filtered
through the canopy. But he could not find a hint of the main
trail anywhere. The hairs on his arms spiked.

Lost in the Evenmeres.

Cyran unsheathed his broadsword, holding it before him. He
studied the trees and the shadows. There was nothing but
boughs and needles and leaves and undergrowth. He glanced
skyward to where a swath had been cleared through the canopy
and more faint light streamed into the forest. Broken branches
dangled straight downward along the swath's margins—the path
of the crashing forest dragon. Surely the beast was dead. Dead
along with its fallen guard and mage. But the archer on the
quarterdeck could have survived.

Cyran clenched his jaw as he studied the path. Given the
position of the morning sunlight, this pathway ran to the northeast. But he looked south. Nevergrace would lie somewhere in
that direction. No matter where he was in the Evenmeres,
heading south should eventually lead him out of the forest.
Thoughts of the outpost and his sister and friends under attack
by dragon fire struck his mind like a barrage of bolts. The
Dragon Queen would surely kill everyone.

He crept along as silently as he could while pains radiated
across his back and down his limbs. He kept a brisk pace as he
traveled south, curtailing his worries regarding Nevergrace as

well as those concerning the fallen dragon he'd been riding and its other archer.

Something to his right rumbled and moved. Cyran leapt aside and brandished his sword. A tree shifted, or was it only its trunk bowing under the winds?

A melody sounded in the distance. Its tune was joyful and yet foreboding, the one Tamar and Jaslin had been singing. A creeping ripple slid up Cyran's arms. Images of a sinkhole opening beneath his feet and trees falling on him bubbled up from the crevices of his mind.

Tamar. Anger rose inside him. Something out here had taken his brother's life and turned his sister against him, but if he attempted to face it now, it would likely take him too.

Cyran ignored the music and continued southward, stepping over bracken and around brush. The melody grew louder. He glanced deeper into the woods, but the branches became snarls of darkness with beards of draping moss.

A light flashed in the distance, at the periphery of his vision. But when he looked over, it was gone. The light had given him the impression of a floating ball. Cyran forced a deep breath. Memories of a ball of light floating behind what he'd thought was a flaming silhouette of a man returned.

"Jaslin, Emellefer, I'm coming," he said with all the determination he could muster. Not that he would be able to save them or Nevergrace from the Dragon Queen and her minions, but he would not let them die without trying to help or joining them in death.

A sharp howl rang in the distance, drowning out the melody. The light flashed again, and a yellow sphere hovered in the distance before darting behind a tree.

"Who is there?" Cyran called out. "I carry a sword."

He continued along his path southward but tentatively approached the tree in question. As he neared its trunk, he stopped for a moment and knocked on the tree with his sword's crosspiece. A thud ran through his hand and up his arm but sounded dull and dead against the wood. Nothing answered.

After waiting a few heartbeats, he crept around the trunk and peeked at its far side. No lights hovered there, and there were no people or animals. Only more branches and hanging sheets of moss that waved in the shadows. A stench of damp wood and rot wafted through the air.

Cyran studied his surroundings and looked up into the tree. Nothing hid up there either. And the distant melody had faded. After convincing himself that whatever had been hiding was gone, he walked past the tree.

Its trunk erupted in purple flames.

The fire seared Cyran's arm before he could jump aside. The snap and pop of burning wood rang his ears, and flames roared up the length of the tree, feasting on its outer bark. The tree shuddered and quaked as Cyran ran from it as fast as he could.

"The trail lies to the west of where you are now," a voice sounded, although Cyran wasn't sure if something had said it or if he'd only heard it in his head.

After a minute of sprinting away through the forest, branches snapping and prodding and whipping at him, he slowed his pace.

"But you must first follow the line of sky where your dragon came down," the voice continued. "Come. Find me. Given your current position, the stream blocks your route to the Evenmeres's trail."

Cyran whipped his head around, but he could not see anyone or anything around him that should be able to speak. The distant violet fire clung to only one tree, its voice more of a muted roar. A crack sounded beside him, and a tree shifted and teetered. It came swinging down in his direction, and Cyran fled, dashing away at an angle before hiding behind a larger tree. The falling tree smashed into several others before cracking and thumping onto the ground a horse length away, quaking the dirt beneath Cyran's feet. The upper branches near him jostled and rippled and then fell still.

Cyran's lungs burned, and he exhaled and took another quick breath as he retreated from the fallen tree. Something similar must have happened to Tamar. But the nyren said there'd been a sinkhole as well. Cyran studied the ground around him as he took long loping strides away. Once he'd traveled a couple minutes south—judging by the direction of the early sunlight—the swath created by the falling dragon again showed overhead like a river of light in the canopy. And it wasn't any more distant than it had been before.

What is happening?

The dragon's descent into the forest started where he now stood and traveled northeasterly. There was no sign of broken trees to the south. A jolt of fear sent a shiver surging through his limbs. He'd gotten nowhere. He'd traveled in a circle or run back north without even realizing it. But he'd always kept the sunlight to his left. He should have always been traveling south.

"Come quickly." The voice was only a faint whisper now, and it sounded familiar and welcoming. "I am dying."

Cyran glanced along the path of the open swath running northward. Somehow, he knew the voice had come from that direction. He spun in a circle, watching for dashing lights and shifting trees, then stalked north. At least he would have a marker to follow if he continued that way.

After walking for ten minutes with the dragon's path of destruction opening wider and wider and falling lower and lower into the forest, Cyran approached an area where the trees had been broken along their lower trunks, their tops and bulk shoved outward. This destruction created a small clearing.

A forest dragon lay on its stomach upon crushed trees,

groaning and breathing heavily. Cyran drew in a sharp breath. If the lower turret had not broken free during the dragon's crashing descent, Cyran would have been dead. Crushed. Even the quarterdeck on the dragon's back was smashed to pieces, as if the dragon had rolled upon landing. The archer was nowhere in sight.

"Vetelnoir." Cyran cautiously approached the forest dragon, one he'd never taken care of but whose name he had heard.

The creature did not answer.

"Can you hear me?" Cyran asked.

Several dragonbolts protruded from the creature's neck and torso, and an entire trunk had punctured one of her legs and a wing. The dragon groaned again. "I am dying. But there is so much pain. And the sharp sting from the broken bond with my *mëris* is crushing my heart and soul."

Cyran ran to the dragon's face. Both of her eyelids sagged over her pupils and yellow irises. "What can I do?" he asked.

"Finish me. Let me leave this world of man and fully return to the dragon realm with my ancestors."

Biting nostalgia and sorrow sank their teeth into Cyran's heart.

"I will die in my home forest, a place I have not lived in or ventured to in over a century," the dragon barely whispered. "This place feels so foreign now."

"It may be the trees. I thought I saw one move. Another one fell toward me, and yet another caught fire as I walked past it."

"It is not the trees themselves. It is something else. Please..."

"I do not wish for you to suffer, but I cannot kill a dragon by myself."

"Use the—"

A presence hovered around the clearing and surrounded it, instilling a trapped sensation inside Cyran. A few crunching footsteps approached from every direction, the noise sounding purposefully created to instill fear. Four figures in reddish brown cloaks swept in from the trees and surrounded the dragon. Swords gleamed silver in their hands.

"They do not wish for me to enter the realm," Vetelnoir muttered.

Cyran pressed his back to the dragon's neck and faced the new arrivals, attempting to give off a confident demeanor. "This is *my* dragon."

"We've come for her scales and claws and teeth." One figure in a draping red hood strode closer. "We will cut them from the carcass. And we'll take the mounted crossbow as well."

"You cannot have them. Vetelnoir is still alive and belongs to Nevergrace. As does whatever remains of her quarterdeck and crossbow."

The figure flashed his silver sword. Intricate runes stood out and ran the length of the blade. "Dragons belong to no one. And the woods around you have come alive. They have even turned against *us*."

"And who are you?"

"The last of the line of Cimerenden. But that is of no significance. Something ancient and dark now stalks these woods. Something that has been growing in potency over the years. A change has come about, and now it leaves its home within the angoias. All of the woods but a small space we can still call our own belongs to it."

Cold blood trundled through Cyran's limbs.

"And anything that enters our woods can be claimed by us," the man said. "Our people made a mistake, a grave one. And we have suffered because we did not take to the dragons. But now we take what we can from such beasts. And from you, human."

Human? Why would another man use that word?

"Draw them closer," Vetelnoir said. "Toward my hind end."

"This dragon lives." Cyran held his arms wide, hoping he

and the dragon would be granted mercy. "You cannot cut apart a living beast."

"We will cut the scales and remove them from her flesh. They will be ours."

Cyran leapt at the apparent leader and swiped with his blade. The tip of his broadsword clashed against the man's silver sword and rang, and Cyran darted toward the forest dragon's tail. The hooded man grunted as he recovered from his surprise, perhaps believing he'd parried the blow. He closed in on Cyran, and the other three of his people followed his lead.

Cyran stopped near the dragon's curled thigh, where a trunk impaled its flesh, and he faced the hooded man. A long slip of golden hair flowed out from beneath the man's hood. The other three closed in around Cyran, trapping him against the dragon.

"It was humans who forced us to reside in here," the leader said. "And it was humans who destroyed all we had. Our city. Your people killed my people."

"I didn't do anything to anyone in the woods." Cyran crouched and prepared for their attacks. He was an excellent swordsman, but he didn't think he could take four trained warriors. And given the look of their blades, these men were no common thugs.

The leader lunged forward, raising his sword and slashing down over his head in a massive arc. His blade glowed blue. Cyran raised his sword to parry, unable to follow a force coming with such velocity and quickness.

The silver blade clashed with his and carved clean through his broadsword, dropping the top half into the undergrowth. Only the extra split second from the drag along the inferior steel saved Cyran's life by granting him enough time to dodge the blow. The silver sword whistled as it swiped downward, and it cleaved into the trunk stuck in Vetelnoir's leg. The blade lodged in the wood.

Cyran leapt at the man and drove the broken blade of his broadsword into the man's ribs, drawing it back and striking again and again. The man grunted and doubled over as blood covered Cyran's blade. The other three cloaked attackers rushed him.

Vetelnoir's massive tail whipped around, clubbing them. Bones crunched, and gasps sounded as ribs broke and lungs expelled their final breaths. Two men were launched into the woods. The spines on Vetelnoir's tail impaled the other, and that man was crushed when her tail landed with a thud.

The leader collapsed, grabbing his side and groaning before falling over in a heap. His silver sword remained embedded in the trunk, glinting in the sunlight.

"Now, please allow me to pass into the realm of my mother's and father's." Vetelnoir's lips barely moved, her voice faint.

Cyran dropped his cloven sword. "And how can I kill a dragon?"

"You could tear a bolt free from my hide and stick it into my heart, but I would not relish the pain of its removal... Use the silver sword buried in the trunk."

Cyran slid his fingers around the sword's hilt, which was wrapped in fine leather. He gripped it and worked it back and forth, levering it out of the wood. The blade broke free with a whisper of steel.

"Beneath my left wing," the dragon said. "Crawl under me and lift my scales."

Cyran squeezed between the collapsed wing and the dragon's torso.

"Lower," the dragon said. "More toward my sternum."

Cyran mashed himself between the ground and the pale-green scales on the dragon's underside. He grabbed the edge of a scale as large as a shield and heaved, lifting it up and bringing a region of scales with it.

"You have found it." The dragon shifted to better expose the area.

Cyran hesitated, looking from the dark flesh beneath the scale to the silver blade in his hand.

"Do it. Release me." Vetelnoir grunted in pain. "Then travel *away* from the sunlight. If you do so, you should find the trail. And do not follow the other lights or the song of the forest."

Cyran raised his sword.

"But first utter the parting words," Vetelnoir said. "Of the elder tongue. Of the dragon realm."

Cyran's sword drooped in his hand. "I do not know such words."

Vetelnoir moaned. "Then repeat the ancient words after me. *Mörenth toi boménth bi droth su llith.* Till the end of days we soar. *Mörenth toi boménth bi nomth su praëm.* Till the end of nights we reign. *Röith moirten íli. Ílith Ëmdrien tiu gládthe.* You honor me. My soul sees yours."

Cyran repeated the words, the last with more emphasis. "*Röith moirten íli. Ílith Ëmdrien tiu gládthe.* You honor me. My soul sees yours."

Cyran plunged the blade into the dragon's flesh. The steel shaft slid in easily, and the beat of a mighty organ thudded against the weapon's tip but gave way. Silver pierced dragon heart. Blood drained around Cyran's arm, and Vetelnoir sighed, her body releasing the last of its tension as it slumped against the ground.

The feeling of a great weight and power rose from Vetelnoir and sifted through some window in the air around them. It slipped away, and the window snapped shut. All it left in its wake was a body and death.

Cyran trembled as he crawled out from under the forest dragon's wing. Four other dead bodies littered the clearing or lay around the edges of it. Men in brownish-red cloaks. These woodsmen feared something in their own forest. And if that was true, it might not be them or others of their kind who were killing travelers who ventured too far from the Evenmeres's only safe path. That could also mean these men and their people were not responsible for Tamar's death, but whatever they feared might be. Cyran vowed to find out either way.

He slipped the tip of his blade under the leader's hood and shoved the hood back. Golden hair spilled out. The man was young, and he was as handsome as anyone Cyran had ever seen. But his bone structure was thinner than most men's. He was also a good deal shorter than average, and his ears tapered to points.

An elf.

Cyran had only heard of elves in old myths and legends. It had been said that elves once walked Cimeren but had departed the lands for another, turning their backs on everyone and everything to leave man to his follies.

A whisper sounded in the distance, and Cyran spun about. A melody rose again, tugging at a thread of longing inside Cyran, calling to him through the midst of his turbulent emotions.

Travel away from the sunlight. And do not follow the music.

Cyran held his silver sword high and stepped away from the dragon's body.

21

SIRRA BRACKENGLAVE

NEVERGRACE'S KEEP LOOMED BEFORE SIRRA AS SHE GUIDED Shadowmar up to its barred doors, her great beast's feet thumping on the ground as she walked. Smoldering fires of orange and black dappled the bailey as the sun climbed over the eastern horizon.

Shadowmar raised her head so that Sirra sat even with a shuttered window in the upper keep. Sirra drew her blade, and black fire leapt up its length, crackling. She drove her blade into the shutters, and the wood and inner glass imploded, blasting into the keep. A scream sounded inside.

"I demand the return of our queen." Sirra peered into the open window, through shards of cracked glass. "Alive. Release her, or I will enter and occupy this keep."

No one answered.

"Your dragonguard and knights and soldiers have been decimated." Sirra glanced back at her four dragonguard and their mounts, who all waited behind her. Only one of the ice dragons had taken a dragonbolt, and blood drained around the lodged projectile and the wound. This same dragon also had a long gash running along its leg where another bolt had sliced through its scales. "You have no choice but to comply."

Footsteps shuffled about inside and then scampered away.

"Then we will burn our way in." Sirra guided Shadowmar's head lower, until she sat even with the front gates of the keep. *"Release your fire."*

Shadowmar roared and sucked in a breath. She spewed black fire, the flames smashing into the iron and wooden gates. Metal heated and flared red before glowing orange and then white. Wooden planks snapped and burned and fell inward. The metal began to drip. In a few moments, nothing remained but the charred stone opening leading into the lower keep.

Sirra swung a leg over her saddle and dismounted, and her dragonarmor boots thudded against the walk as she landed. She strode into the keep, and her guard and archers followed her in tight ranks. The mages remained behind with the dragons.

A score of soldiers with pikes waited in the atrium ahead, and they all charged, lowering their weapons and yelling.

Sirra reached through an invisible window and grasped a thread of the other realm, tugging and snapping it. *Aylión.* She saw faint outlines of each man and where they would move to in the instant after the present. When she stepped forward, she side-stepped each attack, cutting through the shaft of a pike before swiping downward and cleaving two more weapons in half. When the soldiers drew swords, she sliced through their throats or gutted them, her sword snapping and hissing with black flame.

Her guard members followed her and cut down a few stragglers. The last two soldiers of Nevergrace fled up a stairway. Sirra looked past the atrium to a throne room and audience chamber. Empty. She followed the soldiers to the next landing. Two hallways diverged from the stairs, halls with multiple oaken doors. And every doorway was closed, enticing her to break them open.

Sirra strummed another thread—*dramlavola*—delicately, and power surged through her body. She kicked in a doorway. A woman screamed and ducked behind a bed.

"Grab her and bring her down to the throne room," Sirra said to the guard behind her.

Sirra ran with the speed of a bounding cragcat and kicked through the remaining doors. Her guard and archers poured into the chambers behind her. They worked their way up through the levels of the keep, gathering several more people, and a couple archers took them to the throne room as a group. Sirra did not encounter any more resistance until she reached the uppermost floor.

When Sirra stepped inside an expansive chamber, soldiers leapt out from behind statues and columns. She did not want everyone within this chamber to fall. She would not use the dragon voice—*opthlléitl*. Not yet.

Blír. She grabbed another thread from the dragon realm, and she held up her hand. The soldiers hesitated but then continued their charge, their fear wafting from their bodies like an odor. Her fist sprang open. The soldiers catapulted away from her and crashed into the far wall. Another group of people huddled against that wall, behind a statue of the Paladin—a muscular god wielding a sword and shield, his face hidden within an angular helm that molded to his cheekbones and chiseled jaw.

What a hypocritical place to hide.

A few last soldiers stepped before those who were likely of noble blood.

"Call off your soldiers," Sirra said. "Or other innocents may die."

"Stop." A short man with graying brown hair stepped forward. The soldiers too eagerly lowered their weapons and stepped back. "I am the new lord of Nevergrace. Lord Dainen.

Please, speak with me and allow the others here to depart in peace."

"No one leaves this keep alive." Sirra paced around the group of men in embroidered tunics and women in dresses as her guard members formed a wall behind her. The men cringed as she eyed them. "Not until our queen is safely returned to me."

"Your queen is not at the Never, milady." The lord's lower lip trembled. "We cannot give her to you, as you must have already known."

Sirra smirked but kept her black visor lowered, concealing her entire face with a mask that would instill fear in the Paladin himself. "And that is why I have come to your outpost. To hold it until King Igare fulfills my demands. You will all be captives of the Dragon Queen until then, and if your king does not oblige me, you will die. Until my queen arrives, one of you will be killed every dawn and dusk." Sirra motioned for her guard members to take the nobles. "To the throne room."

Women screamed as the guard approached in their spiked and barbed armor as dark as Shadowmar's scales. Sir Vladden took hold of a nyren's arm and pulled him away. Another guard took a clergywoman in white.

There is no conjuror here. Or they are hiding. Sirra stalked around the room as her archers took more of the people and led them away. "Also make a sweep through the baileys and check all the houses. Bring everyone who is still alive inside the keep."

She waited until only the lord remained.

Dainen stared at the floor, his hands trembling. "I will send my swiftest messengers to Galvenstone and deliver your demands to the king."

"Oh, I know you would. But as we now control the last of your dragons, I do not believe you have a swift messenger. You will merely sign any letter I write, if I ask it of you, and I will have it delivered." She waved her flaming sword, and the lord lurched aside, hustling for the exit and the stairway.

Sirra trailed the lord all the way to the audience chamber on the ground level of the keep. She marched behind him and guided him through the chamber toward the throne. When he walked up the dais, Sirra grabbed his shoulder and pulled him back. She shoved him away toward the other captives, whom her archers had lined up against both side walls near suits of armor and busts of past lords.

She turned and sat on the throne, a seat of nothing more than wood and iron with a few dragon's teeth planted along its upper margins. No dragon skin or bone. Nothing of real power. Yenthor stood with his massive arms folded across his chest as he glared at the hostages. Zaldica stood across from him and watched those along the opposite wall, her wiry frame contrasting with her comrade's. Another archer grabbed two young women by the arms and pulled them away, escorting them toward the keep's entrance. One of the women appeared to be dressed as a young lady of the outpost. The other was perhaps a servant.

"Where are you taking them?" Sirra said.

The archer paused and turned, his eyes flashing with fear. "I thought we'd take the spoils of victory. And I did not think it appropriate to do so in this chamber."

"If you take either of them from this room or try anything with any of our prisoners, I do not care if you are a dragonknight or even the legendary Sir Bleedstrom himself, I will remove your bollocks with my blade." She flicked her blade up near her face. Its black fire hissed. "Any flesh wound made with this sword will immediately cauterize, and the burning and pain it will cause would far outweigh whatever pleasure you are seeking. And this pain will also last for much, much longer."

The archer released the women, and his hands trembled.

How did such a man even end up under my command? And when I have so few that every single one of them is important. "The same goes for everyone here. We may kill as we must, but there will be no rape. Not while I lead you. Do not force me to uphold my threat."

She leaned back against the throne, reached up, and plucked a dragon's tooth from its rim. She studied everyone in the chamber as she ran a finger over the tip of the tooth. No one met her eye.

She jammed the tooth into the hand rest, and its sharp point sank deep into the wood. "This outpost is now under the control of the Dragon Queen. Bring me parchment and ink."

22

CYRAN ORENDAIN

A COPSE OF ANGOIAS LAY JUST AHEAD AND TOWERED INTO THE SKY. Cyran's heart beat faster. He didn't think their dragon had flown so far into the Evenmeres.

A cold dread swirled inside him. Could Vetelnoir have lied when she'd sent him in this direction? Given what he'd seen with the other dragon tearing off its harnesses and fleeing after it had lost its mage, he realized Vetelnoir might not have cared about his safety either. She could have even sent him deeper into the woods on purpose. But his conversation with her felt genuine, the emotions and words heartfelt, as if he'd assisted her in an ancient rite of passage. She was a dragon, and she could have been deceitful, but Cyran felt otherwise.

A strong scent analogous to that of wood and leaves mixed with an astringent floated past.

The smell of the ancient angoias.

Cyran had heard the odor described before, but this was the first time he'd ever been close enough to smell it. A reddish haze floated around their trunks. He glanced back at the burgeoning sunlight—still directly behind him. He continued pacing west, and the margins of the angoias passed by on his right, just beyond a few pines.

A memory of something Eidelmere had said to him surfaced amidst the doubts in his mind, something about wanting to smell or touch the bark of his homelands.

It will only take another minute. He strode toward the mountainous trees. Whatever had happened with the attack at the Never, it was probably long over. There was likely little, if anything, he would be able to do now to assist in the outcome. He suppressed his fears of what might be. The guard and soldiers of Nevergrace would be victorious. Once he returned, he would find Jaslin and Emellefer and all his squire friends safe and laughing, asking where he'd been. There could be no other outcome.

He swiped with his new sword, and its blade carved a strip of reddish bark from the angoia. The strip floated downward like a feather, drifting back and forth before gently settling on the ground. Cyran plucked the bark from atop a layer of decaying leaves and smelled its inner face. The strong scent he'd noticed earlier hit his nostrils and caused his eyes to water.

Music sounded quietly in the distance, calling out from deeper within the angoias. The massive trunks overlapped one another for what could have been leagues of forest, leading farther away, making it all appear as a darker and tangled region of the woods. The red haze hovering around the area drifted about as scarves of fog.

Cyran stepped back. A flash of light darted from within the angoias and disappeared behind a trunk. A rush of warning sounded in Cyran's mind. He tucked the bark into his belt and fled the way he'd come. The typical-sized pines and maples looked to be in different locations than they had been only a minute ago. And one shifted before him.

It is *the trees.*

Cyran's blood surged with adrenaline and fear as he sprinted past the trees, keeping his distance in case one started falling or burst into flame. He hurdled a fern and ran on, his mind churning.

But if it was the trees, that could mean everything Vetelnoir had said was wrong or a lie. Parents told their children tales about trees that could think and speak, even move. But no one considered such myths to be based in reality.

Before turning directly away from the sunlight again, Cyran rushed past a pine and swiped along its outer surface. His silver blade sank deep and sliced clean through bark and wood, releasing another strip. The tree did not flinch or shudder, and only a small amount of sap clung to his blade. It was not more alive than a typical tree.

Cyran hurried along for a few minutes before stumbling upon something stark white in the bracken. He knelt and pulled aside a stem loaded with leaves.

A bone waited beneath, an arm and a ribcage. A skull. A human skeleton lay amidst the undergrowth, staring skyward. There was not an ounce of flesh or even clothing on its bones, making it appear as if it had been here so long everything had rotted away. But the bones were not even cracked or dried, hinting at a different story. These bones might not have been exposed to the air for very long.

A howl rang out just behind Cyran. He glanced back, but nothing moved in the woods. Another howl answered the first, arising somewhere to his left. He ran, heading directly away from the sunlight, sprinting and leaping over brush and logs. More howls echoed in the forest around him, and they drew closer. The sound of rushing footsteps, in addition to his own, pounded undergrowth, but when Cyran risked a glance over his shoulder, he could not find whatever pursued him. He raised his blade. Its silver sheen twinkled, creating spots of light, as if it were filled with stars.

Could the sword be cursed and leading something to him? He considered casting it aside, but it was his only weapon. And it seemed he might need it soon.

After Cyran tore through the woods for another minute, the pines parted. A broad path opened up, and sunlight stole down into the forest. Cyran leapt onto the trail, heaving for breath as he glanced around. There was still no sign of anything pursuing him. His pause lasted only an instant before he began walking south.

The howling faded and died out, and after two hours of hiking, the trees thinned. Cyran picked his way eastward so that he would not emerge directly north of the outpost, in case Murgare was now monitoring the trail.

He stepped from the Evenmeres onto the rolling fields east of Nevergrace. After casting one last glance at the woods, he ran for the outpost. His feet pounded down inclines and over dying grasses before he ascended a hilltop.

A shriek knifed at his ears, and he fell onto his side, clutching his head. A shadow blotted out the sunlight, and it swooped over the countryside around the castle as it wailed. Cyran crawled for cover, seeking a mound of rocks nearby.

The dragon—appearing as only a pair of massive black wings, its pale body blending with the sky—wheeled about. Its shadow dragged across the grass around Cyran as he shuffled along on all fours. Its presence grew closer. The shadow grew larger.

Cyran pressed himself against the rocks, wedging himself under the largest. The shadow spun about on the grass and hesitated a moment as it hovered there. Then it flew off westward.

Cyran peeked out from behind the mound. The sky was clear except for rafts of clouds that were being chased by the breath of the Evenmeres. The ever-present sky sea watched over everything, sunlight diffused through its waters.

And so the dragons of the north are not *defeated.* Cyran's heart buckled. Murgare's mist dragon patrolled the area around the outpost, probably hunting for anyone who escaped the attack and the castle while also watching for approaching armies. The presence of the mist dragon probably also meant Galvenstone had not received the signal from the beacon fires.

Jaslin. Emellefer. My friends. A stabbing guilt over his and Jaslin's last conversation sank into his chest. But he could not allow his thoughts to linger on that. Not now.

Cyran crept from his cover and slowly ventured toward the Never, making sure to pick a path that would allow him to keep either a tree or rock nearby. But a couple times he had to dart between open areas. The walls of the castle soon came into view, rising from the hilltop beside the forest. Dragons sat on the battlements, partially concealed by fog and mist. None of these dragons were forest dragons. The drooping heads of a fire dragon and two ice dragons made all three appear to be sleeping in perched positions.

Cyran's weakened heart crumpled, as if it had been struck by the blunt end of a lance. He collapsed to his knees, and he stared blankly at the scene.

The north had taken their castle. The unbreachable walls of Nevergrace had folded. All his friends and family were likely dead. Or they soon would be. Murgare did not keep prisoners, and they tortured those they had. To death. He prayed to the Paladin and the Siren of the Sea and the Hunter and the Shield Maiden that Jaslin and Emellefer were somewhere safe, somewhere far away from the outpost. But if they were not, he prayed they had died quickly and during the confrontation rather than having become prisoners. And he prayed that Jaslin had forgiven him.

He could do nothing now. Not alone.

But who else would come? *Sir Kayom*. Cyran's guard-master was still in Galvenstone with the king. Cyran could ride back to the capital and make the Never's dragonguard aware of the evil that had transpired. Together, they could inform the king and warn him of the impending danger. Then Belvenguard would send as many dragons as necessary to take Nevergrace back.

An idea dawned on Cyran. Maybe his friends and Jaslin were still alive. Murgare might be hoping to use them as hostages. Five dragons, no matter how powerful, were not nearly enough to attempt an assault on all of Belvenguard.

There is hope. Cyran pushed himself to his feet and crept closer to the outpost. It would take him far too many days to travel to Galvenstone by foot, but if he could take one of the Never's horses, he could ride it as fast as it would go, like during the latter part of his and his friends' previous journey to the capital. But if he were caught while attempting to sneak into the outpost, there would be no one to warn the king. Then, even if some of his people were still alive, they would not receive aid.

He steeled his resolve and crept closer, and the veil of mist became easier to see through. A bloody gash on one of the ice dragon's legs stood out where some of its scales had been shorn off—Cyran's doing. There was also a puncture wound where a dragonbolt must have struck the beast but had been removed.

He cautiously approached the front gates of the castle, but no gates remained, only a scorched archway. There were no soldiers standing guard—although a couple could have been hiding in the denser pockets of mist clinging to the walls of the archway. But the north could not have brought many soldiers with them. Cyran paused. The gaping entrance felt more unwelcoming and foreboding than the largest barred gates ever could.

He crept closer to the archway, and the towering figure of a fire dragon slowly swung into view. No wonder the north was not overly concerned with placing human soldiers on watch. No one in their right mind would try to break into the Never now. Maybe a Belvenguard army would attempt to do so, but the north would hear and see such an army coming.

The fire dragon's eyes remained closed, its breath coming in slow rumbles. There was no mage on its back or within Cyran's line of sight. Were the dragons of the north so evil that they also enjoyed what their masters made them do and willingly helped perform such vile deeds? It seemed the forest dragons of Nevergrace would escape and return to the forest if given the opportunity to leave man and his desires behind. That must be the primary reason for the locked gate outside the den, not to mention all the shackles.

Voices sounded from within the walls. Cyran's stomach slumped into his guts as he stepped back. The uppermost portion of the keep's gates and entrance were visible from where he stood, and it also appeared that the keep's doors had been incinerated, the stones around the opening blackened. The Never's steeds had probably all been butchered or fired in battle as well. Or they had been fed to the north's dragons. He shouldn't have ventured this close. While there might only be a few of the north's soldiers spread out around the entire outpost, their dragons were another matter. Perhaps he could find a plow horse in the farmlands around the area and ride it to Galvenstone instead. He glanced over his shoulder, surveying the distant fields for as far as he could see. The dark shapes of livestock dotted a hillside near the horizon.

The breath of a dragon rumbled in the distance.

Cyran froze and slowly turned back.

The enormous shadow dragon lumbered about inside the baileys and approached the area of the den. Its wings and neck extended far above the walls, and it sniffed but then lowered its head, maybe to investigate the den, an opening that would barely be large enough for such a beast. The dragon pulled back, and its neck rose again, its snarling head whipping side to side as if searching for something.

Cyran dropped behind a small mound in the field, although it was not large enough to hide him completely. He peeked over its lip. The shadow dragon sniffed again, its slitted red eyes flashing about and a dark third membrane intermittently sliding across them. After a minute of scrutinizing its surroundings, the dragon contorted and lowered itself, disappearing behind the walls, perhaps into the Never's den. But the vilest beast was awake and watching.

Cyran waited a moment before rising and dashing across the fields.

23

JASLIN ORENDAIN

JASLIN SAT ON A CHAIR INSIDE A CHAMBER PACKED WITH MANY soldiers and knights and servants and woodsmen and farmers of Nevergrace. These people might have represented all of the castle's surviving men, women, and children. But whether these were the last survivors or not, anyone who hadn't been killed in the attack was surely a prisoner now. Jaslin had to hope that more of the Never's people were being held in different rooms within the keep.

The north's dragonguard and archers alternated watch at the doorway of the chamber. There were not many of them, but their dragons waited outside. Jaslin had seen these creatures sitting on the battlements, looking like gargoyles that had bred with the legendary giants dwelling in the mountains of southern Cimeren. And just one of the dragons could kill everyone in this room. The men of Murgare had even threatened that if anyone tried to revolt, the dragons were only one shout away from breaking through a window in this chamber and roasting or freezing everyone inside.

Jaslin twisted the fragment of the crystal decanter over in her hand. The feeling of needing it, of it filling some empty hole in her heart, coursed through her. She also experienced a desire to locate where it came from, its secrets. She had to understand it, to find its voice in the woods. Tamar had given the decanter to her, so her attachment to it did not feel entirely out of place. It was her last link to her oldest brother, his final gift to her. And now he was gone. Cyran was gone as well. Both of her brothers were dead. She had no family left. Everyone she loved was dead. And she'd tried to avoid Cyran upon his return, still angry with him for leaving immediately after Tamar's death. But that was not the only reason she'd avoided him. The temptation of the crystal's secrets also drove her, and it seemed to want her to steer clear of him.

Anger coursed through her heart and flooded her chest. This world took her parents from her, and it took Tamar from her for no reason. Tamar had been the hardest worker she'd known, performing so many extra chores so Cyran could train and become a dragonsquire and she could enjoy her stories. Tamar had been the most giving sibling anyone could ask for. But little good it all did, as it only made Cyran a slave to duty and made her a prisoner inside the Never's keep. Cyran had thrown the last of his life away, taking an oath and spending his final days serving a king Jaslin had never seen, a king who lived in some city beside the lake. Tears swelled and rolled down her cheeks. Cyran's duty hadn't even helped the people of Nevergrace when the time came. And now she was sitting here in this chamber with all the crestfallen of their outpost.

Jaslin reared her arm back, wanting to expel her anger by flinging the crystal fragment like a knife. Hopefully it would bury into the dragonarcher's chest. She could watch him collapse to the floor, and then she'd run free with her people. But then the dragons would burn them all alive.

She sank into despair, and a familiar melody—one that would not leave her mind these past days—pulled at her lips and formed notes when she breathed. Humming the tune was more habit now rather than something she had to focus on.

The howl of wolves sounded off in the distance, probably coming from the forest. Maybe little Smoke and his friends had escaped the castle. There were probably plenty of other wolves in the Evenmeres, but none wandered too close to people and the Never had a much bigger population than any village or hamlet along the woods' southern border.

Menoria, who was sitting beside Jaslin, burst into tears. Jaslin hesitated. This was the young lady of the Never, or at least she used to be before their new lord had arrived. Jaslin furtively watched Menoria's tears overflow from her eyes and track down her cheeks. She slipped her arm around Menoria and hugged her.

Menoria covered her face and sobbed. Her golden hair formed a tangled knot behind her head. "First my father and now this. All I ever wanted was to become a lady of the Never and help my people. To treat them with respect and decency and be treated the same."

Jaslin's anger brewed and simmered. This world might have been unfair to Menoria, but it was just as unfair to her, if not more so. She pressed a fist into her chair. Defeated faces and dejected people surrounded her in droves. Nearly one hundred people sat or stood shoulder to shoulder inside this expansive visiting chamber. Brelle sat beside Dage and Laren—Cyran's friends—but Garmeen wasn't in the chamber, probably another to have joined the dead out in the baileys. Emellefer, the young lady Cyran had a fancy for, worried at something on her hands while she stood quietly in the corner near Dage. Renily sat on Ulba's lap. Even Ezul, the old nyren, was in this chamber, but he did not appear to be making any plans or taking action. He wasn't even discussing anything with anyone.

"There are so many dragons out there," a serving woman

with gangly arms and dangling breasts whispered to another as she stared out the window. "And they must get hungry."

"We will all be fed to them eventually," the other woman replied.

Jaslin glanced around the chamber. Soldiers sat in groups, their eyes downcast. Most were silent, but a few whispered quietly.

"The new lord is probably already dead," one soldier with a draping mustache said to another who was bald.

"Galvenstone will never hear of what has happened," the bald one added.

"Not until we are all long dead," the first replied, and the bald one nodded in agreement.

Jaslin swallowed. Was everyone waiting to die? Given the takeover and presence of many powerful dragons from Murgare, it seemed they had already accepted such a fate.

Jaslin hugged Menoria again and whispered, "What if we start to plan our escape rather than just sitting here waiting to be executed by the Dragon Queen?"

The former young lady of the Never lowered her hands and studied Jaslin with reddened eyes. "Are you jesting? If they catch us, we will surely be the next to die, *if* they don't have a dragon burn everyone."

"We are probably all going to die anyway. The north does not hold captives, remember? And the archers only threatened the use of dragon breath when trying to dissuade us from fighting back."

Menoria glanced at the two dragonarchers by the doorway. They both carried hand crossbows, and swords were strapped to their waists. All of Nevergrace's soldiers and knights were unarmed and unarmored.

Menoria's posture slumped further. "What you suggest would be fighting back. But perhaps in a subtler way." She brushed aside her tears and swallowed. "If you can think up a plan to slip past five dragons, I'll listen."

Jaslin stood and yawned—for show in case one of the north's men watched her—and stumbled over to a desk in the corner. She swiped a stylus and parchment before facing the wall. After tearing the parchment into four equal pieces, she wandered over and sat beside Brelle.

"I'm so sorry about Cyran," Brelle said and hugged her.

Jaslin shrugged her off. "It is not time to mourn the dead or the fate of the outpost. Not yet, or we will join them. We can all mourn together another day."

Brelle pulled away. "What are you getting at?"

The north's soldiers still had their backs turned. Jaslin raised an eyebrow. "Something must be done."

Dage cast her a scowl and shook his head. "The king will come with a legion of dragons. They will burn all those scales off Nevergrace's walls."

"And what if they don't arrive before some of us are executed?" Laren asked. "Their soldiers take someone every dawn and dusk. You could be next. Or it could be me."

"They will come." Emellefer shuffled closer to Dage and puffed up her small chest. "King Igare is just and powerful. His legions can defeat any of our enemies."

"I wonder how the north will execute me." Brelle pursed her lips and shook her head. "I'd prefer dragon ice breath to that of fire. I think some cold burning before going numb sounds like a much nicer way to go than being roasted alive."

"I don't think they make their dragons perform the executions," Laren said.

"Unless some of the dead are meant to feed their dragons." Brelle shrugged.

Jaslin sketched an outline of the keep and the castle walls on one of her pieces of parchment, drawing the dragons' positions where she'd last seen them. Even this simple action reminded her of something from one of her stories, something that heroes often did.

"What are you doing?" Dage reached for the parchment, meaning to tear it from her grip, but she jerked it away and leaned back.

"I'm just trying to get you all to plan something with me," Jaslin said.

"You're going to get us all killed is what you're going to do," Dage said.

"I am no warrior," Jaslin continued, "but I know there are a lot more of our people packed into this keep than there are Murgare soldiers. They will never be able to watch us all. And if we are here long, they will have to allow us to start preparing meals and cooking for ourselves, or we will all starve."

"I wouldn't trust the north to worry about getting any of us fed." Laren leaned closer to inspect her drawing and tapped a finger against it. "The last I saw through the window, the shadow dragon was headed into the den. And that beast hasn't been out on the walls much."

"I haven't seen the shadow dragon out at all," Brelle said. "But I did see some of their guard taking our surviving forest dragons down into the den. Nevergrace still has at least three living dragons."

"If the shadow dragon hasn't devoured them." Laren's face paled.

"And we probably don't have any surviving mages," Dage added. "If there are any left, the north must have hidden them elsewhere. So none of this even matters."

"I agree that we should do whatever they tell us and obey the Dragon Queen's wishes." Emellefer's hands shook as she worried at her tunic. "If we are subservient, we will not anger her. And we will wait for the king's legions to swoop in from

Galvenstone. Sun and rose dragons will fill the sky, and the ice and fire dragons will flee out of fear."

"If that happens, I will jump with joy and kiss you with more passion than any of the young men you chase are willing to use on those lips of yours," Brelle said, and Emellefer grimaced. "But we cannot place all our faith in being saved when the north is executing our people."

Jaslin sketched out the gates of the keep and those of the castle's walls. "We still outnumber them. Even if our only survivors are those inside this chamber, we have a lot more people than they do."

"But they have five dragons." Laren tapped another area on her map. "That gives them the equivalent of five thousand soldiers."

"I know." Jaslin shook her head. "Or five hundred knights. More than the Never has ever had."

"And I believe the shadow dragon probably counts for more than a standard dragon's share." Brelle knitted her fingers together and wrinkled her forehead.

"But if they come marching in here, looking to drag you away, what plan would you like to follow?" Jaslin looked at each of them in turn.

A spell of silence lingered.

"I'd like to run into the forest," Laren finally said. "The Even-meres have been scaring a lot of people lately, but if I were faced with the decision of standing before the Dragon Queen or the forest, I'd choose the forest. I could hide in there."

The woods. The song. Jaslin realized she'd forgotten about the crystal and everything it made her feel for a few minutes, but the sensation and its draw came rushing back. A deep yearning sparked in her heart. Cyran had told her not to venture into the woods until he returned, and despite everything, she'd managed to heed his wishes. Although she had gone to the wood's borders several times and stared in wonder at their depths. Then Cyran returned, and now he was gone. For good. Tamar had discovered something Cyran didn't understand. If she ever escaped this place, she would follow Tamar's lead instead.

"Then how do you propose we distract the Murgare soldiers and the dragons and all make it into the woods?" Jaslin drew a few trees on her map and penned three additional copies on the other torn sheets.

Menoria wandered over and joined them. She examined the parchments. "I will do whatever I can for the Never and its people. I do believe sitting and waiting to die should not be how we go about our apparent defeat."

Warmth blossomed inside Jaslin, and her lips lifted in a determined grin. "We are not that different, you and me. We have both lost members of our family as well as our home, we the young women surrounded by men of consequence."

Menoria glanced up at Jaslin and smiled. Her tears stalled. "We, the daughters who go unnoticed and are told how to live our lives. We, who are told whom we shall marry and where we shall live."

The two young women stared at each other, and Jaslin took Menoria's hand and squeezed it.

"Hope." Laren's boyish grin returned. "That is what this is. A moment ago, we had none. We may be fooling ourselves, but hope can make all this bearable."

The old nyren shuffled over to their group while stroking his beard and watching Murgare's archers, who spoke quietly amongst themselves and devoured a meal consisting of the Never's meats and potatoes. Ezul picked up one of Jaslin's maps and scrutinized it.

Emellefer groaned and slipped through the mass of captives, most of whom were sitting quietly with their heads down. She took a seat on the opposite side of the chamber.

Ezul blinked rapidly, and his wooly eyebrows danced over his eyes. "Now, if I were to outline a plan of escape, I'd suggest forming a few different groups. These groups would each have a different objective, such as distraction or fighting or sneaking their way out of this miserable chamber. Every individual would have to know each group's purpose, and each group would have to act either at a specific moment or within a series of events, the initiation of one event being the signal for the next."

Jaslin's mind swirled with ideas and possibilities. "I will stay with Menoria. As her... handmaid."

Menoria clutched Jaslin's hand. "I think anyone would believe that. Or maybe I should become the handmaid for any who ask."

"Yes." Jaslin winked and squeezed Menoria's hand. "If you act as my handmaid before Murgare starts searching for you, I can convince them I am the young lady of the Never."

Menoria swallowed and nodded. "You are very kind."

But doubts swirled through Jaslin's mind as she looked from her tunic to Menoria's dress. "But the Dragon Queen cannot be a fool. She will not believe us. And your dress is too short for me even if we were to switch clothes. Also, they may execute people of lesser consequence before moving onto others of higher station."

Menoria shut her eyes. "You are probably right."

Ezul paced in a tight circle around them while tapping at his beard. "Since we cannot use our sheer numbers to overwhelm our enemies, not without being scorched by dragon fire, then we must use stealth and distraction." He furrowed his forehead, which caused his hairy eyebrows to mash together. "Or prefer-ably magic, if we had any." He glanced around the group, but everyone shook their head or shrugged.

Brelle cleared her throat. "The other possible exits from this chamber, besides the obvious guarded one, would be through one or both windows. But I don't think we could open either of them, much less climb out, without creating a lot of noise."

"There is an old passageway in Nevergrace." Ezul studied one of Jaslin's maps. "A secret tunnel leading from the keep that was meant to be utilized in times of siege. It has not been opened in centuries."

"Where is it?" Jaslin's excitement and hope swelled, but Ezul shook his head.

"Don't tell me it's in the throne room." Brelle groaned. "That's where the Dragon Queen has supposedly taken up residence."

Ezul shrugged. "I cannot remember."

"What?" Brelle's voice came out quite a bit louder than any of them had been talking. "I thought nyrens remembered everything they ever read."

Ezul nodded. "Following decades of training in our arts and after mastering such skills, a chained nyren can remember all he or she reads and all they are taught. That is why we do not require libraries beyond the southern citadels and the academy. But in this instance, it was only a story that I'd read, and the story did not specify the location of the passageway. The only description of it was that it ran from the keep out into the Evenmeres. The lord and his family were the only ones who were supposed to know of its location."

All eyes turned to Menoria, but it took her a moment to realize why she'd become the focus of everyone's attention. "I was never told of such a passageway."

Jaslin groaned, and she started to draw groups of people around the inside of the chamber they currently resided in. "If someone can escape, they will need to warn the closest village, and preferably Galvenstone."

"The beacon towers." Brelle leapt up. "We need someone to get out there and light them."

Jaslin drew more groups on her parchment and a beacon tower beyond the castle. "I will be in a group with Menoria, as her handmaid. Ezul should stay on watch here—"

Someone ripped the parchment from Jaslin's hands. She gasped.

One of the north's archers stood over her and aimed his crossbow at the nyren's chest. "What is this? A map of the castle and your escape plans?"

"No." Jaslin shook her head, her heart leaping in her chest and racing between heaving lungs.

The archer grabbed Jaslin by the wrist and pulled her to her feet. He also snatched a scrap of parchment from Menoria and tugged her along as well. "Go." He pointed to the doorway. "Or the other archer you see there will bar the doorway and this entire chamber will become the biggest hearth Nevergrace has ever seen."

24

CYRAN ORENDAIN

A BUCKSKIN DESTRIER GRAZED IN THE DISTANCE BEYOND THE Scyne Road. When Cyran approached the steed, he recognized the look and build of it. It had to be a horse from the Never's stables. And more than just this one had escaped becoming a meal for a dragon. Several more horses dotted the fields south of the road. The buckskin carried no tack, neither bridle nor saddle. It wore only a halter, and a lead rope dangled below its head. If Cyran could catch and ride this steed, his journey to Galvenstone would be much faster.

He plucked a fistful of grass from beside the trail and clucked as he approached the destrier. The trained warhorse didn't spook or shy away. It simply continued grazing.

Already over any fright from the dragon attack. The old destriers of the Never were used to the beasts, as much as a horse could be anyway. Cyran reached out, rubbed its neck, and grabbed the lead rope. He tied the rope around both sides of the halter and climbed onto its back before swinging his leg over. Once Cyran found his seat, the destrier lifted its head, and Cyran nudged it forward with his heels. The horse was well trained and started off at a walk. It might come to realize it carried no bridle or bit and that Cyran would not have great control over it if it spooked, but for now, it picked up its pace and trotted along the road.

The beacon towers rising in the distance between them and the Evenmeres had been tampered with. They were not overtly scorched, but no pyre of kindling remained in their upper reaches. All the beacons' wood was probably nothing more than ash and dust, and the mist dragon had concealed any fire until it had burned itself out. And no watchmen remained on duty. The north must have dealt with them too. Cyran pondered attempting to start a fire on one of the beacons, which could lead to Galvenstone answering the call long before he could arrive at the city. But even if he gathered wood, hauled it all to the top of a tower, and lit a fire, which would not be quick, those now in control of Nevergrace would probably see it first. Then that mist dragon would come for him and conceal the flames again. And he didn't know if there were any remaining watchmen on any of the towers along the beacon's path.

He continued riding at a steady trot. The old oak—an ancient tree with a gargantuanly large trunk—crouched alone in the field to the south like a sentinel. A man walked the road in the distance. Cyran urged his mount into a canter, and within a few minutes, they neared the man. Cyran tugged on the reins of the lead rope, and the destrier eagerly slowed its pace.

"There's still a fog lingering over Nevergrace." The old farmer pointed northeast. "It seemed like there was smoke too, but they must have put that fire out quickly 'cause the smoke is already gone. Just the fog from the breath of the Evenmeres still holds on."

Cyran glanced back. Mist shrouded the castle like a cloud.

"You come from there?" the farmer asked, scratching at his grizzled chin and shoving his hat back on his head.

Cyran nodded. "Do not go anywhere near the Never. The

north attacked our outpost last night. The fog is only a cover for their destruction and their dragons. I ride now for Galvenstone. To warn the king. Tell anyone you can, and if there is any way you can assist, please send word to Galvenstone and the cities."

"The people of the Never and its lord have been taken, then?" The farmer's eyes gaped as he scratched his head.

Cyran nodded, and an empty hollow feeling swelled inside him.

"There've been soldiers out here traveling about telling us that it was only a fire that started suddenly," the farmer said. "But they said that everything was all right."

A warning arced across the back of Cyran's mind.

"The unbreachable walls have been breached?" One of the farmer's eyebrows climbed his forehead in disbelief.

Cyran pursed his lips and nodded.

"Well, shit." The farmer paled and shook his head. "I'd hoped I wouldn't live to see that day come."

Cyran kicked the buckskin into a gallop and thundered away down the Scyne Road.

An hour later, a hamlet passed on Cyran's right, a few small wood and stone houses with thatched roofs. No one was about. In fact, the hamlet appeared abandoned at a moment's notice. Embers smoldered in the stubble of a harvested field, and the burning was unattended. Smoke ran in gray wisps into the sky.

A cold chill grasped at the base of Cyran's skull.

The north had ventured out beyond the outpost and tried to convince the few farmers and woodsmen out here that everything was fine. But if those from this hamlet had suspected something was amiss, the soldiers of Murgare might have butchered them.

Cyran debated between continuing on his journey and inspecting the hamlet. But his people and Nevergrace needed him to bring aid from Galvenstone as soon as possible. He rode on at as fast a pace as his steed could manage.

After another few hours, when the buckskin started dragging its feet, Cyran spotted a caravan of people on horseback. They waited ahead, in the shade of an oak alongside the road. Light from the late afternoon sun bore down on the countryside. Cyran rode through an open expanse, and thus the caravan would have already seen him. There was no way to avoid them. Cyran squeezed the hilt of his new sword and slowed his mount's pace, trying to appear as a casual traveler as he approached the company. He hid his sword as best he could beneath the back of his tunic.

"Hail, traveler." A voice called out from the shade of the oak, although the caravan was still many horse lengths ahead of Cyran. A half-dozen men on horseback waited with two women and about a dozen children who milled about behind them. Cyran's nerves settled with the sight of the children, their sizes ranging from teetering about and holding on to another's hand all the way to Cyran's age. Most of their clothing was far too short for them.

Cyran smiled and waved as amicably as he could manage.

"Where are you headed?" the voice asked. The men rode closer to the edge of the road, the women staying back with the children. Two of the men wore torn and stained tunics typical of farmers, their exposed skin streaked with dirt. Two others wore coats of chainmail and had weapons sheathed at their waists as well as empty sheaths on their saddles. The last two appeared to be merchants in their typical lavender robes, and packs of goods were strapped to two burros behind them.

Cyran smiled and shrugged. "I do not wish to be rude, but I cannot stop for idle conversation."

"Can you at least tell us why you are in such a hurry?" One of the two likely mercenaries, a short man with a heavy beard, spoke.

The chill Cyran had experienced earlier returned with a stronger grasp. "Simply to help out my family"—he glanced at the women and the children, who all eyed him warily—"during harvest. They live in the Nicera village. Word is there was an accident."

The men looked Cyran and his buckskin over, and the bearded mercenary said, "Your mount is tired, but he is a fine steed. Mayhap a warhorse by the look of him."

Cyran nodded as he came nearer to them but remained on the far side of the road.

"And you've been riding him hard," the other mercenary—a man with legs that appeared too long for his horse—said.

Cyran shrugged again.

The first mercenary grinned, his dark beard lifting on his cheeks. "Nicera isn't far. You'll be there before sundown. Surely harvest isn't reason enough to lame a destrier."

Cyran cursed himself for not mentioning some village much closer to Galvenstone, although he didn't know the names of the more distant ones. He attempted to look as sheepish as he could. "Well, if you must know, he isn't my horse. I had to borrow him for the journey, trade another horse that'd grown too weary for him. This buckskin was rested at that time. But now I may be looking to trade him for another fresher mount."

The men all shared glances. "Well, the worst of the day's heat is passing," the bearded mercenary said, "and we're about ready to move on until dusk. He is a fine mount. You think you may want to trade him for one of our old rounceys?" The mercenary pointed to his horse and the farmers' and merchants' mounts. "You must be out of your mind. Where did you get him?" The mercenary's eyes narrowed slightly.

"He was grazing out in a field. Abandoned."

The bearded mercenary gave a skeptical huff and stepped his horse out from under the shade, and the others followed him. "Come, ride with us for a bit and we can talk about your horse and what we'd be willing to trade for him." He paused as he looked Cyran up and down and grimaced. "You look like you've been through a battle."

Cyran glanced downward. His leathers were shredded across the arms and chest and legs, the result of plummeting through trees. Stains smeared the backs of his hands, and dirt was lodged under every nail. Blackened areas spotted his tunic. He ran a hand through his hair—matted and littered with bits of needles and leaves. His face probably looked just as bad.

"You've got a warhorse but not even a bridle or saddle." The mercenary's look turned to one of suspicion. "Surely you would have taken those from your previous horse before leaving him in the field."

Cyran hid a wince. "They didn't fit. Not at all. And I didn't want this horse to get terrible saddle sores that would slow him down."

The mercenary was silent for a few heartbeats. "The merchants and farmers have recently seen a few strange things about this area." The mercenary guided his horse ahead of Cyran's, angling to cut him off. "That's why we're suspicious. You say you're headed to Nicera?"

"For a bit." Cyran glanced at the other men and their approaching families, wondering if he should make a run for it and plow between them. No. His mount was too tired to outrun anyone. "You may accompany me, if you wish."

The mercenary nodded, and the women and children slipped out from under the shade and trod along behind the other men. Could these mercenaries be from the north? Hiding amidst a family of farmers and two traveling merchants?

Cyran plodded his destrier along on the far side of the road, keeping as much distance as possible from their troop.

"One of our rounceys could probably run farther and for longer than your hulking destrier." The long-legged mercenary rode up beside Cyran. "And if you rode a rouncey, you probably wouldn't draw as much suspicion from other travelers. Especially with that poorly hidden sword you carry."

Cyran glanced at the mercenary and then studied the man's sorrel mare. "I'll trade you right now, and then I can be on my way."

The mercenary looked over the buckskin. "Not until morning. After I'm certain your mount can still move its legs."

They rode along in tense silence for several minutes.

"Pay my companion no mind." The bearded mercenary kept pace alongside Cyran. He cast a quick glance back at the merchants and farmers. "I am called Jalar. You?"

"Cyran."

"Well then, Cyran, have you heard any rumors of late?"

Cyran tensed. He considered mentioning the Never, but if these men were from the north, they would probably kill him with a crossbow bolt or a dagger in the back before he could even draw his sword. But Murgare's evil soldiers probably wouldn't have brought children along with them. Unless the children and all those in this mixed group had slipped through the Evenmeres's trail. Or maybe the children were from Belvenguard and would be killed if any of the others acted out.

"I only know my own business," Cyran finally replied. "I have not kept an ear out for anything else."

"Then you haven't heard about the strange happenings along the Scyne Road?" One of the merchants rode closer, a man with a bald scalp and ring of graying brown hair around the edges.

Cyran's interest piqued, and he glanced over his shoulder.

"No." Images of what he might have encountered on his last journey along this road flashed through his memories. He shook his head to dispel their horror.

The other merchant rode up on Cyran's far side, flanking him. The farmers' two horses paced faster and moved in front of them. Cyran suppressed his rising anxiety, feeling his new sword jostle against his back in a cold reminder of its presence.

"A merchant friend of mine found a man wandering these fields east of Galvenstone." The bald merchant pressed his horse closer, his voice low. "Said the man appeared to be in a daze, muttering something over and over again. A song maybe. He thought the man may have been humming."

Cyran's blood chilled.

"And this man kept rubbing at some bleeding spot on his head," the merchant continued. "My friend brought the man into his room at an inn along this stretch, hoping to help him. My friend went to sleep, and when he woke, the man was gone."

"What did this man look like?" Cyran asked.

"Young. A woodsman."

Images of Rilar flooded Cyran's mind. *Could it truly have been him?*

"My friend kept an eye out for the man during his travels along this road," the merchant said, "but last we spoke, he hadn't seen him anywhere."

"And not too many fortnights ago," the other merchant, a heavy-set man perhaps in the late second decade of his life, said, "I traveled this road and encountered a man at an inn who insisted he'd met another man who not only wouldn't speak but couldn't. He offered the man a meal, and the mute ate readily. But when the mute opened his mouth, the man I talked to swore he saw the reason for it true as the day is long. The man had no tongue."

More memories assaulted Cyran. *The assassin in Dashtok.* "Did he mention or notice anything else about this man?"

The merchant eyed Cyran. "What do you mean by that?"

"Anything striking about his appearance? A marking perhaps? I just want to stay away from him. I do not trust a man who has had his tongue removed."

The merchant tugged at the roll of his second chin that was covered by a sparse brown beard. "He did mention something about seeing part of a tattoo on the man's throat as he ate. But the tattoo was mostly covered, and the man I met couldn't make out exactly what it was."

Cyran's stomach turned.

"It's said that those in the south of the Rorenlands brand certain of their people with throat tattoos," the bald merchant added. "I don't know nothing more about it than that though. But a man of the Rorenlands without a tongue traveling this country gives me the shivers."

Cyran pondered the possibility. If these men were from the north, and their rulers sent the assassin and controlled whatever lurked in the woods, they might know about both Rilar and the assassin. Maybe they were attempting to trick Cyran into giving away what he knew, especially if he was seeking to spread word about the events at Nevergrace.

"Those are very strange claims," Cyran said and then rode along quietly.

They shared a few other stories that did not remind Cyran of anything he'd experienced, and some of the stories probably had to be escalating lies. But after what Cyran had seen, he could not entirely dismiss any of them. After his buckskin's breathing slowed to a more normal rate, Cyran pressed the animal faster, but it quickly tired again. Twilight fell across eastern Belvenguard, and a lone inn stood out beside the road. Nothing else but the Evenmeres and rolling fields surrounded them. The inn appeared deserted, but Cyran hoped the others would stop there for the night. He intended to press on and would even walk alongside his destrier if that would rest the horse enough to be able to continue at a faster pace in the morning. But there was another horse—possibly a fresher one—grazing in a field just outside a paddock behind the inn. The door to the paddock was hanging open.

The same chill Cyran had felt earlier when coming across the empty hamlet returned.

"It looks abandoned," the heavy merchant, who Cyran had learned was named Cam, said.

"We will sleep here." Jalar veered toward the inn. "There will be an innkeeper. And if not, we may still find beds without having to part with our coin."

The farmers stepped their plow horses before Cyran, cutting him off from the Scyne Road. The mercenaries did the same, riding just around Cyran's horse and guiding his tired mount toward the inn.

The others in the troop followed them. Cyran glanced around. He again considered plowing through them and riding on to Galvenstone as fast as his destrier could take him. But if he stopped, he might be able to obtain a rested horse without even having to wait until morning. He allowed his mount to walk down the dirt path to the inn with the others as he eyed the horse in the field.

25

CYRAN ORENDAIN

CYRAN DISMOUNTED FROM HIS DESTRIER AND LED THE HORSE TO A half-filled trough, where the animal drank deeply. The mercenaries and merchants waited behind him, seeming to keep an eye on him. Cyran met Jalar's eye and nodded.

"You can have him." Cyran unfastened the halter and lead rope from the buckskin. "I still seek a fresher mount." Cyran turned and, as casually as possible with rising nerves, approached the lone horse. He slipped through a fence and into the field where it grazed.

"There's not any man or woman inside," one of the farmer's wives shouted from near the entrance to the inn.

Cyran paused and glanced back. *More victims of the north?*

One of the children wailed. The horse Cyran was attempting to halter bolted and ran over a hill.

"Bloody buggering hell." Cyran whipped his lead rope into the ground in frustration. The weight of his pressing issues, the need to help his people and outpost, landed on his shoulders in full.

"We should not stay here," the farmer's wife said.

"We will be safer in there than beside a cooking fire out in the open night," Jalar replied. "If some bandits drove the innkeepers off or killed them, the bandits may have long left the area."

The men were inspecting the chambers inside the inn when Cyran approached its entrance. A farmer's wife met his gaze, a look of poorly veiled terror lurking in the depths of her eyes. She turned her back to the others and clamped her hands together in a silent plea.

A jolt lanced through Cyran. That look could not have been one born out of trickery. It couldn't. But there was something she wasn't saying. Cyran casually studied the people in the caravan. Maybe most of them were not part of Murgare, but it was likely at least one was. His eyes settled on the other woman. Her hands trembled as she clutched three children to her. If the two merchants were soldiers of Murgare, they had to be the most unfit warriors in their kingdom. The two farmers were dirtied from work and wore torn and stained tunics like most farmers Cyran had ever known. Their skin was also darkened by the Belvenguard sun. The two mercenaries also had tanned skin. They also wore chainmail, but they didn't carry swords or any weapon Cyran would expect them to. Only knives were sheathed at their belts.

Strange. But Cyran could not distinguish them as men from the north. If anything, the fact they didn't carry large weapons on their person made them less suspicious. Cyran's attention swept over the children—boys and girls ranging from approximately a few years old to twenty. The two oldest boys were covered in dirt stains, their tunics torn, but their skin was pale, especially on their upper arms, which were exposed at the margins of their too short clothing. And they both carried heavy packs.

Cyran's muscles turned rigid. These young men were suspicious, and they might have been older than Cyran first suspected, only cleanly shaven, their hair brushed over their upper faces. Were these two about to force everyone into the inn and then kill them all?

"I will sleep outside." Cyran furtively watched the oldest boys as he cleared a spot to make a bed. One of the two gestured at his waist and then to the children.

"We will all be sleeping inside," Jalar said. "I must insist."

The hair on the back of Cyran's neck spiked, but he acted unconcerned. He followed everyone as they entered and spread out across the inner dining chamber. Some of the children and the mothers wandered off to the bedchambers, their fear showing in their shaky movements.

One of the supposed oldest boys sat near the inn's entrance, the other across the way from him.

Cyran stood and stretched as he sauntered over to the entryway near one of the oldest boys, leaving his hands up in the air as if still stretching.

"I must ride on this night." Cyran neared the exit. "There is something I must do."

The boy stood, hefting his pack and pointing its end at Cyran's chest. "You will stay here." Someone quickly moved about behind Cyran.

Cyran jerked his hands down, ripping his elvish blade from its sheath as he did so. The blade sliced cleanly through the man's arm and chest, opening his tunic and ribs. He collapsed, and Cyran bolted outside as if intending to flee. But just as he slipped outside, he leapt to the side of the doorway.

Shouting sounded, followed by footsteps pounding on the interior stone floor. The other supposed boy dashed out into the night, barreling into the open and glancing around, a loaded crossbow in his hands.

Cyran stepped closer and, in one swipe, as the man swiveled around to face him, cut him down. The supposed boy's crossbow twanged, its bolt flying harmlessly away into the night. He toppled over and crashed into the dirt.

Mutters erupted inside the inn before boisterous yelling sounded. But there was no wailing caused by fear or worse. Cyran stared at the dead body before him in shocked silence. Then he glanced at the other. He'd sparred with many hundreds of men, but he had never killed another person. A wave of nausea washed over him and churned in his guts. Two lives taken in less than a minute. They even looked like such young men, if not adolescent boys. But they weren't. They were soldiers from Murgare. Cyran's hands trembled, and his heart rioted inside the cage of his ribs. He swooned and leaned against the wall of the inn.

A strong hand clapped him on the back. "Fine work, lad." Jalar took two broadswords from the boys' packs and handed one to the other mercenary. "They took us by surprise and also rounded up the farming families, who they suspected knew about the situation at the Never. They wanted to keep an eye on all of us and not allow us to spread word about what happened to the outpost. They also threatened to kill the children if we did not comply."

Cyran could barely nod. "And they killed those at this inn and probably at a hamlet to the east... to keep them quiet as well." His voice trembled.

Jalar shook his head. "These men couldn't have reached this inn prior to our arrival. They took us captive soon after they claimed the outpost. From what we learned, we passed by the morning after they arrived."

Cyran glanced up at the mercenary. "And the hamlet?"

"It was abandoned when we passed it as well. The merchants said it made them uneasy, as it had been occupied last they knew. But the northmen didn't care to listen. They were only concerned with monitoring the area and making sure no messengers or survivors passed westward from Nevergrace to report the attack to Galvenstone."

Thoughts swirled in Cyran's mind. The hamlet and the inn were other things he should look into. But his people still needed him. "But they may have been planning on killing all of you inside the inn."

"No, I don't think so." Jalar shook his head, and his beard snapped side to side. "It's possible, but it seemed they weren't keen on killing children to enforce their objective. Although they threatened it many times."

Cyran considered that for only a moment before wiping his blade clean on one of the northmen's tunics and sheathing it. "I must ride on this night. My people are in grave danger. If any of them are still alive."

"Take my mount." Cam had stepped out into the night along with all of the others, and they surrounded the dead bodies, staring at them. "The young mare will be happy to be rid of my heft. And she is known for her endurance. Ride hard, my friend."

Cyran turned.

"Wait." The bald merchant hurried up to him, reaching out a hand and working a ring from his finger. "Take this. It is not much for what you have done, but it is a token of our appreciation." He handed it over.

Cyran studied the insignia of a laden burro on its wooden face. He nodded in thanks, unsure if it carried any value other than sentimental.

"It is a ring of the merchants' guild," the bald man said. "Not worth any coin to a thief, but worth all the information any merchant of the guild carries when shown to one of us. Such a man or woman will share anything they know with you."

"Unless they believe I stole it."

Cam shook his head. "The guild is secret, and there have

been very few reports of any brigands even interested in taking a wooden ring marked with a burro." He cast Cyran a forced smile.

Many of the others thanked Cyran as he saddled up Cam's horse and mounted.

"May the king bring dire consequences upon all from Murgare." Jalar held a hand aloft in farewell.

"And in the words of the merchants' guild, may your travels always bring you joy, wealth, and new experiences." Cam patted his mount's rump as Cyran kicked its flanks and galloped away.

Cyran's new steed heaved for breath as it dragged its hoofs and entered the gates of Galvenstone. Cyran hunched over his mount, having ridden for several days with only brief stops for water, a bite to eat, and quick rests. He attempted to speak with the soldiers beside the gates, but they growled at him and waved him on.

"Be off, beggar," one said, his eyes shadowed under his helm.

It would probably take longer to argue with these men who might hear travelers telling wild stories every day, finally convince them of the truth, and then have them send a foot messenger to the castle rather than for Cyran to just keep riding. His mount carried him up the winding streets through the first tier of Galvenstone.

People parted around them as they passed, and a man muttered, "How did *that* boy ever get a horse?"

"Must have stolen it," another answered.

"Must have."

"Stolen straight out of a stable."

Cyran passed through the crowds of merchants and buyers, and his stomach grumbled. He'd already had to tighten his belt two notches over the past days. He passed into the second tier of Galvenstone, where the people dressed in brighter tunics of a finer cut. Those people whispered even more when he passed. Cyran neared the gates of Castle Dashtok and dismounted. The soldiers there stepped before him.

"The hour for beggars has passed," one soldier said from beneath a shadowed helm.

"I am no beggar." Cyran approached, and the soldiers lowered their spears. "I am from Nevergrace. I have come to find Sir Kayom and to warn the king. To report an attack on the outpost. Please, you must hurry." Cyran clamped his hands together in earnest. "Please. My sister, my friends, and my people are dying."

The soldiers shared a glance. "You'll have to wait here." One called for three messenger boys within the walls, and the others spoke in hushed voices.

Cyran teetered and leaned against his mount, whose coat was layered in dried salt and sweat. What seemed like half an hour passed as Cyran drained the last of his waterskin. His horse wobbled intermittently and drowsed with a cocked hind leg. It needed water and a salt lick, but Cyran didn't dare leave and delay warning the king.

"What is this?" A man whose red and gold armor clanked strode out from the gates, his salted hair waving in the wind. Sir Paltere.

Cyran stood at attention, his look grave.

"You fools." Sir Paltere hurried past the soldiers to Cyran and addressed him. "What has happened?"

"The north has come." Cyran licked his cracked lips, his throat and tongue feeling like a web of dryness clung to all their surfaces. "They attacked the Never and have taken it over. I don't know if any have survived."

Sir Paltere's expression fell. "By the nine gods. When?"

"The assault began days ago. I lost track during—"

"But the beacons. We never saw any sign."

"They used a mist dragon to hide the fires."

Sir Paltere turned and snapped at the soldiers, ordering them to send a multitude of messengers to inform the king. "Now! And care for his mount." The dragonknight faced Cyran and tugged him along into the castle. "How many dragons did they bring with them?"

"Five. And one is the Dragon Queen's shadow dragon."

Sir Kayom burst from the castle doors, hurrying toward them. "Cyran, tell me it isn't true."

Cyran's heart sank. "I will not lie to you. The Dragon Queen has come to Nevergrace."

Kayom's hands trembled, and his voice shook. "Then all are dead. Or they soon will be. I must leave at once." He spun around, searching for anyone within earshot. "Prepare my mount for immediate departure."

"No." Paltere grabbed Kayom's pauldron and guided him toward the castle. "You will forfeit your life with such an attempt. We must hold an audience with the king. He will need to assemble a legion to strike back."

26

SIRRA BRACKENGLAVE

THE AUDIENCE HALL AT NEVERGRACE FELT SMALLER AND SMALLER these past days. Sirra stood from the throne and stepped across the dais. A thud sounded, followed by the thrum of a bolt just outside. She paced over to the closest window, its colored glass panes already open, and she reached out for a cork shield strapped against the outer wall. Her fingers located a steel bolt buried into the shield, and when she wrapped her hand around the projectile, it stopped thrumming.

After yanking the bolt free, she leaned back inside the chamber. As she paced, she unrolled a parchment that had been wound around the bolt's shaft, and she read its message.

"Then what will our strategy be?" Yenthor wiped grease from his lips with the back of his hand and stood, folding his arms over his broad chest. His dark helm was removed, and his long red hair and beard draped over his breastplate.

"We should take our dragons out into the lonely farm country around here and raze a few towns to the ground." A hooded dragonmage lounged on a chair, a knee and ankle extending beyond his cloak. The limb's knobby protrusions showed under his leggings. "We'd catch the king's ear quickly, and we could keep at it until our queen is safely in our hands."

"No," Zaldica said from the shadows of the chamber before stepping forward. Torchlight fell across her wiry frame and her exposed face. Her hair was cropped close to her skull. "We should take Galvenstone by surprise. Before Igare is prepared and ready for us. One way or another, the entire south will learn of our presence here before too long."

"We cannot storm the capital and Castle Dashtok." Sirra stepped down the dais. "Not with so few dragons."

"But we have you, my Dragon Queen." Zaldica sliced a chunk off an apple in her hand before using her knife as a utensil to slip the chunk into her mouth.

"I will not be able to change the tides of such a war." Sirra shook her head as she strode along the chamber's central walkway. "Igare has probably been preparing for our retaliation since the moment he and his council plotted to take our king. They may not have fully amassed their legions, but they will be ready. Galvenstone alone has at least a hundred dragons at its disposal. Attacking them would be a death sentence for us and for our queen." She looked to Sir Vladden. "You are uncharacteristically quiet."

Sir Vladden bowed his head. "I wish for vengeance as much as any of us, but I cannot foresee a better method than holding this outpost and using its hostages to bargain with their king. If we set out burning the countryside, not only will Belvenguard learn of our location sooner, our dragons may not be here when their legions arrive. Then Belvenguard would have to expend less effort in taking their outpost back."

Yenthor returned to chewing on a haunch of fired meat and spoke through a mouthful. "As much as I want to kill everyone involved in King Restebarge's assassination and the abduction of Queen Elra, I think charging head-on into the fray is not wise."

A minute of silent contemplation settled over the chamber.

"My Dragon Queen," an archer waiting by the open window said. "The storm dragon is still circling low."

"The time has come to send a second message to King Igare, one with a different... tone." Sirra penned a message and rolled the parchment up around the steel shaft of the messenger bolt. The archer held out his palm. "No. I will deliver this one." She took the crossbow from the archer and paced toward the chamber's exit. "I do not want too many messages being sent from here. Not even these we send to Northsheeren. The more times the storm dragon comes, the more likely Igare will know where we are and what we are plotting. We will hold our location secret for as long as possible, hopefully until the queen is to be delivered."

"Dragon Queen." An archer rushed into the chamber. "Some of our captives have been plotting to escape and send word to the neighboring villages and Galvenstone. They've drawn out plans and passed them around. We only just discovered this." He handed a folded parchment to Sirra.

Sirra unfolded the parchment, and its dry surfaces crackled. There were drawings of potential routes to take around the outpost to reach the Evenmeres. A tree labeled as the old oak, and the beacon towers, were reference points. A note suggested one group of people was to go and light the beacons. And so these captives didn't know that Sirra's dragons had already dealt with the fuel and soldiers associated with the towers.

Sirra crumpled the plans, and she lifted her sword a handsbreadth from its sheath. The black fire on the blade rolled outward, and the parchment burned atop her palm without singeing her gauntlet or heating her skin. "I presume one of the dragonsquires drew this."

"No. It was primarily two young women. The former lady of

the Never, one Menoria, and her handmaid, a girl called Jaslin. The Never's nyren was seen assisting them."

Sirra shook her head. "First, bring the two ladies here. Then I will deal with the nyren."

The archer stamped his foot and pivoted about before marching out of the chamber. Sirra turned her fist over and let the ashes of the parchment drift to the floor. All the archers and guard in the chamber watched her, waiting on her next command or even her slightest whim. But she could do nothing to speed the response of a king, nothing but kill her hostages if Igare continued to ignore her demands.

The clatter of armored boots sounded, and two archers led two young women into the chamber. The returning archer said, "These are the two we discovered discussing the plot, and we found this one trying to hide a parchment in her skirt." The archer pushed one of the girls forward.

The girl was probably no more than ten and six, the younger of the two. Auburn hair and blue eyes. A stained and torn tunic. Her hair was tangled, and dirty streaks ran across her face. There was nothing refined in her dress or demeanor. A simple young lady. "And you are?"

"Jaslin." She eyed Sirra with dilated pupils, but she did not flinch.

Impressive. More than half the warriors who stood before the Dragon Queen cowered. "Did you believe you could escape your chamber and this outpost and then warn your king? With my guard and dragons and mages and archers all watching?"

Jaslin swallowed, and she seemed to grow younger, too young for all of this. "No. I did not."

Sirra arched an eyebrow as she stalked around the two women. "Then why resist? You must know it could mean death."

"Because I *hoped* we could escape and warn Galvenstone," Jaslin said.

Sirra concealed a smirk. *Brave indeed.*

"And both of my brothers are gone, as well as some of their friends." Jaslin folded her arms over her chest. "And you or your men took at least one of them from me. I may as well die too. And I would willingly do so to save the Never from ruin." She started to hum a quiet tune, something ancient that even Sirra had a hard time placing, although she knew she'd heard it before. Jaslin also held something reflective in her hands.

"What is that?" Sirra didn't grab for the object, only indicated it with a gesture.

At first, Jaslin tried to conceal the item, but it only took another moment for her to hold it out. A translucent shard of crystal lay on her palm. It was carved in an ancient style with dancing men—no, elves—on its face.

"And how did you come by such an old relic?" Sirra studied it but didn't move to take it.

"My brother gave it to me."

Sirra pursed her lips, feeling some power emanating from the item. "Be careful of anything it seems to tell you."

Jaslin whipped her head up to stare at Sirra. Surprise reveled in the young woman's eyes, but she did not respond for a moment. "Do what you must with me, but do not harm Menoria. She is a much more important hostage than I am, and I will not stop trying to save this outpost. Death no longer scares me, as I hope to find my brothers there."

Sirra paced about and studied the two young women and this chamber. The blood of great guardians and sentinels did flow through at least some of those still at Nevergrace.

"And you, young lady." Sirra addressed the other woman.

Menoria stared straight ahead at the throne without blinking, but her lower lip trembled and her cheeks flushed. Her laced dress of violet was stained, her fine strands of golden hair unkempt.

"I've learned that not long ago, you were the young lady of this outpost," Sirra continued. "But a distant uncle has now taken over as lord of these walls. And so what will become of you and the Never?"

A tear rolled down Menoria's cheek, and her chin quivered. "I will accept whatever fate befalls my station, but I will not accept the turn of fate the Never has seen these past days."

Sirra ran a gauntleted finger over the fletching of the steel messenger bolt, watching the individual fibers spring back into place.

"I convinced the young lady of the Never to help me in my plot to escape and warn Galvenstone." Jaslin took a step back and stood beside Menoria. "She thought we shouldn't pursue such a plan. I made her assist me."

Menoria paled, but she remained silent.

Sirra continued strumming the fletching of each vane on the bolt and allowed her heavy boots to bang against the stones as she walked. She paused and inhaled, a long and slow breath. "You two may go about plotting whatever you believe may save you while realizing nothing will ever happen. The only thing that can save your lives is if King Igare delivers our queen to us unharmed. And the sooner Igare does so, the more likely both of you shall live." Sirra motioned for the archers to escort the women away.

Jaslin glared at Sirra as the archer took her by the arm, the handmaid's expression full of anger but laced with curiosity and bewilderment. Tears cascaded down Menoria's cheeks as she trembled and fought off sobs while hurrying away.

"Sir Vladden." Sirra strode toward the exit.

"Yes, Dragon Queen?" The guard followed her.

"Bring Nevergrace's nyren to me. I wish to discuss strategy with him."

"Of course."

Sirra marched out of the audience chamber and headed for the stairs leading to the upper keep.

"And where should I deliver him to?" Vladden asked.

"The roof of the keep. I will be waiting up there."

Vladden nodded somberly and departed as Sirra climbed the stairs. She wound around and ascended the five levels of the keep before stepping out onto a landing. Wind whipped the loose ends of her hair and streamed them across her face and around the sigil of the rampant shadow dragon on her breast-plate. She climbed the last stairway outside and walked across the roof, staring past the merlons and crenellations at the dense canopy of the forest beyond. Walls of angoias rose like spiked mountain peaks and stabbed into the clouds, their reddish bark darkened by the distance. Their pale leaves showed like dirty snow. Sirra had walked the land they now resided on when there were no angoias but only pine and maple and oak, when elves thrived in their shining city. Before the time of the Dragon Wars. Before the genocide of the elves. Long, long ago.

Sirra nocked the steel bolt on the crossbow's rope and glanced skyward. Way up there, a blur with a bluish hue circled over the margins of the woods, sweeping out toward the outpost. The relatively tiny storm dragon and its mage and guard were not being as careful as she'd asked them to be. Maybe Oomaren —Restebarge's brother—wanted to keep an eye on her, and that man found ways to influence certain riders and dragons by holding whatever he needed over them. She lifted the crossbow and aimed at the dragon before squeezing the trigger handle.

The crossbow's arms jolted, and the steel bolt launched away, its bright yellow fletching appearing like shooting fire. The bolt sailed high but gradually slowed in its arc. As it flattened out far above the keep, the storm dragon swooped in. The dragon's guard, who would be bundled in masses of furs but nearly unarmed and unarmored—the only way a guard and mage could ride the small storm dragons—caught the bolt as it hovered and turned downward, plucking it from the wind and sky. Another one of her messages had been sent.

Sirra gazed back over the Evenmeres. Now she had to trust that Igare would do the right thing. The lives of those two young women depended on it.

Footsteps shuffled on the stairway, and the white-bearded face of a nyren emerged over the battlement. He stepped onto the roof, and the wind caught his red robes and rattled his chain. Vladden waited on the stairs behind the man. This nyren's life could be the next to be taken. Sirra smiled as she strode up to the old man. He paused, remaining at the lip of the battlement.

He is not as wise and cunning as a nyren should be. He should know to stay away from the edge.

27

CYRAN ORENDAIN

KINGSKNIGHTS IN GLITTERING GOLD AND SILVER ARMOR WITH RED capes, court attendants in embroidered tunics, and dragonguard filled the audience hall of Castle Dashtok. Cyran marched beside Sir Kayom and behind Sir Paltere. Guard and noblemen and women parted as Paltere strode through their ranks along the carpeted walkway toward the throne.

A nobleman in yellow stood before the king, reading from a scroll. The king's orator, Riscott, waited on the king's right, his fingers tapping at the side of his robe with impatience. Two adolescent girls whispered to each other from their seats near the king, and a young man sat between them.

"We at Progtown have kept an eye on the Rorenlands as well as any could ask of us," the man addressing the king said, "but the traders have been passing by—"

The king stood when Paltere stepped beyond the line of kingsknights, and Igare's gray-streaked locks fell over his ears. The speaker from Progtown fell silent. A hush rolled through the chamber, causing the shuffle of feet and a cough to ring loudly. The queen—a voluptuous woman with curly brown hair and a red dress with gold trim—slowly rose beside her king.

"What is it?" King Igare's expression turned grave, as he likely sensed the urgency in Paltere's manner. Igare held a rolled-up parchment, one small enough that it barely extended beyond his clenched fist. His knuckles were blanched, and the edges of the parchment were crumpled and frayed, as if he'd been clutching it for days.

"There's been an attack on Nevergrace, milord." Paltere stepped aside and allowed Kayom to escort Cyran closer. Murmurs and whispers roamed around the chamber. "A dragonsquire from the Never has come to report the event to his king."

Cyran stepped up and stood beside Paltere.

"Speak, boy." Riscott stroked his goatee and strode one step down the dais.

"Nevergrace was attacked, milord." Cyran's gaze flashed around. All eyes were locked on him. The king's conjuror shifted and rubbed her fingers together, and her white locks rolled around her shoulders. The young priest of the nine and the king's nyren both stood from their chairs. "At night. By dragons from the north."

"Pray tell us how many—" Riscott began, but the king cut him off with a grunt and a wave.

"Dragonsquire of Nevergrace." Igare stepped down the dais. "How grave is the matter for the brave soldiers and lord of the Never?"

"The outpost has been taken," Cyran said, and rumbles of astonished conversation arose from the court attendants.

Riscott frowned. "Then we must assume that every one of our men and women there are dead. The north does not take prisoners."

The sensation of a kick to the gut landed on Cyran.

"Did any others escape with you?" Igare asked.

Cyran shook his head while trying to curtail thoughts about

what might have befallen Jaslin and his friends. He absently toyed with the merchant ring on his finger.

The orator paced back and forth across the step, knitting his fingers together before resting his hands against his thighs. "And please, will you expound upon how you managed to survive and flee when all your kindred must have lost their lives defending the Never?"

"I—I went down on a dragon." Cyran's stomach felt as if it were filled with lead. Had he left them all to die? "I was asked to man a turret crossbow because Sir Ilion's archer was killed. Sir Ilion and his mage were later lost to lance strikes, and our dragon took many bolts. We crashed in the Evenmeres. I was the only one to survive the landing, and when I returned to Nevergrace, the north's dragons watched over its walls."

"Further proof the Evenmeres are not haunted and that something does not kill anyone who ventures too far into them," Riscott said.

Cyran wanted to mention something about what he'd seen in the Evenmeres, but Igare turned to his curly gray haired and bearded nyren and whispered something before facing Cyran again and asking, "How many dragons did Murgare bring?"

"Five, I believe."

"And what types of dragons are these five?"

"Two ice, one of which may have been their only mount to be wounded. One fire. One mist. And a shadow dragon."

Gasps pinged around Cyran.

"A shadow dragon?" The conjuror rose and sidled up beside the king.

Cyran nodded.

"Bless the Paladin and the Shield Maiden," the clergyman said, a young man not much if any older than Cyran.

King Igare gestured to his advisors and to Cyran, Paltere, and Kayom. "Come. Follow me. We must discuss this further."

The king led them past the queen and adolescent nobles and through a doorway across from the throne. Once they had all passed between two kingsknights, the knights shut and sealed the door behind them. Igare strode to the head of a long dark table. Maps and figurines littered its surface. The king did not sit, but he motioned for everyone else to take a chair around the table as he made brief introductions.

Paltere and Kayom did as instructed, and Cyran sat between them. The conjuror, Cartaya, muttered something and rubbed her fingers over her palm. Violet flames sprang to life on her skin. She lit several tapers and placed one on the table before each person before sitting with the others.

"Now," Igare said. "Let us discuss everything openly. We are among those we can trust to not spread fear. For those of you who have not sat at this table before, this is where I attempt to understand our strange world and its even stranger people before arriving at my final decision on matters of great importance." He paused and looked around the table before focusing on Cyran and offering him a brave smile. "Dragonsquire, you mentioned that a shadow dragon may have attacked Nevergrace."

"I did."

"Then are you claiming that the Dragon Queen herself has come to Belvenguard?" Lisain, the clergyman, asked.

"It was probably a large moon dragon," Tiros, the nyren, said. "The dragonsquire stated that the attack was initiated at night. The north would have used a dragon best suited to the timing of their assault. And if it was dark, and fear and chaos had already spread, it would be easy for a young lad to confuse the two types of dragons, in addition to much more."

No one responded.

Cyran cleared his throat. "I believe Sir Ilion said it was a shadow dragon."

"You 'believe' he said that?" The orator arched an eyebrow.

Cyran's mind ran wild with memories of that fateful night. "It was my first time in a turret, and there was quite a bit going on around me. As best as I can remember, Sir Ilion said it was a shadow dragon and the Dragon Queen was likely riding it."

The nyren rubbed at his lower lip, and his eyes scrolled over his thoughts. "Even if it were a shadow dragon, that doesn't mean the Dragon Queen has come."

"Shadow dragons are the rarest of the species, and they are *much* larger than moon dragons." Cartaya reached out with open palms, parting her mauve cloak as she did so. She rested the backs of her hands on the table as flames flickered across her skin. "Not to mention dangerous, if not impossible, to raise or capture in the wild."

"And evil." The clergyman folded his hands, a distant look glazing his eyes. "As we have learned. We are always under the watchful eyes of the nine, and that is why Belvenguard will never allow such a dragon, not even one of its eggs, inside our kingdom. By penalty of death."

"Yet the north does not have many shadow dragons either." Cartaya shook her head. "If one has come to Nevergrace, there is a very good chance it is the Dragon Queen's beast, Shadowmar."

"Would Murgare send her for such a brash assault?" Tiros's chain rattled as he shifted in his seat. "The Dragon Queen would know there is a decent chance she will find herself so badly outnumbered that she could be killed. I understand the north is angry and may make quick decisions based on emotion rather than reason, but to risk one of their prized shadow dragons, much less their Dragon Queen, seems unlikely, even for them."

"I will seek the Hunter's and the Siren of the Sea's advice pertaining to the matter." Lisain smoothed his white robe. "We can find all truths with them."

"Wait." King Igare raised his hands. "Dragonsquire, do you have any idea how these five dragons, one potentially being a gigantic shadow dragon, could have arrived in Belvenguard without being spotted by Galvenstone's watchtowers?"

Possibilities played out in Cyran's head. "I awoke to the commotion of their fiery and icy breaths as they attacked the Never. I did not see how they arrived. But given Nevergrace's location, I assumed they must have come through or over the forest."

Riscott scoffed. "They would be just as likely to come through the forest as over the sprawling walls of angoias. And no dragon would ever be able to fit on the Evenmeres's trails."

The heat of embarrassment licked at Cyran's cheeks. He had not spent time reasoning out where they had come from, as it hadn't mattered in the middle of the attack. Maybe he should think more before answering in front of the king and his council, who now stared at him. But what other possibility was there? "If not over the forest or lake, what other route could they have used?"

"The men of our watchtowers definitely should have seen five dragons flying over the Lake on Fire." Tiros wagged a finger as he tapped the table with his other hand, lost in thought. "But only a storm dragon that can sleep in the sky—sleep while it rides the air currents—could fly an entire kingdom's width over the Evenmeres without having to stop in the forest for respites. And that forest may not offer safe havens, or havens of any kind, for such a need. And only storm dragons can fly over the angoias where the air is so thin. The legions of Belvenguard attempted the crossing decades ago. Only storm dragons could manage it."

"But we do not hold the power of the north," Cartaya said. "They are the ones who cursed the woods and may be able to manipulate it for their own gain."

"Unlikely." The nyren licked his lips. "Why wait centuries to use this power when they have long despised us and everything we stand for?"

"Also, we must consider that Belvenguard has not housed a shadow dragon in centuries." The wisps of flame on Cartaya's palms turned to embers. "Not since the first... Not after what happened. So we do not know if a shadow dragon could make the crossing."

Tiros's face contorted with incredulity. "I concede that shadow dragons are more powerful than others, but they must be too large to excel at flight. Maybe it was only a few storm dragons who looked dark in the night and who took the outpost by surprise. Maybe Murgare even colored the dragons to try to make them appear as something else."

Sir Kayom's face reddened, and his tone came out thin and sharp. "You insult my outpost, my soldiers, and my guard, nyren. A few storm dragons could not take the Never. Not with surprise or treachery or even if they had every one of our dragons killed beforehand. I stake my honor on that fact."

"I second Sir Kayom's assertion." Sir Paltere's gauntleted fists clenched as he eyed the nyren and then the orator. "And storm dragons do not breathe fire or ice."

"Then perhaps the Weltermores have turned against Belvenguard, and they sent their dragons to Nevergrace." Riscott dropped a flat hand onto the table, creating a bang and drawing everyone's attention away from Kayom. "The bloody Weltermores king just recently sent a message to Igare, hinting at some of his desires that could empower his throne. The most likely route dragons could use to reach Nevergrace without being spotted would be from across the Scyne River. Even if the north came through the spires or over either sea, they would have been seen."

"But even considering the recent demands from that damn brigand of a king, why would the Weltermores wish to bring war against us?" Igare paced at the head of the table, looming over those who were seated. "It must be an attack from the north in retaliation for what happened to their king."

"Maybe it was simply pure rage that drove the north to press some of their best dragons to cross the forest." Cartaya closed her fists and extinguished the last of the embers smoldering there. "We do not know how many more may have died trying to make the crossing under the fiery whips of their masters. Revenge and anger are strong motivators."

Sir Kayom stood. "Does it matter how these dragons arrived? We waste time here discussing possibilities while the Nevergrace has been taken, her people captive or dead. We must act quickly. Please, my king."

"The guard of the Never is right," King Igare said in a conclusive tone. "The discussion of how is over. For now. There is also something else more pressing. I received a message from the north. The day before yesterday. It declared they had taken hostages somewhere in Belvenguard, but they kept their location secret. They also claim that if we seek them out or send a full legion in retaliation, they will kill all of their captives."

Cyran lurched in his seat. *Captives? Maybe Jaslin and my friends are still alive.*

"I thought it was a ruse," Igare continued. "Until now. These brigands of the north likely fear that we will discover their location and wipe them out. But we cannot risk the lives of any of the Never's survivors."

"But now we know for certain where they are and what and who they have taken." The orator grinned ruefully. "They would not expect a boy whose dragon crashed into the Evenmeres to survive and reach us."

"It would be the way of the Paladin to send a legion and wipe them out," the clergyman said. "We should not negotiate with them."

"Please, not if they hold hostages," Cyran said quietly. "Then the raiders from the north will kill the rest of my people."

Everyone at the table stared at him again.

"I concur with the squire," the nyren said. "Not only because of the hostages, but also because it could be a trap. A diversion. If we send a large legion away from Galvenstone, will we find that there are other, much larger, Murgare legions coming at us from the far side of the lake? The north may plan to spread our forces thin before launching their main assault."

"Or they could simply be positioning a legion at Nevergrace in order to flank us." Riscott stared into the flame of his taper. "Maybe the hostages are a farce. They could already all be dead."

"In the north's message, they also demanded their queen be returned to them." King Igare's head drooped as he removed his golden crown from his head and held it before him. "And they affirmed they would kill a captive every day and night until we comply."

Sir Kayom stifled a groan by biting his lip. Most at the table glanced at each other with wide eyes. Silence crept out of the shadows and hung over them like a pall.

"Then what shall we do?" Cartaya finally asked, shattering Cyran's ponderings of where each decision could lead them. "Tell these raiders the truth concerning their queen and risk the captives—if the north's men haven't already killed them all— being tortured or put to death? Or shall we attack them outright and raze Nevergrace to the ground?"

"Both of those options are too dangerous." The orator stood and paced around the table. "I trust this bedraggled squire saw dragons and that the forces behind said dragons have taken over the Never. But relying solely on the opinions of a greenhorn, who was abruptly awakened, new to flying, and likely terrified at the time, poses a great risk to Galvenstone. He cannot even remember for sure if Sir Ilion said there was a shadow dragon. And, in the midst of battle, he could have misheard the guard. We should gather more information before deciding how to best deal with the matter."

"I know what I saw." Cyran glared at Riscott, realizing he was likely the most disheveled young man that had ever sat at this table. "The Dragon Queen and her shadow dragon have claimed the Never."

"A small scouting party *would* be a wise consideration," Tiros said. "We would not have to spare many dragons, in case the legions of the north are flying and sailing over the lake as we speak. And this scouting party could confirm the number and types of dragons currently residing at the outpost." He faced Cyran. "Besides your dragon that died, do you know if the north killed the other dragons housed at Nevergrace?"

Cyran's mind turned. "The Never's dragons—"

"All of Belvenguard's dragons are the *king's* dragons." The orator flashed a sly grin. "The crown only loans them to certain guard and outposts as he deems appropriate."

"Enough with the frivolous remarks," Igare snapped at his orator. "We discuss matters of a much more serious nature."

The orator fell silent and bowed his head before taking his seat again.

"I was simply trying to determine if the invaders were considering taking the forest dragons and retraining them as their own." Tiros pressed his steepled fingers into the flesh under his jaw. "They may plan on adding to their legion before flanking Galvenstone."

"Besides Vetelnoir, I do not know how many others died," Cyran said. "I saw another dragon's guard and mage be unseated, but the dragon tore off its quarterdeck and fled."

"A typical response for a mindless beast frightened by battle," Riscott said.

"And I did not see any dragon carcasses around the Never," Cyran added. "Not even the bones of one that had been feasted upon."

"Then those we send to the outpost could also attempt to add more dragon allies to their numbers." Riscott's smirk contorted, and an eagerness widened his eyes. "There could be as many as three forest dragons still there. We simply have to reclaim the dragons the north is harboring and could do so by supplying three extra mages."

"Another argument that favors sending a scouting party." Tiros jostled the chain at his waist. "If the Never's people still have a dragon, or dragons, willing to fight for them, we may only need to send a few others to free them from the den or wherever they are being held. Together, they could take back the outpost. It could become a surprise attack of our own with the ability to double the party's numbers and not risk weakening Galvenstone too much."

The king nodded as he stared into the depths of his crown, mulling everything over. "I am almost hoping the north makes their move. The waiting is worse than anything. And if they do attack, it may be their last offensive before they splinter apart. Without a strong king, all the lands of Murgare cannot stay united." He swallowed. "Unless the Dragon Queen usurps their throne."

"But there are still the other issues, my king." Tiros's cloudy eyes narrowed.

"Do we discuss them here?" Riscott asked. "With the guard and the boy?"

The king dropped his crown, and it clattered onto the floor and wobbled on its rim before settling. He didn't move to pick it up. "We shall discuss everything that will affect Nevergrace and our decision of whom to send to the outpost. And we will do so here and now."

Riscott stroked his goatee with thumb and forefinger as he glanced between Kayom, Paltere, and Cyran. "Then let it be known we've discovered that a traitor has been hiding in our midst. We were aiming to use the queen to help unmask this person, but as you know, the queen's life was taken."

"I hope you are keeping that bit of information behind closed doors." Sir Kayom scowled at the orator. "If Murgare still believes their queen is alive, that may be the only reason the people of the Never have not all been executed."

Another moment of quiet lingered as Cyran's flame wavered before him, its reflection dancing in the table's varnish.

"As I was saying," Riscott continued, "we did not uncover the traitor's identity, but we now know they were housed at Nevergrace."

The base of Cyran's heart twisted on its axis and ripped at its stalk.

"All we could wheedle out of the queen was that we would never find *him* before the north brought their vengeance upon us." Riscott exhaled in frustration. "She implied this man would flee, and now we know the event he was fleeing from."

Cyran's mind flipped through people he'd known and seen, trying to summon up an image of a questionable character. None surfaced.

"This person provided knowledge of our defenses to the north." Riscott stood again and paced with his head lowered. "When you are sent back to Nevergrace, and if the opportunity arises, make an attempt to determine who was not there for the attack. I understand this will likely be difficult with so many casualties, especially if the dead have been gobbled up by dragons."

Anger seethed inside Cyran, and Kayom's face flushed again. Either the orator was trying to prod them, or he had no notion of tact.

"Then it is time to decide." Igare gazed down at his crown.

"There is yet one other matter, Your Grace." Cartaya's candle flame burned as white as her hair when she spoke. "A hamlet in the north. Near the beacon towers."

"What else is happening to my kingdom?" Igare scowled.

Images of the empty hamlet and inn Cyran had seen flared in his mind. He and his companions also experienced that bizarre night when Rilar went missing soon after passing a hamlet and a beacon tower.

"One of my informants spoke with a girl from the hamlet." Cartaya shifted uneasily in her seat. "The girl insisted the forest and its monsters came for her people. Not *only* monsters lurking in the angoias, but some of the trees themselves. She said the woods shifted about and crept toward their homes. She could not describe the monsters other than they were hunched and swept through the area. Most of the hamlet's people bolted themselves in their cellars after the ground shook and the trees moved. These people didn't come out for hours after the commotion died, and when they did, they couldn't locate two of their woodsmen. It was as if the men or their bodies simply vanished."

"The accounts of simple minds stoked by fear and drink," Riscott said.

"I've seen something similar." Cyran stood without thinking. Maybe the north wasn't responsible for all the killings in the countryside. "An abandoned hamlet and inn, as well as something during my previous journey here. We were charged with taking a farmhand to the nyrens of Galvenstone for advanced medicinal care. This young man had ventured out into the woods, and he suffered some kind of wound to the head and would not wake. One night during our travels, when a companion of mine went to wet the farmhand's mouth, we found the litter empty."

The eyes watching Cyran now either gaped or narrowed with scrutiny.

"We searched about but couldn't find him." Cyran sat down. "I... some of us thought we saw a burning shadow and a ball of light moving about the area. But it was dark and raining heavily. Then, when the dragon I was riding went down in the Evenmeres, I thought I saw a few trees move. I cut into one of them, but nothing happened." He paused and took a deep breath. "I also encountered several elves in the woods."

"Elves?" Cartaya shoved her hood back and studied him. Her young-appearing face seemed unnatural somehow, although Cyran could not say exactly why. "There has not been a confirmed sighting of elves in nearly five hundred years."

Riscott chuckled and shook his head. "Somehow this squire has managed to see the Dragon Queen, a shadow dragon, moving trees, and now elves. And might I remind you, two of these he did not mention until someone else brought up their notion. Our favored dragonsquire of the Never may feed on attention, namely the king's."

Cyran's anger erupted, but he dug his fingers into his leggings and remained silent. "I have a sword that—"

"Is that a threat?" Riscott raised an eyebrow. "If you draw a weapon in these quarters, the kingsknights will slay you."

"It is from the elves," Cyran said. "Proof. I did not intend it to be a threat."

"A sword you carry, even if it was given to you, proves nothing about the presence of elves," Riscott continued but paused in thought. "I am not making any accusations at the moment, but if we were searching for a traitor from Nevergrace, it seems this young man would be a likely suspect."

"Impossible!" Sir Kayom leapt to his feet. "Cyran has been at the Never long before he was a squire. He would never assist the north, and he didn't have the opportunity under my watch."

"Enough!" Igare glared at everyone with smoldering eyes before studying Cyran. The king's eyelids dropped like falling portcullises. He took a deep breath and repeatedly stomped his crown, crushing its gold flat. The echoes created by the dying crown rattled around the room. Rubies and emeralds slipped out of fastenings and rolled away. "I despise the north, but I intended to keep my kingdom safe and prosperous throughout my reign. I believed passing up the only chance of taking the Murgare king in my lifetime would be folly. I hoped to ease our worries and the evils of this world. But now I am failing Belvenguard." He slumped into his chair.

Tension lingered and rolled around the table, gaining weight and density as feet shuffled and candle flames guttered.

"Something strange is at work in our lands." Igare rubbed at the red mark on his forehead where the crown had sat. "I will send a swift dragon to the hamlet to look into the matter. But we cannot spare many from our legion. I will send another couple to Nevergrace with Sir Kayom. They will confirm the number and types of dragons involved in this recent takeover, in addition to the presence of the Dragon Queen and any captives. Sir Kayom and those I send with him will also attempt to recover any of the Never's surviving forest dragons to use in a retaliative assault." He glanced to the young priest of the nine. "And we will all pray to the six righteous gods and the Dragon that the north does not use this opportunity, this moment of weakness, to launch their full assault. We will also attempt to keep the Assassin and the Thief unaware of everything that has been said in this chamber."

28

PRAVON THE DRAGON THIEF

THE DARK MIST CLINGING TO THE OUTPOST OBSCURED ITS FRONT gates and much of its walls, but torchlight still bled through its swirling depths.

"Mist dragon breath," Pravon muttered.

"I'd bet all the Murgare king's gold crowns the gates are gone." Kridmore's white teeth flashed beneath his draping hood. "Burned by dragon fire."

"You realize, we'd never even know if the Murgare or Belvenguard kings died," Aneen said. "Not with our contracts and how we have to remain out of touch with everyone but our contact."

Pravon had similar worries, but it wasn't as if he'd had a choice in accepting his contract. Kridmore and Aneen probably hadn't had a choice either. He scrutinized the silhouettes—battlements, flags, dragons—showing through the fog. He could not make out the types of dragons, nothing more than general shapes. The light of the moons barely pierced that mist.

"We can use the fog to our advantage." Aneen grinned. "They are trying to hide something, and we wish to conceal ourselves."

"After you, my lady." Kridmore bowed his head and held a hand out in the direction of the castle.

"I'd almost feel flattered if I weren't worried about getting a dagger stuck in my back." Aneen crept closer to the outpost. "Or if I weren't concerned about being offered up as the fool meant to spring a trap."

"Why would the dread king even want us to go through with this?" Pravon followed behind Kridmore.

"We are not in the position to question our employer." Kridmore moved without creating even a rustle from his shadowy cloak. "I was jesting when I asked our contact how he tracked us down when the village was burning, but I do not doubt the man has the ability to find us by less tangible means."

Pravon shivered. This was his style of work, but he'd never been so in the dark about his true objective before. He and his comrades slipped into the fog and through the archway of the outer gates that were nothing more than ash and dust blowing in clumps across the ground. Dim torchlight glowed in the distance.

"Do you still question everything I said about this place?" Kridmore asked.

Neither Pravon nor Aneen answered as they slipped into the bailey and slinked around the margins of the inner curtain. Sleeping dragon sentinels perched on the battlements around them. A few sentries patrolled the grounds as well, their figures only visible through the mist when they moved. Only fools and those who were otherwise already dead would dare sneak into this place. And there was a good chance their group's contact must have predicted or known this outpost would be captured. Their sole reason for coming here might have depended on it.

"Put on your shadows." Kridmore tugged his black cloak tighter about his frame, and he almost seemed to become ethereal as he moved.

Pravon did his best to emulate the assassin, and the trio crept around chopping blocks and stacks of wood as well as empty soldier houses and servants' quarters. Scorched earth lay all around them, and the bailey was littered with blackened logs, shields, and the remnants of weapons. The entrance to a den passed by on their left.

Pravon's blood spiked with adrenaline, and his skin tingled with excitement and fear. *Dragons.* His previous employers usually only focused on his abilities that pertained to such beasts.

"On our way out, I may take a quick detour and slip in there for a moment." Kridmore nodded toward the den. "But we have to fulfill our obligations first."

Anticipation and eagerness sheeted off the assassin now. Was Kridmore enthralled by dragons as well?

The trio slowed their pace when they approached the keep and avoided the wall and grounds silvered by the brightest moonbeams. A clatter of booted feet sounded far up on the roof. Torchlight fluttered through the glass and shuttered windows of all the lower chambers, while many of the upper stories remained dark.

"How should we best use the darkness to find our target?" Aneen whispered, her twin blades shining under pale moonlight. "Before the sun rises or we wake a dragon?"

"Follow me." Kridmore grinned.

He led them to an unshuttered window and quickly stole a glance inside. Kridmore pulled back but did not acknowledge Pravon or Aneen or show any indication of success or disappointment. He crept away to the adjacent window and continued his peeping.

Marching footsteps sounded near the keep's entrance, and Kridmore pressed himself against the wall, becoming nothing more than shadow and stone. Pravon ducked behind an overturned cart, and Aneen hid with him. Two dragonarchers carrying hand crossbows muttered to each other and laughed as they paced by. After they were gone, Kridmore continued his methodical investigation of the windows, peeking through tiny slits or cracks in the wood of those that were shuttered. Pravon often stole a glance through the windows after Kridmore had moved on. Some rooms held cots with sleeping guard members and mages. Others were filled with captives—unarmed soldiers, knights, servants, farmers, woodsmen, and nobles.

Once they had circled the entire keep, Kridmore grinned again. "Time to go up."

"Scale the walls of this keep?" Aneen asked. "With dragons sleeping within earshot? Can't we just burn it down? That seems to be your style."

"Are you two thieves or not?" Kridmore pulled climbing blades out of his cloak and strapped scaling spikes to his feet, which had sharp protrusions extending from the toes and inner edge of his boots. "If not, I am unsure why you've been sent here with me. Get your spikes on. Burning the new residence of the Dragon Queen would get you tortured and killed before the dread king could even catch us."

Kridmore buried a thick but sharp and tapering spike of a blade into a gap between stones. He jammed the spike around and pulled against it until it was stable. Then he hoisted himself up, using the prongs strapped to his boots and his other blade to climb the wall like a spider. Pravon motioned for Aneen to go next as he prepared. Pravon could climb with the best of thieves, but it was a skill he preferred to use when dragons could not pluck him from the stones and swallow him whole.

Aneen moved almost as fast as Kridmore, and Pravon sank his blades into gaps and crumbling mortar, stepping and pulling himself up in quick bursts. A dragon snorted from somewhere in the fog, and Pravon froze. A wing stretched out from a cloud of mist and trembled. Pravon swallowed, his mouth suddenly as dry as cracked parchment. The only dragon he ever wished to encounter was a sleeping dragon. Only in that state would he take his chances with such a creature.

A heartbeat or two passed, and the dragon's wing retracted. The great beast lumbered and turned about on the battlement before falling still, its raspy breathing growing rhythmic again. Soon after, Pravon reached the second landing, and his companions worked their way around the balconies and windows. Pravon traveled around the keep in the opposite direction as Kridmore. Aneen continued scaling up to the third level. After being unable to locate their target, they climbed higher. Once outside the fifth and uppermost story, Pravon peeked through a window wherein many lighted tapers burned on a chandelier. A short man with graying brown hair and a woman slept inside, the man in a bed, the woman on a cot against the opposite wall. Two archers sat near the chamber's doorway, one ripping bites from an apple as he rolled dice on the floor between them.

"Is it them?" Aneen lowered herself from the fifth-story balcony. "I don't want to have to kill the watchman on the roof, but I am growing weary of this search and I keep hearing his coin purse jingle."

"They are inside," Pravon said.

"Good." Kridmore was suddenly on the wall beside Pravon, which made Pravon lurch with surprise. "I'll create the distraction. You two fulfill the order." He descended before Pravon could even protest, the master assassin moving down the wall so quickly it appeared he had a rope and was gliding down.

"What? Don't you feel like killing nobles?" Aneen sheathed a spike blade and pulled out a dagger.

Pravon removed a tool from an inner pocket in his cloak and unfolded it into long and thin lengths. He eased the back of his hand against the window and gently pushed. It had less than a finger's width of give. More than enough.

Firelight flared in the distance of the outer bailey, and the roof of a curtain house burst into flame. Smoke plumed into the night. A dragon hissed and roared. Wings beat. Shouting arose outside the keep, and the pounding of armored boots rang on the stone walks far below.

Pravon peeked back into the chamber in question. The two archers were standing and motioning wildly before they both disappeared behind the doorway. The man and woman had awoken and were glancing about. Pravon shoved on the window as hard as he could, and the panes hit the inner latch and rebounded outward. He slipped his tool into a tiny gap between the window and the stones and twisted and turned it until its flared tip flipped the latch. Then he shoved on the panes again, and both flew inward as he leapt inside the chamber.

The man inside shouted and pointed as Aneen landed behind Pravon with barely a sound. One of the archers dashed back into the chamber, his crossbow leveled and ready to loose.

Pravon hurled a throwing knife before he'd even realized he'd unsheathed it. The weapon buried itself up to its hilt in the archer's throat. The archer collapsed, and when he hit the floor, his crossbow slid across stone. Its rope sprang forward, sending a bolt bouncing off the floor and ricocheting around before lodging into a post on the bed.

"You were not supposed to remain here." A sucking feeling pulled at Pravon's guts. He should not have killed *her* men. "You were supposed to go check on the fire."

The man on the bed screamed and fell back, tearing at the covers and lifting them over his body and face. His fingers and white knuckles were clamped onto the edge of the sheet and were still visible. Pravon scoffed and almost shook his head.

Too easy. The targets themselves were almost always too easy.

"Finish him before his screaming brings more archers." Aneen stood over the woman's body. Blood ran from her victim's throat.

Pravon lunged over to the cowering man and reached out to draw the covers back.

"Hurry!" Aneen leapt out the window.

Pravon's hand stilled, and he left the covers in place, noting the outline of the man's form and area of his face from the flutter of the sheet where he breathed frantically against it. Pravon aimed for the man's heart, and when the deed was done—with a few extra strikes for certainty's sake—he retracted his dagger and wiped it clean. Then he slipped out the window without a sound.

29

CYRAN ORENDAIN

THE DEN SMELLED OF FIRED GOAT AND OX MEAT. CYRAN PUSHED A barrow holding a raw sheep carcass down the length of the aisle, eyeing the stalls and dragons of so many sizes, shapes, and colors. He stopped when he spotted a familiar forest dragon.

"This time you come bearing a meal." Eidelmere's eye popped open, and the wizened old dragon studied Cyran under firelight.

"I was asked to hurry and not stop for anything, but I remembered our last encounter and didn't want to upset you again."

Eidelmere narrowed his eye and sucked in a breath. He paused, and his nose twitched. "And what is that other smell?"

Cyran glanced down and dusted off his stained and torn tunic. "I went down on Vetelnoir in the Evenmeres and had to ride here. I haven't taken a bath in some time."

"No." Eidelmere's massive snout pressed against the bars of his stall, his nostrils sticking through. The dragon sniffed, starting at Cyran's face level before sweeping downward and stopping at his waist. "That is something I have not smelt so closely in an age."

Cyran noticed the strip of angoia tree bark he'd tucked into his belt, and he drew it out.

Eidelmere's eyes grew wide, and the dragon took the bark gingerly in his yellowed and cracked teeth. "Is this a gift? For me?"

Cyran nodded. "I unintentionally passed far too close to the angoias when I was in the forest."

"An angoia of the Evenmeres." Eidelmere breathed the scent of the bark in and then used his tongue to grasp the strip. He turned and rubbed the bark over his cheeks and then along the scales of his neck and shoulders. The dragon's eyes turned distant and cloudy.

"You seem more overjoyed with that little strip of bark than you do with your meal."

"What do you know of it?" Eidelmere snapped as he lunged out and bit the air before Cyran, the dragon's teeth scraping along the bars of his gate.

Cyran leapt away and fell onto his backside. He steadied himself for a moment until his heartrate slowed, and he held out a hand in peace. "I... did not mean to rouse your anger."

The distant look in Eidelmere's eyes had hardened into a more familiar resentful appearance. The dragon sucked in a breath and blew water over the sheep carcass, splashing Cyran with much of it before Cyran could roll away. "Vetelnoir has indeed entered the other realm for eternity, then?"

Cyran nodded.

After the forest dragon feasted, Cyran, in his dripping wet leathers, led the dragon up the incline toward the den's exit. Eidelmere's tack was not stored in the harnessing chamber of Castle Dashtok. The dragon did not say another word but kept the angoia bark between his teeth. Once they exited the den, they found others waiting for them.

Sir Kayom marched up to Eidelmere and waved to a few

squires, who rolled over a frame holding the dragon's quarter-deck and saddles. Sir Paltere whistled absently as he walked with Kayom. Morden—Kayom's dragonmage—waited under a brown cloak, leaning on his staff and speaking with five other mages. Two additional guard in red and gold armor spoke together near the mages.

"Three dragons will not be enough to take back Nevergrace," Kayom grumbled. "Not if Murgare has five at our outpost. This is a fool's errand."

Paltere clapped Kayom's armored back and, in a light tone with a smile, said, "A guard is not supposed to question his king. Igare believes three dragons shall be more than enough to swoop over Nevergrace, assess the situation, and report back. Maybe you can even recover some of the Never's lost dragons, and *if* it is then reasonable, attack and take your outpost back."

Kayom huffed. "If we indeed still have three forest dragons remaining and we reclaim them, we could then attempt retalia-tion. But together we'd barely outnumber the raiders."

"But they cannot have many, or any, soldiers and knights with them. No matter which route their dragons came by. And your surviving soldiers and knights can aid you with your revolt."

Kayom studied Eidelmere's cracked scales by running a hand over them. "But none of what we do will matter if one of their beasts is a shadow dragon and the Dragon Queen occupies the Never."

"In that instance, you should simply report back to Igare." Paltere checked the harnesses on Eidelmere's quarterdeck and on the mage's saddle as the squires rolled the frame out over the dragon's back. Cyran scaled the frame and assisted them. "If the Dragon Queen is residing in your castle, Igare will send a much larger legion."

"I wish you and your sun dragon were coming with us, dragonknight." Kayom clapped Paltere on the pauldron and looked up to address Cyran. "Are you certain it was a shadow dragon that you saw?"

Cyran nodded as he used a rope and pulley to help ease the quarterdeck onto Eidelmere's back. "I also saw its guard flying without a mage. If it was not the Dragon Queen, it must have been another dragonknight in armor contoured for a woman."

Kayom's eyes closed as he groaned. "You are no fool, Cyran. I fear we will not return from our expedition."

"I wish to fly with you," Cyran said as he stepped up before Kayom, and Paltere chuckled wryly. "I've flown as an archer now, and I may be able to help guide us and point out certain things concerning the attackers. I'm the only one who has seen them."

Kayom shook his head. "I know of your unmatched prowess with the crossbow on the ground, squire, but you need a lot more experience in the air before I willingly send you into battle. I have well-trained archers. I appreciate your eagerness, but it'd be best if you wait for us here at the castle. Here you may survive to see another day." Kayom turned to address a group of messengers waiting along the wall nearby. "Find my archers. We depart in an hour."

Three messengers sprinted away as the sun sank low in the west.

Groups of squires led two dragons—a silver and a black moon dragon—from the den while others rolled over frames supporting quarterdecks and saddles. The two nearby guard in red and gold armor approached the dragons, checking tack and harnesses.

"A damn silver?" Kayom said. "Sure, it's much stronger than a forest dragon, and the moon dragon is a great choice for this death mission at night, but a *silver*? The Dragon Queen's men will see it coming from a league away."

"Perhaps Riscott thought your group needed more strength

and fire." Paltere's tone carried a false air of optimism. "Just in case the dragons occupying the Never come after you."

"Then send you and your sun dragon with us." Kayom's fist clenched on his sword's hilt. "Damn this day and these circumstances."

"I know you seek justice, but perhaps you should stick with scouting out the situation from high above or only with the moon dragon while keeping the silver back. Unless you need him. And the night you should arrive is supposed to be when most of the moons are new and their light is at their dimmest. The moon dragon is a wise choice."

"That's the damn squire we paid but who didn't end up feeding our dragons." A familiar squire stood nearby. Two others watched with him. They were the young men who had given Cyran coin to feed three dragons during his last visit to Galvenstone. The squire pointed at Cyran, and his friends sneered. "Got me three lashings."

Cyran remembered receiving their coin and then being called back into the castle to hear about the queen's death after feeding only two of the dragons. Almost immediately after that, he'd been sent back to Nevergrace. His stomach turned. "I am sorry for—"

"Be off!" Paltere waved at the squire who had accused Cyran, and the dragonknight marched toward the trio. The three young men turned and ran into the crowd. "This squire is serving his king, and he did not survive an encounter with the Dragon Queen only to be hounded by you."

Archers for the other two dragons slipped on chainmail and ran back and forth, stocking dragonbolts and checking their crossbows. Soldiers and knights gathered around the margins of the square, standing at attention while the dragons were harnessed and weaponized.

Several men and women carried pipes and flutes. One

woman held a bagpipe, and they all played a melancholy melody that crescendoed into tunes of overpowering triumph. The music instilled hope and bravery in the men as they worked, and its tones called others out from the keep. Cyran flung Eidelmere's harness straps over the dragon's far side.

"If you will, play the song of the endless Never," Kayom said to the pipe players once their initial melody faded. The bards began a song with a slow tempo, one that Cyran recognized but had never learned to play on his lute. He tried to memorize the notes as he fastened the harnesses.

When the music belted out sad, longing chords that echoed off the walls, Kayom paced before the dragons and began to speak, his altering pitches matching the lower notes of the song. "The history of the people of the Never is a vast darkness without perceivable depth or detail. But echoes still rattle amongst those shadows. Voices. Songs. Legends. We are a people of music and dance and tales. Of war and love. Defenders of the realm. We maintain pieces of our past, and we pass these along to others who venture within our walls. And we will never be forgotten. Not then. Not here. Not now. We have taken as much from our enemies as they have from us. At least until this day. And the day is not over."

Those who had gathered around cheered, and women arrived bearing flowers. They flung handfuls of bright petals into the square.

Kayom checked the saddles in addition to the cinches and harnesses of Eidelmere's quarterdeck, and a messenger arrived and spoke quietly with him. Kayom shook his head. When Cyran's guard-master was satisfied with the tack, he motioned, and Morden approached and climbed into his saddle. Eidelmere moved his neck to better accommodate the mage. The other guard and mages and archers mounted their dragons, and after they had taken their positions, Kayom climbed into his saddle. The sun collapsed into the horizon.

"We will wait no longer." Kayom glanced at Cyran and pointed to the unmanned crossbow on his dragon's back. "Squire, you will take up the position on the quarterdeck. For Nevergrace."

The hair at the base of Cyran's neck spiked and tingled. The archer in Eidelmere's lower turret finished strapping himself in, but there was still no archer approaching to take the upper post.

"Hurry, squire." Kayom waved him onward. "We fly with or without you. The Never is waiting for us."

Cyran glanced around before hurrying for the rope ladder hanging from Eidelmere's quarterdeck. Cyran swallowed and moved to haul himself up to the quarterdeck, but he paused and faced Kayom. "Why are you taking me now?"

Kayom leaned back, and Eidelmere's neck swung around, bringing the dragonguard closer. He whispered, "My archers were both here, ready to fly, until I explained the situation. I simply told them and Morden about our scouting party and the shadow dragon. Now the messengers cannot find Blain. He does not deserve to fly back to the Never on Eidelmere." Kayom sat straight and raised a fist in the air as he turned to the crowds and shouted, "We *will* reclaim Nevergrace. *And* our lost dragons!"

Men and women cheered while the music played on.

Cyran reached for the rope ladder, but a hand clamped onto his shoulder.

"You should have these if you are going into battle as a dragonarcher." Sir Paltere held a suit of shimmery chainmail and a longsword.

Cyran took the chainmail and slipped it over his head and tattered tunic. Then he reached for the sword. "I already have a sword."

"But you should no longer carry a squire's broadsword..."

Paltere glanced at the weapon strapped to Cyran's waist, and Paltere's eyes narrowed. "What kind of blade is that?"

Cyran drew his sword halfway from its sheath, and its silver sheen glinted.

Paltere's eyes widened. "Not a dragonblade, but... where did you get that?"

"Like I told the king"—Cyran slid his weapon back into its sheath as others began to stare—"I saw an elf. And after he died, I took it from him."

Paltere grinned. "Then you won't be needing the longsword of a soldier." He tossed the weapon to another squire nearby. "Remember whatever you can from Kayom's and Ymar's teachings, and maybe some of the words we shared. Forget the rest. Trust your instincts." He clapped Cyran on the shoulder and gestured to the ladder. "Time to climb, dragonarcher."

Cyran squeezed a rope rung in his fist and hauled himself up.

30

PRAVON THE DRAGON THIEF

THE DEN WAS MUSTY AND DANK. ITS TUNNELS WERE ALSO QUIET AS Pravon snuck through the darkness and down the rampway. Maybe too quiet. But faint firelight blazed down below. Aneen and Kridmore followed him now. This potential exploit was what he knew best, why the dread king must have sought him out and sent him on these tasks. He moved without a sound as he snuck along the walk. The smell of dragon lingered in the air.

"We must hurry," Aneen whispered, her voice carrying a hollow timbre as it trundled away into the darkness. "Soldiers will never think that a group of thieves would want to hide in their dragons' den, but they *will* eventually come down here."

Pravon held up a hand. "In these kinds of endeavors, surprise is our best ally. Do not make a sound."

He snuck along, maintaining as quick a pace as he could without his boots scuffing the stones. The first stall along the walkway was empty, but the harsh breathing of dragons sounded ahead. One of the beasts near the end of the long chamber shuffled about and groaned, making strange noises Pravon had never heard a dragon make. Its talons scraped the floor as it twisted and turned, and it gave off the impression that it was also much larger than any dragon Pravon had encountered.

Pravon held up his hand again before whispering, "There is a massive dragon down here. And it is fully awake and agitated."

"Then we take the others." Kridmore slipped past him and stopped outside the next stall. Pravon crept up beside him. A forest dragon slept in its links, its head hanging and pulling its chains taut, its breathing slow and steady. "This one is mine." Kridmore unrolled a bundle of lockpicks and went to work on the stall door.

Pravon shook his head. *He is mad. Can he even steal a dragon?*

Pravon crept to the next stall and the next. Two more stalls held forest dragons, one for each of them—the master thieves— if his two comrades knew anything about stealing dragons, a rare skill indeed. At the end of the hall, multiple gates were strewn along the walk and either mangled or flattened. And the walls of at least two stalls were knocked out, their stones having spilled outward. For certain, a massive dragon was housed down there, and it didn't appear to be contained.

Aneen slipped into the stall of the forest dragon housed between Pravon and Kridmore.

The dragon at the end groaned louder, and the forest dragon before Pravon bounced its head. Its eyelids fluttered. Pravon slid his pick into the stall's lock and, within a few seconds, popped it open.

The dragon before Pravon snorted, and its eyes twitched under their lids. Pravon's pulse thundered in his ears as he shoved a finger through a tiny slit in the top of his boot. He pulled out a spike from a hidden sheath. The spike he held was as long as his forearm but only as big around as a finger, with a needlelike tip.

The dragon before him settled, but its breath was shallower than it had been. Pravon carefully removed a thin vial from a pouch, unstoppered it, and dipped the spike in, taking care not to waste a drop. The black liquid inside had been diluted by a master alchemist but was still worth more coin than a dragon egg. He stoppered the vial and tucked it away, holding the needle in a backhand orientation, like a dagger. Something shuffled in an adjacent stall, and the dragon before Pravon groaned. Pravon froze, holding his breath. The beast snorted, and its eyelid cracked open.

A rush of terror surged through Pravon. He lunged forward, hunting for the groove that ran near the bottom of the dragon's neck. Where its jugular vein would lie. The dragon shook its head, and Pravon grabbed onto one of its spines. The dragon grunted in surprise and whipped its head upward, lifting the dragon thief into the air in the process. Pravon quickly slipped his spike under a scale and lifted the scale upward, his heart racing as he attempted to study the flesh beneath. If he didn't hit a large vein directly, the beast would kill him before it was affected.

The pale skin beneath the scale was far too shadowed for Pravon to be able to determine its contours, and the dragon grunted again and inhaled a vast breath.

Pravon jammed his spike into its flesh, sinking its tip deep.

The dragon snarled and shook, trying to dislodge him.

Pravon withdrew his spike and climbed the side of the dragon's neck. When he reached the crest running down its topline, he stood and rushed forward as the beast groaned and flailed, coming fully awake. He slipped through the spikes rimming the back of the dragon's skull and slid onto its head and then down between its eyes, landing on its muzzle—the safest place to be on a dragon. Its nostrils flared. But its breath could not strike him here, and if he pressed himself close to the beast's eyes, it would not viciously claw at him with its wingtips or talons.

Pravon clamped his eyes closed as he gripped onto the

rougher scales between the dragon's eyes and held on tight. Now all he could do was wait. If he hadn't hit his mark, he would be killed. Very soon.

The dragon's blinking eyelids slid against Pravon's arms as he held his breath. The dragon reared its head back to roar, and Pravon cringed. If the beast alerted the other dragons down here, Pravon would also soon be dead.

The next second passed like an hour. The dragon's roar fizzled out of its mouth in a raspy groan as its neck collapsed onto the floor. It began to writhe.

"That is the diluted poison of a shadow dragon coursing through your veins, my beast," Pravon whispered. "The bond you held with your mage has been severed. That is causing you pain, and for that I am sorry." He stroked the dragon's scales. "The poison is also causing the muscles of your heart to cramp, and your soul is being cut off from your realm. But your heart will not fail. Nor your soul. Not yet. You know what I speak is true."

The dragon released a low growl, shock and then anger rising in its atavistic voice.

"The antidote for both ailments, only I carry." Pravon spoke in soothing tones, as if he were speaking to his favorite pet, and the guilt he always felt for having to use the poison never failed to gnaw at his conscience. But the method was the only way he could control any dragon. "I will release you from the pain, allow you to live, and allow your soul to continue to wander both realms *if* you do exactly as I ask."

The dragon's grumbling stilled, but its anger roiled just beneath its eyes.

"You must also understand, my well-being is linked with yours." Pravon's fingertips relaxed on the dragon's scales. "The dose I've given you will only allow you to live for a few hours. After that, your heart will seize up and you will die. And if I die, you will never find the antidote in the multitude of poisons I carry on my person. So it is in your best interest to protect me at least as well as you protect yourself."

The tension in the dragon's face ebbed, and its body became something akin to clay, waiting to be molded by the hands of a master sculptor.

"Now, we will exit the den quietly." Pravon pushed himself back from between the dragon's eyes. "And we will fly away from the outpost as soon as you can spread your wings."

The dragon swung its head around but did not reply. It always took the beasts a minute to work through the options, as initially they only focused on their desire for revenge. Pravon unfastened a leather strap that wound many times around his waist and across his shoulders. He crawled back behind the dragon's head and flung the strap under the creature's neck. He caught the strap's end and clinched it down tight. After taking a seat in a gap between the beast's scales, he slipped his thighs into loops on the leather strap and grabbed onto its handles.

"When needed, I will guide you with my legs and hands by squeezing or tapping your scales to indicate speed or which direction to travel. Similar to a horse rider with spurs and reins." Pravon laid his palms against the dragon's neck. "By now you must understand what we're about to do."

The dragon exhaled a raspy old breath and lumbered from the stall. The walkway was empty, neither Kridmore nor Aneen having emerged from the stalls they had entered. Did they truly believe they could steal a dragon for themselves just because the quiet and unassuming Pravon was attempting it?

The enormous dragon at the rear of the den roared, vibrating the air and shaking the walls as it stomped around. Its nostrils and muzzle of black scale stretched out into the faint firelight of the walkway, and the beast sniffed. Pravon's blood ran cold. He drove his mount onward, and they hurried down the walk and up the incline.

Beyond the den's entrance, men yelled as they threw buckets of water on a second smoldering house along the outer curtain, one across the bailey. Was that fire also the work of Kridmore? Somehow timed to create a later distraction? The house that had first been set aflame was encrusted by dragon ice, and an ice dragon approached the second burning building. More shouts arose inside the keep, and archers and dragonguard in black darted around the bailey and to the well. As soon as Pravon emerged from the den riding his dragon, a guard pointed at them and bellowed.

Pravon glanced over his shoulder. The den's rampway was still quiet and dark. Nothing in the contract he'd accepted stated that he had to make sure his companions, whom he'd just met on this venture, survived. Pravon spurred his forest dragon on, and the dragon's wings beat the air. Other dragons around the battlements shrieked as Pravon rose into the night. But none of the other dragons lifted into the air. They would need their mages first. Pravon had only until those mages climbed into their saddles before a pursuit began. He had been in similar situations before.

He rolled the forest dragon over the outer curtain, keeping as far away from the sentry dragons as he could. Those dragons screeched and snapped their jaws from a distance. Pravon swooped away through a mass of fog before sailing out over the moonlit plains.

Beating wings sounded behind him, and he glanced back. A dark silhouette trailed him. *Bloody Thief's hell. Not already.*

Pravon veered his forest dragon toward the Evenmeres, the place he'd hoped to avoid even more than the keep. He weaved his dragon back and forth and bobbed and dipped, hoping to avoid any dragonbolts, although he prayed to the Thief that the archers hadn't been ready or as close to their dragon as their mage must have been. The lines of pine and oak drew near, and Pravon banked west, hoping to skim the forest.

"Don't go into the woods!" a familiar voice shouted from behind.

Pravon glanced back again and slowed his dragon's flight, commanding the beast to hover over the trees. Aneen flew up to him on another forest dragon, and Pravon had to hide a gasp of surprise. Aneen studied him and he her, as if they had just seen each other's true selves for the first time. No other dragons pursued them, but screeches rang over the outpost as some took flight and circled about.

"Then you are also a dragon thief." Pravon nodded to her. "Or a dragonmage." What were the chances? He'd only heard of and met with one other of his kind, and that was an arranged affair.

"I am no sickly mage." Aneen grinned, lifting both her arms to display her toned body. "But if I were and were also strong enough to become a dragonknight, I would despise the expected duty and subservience. Therefore, I am a dragon thief. As are you. Coincidence?"

"I don't think so." Pravon shook his head.

"The dread king or his conjuror must have found us specifically and plotted all this from the beginning."

Pravon could barely nod his agreement. She was like him. He'd never shared his abilities with anyone he knew, other than during that one meeting. And this dragon thief was a woman. Attractive too...

Beating wings dived down at them, and Pravon's heart lurched and banged against his ribs. He wheeled his dragon around.

"We should land over there." The man on the dragon above them said. *Kridmore.* He glared down at them from the back of the last forest dragon that had been housed in Nevergrace's den, only his teeth and shovel chin showing beneath his hood that rippled in the wind. He pointed into the distance. "We should be on the ground for what comes next. For the concluding task our employer requested."

Pravon swallowed his shock and fear. *Another* dragon thief. "I do not want to be sitting out in the open, waiting for the sentry dragons of the keep to swarm out and find us."

Kridmore shrugged. "Their dragons probably aren't going to travel far from the fogged cover of that outpost. They may fear that Belvenguard will learn where they are and what they have done."

Pravon studied the castle and the mist clinging to its walls, the light within having dimmed after the fire Kridmore had set died out. Two dragons flew in widening circles around the outpost. "We fly a bit farther, and then we can stop and discuss what kind of message to leave behind." Pravon swooped away and flew for another few leagues, not caring if Kridmore left him this time. He would not again allow that man to decide the fate of their group. But Aneen and Kridmore followed him, and he eventually settled his dragon down in the grass beside the Evenmeres.

His companions landed beside him, and Kridmore immediately popped out of his harness and strode along his dragon's back to the quarterdeck that was in place there.

"How did you ever get a quarterdeck placed on your dragon?" Pravon asked, incredulous.

"I just moved faster than you." Kridmore wound the crossbow's windlass until its rope clicked into place. He loaded a dragonbolt. "I stole the bond between this dragon and its mage on our side of the realms. By another method." He pointed, and the sleeve of his cloak slid up past his wrist, revealing a golden band that ran up his forearm. But he was indicating the hilt of a similar gilded dagger that was buried in the scales at the base of his dragon's skull. A dark gem protruded from its hilt. "Of course, this dragon is also in pain and will die soon, its soul to be severed from the other realm. And so it loathes me. But wanting the quarterdeck placed is why I took the first occupied stall and got my beast out quickly. I rushed him into the harnessing chamber, but you both beat me out of the den."

A shout of warning echoed in the back of Pravon's mind. *Another method? A simple dagger?* Such a weapon should barely harm a dragon. The only other option Pravon knew of that could accomplish such a feat was the magic of a dragonmage. Or were the wristband and dagger some kind of magical items? He shook his head. *Never trust another thief, especially one you don't know. Moreover, a dragon thief.* "What do you intend to do with the crossbow?" And why did he take all the extra time to make sure he had the quarterdeck, given the extra risk involved?

Kridmore paused and flashed a grin, his white teeth the only visible thing beneath the shadows of his hood. "What I couldn't do in the den with that monstrous dragon nearby and you two fumbling about trying to steal more dragons." He swung the crossbow around until it pointed at Pravon. "Leaving a message."

Pravon flinched and ducked to the side as Aneen stifled a shout of surprise. Pravon's dragon flapped its wings, ready to take flight. But a few heartbeats later, still nothing had happened.

"Look at me, dragon," Kridmore said, and his dragon bowed its long neck around as if it were trying to bite at its flank. Then the creature tilted its head up and studied the man behind the crossbow.

Kridmore squeezed the trigger handle, and the crossbow twanged. The bolt launched straight out into Kridmore's dragon's head. The projectile struck the beast in the center of its head, right between its eyes. Bone crunched as steel pierced skull and then brain. The dragon dropped like a stone, crashing onto its side. Kridmore leapt from the quarterdeck and landed on the ground, rolling to break his fall. He came up on two feet, hopping to a stop.

"What in the bloodiest whorehouse in Tablu?" Aneen's jaw hung open. "A dragon thief does not go through all the risk and effort to steal a dragon just to *kill* it. Just one of these beasts is worth more than that entire keep back there."

Kridmore smiled as he approached Aneen, and violet light bloomed in his fist, extending outward into a lance. Aneen's dragon retreated from the man and reared up, exposing its neck. Kridmore lunged forward and jammed his lengthening blade of light into the dragon's chest. The weapon created no sound when it pierced scale, but the dragon's eyes immediately shriveled and turned black. And the beast fell just as quickly as the first dragon had, as if the blow had severed a vital spark inside it.

Aneen cried out as she toppled over with her dragon. Kridmore then spun to face Pravon, whose dragon beat its wings faster and began to lift into the air.

"We cannot take dragons with us around the countryside, you fools." Kridmore reared back and hurled his magical lance.

The weapon sailed through the air and impaled Pravon's dragon's chest before disappearing in a flash. The forest dragon dropped the height of two men and crashed, jarring Pravon's bones and flinging him away into the grass.

"This is why we stopped," Kridmore said. "I thought you'd prefer being close to the ground rather than falling a league out of the sky." He ripped the golden dagger from the base of his dragon's skull, flinging a trail of blood in its wake. "And do not *ever* attempt to remove this weapon if it is embedded in a dragon. You will not be able to do so, and it will kill anyone who touches it. Anyone but me." He turned and strode away. "Now, come. We must find a village around here where we can bide our time until our contact shows." He glanced over his shoulder, a wicked grin lighting up above his chin. "I don't know about you two, but killing dragons always makes me thirsty. And I was employed for only one reason. I am *not* a dragon thief. I am a dragon assassin."

31

JASLIN ORENDAIN

Jaslin gazed out the window at the silent battlements, then studied the people of the Never who were crammed inside the chamber. Odors of sweat and the pungent stench of urine mixed together and hovered around them. Fortunately, the Murgare archers let them dispose of most of their waste by using bedpans.

A Never soldier sat on the ground nearby with a score of others, their cheeks more sunken than they had been. The looks in their eyes screamed defeat and acceptance. Water jugs sat around on tables, but food was scarce. And because the Never's people weren't allowed to eat enough, it created a sense of despair and sapped their energy, a tactic likely employed by Murgare to help keep them subdued. The dragonsquires were hardly any more optimistic than the soldiers, and Ezul had still not returned after an archer brought him away.

One of the Dragon Queen's sacrifices?

Jaslin returned to the book in her lap, one she'd found on the shelves of this room along with several others. She'd never been in this chamber before, had not been inside the keep often, but someone had said this was Ezul's study chamber. There were so few books in here compared to what she imagined a nyren should own. But then again, it was rumored that the rare elite scholar who became a nyren mastered the skills necessary to remember nearly everything of importance they had been taught or read. They no longer needed books related to their areas of specialty, or many books at all for that matter. Such assertions about nyrens made them sound more like a strange group of mages rather than scholars with honed skills of the mind.

The only books Jaslin had found in this chamber were those for pleasure reading or those pertaining to obscure topics Ezul likely had never studied. She turned a page, reading about a shining city of mythical elves. This story had all the components of a fairy tale, but it claimed it was based on the realism of the past age.

"It says the shining city was east of the lake." Jaslin shook her head, but Menoria wasn't really listening, her eyes lost in some other world of thought. "But all that is east of the lake is the Evenmeres."

Jaslin's mind wandered as it often did when the long hours and days inside the chamber lingered. Her thoughts returned to Tamar and Cyran. Pain swept through her and threatened to buckle her knees. Wolves howled out in the Evenmeres, Smoke's familiar tone still catching her ear. But Smoke and his companions' voices had changed, becoming more feral and demanding. Maybe even desperate. She gritted her teeth, and a rush of anger followed. Both her brothers were gone, and Smoke could soon be gone as well. A familiar tune worked its way through her burning rage and settled on her lips. She hummed as she pulled out her crystal fragment and studied the dancers on its face, a web of cracks running through their bodies. There were woods behind them, and the faint outline of a dragon. Jaslin shuddered.

"How can you sing at a time like this?" Menoria asked.

"How can you not sing if you've got the energy for it?" Brelle started humming her own tune, even louder than Jaslin's. "I'd rather say something humorous or unexpected, but I can barely think."

Men shouted outside in the bailey, and Jaslin peered through one of the windows of the chamber. Murgare's archers ran about yelling for dragons while hauling buckets to and from the well. Firelight reflected off the outer curtain. A blaze had to be burning somewhere beyond the keep.

Jaslin whirled about to assess the situation and those guarding their doorway. The two archers there discussed something before slamming the heavy oak door shut. Its wooden planks shuddered a moment later.

They've barred us inside.

"They will bring their dragons upon us." Dage hustled to the other window and glanced out before spinning on Jaslin and Menoria. "What have you two done?"

"This isn't anything I could have done." Jaslin craned her neck to try to see around the margins of the window.

"Then perhaps Galvenstone has come," Ulba said as she pulled herself up, and little Renily slid off her lap, waking from a nap, her eyes wide, her red hair disheveled.

"It could be true." Dage shook his fists triumphantly in the air when he spotted the firelight. "The dragons of Galvenstone are here."

"The Siren bless the king!" Emellefer's eyes streamed tears.

A mass of the Never's soldiers ran at the door and began beating its planks and then ramming it with their shoulders. The wood didn't give.

"I do not hear the cries of attacking dragons," Jaslin said to Menoria. "And the Dragon Queen seemed to believe that Igare had taken her queen. She hinted that she may release us if there was an exchange of prisoners."

Menoria's eyes rolled across her thoughts. "But this doesn't sound like a friendly transfer or negotiation."

Jaslin shook her head. "No. It does not. But it also doesn't sound like a legion of dragons has arrived to free us and take back the Never."

"Then those archers who were at our door are sending word to have their dragons cook our arses or make this chamber as icy as Frozen Fist Mountain." Brelle hammered a fist on the window. "We should break the glass and start climbing through. At least some of us may be able to escape incineration."

Laren stepped up beside her. "Without any tools or weapons, the iron mullions are going to make it difficult for us to squeeze through."

Brelle grabbed a chair and swung it at the window. Glass shattered and exploded out into the bailey, but the mullions barred their way.

"Stop, please," Emellefer said. "We may be saved soon."

A few soldiers or knights, now indistinguishable as they wore no armor and carried no weapons, broke the other window with the legs of a desk and pounded against the mullions. Brelle and Laren alternated swinging chairs. Dage shouted as he lifted a desk and ran at the window, holding the desk over his head. The others stepped aside as thick oak rammed into iron. The iron bars bent outward with a screech but did not snap, and the force of the impact and sudden stop flung Dage backward, sending him crashing onto the floor. The desk fell on top of him with a thud. Laren and Brelle lunged over and lifted the heavy piece of furniture off him.

Jaslin and Menoria shoved on the bent mullions, but their iron was far too thick and strong and did not give way.

"I never thought I'd say this," Brelle muttered, "but damn the

Never's accomplished and drunken blacksmiths." She faced Dage and, in her best imploring voice, asked, "One more time? I'll try to catch you if you rebound again."

Dage shook his head, his eyes vibrating and unable to focus. He rubbed at his scalp. Their fellow captives' pounding on the door grew louder, but no splintering or cracking answered.

"You want to take a stab at it?" Laren asked Brelle, and she nodded. Dage growled and climbed to his feet as Laren and Brelle lifted the desk onto their shoulders and charged the mullions. Dage braced his hands and arms against the end of the desk and helped propel it.

Wood rammed the mullions again, and their iron bowed. Rivets connecting the mullions to the surrounding stone popped out. The upper portions of two mullions gave way and creaked as they bent outward. Laren, Brelle, and Dage were not flung back this time, and they dropped the desk and assisted Jaslin and a few soldiers in pushing the iron rods outward until there was enough space for a person to slide through.

"I'll slip out and assist others in escaping," a soldier with a draping mustache said as he climbed through the window. A second soldier followed him before they both landed outside and turned around, reaching for others.

"Renily"—Jaslin took the little girl's hand—"and Ulba should go next."

The old cook neared but shook her head. "Take the little girl, but leave me. I am the last one who could be of any help against the north."

Jaslin eased Renily through the gap, and the soldiers outside pulled her through.

"Go with her." Brelle took Ulba's hand, and she and Laren assisted in shoving the protesting old woman out the window behind the girl.

The piercing cry of the mist dragon rang over the castle,

muffling any other sound. People fell to their knees or collapsed completely, covering their ears and trembling. Ulba fell outside.

Jaslin hauled herself to her feet, her knees still quaking as she helped Menoria grasp onto the sill and pull herself up. Menoria's hands and arms shook violently. Jaslin pressed herself against Menoria's back and said, "Go!"

The head of a snow-white dragon snaked down from above. Its teeth flashed as its massive jaws gaped, and it snatched Ulba, biting her in half just outside the window. Only the old woman's legs remained behind, along with a spray of blood. Then the beast blasted its icy breath, which coated both soldiers and froze them, making them appear like blue-tinged statues covering their faces and holding up hands in defense.

People screamed, ringing the chamber nearly as loud as the mist dragon's shrill cry. Menoria slid back inside and cowered below the sill. The deep blue eye of the ice dragon swung closer and pressed against the remnants of the mullions as it glared inside the chamber.

Soldiers yelled and dived for cover behind desks and chairs. Some hid behind others. Laren, Brelle, and Dage stood just inside the window, all three of them petrified with fear. Jaslin turned and pressed her back against the wall beside the window, hoping to shield herself. She smashed her eyes shut and waited for the gale of deadly cold.

32

SIRRA BRACKENGLAVE

"AND HOW DID WE LOSE THE THREE FOREST DRAGONS WE JUST recently acquired from this outpost without even having to kill the creatures?" Sirra stroked the armrest of the castle's throne along its stained wood, and she dug her fingernails into it. She gripped a parchment and the steel-shafted messenger bolt in her other fist.

"I am not certain, my Dragon Queen." Vladden stood before her, his voice shaky. "A few people must have snuck into the outpost."

"And so you believe some crippled dragonmages prowled about like bandits and hid and then outran all our archers and guard?"

"We don't have anywhere close to enough men to watch an entire castle." Vladden glanced at the stone floor. "Including myself, we only have the four guard, four mages, and the archers for each dragon. It is barely enough men to take shifts watching all the captives. There were fires burning, and one of the ice dragons could not assist as it had to remain close to where those prisoners keep attempting to escape from."

Sirra sighed. "And the new lord and previous lady of the

Never are dead as well. Both assassinated in their upper chambers. What do you make of that?"

"It has to be the work of master assassins. Brave ones. Not dragonmages."

"Then you suggest the south learned of our whereabouts and sent these master assassins to kill only certain captives, specifically those who are worth the most to King Igare? Would Igare do such a thing rather than send a legion of soldiers and dragons to recover his prized outpost on the northern border?"

Vladden shook his head. "I do not claim to know who sent them."

"And what do you make of it all, Quarren?" Sirra asked Vladden's mage, who sat on a chair against the wall.

The woman stood when she was addressed. "I do not believe mages could have done this—come to the outpost without a dragon carrying them, snuck in, slipped down into the den, and stole dragons." She hobbled about to emphasize her point. "There are simply no mages this agile."

Sirra nodded. "Please, sit."

Quarren did so, easing her hips onto the chair, her tawny hair shimmering under the light of the chandeliers. Her long and twisted fingers and crooked nails wrapped around her staff. "And so it could have been three or more dragonknights who—"

"There are hardly that many dragonknights in all the north." Sirra crumpled the parchment in her hand. "The southern kingdoms are more populated, but would they gather three such knights together and send them on a risky venture without their own dragons? I am incredulous, to say the least."

"There is another kind." Quarren wrinkled her forehead in contemplation. "A new and rare skill has arisen and has also been honed over the past few decades."

Sirra leaned forward. With how long Sirra had lived, and with everything she'd seen and encountered, she considered herself wise, but perhaps she didn't stay as well informed as she should on particular current affairs.

"There are others who are not crippled but who have learned a method of controlling the dragon." Quarren's eyes grew distant, as if she walked the landscapes of the dragon realm now. "Those who do not need to enter the other realm to tame the beasts."

"Who are they?" Sirra asked.

Quarren jerked, and the distant look in her eyes fled. "They are those who are rumored to have started a guild, although the legitimacy of this guild is in question."

Sirra stood, a sensation she hadn't experienced in decades settling over her in a cloud of hungry anticipation. "And what have these outcasts, these middle mages if you will, done?"

"They are thieves. Dragon thieves."

Dragon thieves... I should have anticipated their coming in Cimeren. Humans would not go long without attempting to steal what was most valuable. No matter the risk.

"They exploit poisons concocted by dark alchemists and slip these poisons into their quarry through blades, severing the bond between the dragon and its mage," Quarren continued. "Their poison acts by slowly killing the dragon, and these rogues only offer the antidote should the dragon obey their every wish. There are more than a few lords and nobles who offer contracts paying heaping sums of coin for any who can steal a dragon from another kingdom. Or even steal one of the creatures from other cities and fiefdoms in their own kingdom. It has happened in the north, and I do not doubt that this guild and its ways have spread to the south, if it did not begin here."

Ideas exploded in Sirra's mind. "And these thieves would certainly be able to assassinate human targets if they are adroit enough to sneak up on a dragon and prick its flesh with a poisoned blade."

Quarren nodded. "If they can steal a dragon, they can surely assassinate a man."

"I cannot believe three such rarities could have already resided at or near Nevergrace." Sirra held the crumpled parchment up. "And now I believe I know who is behind the events. This message mentions Oomaren's recent... activities in Murgare. Those he's taken up during our absence."

"King Restebarge's brother." Vladden shook his head and took a seat opposite Quarren.

"Oomaren is seeking to act as the interim king during the queen's absence." Sirra sipped from a tankard beside her, and a light and fruity wine washed down her throat. The wines of the south were much more elegant and flavorful than any from their lands.

"But while Queen Elra is being detained, the princess—Kyelle—should be Murgare's acting monarch." Vladden picked up a plate holding a fired meal and bit off a hunk of bread.

"She is too young to reign without an overseer, but the throne is rightfully hers, if the queen does not return." Sirra took another long gulp. "I fear Oomaren either wants to establish himself as her overseer, or he wants to instill the idea that he is now the king in the minds of our people."

"Indeed." Quarren dragged her nails over her staff. "He has always sought the throne."

"And that is not the only announcement from Northsheeren." Sirra squeezed the crumpled message in her hand. "There is an uprising out in the Eastern Reach. Along the sea. Word of the king's death is spreading, and the bolts of Murgare are loosening. The loss of Restebarge may cause some in the north to start fighting amongst themselves. Perhaps we never should have come here. The anger and vengeance we wished to bring upon Igare may not be worth the cost."

"But you could unite the north upon our return." Sir

Vladden rose, his fist clenched to the sigil of the rampant shadow dragon. "And we could still avenge King Restebarge's soul. You hold the same power as our late king and can bring the north together, no matter who tries to tear it apart."

Sirra closed her eyes. "If I wanted that, maybe. But it is Queen Elra's right, and then Kyelle's."

"Sometimes rights are won with power and might." Vladden gripped his sword. "If Oomaren seeks to disrupt the old ways, and others begin to follow him, we will do what we must."

"But we are not leaving this outpost or Belvenguard without the queen." Sirra ran fingers through her long brown hair and then rested her hand atop her helm, which was sitting on the arm of the throne. "Elra is our best hope of keeping the north united and relegating Oomaren to his rightful place as another piece of useless palace furnishing. *But* with the recent loss of our best bargaining chips, the two hostages Igare would have most likely traded for the queen, I do not know if we will succeed. He may not exchange Elra for all the others here. Three forest dragons may have also piqued his interest, but those have been taken from us as well."

"Perhaps there is another way." Quarren shuffled across the green and gray runner that divided the audience hall, its surface stained with dirt and mud. She moved in a hunched manner, reminding Sirra of a witch in some old myth. "A way to still retaliate against Belvenguard and free the queen."

"What do you propose?" Sirra asked.

"There are other kingdoms here in the south." Quarren smirked, revealing crooked and broken teeth running along one side of her mouth.

"Dragon Queen." Zaldica paced into the chamber with Yenthor trailing her, but Yenthor waited near the entryway.

Sirra cocked an eyebrow.

"The young lady of the Never and the handmaid of hers who

were caught trying to escape are now pleading to speak with you." Zaldica's tone carried a heavy dose of skepticism, but her expression did not reveal any emotion. "I would not typically bring such a request to you, but they insisted it could prevent another attack."

Sirra lifted her dragonsteel sword just out of its sheath, and its fire licked and chewed at the parchment in her hand before the parchment ignited. She dropped the flaming black ball onto the floor and watched it burn. Those two young ladies—or at least one of them—seemed to be the true leaders of the captives. "Bring them in."

Zaldica motioned, and Yenthor stepped to the side, making way for Jaslin and Menoria. The two girls paced up the length of the hall, walking side by side before stopping a few strides beyond Quarren.

"We have a proposition for you, Dragon Queen," Menoria said, her voice quavering. Her fine blond hair was tangled. "And we hope to reach an agreement before any more hostages are killed."

"I'd love to hear this proposition." Sirra folded her arms over her breastplate. "And from you two, no less."

"Those who remain at the Never are willing to forego any attempt to escape and warn King Igare as long as no more of us are put to death. We will also not seek retaliation when the time comes. We simply do not want to lose any more of our people. And in return, we also promise that no more fires will be started around the castle."

Sirra studied Menoria, and Sirra reached out into the dragon realm and strummed a thread—*desirité*. Sirra sensed the beautiful young lady's lie and her feigned air of courage, an emotion that was nearly as superficial as the fine hair on her arms. Menoria hid another objective, and fear emanated from her bones.

Do these two truly believe they can fool me? "Unfortunately, all I am interested in is receiving our queen alive. And King Igare is not answering my demands. A trade of some sort would suffice, either people or what is left of this outpost for Queen Elra." She paused and looked beyond Menoria to the young lady with auburn hair that had sun-faded ends. "And whose idea was this? Yours or your friend's?"

"I am her handmaid." Jaslin's posture didn't break, and her tone was even and calm as she met Sirra's gaze. She stood much taller than Menoria.

Another lie.

"If not for your dragons," the supposed handmaid continued, "there would not nearly be enough of you to watch over all of us and keep us from trying to escape. If everyone inside the keep revolted, yes, we would lose more lives, but we would overpower you. And the Never would be ours again."

Sirra smirked at the threat and allowed a long minute of tension to fall over the chamber.

"It was my idea," Menoria said, and another sinking sensation from an untruth fell against the thread Sirra held in the dragon realm. "I am also willing to ride to Galvenstone for you. To speak with the king himself. He will listen to me. I can get you your queen."

"I will not permit anyone to leave the castle grounds," Sirra said, "especially not one as important as you."

"Then send me." Jaslin stepped closer. "I am no longer important to anyone. Both of my brothers and all of my family are dead. I will demand to see the king."

Truth, but the real young lady of the Never also lost her family. Sirra tapped her chin. Menoria appeared to be dressed as and to behave as a lady, but suspicion brewed inside Sirra. She needed to rule out any deception these two were attempting, such as if the young lady calling herself the handmaid was actually the previous young lady of the Never who had swapped identities with the other. Two of her archers had been ordered to consider similar deception—disguising themselves as people of Belvenguard—when patrolling the countryside and seeking anyone hoping to inform Galvenstone of the north's takeover. Maybe these two young women intended to deceive the north and have Sirra believe the wrong woman was of lesser value to Igare and could be sent away. A wise person might attempt such a thing... but an even wiser person would realize they could not pull it off without extensive training as a lady of the castle. And a person of high intellect might decide to try tricking a fool, but not someone who paid attention to details.

Sirra glanced at Menoria's dress and Jaslin's tunic. The bottom of both garments were ripped and torn, making it impossible to determine how long each had been before the damage occurred.

An intentional alteration. These two meant to try to confuse her and her guard. "And you are the former young lady of the Never?" Sirra asked Menoria.

A look of bewilderment settled over Menoria's countenance, but she nodded.

The motion was not enough of an acknowledgment to stir the threads of the dragon realm and allow for detecting a truth or lie. Such detection required speech. But Sirra did not want to be so blatant as to force either of them to make a statement, or they might grow too suspicious of her intentions. These two young women reminded Sirra of herself and something she'd done as an adolescent centuries ago, but her curiosity began to wane. In the aftermath of the recent events at the outpost, the former young lady of the Never was probably Sirra's most prized captive, her best hope of still making an exchange with Igare. It would behoove her to better understand what drove each of these women before making a decision. One of them was riling up the captives, but leadership and courage did not always stem from lineages, no matter how much those of the nobility wished for such a thing to be true.

"If one of you could convince us to leave your outpost without any more death, your king may grant that person a title and sole ownership of the Never." Sirra watched closely as a light flickered in Menoria's eyes. Desire flooded from her and soaked into the dragon realm. Jaslin remained unfazed. Sirra slowly reached into a pouch at her waist and pulled out a ruby the size of an eye. She held it out toward Jaslin. The supposed handmaid still didn't burn with desire, and no more than a touch of awe leaked into the other realm. The feeling that the jewel evoked in Jaslin was much weaker than what it evoked in Menoria. "This gem could be yours. If you can convince your king to bring us Queen Elra."

Jaslin did not attempt to grab it, and no rush of emotion escaped her.

Then what drives you, handmaid who isn't a handmaid? This young woman was still naïve enough to carry hope and was more resistant than the soldiers and knights of this outpost. "I would offer the ruby to Igare as a token of my sincerity in resolving our dispute, but I fear neither of you would make it to Galvenstone if you carried such a jewel." Sirra closed her fingers around the ruby and slid it back into her pouch. "Someone would hear of it or see it, and any man even slightly prone to the influence of coin would betray you."

Neither lady spoke.

"Dragon Queen." Zaldica stepped forward. "The handmaid is often seen reading from the nyren's collection of books."

A swath of nervous regret sheeted off the supposed hand-maid and strummed the threads of the dragon realm. *Books are what you desire? Interesting.*

Zaldica approached Sirra and handed her a tome. Sirra

thumbed through it. It wasn't even history or the study of magic or any other skill or art, merely a collection of stories—fables from the time when elves ruled Cimeren and the city of Cimerenden shone like a beacon over these lands.

Even if Jaslin was not the young lady of the Never, would anyone in the farmlands around here believe her if she told them what had happened to her outpost? Would Igare even grant her an audience? Keeping the location of the outpost Sirra and her legion had occupied secret was probably the only reason an army of sun and silver and rose and forest dragons had not already driven them back to the north. That and their hostages.

"If you are both still alive when my queen is brought here, you will be released," Sirra said. "Not until then. Try whatever you can to escape or fight back, but it will not work." Sirra pulled her sword from its sheath, and its black fire snapped and crackled. "And your actions may cause more than the old cook and the new lord to die."

Menoria paled, and her lower lip quivered. Jaslin's eyes gaped before she recovered and hid any further emotion.

"Yes," Sirra continued. "It is true. The lord is dead as well. We are few, but we are much more powerful than we look. And we will continue to make sacrifices until our queen is in our hands." She handed the storybook to Jaslin and addressed Zaldica. "Take these two to the lord's chambers and keep them there. May the recent deaths of their nobles remind them of what their plotting has brought upon their outpost."

Menoria stifled a gasp and a sob.

"And what will happen if your queen is not brought to you?" Jaslin asked as Zaldica took her by the arm.

"Then Belvenguard will not receive any of you alive."

33

CYRAN ORENDAIN

"THIS IS A GOOD NIGHT TO DIE." SIR KAYOM SAT TALL IN HIS dragonguard saddle. They flew through faint splatters of moonlight, across the countryside east of Galvenstone.

Cyran maintained a white-knuckled grip on his crossbow but managed to practice pivoting around on the quarterdeck. So far, this position was less harrowing than the one inside the turret. And he was enjoying the dragon's flight much more, watching the shadowed fields and trees blur by, feeling the rise and fall of the dragon beneath him, the warm wind on his face, the slow and steady beating of enormous wings as they filled with air. So fast and yet so powerful. It was a feeling unmatched by anything he'd experienced, and this time he noticed it on a deeper level because he was not terrified of plummeting from a broken turret in the midst of battle.

"Eidelmere cannot see well." Morden, the dragonmage, hunched in the saddle just behind Kayom's, but Morden's voice was barely discernable over the wind whipping in Cyran's ears, a warm, late-summer wind. "Not on this night with so many new moons floating over the sky sea. The silver probably cannot see well, either. We should let the moon dragon do its work alone."

Kayom cursed under his breath. "This venture only has one real opportunity—information. Once I saw the damn silver dragon, I realized we'd never stand a chance of taking the outpost back."

"Silvers have some pretty hot fire," the archer beneath Eidelmere said. "Igare, or I guess it was Riscott who chose the team, probably wanted to make sure we had some muscle behind us. Like Paltere said, in case we run into trouble."

Sir Kayom did not acknowledge the archer.

"Wouldn't a sun dragon have the same weaknesses as a silver?" Cyran asked. "A sun dragon could also easily be spotted at night with its golden scales."

Kayom didn't turn around. "I know what you are getting at, squire, but I would have taken Sir Paltere and his sun dragon over *any* others."

The breath of the Evenmeres whipped around them as they swooped across the plains.

"What actually happened to you?" Cyran asked his guard-master. "At Castle Dashtok? You never told me why you weren't there when we arrived for the queen's trial."

Kayom grunted. "I was there."

"When we arrived?"

"That is right."

Confusion pinched the flesh between Cyran's brows. "Then why did the soldiers tell us you weren't?"

"I've been wondering that and occasionally looking into it since my squires departed for the Never and I was forced to remain behind to help watch Galvenstone. The best I could tell was at least one of the young messengers of the castle reported my absence to the soldiers because he thought it to be true."

"But you are skeptical about this. About the 'he thought it to be true' part."

Kayom released a long breath. "I received a sealed letter just after I arrived in Galvenstone."

Eidelmere veered hard to the left, whipping Cyran to the opposite side. Only his harness and bootstraps kept him anchored to the quarterdeck. The branches of a maple skimmed Eidelmere's right wing.

"He didn't see that one coming," Morden said.

"Be wary this night," Kayom said over his shoulder. "Logically, the presence of all the new moons should aid us, but a warning stirs in my gut. The Never's lands feel different. More so than simply being overtaken." He glanced about, his dragon-armor and shield glinting in a pale beam of moonlight. Then louder, he said to his legion, "Send the moon dragon ahead. We will wait over the fields away from the castle."

"Make for the outpost," the guard on the moon dragon said, and the mage behind him angled his staff. The moon dragon's eyes were tiny little dark beads and didn't function. The dragon opened its mouth and emitted a blast of a shriek that Cyran couldn't hear. Supposedly its cry rebounded off everything ahead of it and returned to the dragon, giving it a mental image of its surroundings without having to see at all. The dragon's wings beat faster, and it streaked away, skimming low over the field. The moon dragon flew much faster than either a silver or forest dragon could fly, and it was also more agile.

Kayom adjusted his shield as Eidelmere hovered in place.

"I—I mean we, some of your squires, received a similar letter," Cyran said. "What did yours say?"

"It warned me to be wary of someone in the king's council." He scoffed. "As if I weren't wary of all of them already. And it told me not to speak of the message to anyone."

Cyran's mind whirred. Who would send Kayom and then his squires such a message? This person might have also sent a letter to Dage before any of the rest of them.

The silver caught up to them and hovered beside them. "I pray the outpost stays as quiet and peaceful as it looks now," the guard on the silver said.

Kayom nodded. Only the flickering light of a few torches showed inside the walls of the castle. But mist still clung to the battlements.

"I imagined this outpost would be on fire," the silver's guard said. "And every house along both curtains would be smoldering and belching black smoke. Bodies would be strewn around outside and in."

"The north would have you believe that everything is as it should be," Cyran said, tucking away his thoughts about the letters for the time being. "So they can hide until they get their queen back. Which will never..." Cyran let the thought and its implications go.

"Maybe we should fly in a little closer," the silver's guard said. "Have a better look."

"No." Kayom's tone made it clear he wanted no further discussion on the matter. "We stay until the moon dragon returns."

"But I heard there may not even be a shadow dragon here." The silver's guard shifted about, trying to find a better view in the darkness. "I also heard the outpost was initially taken by surprise, when most of its guard and soldiers were sleeping. With our three dragons, we could do the same—take them by surprise this night. We could teach Murgare a lesson."

"No." Kayom lowered his visor to further instill the notion of not wanting to discuss the matter. "It is hard for me to look upon her again. The Never. I was not there the moment she was attacked. So many long years I've spent waiting and defending the border, and I was sitting in Galvenstone when I was finally needed here."

Cyran's thoughts churned. The outpost seemed so calm and

peaceful. Almost normal, except for the fog. He imagined he could just walk in and find Brelle, Laren, Garmeen, and Dage oiling saddles and mending quarterdecks, and Jaslin would be hiding in her room reading. Tamar would be performing work for both Cyran and Jaslin, tending to the pigs and oxen, repairing walls and fences. Cyran should be able to enter through the front gates and find his squire house and cot and fall asleep and wake from this nightmare.

A dragon screeched somewhere inside the outpost, and wolves howled in the woods beyond.

Smoke.

Another dragon roared.

"The moon dragon and its riders are in trouble." The silver's guard wheeled his lance up into an attack position. "And we are here to protect them." The guard spun to his mage and whispered some command.

"No!" Kayom angled his lance straight out to the side, placing its length in front of the silver's guard. "We stay here until the moon dragon returns."

"Maybe those at the Never do not assist their comrades when they are in need, but that is why I was sent." The guard slammed his visor closed and shoved on Kayom's lance, sending the weapon pivoting away from him. The silver dragon flapped its wings and turned away before flying off over the field.

"For the love of the Shield Maiden." Kayom barked an order to Morden, and Eidelmere trailed the silver. The silver dragon's back and wings glowed under faint moonlight, making the creature appear like a flying lake. The walls of the Never, its battlements silhouetted by torchlight, raced closer as they skimmed over the fields.

"The old oak is somewhere up ahead." Cyran pivoted around on the quarterdeck, his crossbow cocked and a bolt loaded as he squinted and tried to make out the tree. "But I cannot see it."

"The Assassin's bloody ass." Kayom flung open his visor. He cupped his hands to his mouth and mimicked the hooting call of the forest dragon. "He's already too damn far away. And I cannot yell at him, or we're all dead."

Eidelmere climbed higher, the movement and motion of the beast not affecting Cyran's stomach as much as it had previously. But the silver dragon racing over the field ahead didn't rise in altitude. They were probably trying to stay low to the ground to avoid blotting out the moonlight. Cyran had to consciously remove his hand from the trigger handle of the crossbow as his grip grew tighter and tighter.

The old oak...

The silver dragon released a gasp and angled sharply upward, the pace of its beating wings escalating. It swooped up, but it collided with something, and cracking rang out in the night. The tops of a hundred branches snapped. The silver's wings smashed through more leaves and boughs, and the dragon shrieked before rising over the remainder of the oak's crown.

Eidelmere glided closer as everyone on the dragon held their breaths. Cyran strained to listen, but the night turned as quiet and dark as a cave. Eidelmere banked to the east to keep their distance from the outer walls of the Never, and Cyran released a long overdue breath, the rasp in his throat sounding nearly as loud as dragon fire. The silver veered westward just before reaching the walls.

Kayom sighed. "We may have gotten lucky, but we never should have accepted a guard who would not listen to my orders. Especially one who has never seen the outpost in the daylight."

A piercing shriek burst from behind the walls of the Never and rolled out over the fields. Cyran's blood turned to ice in his veins, and his limbs were slow in responding to his wishes.

Another shriek sounded, and another. A pale body with only silhouettes for wings rose over the curtains of Nevergrace.

"The mist dragon." Cyran cursed the Thief and the Assassin under his breath.

Another dragon trailed the mist dragon, also pale but much larger. These two turned and circled in opposite directions over the Never before the mist dragon's shrill cry rang again. The ice dragon wheeled about and flew into formation beside the mist dragon. The two Murgare beasts soared after the flying glow of the silver. And a dark red dragon ascended from behind the walls and rose into the sky.

"To the silver." Kayom pointed west, and Eidelmere angled his wings, the massive leather flaps catching the wind and snapping and spinning them about.

Three Murgare dragons flew straight at the silver, the attackers' lances leading their way. Eidelmere flapped faster, but their companion was too far away. The Murgare dragons overtook the silver. Given the distance and darkness, Cyran couldn't tell if the silver's guard or mage was unseated or if the attackers' lances skewered the silver, but the snap of crossbows followed. The north's dragons careened away, and the whistling of flying bolts ended abruptly in thuds.

The silver shrieked, and its flapping grew erratic. A dark shape passed overhead. Cyran glanced up, aiming his bolt along his line of sight. The silent moon dragon swooped away from the outpost and vanished into the night.

"The moon dragon heads south," Cyran said.

The silver shrieked again, and its thrashing wings faltered as the other three dragons swarmed it with claws and lances. The silver fell in a tight spiral around one flapping wing and smashed into a field with a thump.

"Shit," Kayom said as they swooped farther west and soared over the outpost. "We must flee. To the north, away from those three dragons." He pointed. "Fly low over the Evenmeres and swing us back around to Galvenstone. Hopefully the moon dragon saw what it needed to."

As the inner bailey and center of the outpost passed below, Cyran imagined Jaslin and his friends down there, but the black form of a dragon almost the size of the keep stole his attention. The creature flapped its wings and pressed itself against the keep's upper walls and roof. And flickering torchlight on the roof revealed a lone figure racing toward the dragon and leaping onto its neck.

Cyran's heart plunged into his bowels. "The Dragon Queen comes!"

Kayom glanced down as Cyran whipped his crossbow around, but the shadow dragon was largely covered by its position on the far side of the keep.

"It is a shadow dragon." Kayom cursed.

Eidelmere picked up speed, and they ascended and banked to the north. The shadow dragon rose over the keep and roared before pursuing them. Cyran wheeled about and took aim, navigating around Eidelmere's tail and waiting until he had a clear shot. But Eidelmere whipped side to side, and Cyran had to correct for each movement. They veered farther north before heading westerly. The shadow dragon mirrored each turn they made, and the other three Murgare dragons now hurtled toward them.

Eidelmere swung around and headed northeast, away from Galvenstone. They flew for several minutes, and the margins of the Evenmeres began to blur beneath them as the shadow dragon's shrieks grew louder.

"We cannot outrun this dragon." Kayom kept glancing over each shoulder as the Dragon Queen somehow rose higher into the sky but also closed the gap between them. "And it doesn't seem like keeping the treetops so close is going to make her lose sight of us."

"They say she can feel any dragon within a league around her," Morden said. "Our flight will only tire Eidelmere before our inevitable confrontation."

Kayom grunted in frustration. "Bring him around."

Eidelmere's flapping slowed, and the dragon swung about in a wide circle and faced their pursuer. They hovered over the boundary of the forest to the northeast of Nevergrace.

"Are you mad?" The lower archer's voice bordered on hysteria. "If Dragon Queen herself rides that beast, we cannot face it in battle."

"I do not intend to fight her." Kayom raised his visor and angled his lance so that its long shaft pointed upward.

The shadow dragon circled them from above before diving downward in a rush of wind. The beast streaked closer.

Cyran tried to find a clear shot around Kayom and Eidelmere.

Just before the shadow dragon rammed into them, the beast raised its wings and braced itself against the wind. It came to a thrashing halt and hovered just before them. The enormous bulk and wings of the dragon made Cyran feel like he rode a pony but was about to joust against a destrier. His mouth went dry like old saddle leather under the summer sun.

"Will you speak with a guard of the Never, Dragon Queen?" Kayom asked in a bold tone.

The Dragon Queen slowly rose in her saddle and stepped from behind her lance and shield. She stalked forward, slipping through the tangle of spikes on the back of her dragon's head, stepping with confidence, as if she knew every scale of her beast and knew exactly where those scales would be as she strode forward. Her dragon's head lowered and tilted. She did not miss a step or slow her pace, and her mount's movements aided her in coming closer, the dragon obeying her every whim. She wore no armor and no visor. Only pale undergarments clung to her hips and chest. Her long brown hair stirred in the wind and streamed out to the side like a banner. She was a tall and svelte woman only several years older than Cyran, maybe in the mid to late third decade of her life.

How can this woman be the infamous Dragon Queen? The Dragon Queen was supposed to be hundreds of years old.

Cyran attempted to keep his bolt trained on her, but Kayom's bulky armor and shield blocked any shot. And Cyran's hands shook. Instead, Cyran aimed at one side of the shadow dragon's enormous head, which extended beyond either side of Kayom's shield and lance.

"You've come to bargain, former guard of Nevergrace?" The Dragon Queen stepped past her dragon's eyes and onto its snout but did not stop her approach until she stood between its nostrils. She folded her arms across her chest. Murgare's other three dragons stopped advancing and hovered in the distance.

"I am here to simply beg you to free the people of the Never," Kayom said.

"Did you bring my queen?"

Kayom hesitated.

"I understand how hard it is for a man of your stature to beg, but the only way I will free any captives and leave this outpost is if my queen is brought to me." Her bronze eyes burned with the same fire that her dragons had unleashed on Nevergrace. "Then my legion and I will fly back to the north."

Kayom's green and gray armor creaked as he shifted in his saddle. "Then I ask you to give us more time before killing any more of our people."

"So you or another with you has not brought my queen. Then, please, tell me why you decided to undertake such great risk and venture out here without the one person I asked Igare to send to me?"

"To save my people. They are brave and hard working. They have—"

"What makes you believe any of them are still alive? And if you haven't come bearing the queen, then you must have flown in with the notion of attacking us, which means you will die. You have only decided to plead now that you've lost your silver and are badly outnumbered."

The shadow dragon's head whipped to the side, and suddenly the Dragon Queen was in full view, remaining as steady as if she walked a well-worn road. Cyran moved to swing his crossbow around, but she turned to regard him. Her bronze eyes burned brighter and widened when she first noticed him, then they narrowed.

"Situations where life and death teeter on the edge of a blade are no place for such a young man," she said. "And you should not ride a dragon with a crossbow trigger in your hand. Stick with horses and swords. Unless you desire to return to your Never and join the north, boy who has fallen from the sky with a dragon."

Cyran's heart leapt into his throat, but his fingers found the trigger handle and began squeezing it. The shadow dragon rolled its head away and bobbed lower, taking the Dragon Queen out of Cyran's view.

"Have you seen my queen, former guard of the Never?" the Dragon Queen asked.

Kayom hesitated again before answering. "Yes."

"Where?"

"At her trial."

"And when was this?"

"Well over a fortnight ago."

"Is she still alive and well?"

Kayom nodded. "Yes."

A minute of silence dragged out between them, and Kayom

shifted again. The Dragon Queen's tone sharpened with animosity. "You lie to me, guard of the Never. Do not doubt I can tell. Such lies lead me to believe my queen is not well, and that possibility angers me. Where is she being kept?"

"I cannot say."

"Then our talk is over, and I fear for my queen's safety. You have come in an attempt to reclaim your outpost and its people utilizing stealth, without an exchange. You leave me no choice. Now prepare yourself, or attempt to flee." The Dragon Queen spun around and stalked back along her dragon's face as the dragon drifted away, moving in sync with her until she took her seat.

"What do we do?" Morden's words came out riddled with terror.

"I will face her." Kayom lowered his visor and grasped his lance, his tone carrying an accepted finality. "We cannot outrun this dragon. Nor her." He leaned forward and braced himself against the lance's mount as he lowered its tip. "Charge that beast. I will unseat the Dragon Queen and we will win the Never back. All I am lies within her walls."

"This is madness." Morden glanced around. "I don't care if Nevergrace is all you have. There *must* be another way." His gaze settled on the angoia copses rising like dark walls in the north. "We could lose her in the angoias. Her dragon is too large, and we ride a forest dragon who once called those woods home."

"We'll never make it," Sir Kayom said. "Prepare Eidelmere! She is coming."

The shadow dragon circled around and streaked toward them without slowing. Cyran's throat felt like strong hands were wrapped around it and strangling him. The words Paltere had shared with him about a dragonknight being able to adjust their mount's movements and speed at any moment while a guard had to work through the middleman of the mage resounded in his head.

Eidelmere's wings snapped and billowed, and they soared straight toward the Dragon Queen. Cyran whirled about in his pivoting frame, once again trying to find a clean shot around Kayom.

Time slowed as the world wheeled around them, the trees spinning, the sky all around them and nowhere. The ground was no longer simply below. The Dragon Queen and her black beast seemed to be everywhere, swinging side to side and dipping and rising all at once. Then their enemy was upon them, and dragon necks bowed. Scaled heads turned aside as lances struck targets and shattered. A thunderous bang sounded when the Dragon Queen's lance clashed with Kayom's shield, the blow exploding his shield into splinters and catapulting the guard over Cyran's head. Kayom's lance made only a glancing blow and shattered against his attacker's shield, causing nothing more than a faint grunt from the Dragon Queen when she absorbed the impact.

Fuck. Cyran squeezed his crossbow's trigger. The dragonbolt screamed through the air over the hunkered mage, and the bolt slammed into the shadow dragon's rising cheek. The beast bellowed and thrashed as it sailed straight upward and curled about. Cyran cranked the windlass, his arm winding against its resistance. His muscles burned when the rope clicked into place, and he yanked another bolt from a bundled stack.

The shadow dragon dived. Cyran hurriedly nocked the bolt.

Their attacker's lance flashed and struck Morden on his side with a hollow thump as Cyran swung the crossbow around. The mage flew away into the night, and the shadow dragon streaked past their side.

We lost our mage... Memories of the dragon Cyran had seen lose its guard and mage flashed before him.

The archer below shouted and loosed, but his bolt sailed too late, missing its target. "Eidelmere is no longer bound to us. He will fling us away."

Cyran tore at the restraints on his harness, his fear-ridden mind hoping that he would not be connected to the quarterdeck when the dragon dropped it. Eidelmere ducked and swooped high over the forest, making for the angoias in the east, his leg rising and tearing at the harnesses and cinches running across his belly. The shadow dragon circled back toward them, and Cyran's throat squeezed shut, not allowing him to breathe against the keening wind.

Eidelmere's erratic movements jerked Cyran back and forth and up and down, throwing him against the end of his harness and off-balance as he struggled to free himself. Then his terror settled a notch. What could he hope to accomplish by releasing his harness? To not be crushed beneath a quarterdeck? A vision of what happened with Vetelnoir—when the dragon crashed—flashed through his mind. But Eidelmere was not plummeting and would not land atop him. He glanced down, the dark mass of pines below looking like a sea. He would never survive the fall. Nor would he survive facing the shadow dragon.

Dragon claws raked at straps. Leather snapped, and the quarterdeck tilted beneath Cyran's feet. His stomach teetered as he leaned far to the dragon's right.

The archer below screamed.

"Stop this, Eidelmere!" Cyran shouted. "You will not throw your last riders." He glanced at the approaching line of angoias. The dragon was on course to barrel into the trees at full speed. And suddenly, Cyran knew where Eidelmere was headed—to his home. Cyran felt each of the dragon's sways and dips and rises differently, perceiving them somewhere deep inside him just as they happened.

"Get out of my head, boy!" Eidelmere's right leg rose, its

blade-like claws flashing as they extended and swung toward Cyran. "My *mëris* is dead, our bond torn and shattered." Cyran seized the dragonbolt from the crossbow and stabbed at the attacking limb. The bolt's tip impaled the closest toe of the forest dragon, and Eidelmere screeched and swung his foot away.

Then the dragon rolled, twisting and turning upside down in a full rotation as he sailed along and climbed higher into the night. Cyran's stomach swung about and landed within his chest and throat like a stone at the end of a twirling sling. The quarterdeck rolled farther to the dragon's side.

"Get off my back." Eidelmere's malevolent voice rang only inside Cyran's head now, vibrating the dome of his skull.

"You will not throw us," Cyran replied in his thoughts, and a ghostly light surfaced in the recesses of whatever world they spoke in, a world that looked like fields of blurring trees and sky. The light swung about and plummeted, trying to avoid Cyran, but he reached out and grabbed it with his thoughts.

"Stay away." Eidelmere spun and dived. "You are not Morden, and I do not particularly like you."

Cyran was jerked back against his harness and bootstraps. The ghostly light appeared like a crevice and was just out of reach, darting and diving around the periphery of the blurred world in Cyran's mind. Eidelmere's wings braced, and they slammed to a halt, the wind grabbing the dragon's wings and lifting them in the opposite direction of their diving force.

But this time Cyran realized he knew what Eidelmere would do, and he knew where the chasm of light they shared would slip away to. He caught it, sinking an ethereal hand into its gap. Tense fibers bowed under his fingers as he grasped around blindly in the light.

Eidelmere shrieked.

Cyran slipped into the crevice. The world around him appeared similar to what he remembered of the area, but it was composed only of shining light and shadow. The glowing dragon dipped and dived, but he knew where it was headed and what it thought to do. A fiber of feeling in his core paralleled the feeling of one of the threads running through the world around him, and he reached and grabbed it. Power surged through his arm, and thoughts and memories exploded in his mind. He released the thread and gasped as Eidelmere cursed him in the words of the elder tongue, which he now understood.

Another fiber pulsed within the dragon beneath him, and Cyran reached through the scales and flesh of the forest dragon and grasped the thread—taut as crossbow rope cocked tight. Cyran's fingers settled into its substance, and Eidelmere raged.

"*Eidelmerendren,*" Cyran said in his mind. "*That is your true name.*" The dragon's tension and fight broke beneath him like water pooling and falling from the sky. "*I hold your true name in the palm of my hand, and I command you to stop.*"

Eidelmere's wings stabilized, and they leveled out into a steady glide over the Evenmeres far from the Never. Cyran heaved a sigh of relief but waited a minute to make sure the dragon did not try anything else before he unfastened his bootstraps.

The Dragon Queen still pursued them, the encompassing silhouette of her dragon swiftly approaching from the south. Cyran unclipped his harness and crawled and then scaled up Eidelmere's neck until he reached Morden's saddle. He took the dragonmage's seat, not knowing how any of this worked. He had no staff, but he reached out and placed his palms against the dragon's scales. A rush of emotion smacked into his chest, as if their two souls collided and intertwined. The dragon realm blazed around him, but Cyran ignored it, focusing on the shadow dragon pursuing them.

A volley of bolts whizzed through the sky. Cyran caught reflective glimpses of the projectiles. From experience, he gauged their trajectories, and instinctively he imagined a course needed to avoid them. Eidelmere banked hard to the left, just as Cyran had imagined. The bolts whistled behind them, narrowly missing their target, but one tore through the tip of Eidermere's tail. The forest dragon wailed and tried to roll, but Cyran held him still.

"You allowed me to take a bolt," Eidelmere said in Cyran's mind. *"I will not forget that."*

"We cannot outrun them, or outshoot them." Cyran's attention settled on the wall of angoias as the shadow dragon closed in behind them.

They raced along for another minute before the Dragon Queen shouted, and the blunt end of her lance lunged for them. Cyran commanded Eidelmere to dive as Cyran slipped his feet into the saddle's stirrups and gripped with his thighs. A dark trail of dragon blood streamed upward in their wake, flying from Eidelmere's tail.

"Our only hope is to use their size against them," Cyran said.

Eidelmere dived low and swung about, his wings like billowing sails as they veered for a gap in the approaching trunks the size of towers. Just before they collided with a tree, Eidelmere swooped vertically and skimmed between the bark of two angoias. The shadow dragon roared in outrage and then shrieked as it tried to slam to a halt, but the beast was traveling too fast and had to swoop aside. It collided with tangles of branches and pale leaves.

Eidelmere dodged and weaved around red trunks, slowing his flight and then bracing with raised wings. They settled to a drifting pace and spiraled downward around a tree to the forest floor.

34

CYRAN ORENDAIN

EIDELMERE CRUNCHED INTO LAYERS OF FALLEN LEAVES AS HE settled onto the ground. A pale dawn lifted in the east, and angoias surrounded them, extending much farther into the heavens than Cyran could see.

The cries of the shadow dragon faded into the distance.

"What do you wish to do now?" Eidelmere asked Cyran aloud this time, his tone filled with sorrow. The dragon's splayed feet clomped through foliage as they walked along. The archer in the turret hadn't made a sound since the Dragon Queen chased them into the woods.

Cyran's mind whirred.

"You could dismount," the dragon said.

"No. Or you will leave us."

"I cannot leave you now. At least not while you remain in my vicinity. And I cannot lie to you. Not to one of the *mëris*."

Cyran's breathing paused, and a cool rush of realization flowed through him. He *was* a dragonmage, one of those rare people who were able to bond with the mystical creatures and ride them. He could not fully comprehend its implications now, but he sensed what Eidelmere said was true. He slid a foot out of

a stirrup and swung himself over to one side. Eidelmere lowered
his head and neck, making it easier for Cyran to dismount. Cyran
only had to lower himself a half a leg's length to reach the ground.

"And why is there so much sadness and pain lingering
around you?" Cyran asked.

"You can feel it—my emotion—in the other realm."
Eidelmere's head hung. "I am now one of the *siosaires*. The lost
ones. One whose soul has experienced the severing of a bond in
both realms. It is a wound and pain that can never fully heal.
Morden is dead, but I will linger on."

A sweeping despair bombarded Cyran, and his heart ached
with sympathy. He'd recently experienced a similar type of loss.
"Does our new bond help ease the pain at all?"

"Our bond is nothing compared to what Morden and I
shared," Eidelmere snapped. But then he pulled back, and his
eyes turned distant. "But your heartfelt sympathy is comforting."
The dragon swallowed, his voice sounding far away. "I knew
what you were the day you came to the den but did not bring me
a meal. It is the only reason I bothered speaking to you. But I did
not want you to realize any of it. And just because we are now
bonded does not mean I accept or even like you." The dragon's
eyes focused and narrowed as he glared at Cyran. "I still despise
you, boy. *And* you allowed me to take a bolt."

Cyran looked up at the dragon's bleeding tail. "But a bolt to
the tail is far better than one to the chest or heart. I will dress the
wound once we arrive somewhere safe."

The archer in the lower turret remained silent, his eyes
gaping, his body paralyzed by fear. His breathing came in
shallow bursts.

"Are you all right?" Cyran asked as he approached.

The archer didn't respond. Cyran gripped one of the poles of
the turret's frame and hauled himself up.

The archer's face snapped around. "Get us out of here. The shadow dragon!" He worked frantically at his bootstraps and then his harness, tearing himself free.

"Calm yourself, my friend." Cyran laid a hand on his shoulder, but the archer leapt away, falling out of the turret and toppling to the ground. Cyran leaned over. The fall had been less than the height of a man.

The archer thrashed about in the pale leaves and screamed before rising and racing away.

"Wait!" Cyran said. "Stop. We are in the angoias. These lands are dangerous."

The archer didn't slow his wheeling legs. He bolted around a trunk and into the swirling reddish mist of the angoias, his crunching footsteps fading into the forest as Cyran climbed down from the turret.

"We have to go after him," Cyran said.

"That would not be wise." Eidelmere turned his head and eyed the trees.

"Because we have to warn Igare of what has happened?" Would the orator and the others believe him this time? Or had the moon dragon escaped and returned to Galvenstone?

"No. Because we roam the angoias. That man is as good as dead."

A chill slithered through Cyran. He remembered he needed to travel away from the sunlight to find the Evenmeres's main trail, but he didn't know if that rule also worked within the angoias. The red mist suffused with pale sunlight and rolled and twined around them.

"But the pines and oaks are just beyond these trunks." Cyran patted the bark of the closest angoia.

"I am too big to travel through areas where such trees grow so—"

A rumble shook the earth, and beyond the mass of angoia trunks, a few pines might have shifted about.

"The rest of the forest is no longer any safer," the dragon said. "Here with me, you may survive."

"I thought I saw the trees move." Cyran pointed. "The same as I did the last time I was in these woods."

"Something stirs in this forest. Something that was not here when I lived beneath its boughs." Eidelmere slowly stepped around an angoia trunk. "It all feels so hostile and angry *and* hungry."

"Then it *is* the trees themselves." Cyran spun a slow circle. "They are alive."

"No. It is not the trees. The pines and angoias are no more alive than any other plant. It is something else. Many somethings."

Cyran drew his elf's sword and ran past the closest angoia to a twisted oak that he believed had shifted position. He ascended a steep incline and heaved for breath as he reached the base of the trunk and asked, "What do you want?"

Only silence greeted him, and he took a swipe at the trunk. His blade sank deep, but the tree did not flinch or make a sound. Cyran tried to yank the sword out, but it was stuck fast.

Damn my foolishness.

He wrenched his weapon back and forth, slowly freeing the blade, and the ground rumbled again. Trees shifted and moved. Cyran yelled in surprise, jerking his sword free before falling and tumbling down the incline. A monstrous crack sounded behind him in the angoias. Wood creaked and groaned. A heavy mass whistled through the air, the sound lingering for many seconds as Cyran crouched and spun about. The whistling ended in a thunderous thud as an angoia toppled and struck another trunk beside it. Cyran ran for cover behind another trunk. The falling tree sheared branches off the other before being deflected aside, its canopy swinging downward and squashing pines and ramming into the earth with a boom that might have carried to the heavens. The ground bucked and rolled in response to the crash, the impact throwing a wave of earth outward and launching Cyran away from the tree he hid behind and into another. He struck the tree with his back, which knocked the wind out of him. The wave and a few trailing ripples in the earth passed on through the forest as decaying leaves and needles that had been thrown into the air drifted back down.

Cyran sat on his backside in a daze, but he imagined the quake reaching the Never, as similar ones had in days past. He rolled to his side and slowly climbed to his feet. "Eidelmere!" He stumbled as he ran past the first angoia trunk, praying the dragon had not fled and abandoned him.

Eidelmere clung to an angoia like a lizard to a rock, his belly pressed against its red bark. His talons raked the wood, and his wings wrapped around the trunk, the claws at the tip of each wing anchored into the tree.

"What are you doing?" Cyran asked.

"We must be wary," the dragon whispered as he scampered up the trunk. "It draws near. And these trunks are too large and are packed too closely together for me to be able to fly well in here."

A melody carried through the trees, and the hair on the back of Cyran's neck prickled.

"Even I am not safe in this place, my natural environment," Eidelmere said. "We should go up. Whatever approaches may not be able to reach us there."

"You mean to scale the angoia?"

"Yes, boy. Hurry. Or I will leave you."

"I can command you now, dragon."

"Yes, but that does not suddenly mean you are wise!" Eidelmere snapped.

Cyran retreated a step as he glanced around. Maybe the dragon was right. "Very well. We shall..."

A light darted around the trunks in the distance, creating flashes as it moved and then faded into the woods. A moment later, it reappeared in another location far from where it had vanished.

Cyran ran to the dragon and clambered up its tail, using its spikes and scales like tree branches and footholds on a stone face. Eidelmere started to ascend the trunk like a cat, or a bat, if bats could climb trees.

"Remove the quarterdeck." Eidelmere paused, and his eyes narrowed as he peered around the woods.

"Sir Kayom says a quarterdeck is worth ten squires and we have to care—"

"Sir Kayom is dead, and I cannot climb fast enough with that thing swinging about and weighing me down."

Cyran scrutinized the tangle of straps and cinches around the dragon's torso. Howls sounded in the distance, and many more answered. These were not the howls of Smoke or other wolves, but of something else entirely. Cyran pulled himself up and along Eidelmere's side, grabbing straps and unlatching buckles as he climbed higher on the dragon. When he released the last cinch, the dragon shook, and the quarterdeck jittered and teetered. It slid off to the side before plummeting downward, its descent ending in many simultaneous cracks as planks and framing wood exploded and broke free.

Cyran scaled the dragon's neck and reached Morden's saddle, where he planted himself in its seat and hunched over like every mage he'd seen. Eidelmere scampered up the massive tree, the size of its trunk compared to them making Cyran feel like Eidelmere was nothing more than a squirrel scrambling up an oak. Soon, they passed above the canopy of the nearby pines. Their ascent continued for ten minutes and then longer, and Eidelmere's ribs heaved with exertion.

"I have not climbed in centuries," Eidelmere said between breaths. "All I do for the Never is slumber in my stall and fly about the countryside. But I once called this forest home. Before men came and captured me. When I was barely more than a hatchling. And I've lived with men ever since. At several castles and through *so* many lords."

Cyran imagined the old dragon as a young and curious creature darting around the trees.

"If there are still other forest dragons living in this wood kingdom, they would reside in the canopy," Eidelmere said. "The forest floor is too full of terrors."

Cyran shivered. What possible horrors could drive even dragons up into the trees?

They finally passed the first branches of the angoias, which jutted out the length of an oak, and each of these would-be oaks had hundreds of branches of their own.

"Wait," Cyran said. He remembered Jaslin had once told him about a tale of a dragon in the old growth forest who had been wounded. The dragons used leaves as bandages. "Can we venture out on that limb?"

Eidelmere turned to eye him. "We should climb higher first."

"It'll only be for a moment."

"You are as unwise as a hatchling." Eidelmere crawled out onto the limb and glanced about before rushing along its length and stopping where it first branched.

Cyran imagined Eidelmere swinging his neck out over the leaves on the closest branch, and the dragon did so. Cyran grabbed the base of a pale leaf that was longer than he was tall. He used his sword to sever its attachment as he held on to the remainder of the stem with his other hand. Once the leaf was cut free, its full weight pulled against him, but it was not enough that he couldn't lift it. Cyran bade Eidelmere to curl his tail forward, and Cyran wrapped the dragon's wound with the leaf, which clung to dragon scale and blood as forcefully as sap to skin.

Eidelmere turned his head to inspect the bandage. "The leaf of the old blood and of dragon fire. It carries healing powers." He eyed Cyran. "A lucky guess, boy. And the wound would not have been there at all if you hadn't let the bolt strike me."

Cyran tried to ignore the dragon's bitterness, feeling a sense of profound sadness still surrounding the creature. He thought distracting the dragon and taking its mind off the cause of its sorrow might make it feel better, like with Jaslin. "Why are your scales green if you once lived in the Evenmeres, which have red bark and pale gray leaves?"

"My ancestors did not evolve in the Evenmeres." The dragon whipped around and bounded back up the limb to the trunk. "They came here after the forest grew. And in times long past, they lived on the forest floor as well as in the canopy."

They climbed higher and higher into the boughs where no dragon could ever fly, not in such dense foliage. Sunlight sifted through the pale leaves around them as the sun hovered over the distant horizon. Cyran caught glimpses of the vast pines and oaks of the Evenmeres sprawling for leagues in all directions, far, far below. The faint outline of the watchtowers of Nevergrace stood against the morning light far to the west, the outpost residing between their current location and Galvenstone. That was the direction they had to travel while avoiding all of Murgare's watching dragons. Cyran shuddered. How beautiful this world was, and yet how horrific.

Memories of the failed scouting expedition flooded Cyran. He saw images of the Dragon Queen and of the silver dragon and its guard who gave their party away. *Sir Kayom...* He silently vowed to avenge the death of his guard-master.

By the afternoon, they reached the even denser canopy of the angoia, and clouds drifted beyond its red-stemmed branches. The sky sea was probably not much farther above them.

"Where are you taking me?" Cyran asked.

"West. Toward Nevergrace and Galvenstone." Eidelmere scampered out onto a branch. When he neared the end of the bough, he leapt into the air and let his wings snap open. But he didn't flap his wings. He simply glided along, steering them until he landed on a branch of the adjacent angoia. The dragon ran along the bough, past the trunk, and out onto another branch pointing west. He leapt again and sailed to the next tree.

"The life of a *mëris* is not an easy one." Eidelmere's ever-present resentment lightened, and as he climbed and glided, his voice took on a different air. In a few instances, he did not even sound angry or resentful. And the overwhelming feeling of sorrow that lingered around him eased a little as he moved. "But dragons do not wish to take part in the wars of man. We only became linked to your kind because of the first taming on Frozen Fist Mountain, where a barbarian of the north and his crippled boy, who wielded a power similar to yours, discovered how to enter the dragon realm. Word spread after that event. And it all eventually led to the great Dragon Wars of the past age, an age when these woods were not here and the shining city of Cimerenden sprawled across the area."

Cyran glanced behind them, trying to imagine these dense and dark woods as something else, but the size of the trees made it impossible for him to believe anything else—especially a city —could have resided here.

"A century before the Dragon Wars began, the drag-onguard were developed." Eidelmere spoke as he ran through the trees like a much younger dragon and glided, sometimes traveling farther distances than needed before landing again. "The dragonguard were the peacekeepers of all the lands. North and south. Those who united against common evils. But some began to disagree on what or who should be considered evil. Then the great wars raged, and afterward, Cimerenden was no more. The divide between those who fought for and against the elves of the shining city ran too deep. The guard has never healed. Now they wage war and hunt each other across the kingdoms. And they will continue to do so till the end. Or till the last of your humankind dies or departs Cimeren forever."

The weight of such a history, one Cyran had only heard parts of before, and its implications fell upon him like a boulder. But were the other parts true? "You allege that the north was once aligned with Belvenguard?" His forehead contorted with disbelief. "And their dragonguard fought alongside ours? I cannot fathom that."

"Because of their recent attack on Nevergrace?"

"Because of everything I've ever heard about them and their twisted ways."

Eidelmere remained silent for a minute before continuing, "After the Dragon Wars, some of the guard grew greedier and took more and more dragons from the lands, seeking ultimate power through control of my kind. The guard began to battle over dragons, fighting for certain types they believed held advantages over others. And kingdoms allowed rulers who were more domineering and better able to influence the guard to reign. Now the dragonguard is nothing more than a blade for whatever kings sit on the thrones, the Evenmeres and the Lake on Fire the great dividers between once connected lands."

The tale spun some web of awe inside Cyran. Much of it sounded familiar, like something Jaslin had once read and kept telling him about over and over again when they were children. But no adult had ever confirmed some of those details.

"Your blood is that of a *mëris*," Eidelmere said, "but you should never take up the dragonsteel sword or lance of the guard, or you will never be able to go back."

Cyran's heart split along its base and spilled its dreams. *But to become a guard is all I ever wanted.*

"Your father was one of the guard, but not a *mëris*." Eidelmere ripped a hunk of bark off an angoia as he clambered around its trunk. He chewed the bark and seemed to savor memories, the look in his eyes turning more distant, his voice beginning to sound as if it were farther away. "But your father was killed during an attack when you would have been very young. Your mother was taken prisoner and later killed with many others, not too many years after your sister was born."

Cyran nearly fell out of his saddle, his mind swarming with disbelief. "I was told my mother got sick and died of the summer scourge. And that my father was already dead when I was born." Cyran swallowed. "And how do you supposedly know so much about my family?"

"A dragon who has lived for centuries has heard and knows many things, including details of the lives of specific people who resided at the same castle as that dragon."

Cyran's attention settled on Kayom's saddle sitting empty before him. His gaze strayed to the shattered mount meant for a lance, but no weapon was attached to it. Kayom's shield was gone, having splintered to fragments. Only a simple sheath remained on the saddle, its leather strapped near to where Kayom's left thigh would have been. But the sheath was also empty.

"He preferred to carry his blade at his waist," Eidelmere said.

"Sir Kayom?"

"Yes. I feel your longing to wield his blade and take no heed of my warning. The sword would have been with him when he fell, and we are headed in that direction now." Eidelmere sniffed the wind and seemed to ponder something. He leapt into the open air and filled his wings with sky before spiraling downward.

The vast expanse of Belvenguard carried as far to the south and east and west as Cyran could see. There were roads and fields with patches of trees and hamlets and villages.

"But if we find what you seek, you must make your decision quickly," Eidelmere said. "And you must act even faster."

"What do you mean?"

"You may come to see."

They landed along the boundary where the angoia copses were bordered by more typical trees. Eidelmere snaked around trunks, sniffing the ground until he stopped cold.

"There." The dragon gestured with a flick of his head. "Dismount."

Cyran did so and advanced. Something white lay against the base of a pine. As he approached, it became apparent this white thing was a skeleton, reminiscent of the one he'd seen after his last unwanted fall into the Evenmeres.

"Why did you take me here?" Cyran turned back.

"Hurry!" Eidelmere glanced around.

A distant melody emerged, slipping through the darkness of the deeper woods. Cyran swallowed his doubts and rushed to the skeleton, unsure of what he was supposed to see or do. The skeleton had no remaining flesh, no blood. There were no organs or remnants of clothing or armor. How long had it been here? Years? Decades? But again, its bones were not dried and cracked.

Cyran froze. A sheath rested beside the body. The belt it should have been strapped to was gone, as if whatever had done this had stripped the body of everything touching it. But it had left the man's sheath unspoiled. Cyran grabbed the sheath and slid its end out of a pile of leaves. It held a longsword as tall as any he'd seen. An intricately crafted hilt with golden filigree and swirling runes protruded. His fingers slowly reached for the hilt, but he hesitated, recalling everything Eidelmere had just told him about the guard.

"Your decision must be quick," Eidelmere snapped.

A howl sounded off in the distance, and similar calls answered from different areas of the woods.

"This is Sir Kayom." Cyran's words barely caught and formed in his throat as disbelief swirled through him. "The skeleton is Sir Kayom."

"He was dragged here. By now, the archer who ran off is in the same state. Decide! Unless you wish to join them."

Cyran grasped the hilt and unsheathed the blade, holding it before him. Steel forged with dragon scale shimmered beneath the boughs. It was The Flame in the Forest, the blade of Sir Kayom. And it glowed with green light, the color of a forest dragon.

35

CYRAN ORENDAIN

CYRAN STARED AT THE SKELETON FOR A MOMENT, TRYING TO comprehend that these could be Sir Kayom's bones. Had the same thing happened to Rilar, the wounded farmhand the squires were bringing to Galvenstone? That man's bones might also be lying in the Evenmeres. Something could have dragged the unconscious farmhand out of the litter and into the woods. Or maybe Rilar's disappearance had to do with the wound that had been found on his head, and he was taken by the forest after disappearing from an inn some merchant had brought him to. Cyran had heard that tale from the merchants in the caravan that traveled along the Scyne Road. He rubbed at the wooden merchant's ring he'd received.

A ball of light flashed through the trees, and a familiar foreboding and yet joyous melody returned. The light floated in place for a spell, and Cyran could only stare in wonder. It bobbed and darted back and forth, as if it were attempting to communicate with Cyran or draw him closer. He recalled seeing a similar light behind what might have been a cloaked figure who burned with purple flame when he and his squire friends traveled to Galvenstone.

His leg extended of its own accord, but this time he caught himself and fought against something inside him that desired to drive him on. He paused, but the music continued.

The song Tamar was humming before he died. And then Jaslin had started humming it. Whatever this light was, it probably had something to do with Tamar's death.

"I will not follow you," Cyran muttered. "Reveal yourself."

The light flickered and dropped, falling into the undergrowth like a stone. The forest fell silent. Cyran cocked his head. Howling echoed through the trees, and the cries quickly drew closer. Cyran turned for Eidelmere.

"I told you, your decision had to be quick and your action even quicker." The dragon waited in the distance, hunched against the base of a trunk, his eyes wild with panic. "They have already arrived."

Fear spiked Cyran's blood. Footsteps crunched through the vegetation around them, and Eidelmere was not close. Cyran gripped The Flame in the Forest in both hands, and its green glow intensified as he sprinted for the dragon.

A dark figure hovered in the undergrowth off in the distance, watching. A smoldering purple glow showed behind them, but their face was partially visible... And something about this figure was familiar, although Cyran wasn't sure whom it reminded him of.

Something caught Cyran's ankle and tripped him, sending him sprawling into the brush and fallen leaves. He rolled onto his back to defend himself. The foliage shifted all around him as things moved beneath leaf and stem, the waves created by their movements racing closer.

Cyran climbed to a knee. A sharp pain bit into the back of his calf, and he cried out and wheeled around, swiping with this blade. His sword sliced through something, and a distorted head sailed away and sank into the foliage. A short body collapsed beneath the bracken.

"What are they?" Cyran asked as more footsteps tore through the brush around him.

"Something that shouldn't live under these boughs." Eidelmere swung his tail around, whipping at the plants. Cries and wails, as well as what sounded like the snapping of teeth, created a jarring tumult, but whatever created the din remained hidden.

Cyran rushed for the dragon again, but the undergrowth between them wavered. He could make out small portions of creatures lurking in the bracken, tusks and rows of sharpened teeth, beady eyes, wrinkled gray skin. Jagged blades gripped in hands with long black nails.

Cyran's limbs trembled. He'd sparred with various peoples, and now he'd even killed two men and hit a shadow dragon with a bolt, but he'd never faced things so unnatural and monstrous. And the dark figure still watched. The creatures rushed in, stabbing with their weapons, their massive jaws threateningly chomping at the air. Cyran dodged a strike and severed the arm of one of the creatures before swinging a backhand and beheading another. But more took their places, and the brush swarmed with them. The monsters closed in behind him, and Cyran unsheathed his elven sword. He reached out with both blades and spun and took quick swipes to keep the lot of them at bay.

"Eidelmere!" Cyran said. "There are too many."

"We must climb," Eidelmere answered in Cyran's head as the dragon clawed and smashed the creatures with his wings. He leapt onto the trunk of the closest angoia, a dozen of the creatures clinging to his limbs and biting his scales. The dragon roared in pain as he scuttled upward so that only his tail hung

down and beat at the monsters. He shook, and most of the beasts gripping onto him were flung from his body.

Cyran stopped his rotations and ran straight for Eidelmere, chopping down foliage and creatures as he went. The point of a dagger stuck him in the thigh. He cleaved the attacking monster in two, The Flame in the Forest slicing through its flesh as easily as slicing through cream. Another's sword sliced across his stomach, but his chainmail kept the edge of the blade from cutting him. Only the sharp punch of its impact landed in his guts. Cyran cut off that creature's leg with a single slice from his elven blade, the weapon's edge keen but carrying less weight and force behind it than Kayom's sword. The monster toppled over and thrashed about. Cyran parried two strikes and killed a few more creatures, both of his blades hewing through their weapons when they tried to block his attacks. Another score of creatures took each dead one's place, their blades hacking and jabbing.

Cyran would not make it to the angoia. He cursed and glanced back for the nearest oak. Could he scale a tree and avoid them? Or would they simply wait him out? He cut down three more creatures, stabbing one through the eye, but he took a bite to the back of his leg. If only his dragon could breathe fire...

He paused for an instant and imagined Eidelmere unleashing his watery breath. Then he commanded the dragon to do so through the other realm. Eidelmere sucked in a heaving breath and snaked his head around before blasting out a river that swept through the undergrowth in a line just to the side of where Cyran stood. The deluge knocked the bracken flat, and creatures were hurled aside or thrown over.

Cyran ran along the sopping wet trail that had been cleared, swiping along both sides before sheathing his elven blade and leaping up onto Eidelmere's vertically hanging tail. He cut two monsters from the dragon's leg and scaled the dragon just as he had when Eidelmere tried to throw him and the other archer.

The monsters howled below them and snapped their tusks and teeth. The dark figure glided closer.

"Climb." Eidelmere scampered up the trunk. Cyran breathed a sigh of relief, but a half-dozen balls of light whirled out of the trees and flew at them. Cyran commanded Eidelmere to lift his tail so that he could stand on its now horizontal length. He swiped at the lights, but they darted aside, their eerie melody still humming around them. *"Faster."*

One of the lights swung around and hit Cyran on the shoulder and whizzed away. Pain lanced up his arm. A gaping hole with what appeared to be teeth marks had torn through his chainmail. He used the flat of his blade to swat at the rest of the lights as Eidelmere rapidly ascended.

One light struck Eidelmere on the flank, and the dragon growled and hissed. "Keep them off me."

Cyran swung his sword, and his blade struck a ball of light but glanced off. The light darted away, seemingly unharmed. Cyran curtailed his surprise and switched out his swords in hopes that the elven blade would prove more deadly for this new foe. Another light whisked around his head, and he pretended not to notice it until it darted in for a strike. Cyran's coiled arm snapped up and sliced the ball in half. Its light winked out, and something dropped, something very small but with dragon-like wings and large teeth.

Either the tiniest dragon the world has ever seen or a corrupted fairy unlike any of those in Jaslin's stories. But it had been susceptible to the elven blade, not dragonsteel. After the one light fell, the others whizzed away into the woods.

The dark figure glided closer to the base of the tree, and their face again struck some chord of recognition in Cyran. But Cyran's gaze was drawn to something else. Under an oak beyond the horde of monsters, another shadowed man in a cloak stood there watching, tongues of purple flame writhing across his shoulders. This figure was much taller than the first. Cyran's bones chilled and trembled.

The taller figure's flames crackled as he shrieked and spoke in a hollow and yet deafening voice that blasted inside Cyran's head. *"These woods are my kingdom."*

Cyran winced and clutched at his ears. Eidelmere's cry of alarm inside Cyran's head immediately followed, and the dragon's legs moved faster. Behind the figure, the trees shifted—but this time Cyran noticed the ground beneath the trees. The earth and soil rolled about in a wave, like the one caused by the quake of the falling angoia. But this time it formed a weaving line.

Something enormous moves beneath the forest floor.

The taller burning figure floated across the bracken to the base of the angoia and touched a spectral hand to its trunk. The bark ignited in violet fire.

"Eidelmere!" Cyran shouted.

"I feel it." The flames leapt up the trunk, pursuing them and rising faster than the forest dragon could climb. Eidelmere cleared the canopy of the typical forest, and the monsters vanished beneath the boughs. Flames licked at the dragon's tail. Eidelmere gasped and pushed off the tree. He unfurled his wings, catching the wind and gliding over to the adjacent angoia. Purple fire raced up the trunk they had been climbing, charring the red bark and causing it to curl and wither as it blackened. But the fire did not spread to the trees around it. Eidelmere's heart thumped in Cyran's ears through the other realm, and the rate of its beating began to slow.

But Eidelmere did not stop climbing. Blood drained from a few areas on the dragon's legs and tail, and Cyran used his waterskin to wash them clean.

"Those little biters have wicked teeth," Eidelmere said in Cyran's

mind, the dragon's breathing too ragged to speak aloud. *"They can chew clean through dragon scale and likely Sir Kayom's dragon-armor, but their bite carries no venom. Forest feeders—I heard the term centuries ago, but back then they were only myth."*

Forest feeders. Cyran washed out his own wounds, stopping when he came to the one on his shoulder that had torn through his chainmail and leather tunic and bruised but did not break his skin. "And why do you mention venom?"

"Because I can feel it coursing through my blood. From the bite of... what I shall simply call the dragon fae—those of the dancing lights."

"There is poison in the fae's bite?" Cyran inspected his wound closer. "Will you live?"

"Forest dragons are immune to almost all poisons and venoms, as we evolved in the woods where so many types are prevalent. Immune to all the poisons I know with the exception of the venom in a shadow dragon's barbed tail. I will not fall unconscious."

"Unconscious? And why do you suspect that would be the outcome?"

"I can feel the venom's dirty fingers trying to knead my mind. If I were not immune, it would put me into a deep sleep where it would corrupt my conscience before allowing me to wake."

Cyran examined the sheared links of his chainmail again and the toothmarks running along the bite's edges. The same mark that Rilar had on his scalp. If the dragon fae had punctured Cyran's skin, he would probably be unconscious by now. And later, he might wake only to wander off or sneak away.

"I wish I would have kept one of the forest feeders' limbs, or the body of a dragon fae." Cyran wiped off his elven blade and sheathed it. "I will probably need to show Igare's council—particularly Riscott—something to receive support in defending against what we now know lurks in the Evenmeres."

"It is indeed much more than brigands of the north." Eidelmere's clawed wings hauled them upward as his legs took long sweeping strides, and his talons raked and shredded the bark. "But we can always take a souvenir during our next encounter with the creatures."

Cyran scoffed as he climbed up the dragon's back, using scales and spikes like a ladder. "I sure hope there is no next time. Did you notice the earth moving behind that burning figure?"

"I felt its rumble in the other realm."

"And what do you believe lurks beneath the moving trees?" Cyran slipped into the mage's saddle.

"I do not have any inkling."

"And what about the burning man?"

"The rumble from whatever lies beneath the earth was nothing compared to the voice of the *radengúr*, one of the Harrowed."

A tingling cold jolted down Cyran's spine. *The Harrowed.* He thought Jaslin might have mentioned that name at one time. "What are they?"

"I do not know. They are more akin to your kind than mine. But he is something I hope to never encounter again, even if I should live another five hundred years."

"I thought I recognized something about the first figure." Cyran's turbulent brain rolled through memories, and he recalled someone he'd just thought of. *Rilar.* He swallowed and took a deep breath to steady his voice. "I know who the smaller of the two figures is."

36

CYRAN ORENDAIN

Darkness swept across the sky around Cyran and Eidelmere, who walked the upper branches of the angoias. The Flame in the Forest was sheathed against Cyran's waist, but the blade seemed to pulse with a life of its own.

Cyran's thoughts had run rampant for hours with memories of the creatures in the woods and of Rilar and how the man had disappeared from the litter they escorted to Galvenstone. Now the man was something else entirely, part of what haunted the Evenmeres. And all of those things that were involved in the haunting terrified Cyran. He clenched his jaw. He could not dwell on this. Not now. The fate of his people still balanced on the edge of a blade. He could delve into the other matter once Nevergrace and its people were again safe and under the control of Belvenguard. Then those of the Never could all focus on what lurked in the Evenmeres.

"We must return to the outpost," Cyran said.

"I thought you wanted to travel to Galvenstone and inform the king of what has transpired at Nevergrace." Eidelmere settled onto an outer branch, and they overlooked the world of twilight so far below. The sorrow lingering around the dragon lay just as thick as it had when Cyran first sensed it, but the dragon hid it well, burying his pain under a mountain of bitterness and twining fear related to what they had recently seen.

"I do. But if there's a chance that Jaslin and my friends are still alive, I have to try to save them. After I went down on Vetelnoir, I returned to the outpost without waking a dragon. But at that time, the need to warn the kingdom was much more pressing than my need and the huge risk of me alone trying to help those inside a castle overrun with dragons."

Eidelmere grumbled. "This is another unwise decision."

"But you must do what I wish."

A dark cloud passed over the connection between Cyran's soul and the dragon's in the blurred world of the dragon realm. "I wish you would have never been able to discover my true name," the dragon said.

Cyran winced in response to the resentment in the dragon's tone.

Eidelmere leapt from the bough and soared out over the Evenmeres, riding wind currents and slowly drifting west toward the faint torchlight of Nevergrace. As they circled and sailed lower, thoughts and mixed emotions over all that had happened returned and exploded in Cyran's mind. It became a tangled mess he would not be able to sort out for days— commanding Eidelmere, Sir Kayom's death, an encounter with the Dragon Queen, a host of monsters in the Evenmeres. But Jaslin and his friends and people might still need him. That thought remained paramount and surfaced above all the others.

"I sense a vast pain inside you, along with a maelstrom of other emotions," Eidelmere said in Cyran's mind, his bitterness only slightly lessened.

"And I can also feel yours. I am sorry for it all."

Eidelmere fell silent and turned distant as the night swirled around them.

After an hour of gliding through dark skies, Eidelmere settled onto a field just west of the Never and said, "I will be ready to fly to Galvenstone as fast as my old bones will carry us, as I suspect I will soon see you running away from the outpost as quickly as you can. But if you do not return because you have died, I will be free of you, and for that I will thank the Dragon."

Cyran ignored the comment and tugged off his chainmail. His finger slipped through the gaping hole in its shoulder, and he dropped it on the ground.

"You cast aside the closest thing you have to scales." Eidelmere's brow steepled over his eye.

"I don't want a repeat of what happened with the silver. Steel armor under moonlight seems like a bad idea for sneaking around. And if I am seen, a suit of chainmail will not save my life." Cyran gripped the hilts of both his swords, which he now wore strapped across his back, and he stooped over as he jogged toward the outpost. The night was dark, only a few shades lighter than the previous night. The fields he crossed were blanketed in shadow, and he stepped in several holes as he ran, mildly twisting one of his ankles. When he neared the mist-covered front gates of the Never, he darted for the outer wall and pressed himself against its stones. After listening for any voices or footsteps and hearing nothing, he stalked closer to the entrance. Would a single day's passing since the scouting mission had gone awry be enough for the north to have relaxed their watch? If not, he prayed the Murgare dragons would be tired and sleeping. At least with the scouting mission, King Igare would be able to surmise what had happened if neither Cyran nor any of those sent with him returned to Galvenstone. And the moon dragon might have fled to Dashtok.

Cyran peeked through the archway, but swirling mist backlit by firelight obscured the interior. No sounds or voices carried out. The Never now felt more akin to a dragon's lair—the abode of an evil dragon lord. Cyran shivered. But the mist would also aid him, a lone man attempting to slip into the outpost unseen.

Something moved in the fog, and Cyran froze. A lone sentry paced under the far side of the archway. Cyran cursed under his breath. He could try to kill the man and hope no other soldiers or dragons heard him, but his prowess as a would-be assassin was probably lacking. Certainly his skill in that arena would not come close to matching his aptitude with the sword.

He plucked a stone from the ground and lobbed it into the air. It struck the outer wall across the way and clunked, and the shadow of the sentry slipped closer and then turned to investigate the sound. After taking a deep breath and slowly expelling it, Cyran slipped through the archway. The stones of the gateway dragged along his left side, tugging at his tunic and giving off a cold all their own. On the other side of the arch, he pressed his back to the wall and slid out of the densest portion of the mist. Torchlight flickered at intervals along the outer curtain. Dragons —only outlined by moonlight—sat on the battlements. None of them moved.

Cyran stalked along the perimeter of the wall with his back pressed against the stones. The outer bailey's quiet was broken by the occasional soft grunt of a pig or cluck of a chicken as he passed. He darted from behind an overturned cart to a pile of hay and then to an animal pen. None of the houses along the outer curtain were occupied, and he only spotted a couple archers atop the walls. He stooped over and dashed across the bailey, then wedged himself between a forge and heap of horseshoes that had been piled against the inner curtain.

After waiting to make sure no cries of alarm followed, he prowled about and found the entryway to the inner bailey, its gates also gone, the stones blackened. Nearby, the doors to the stables lay open, their wooden faces charred. No horses mingled about in the paddocks. Hay and water hung as if they had been abandoned at a moment's notice, but not a single horse remained. If he'd attempted to slip into the outpost the last time he was here, it probably would have been for naught.

He stepped through the smaller archway of the inner curtain and repeated his process of mashing himself to the wall and traversing the perimeter, using wood piles and crates to hide behind.

A pale dragon slept outside the keep, just beyond a lighted window, its bulk rising and falling with each raspy breath. The beast's tail curled around to the keep's entrance, where two archers waited. Light streamed through the glass or shutters of most of the windows in the lower keep. Some of the chambers in the upper keep were lighted as well. But it didn't matter—with an ice dragon and archers on watch, Cyran would never be able to make it inside without being noticed. His heart turned brittle and almost shattered. Jaslin and his friends could be in there. Some of his people could still be alive. But without a lot more people aiding him, or some other skillset at his disposal, he was wasting precious time. His best option would be to fly to the Summerswept Keep as fast as Eidelmere could take him. Then he could return with a legion.

"Wait," Eidelmere's voice sounded in his head.

Cyran paused. *"I can hear you."*

"That is because we are not far apart in your world." The dragon grumbled something incomprehensible. *"I feel... obligated to make you aware of something that may interest you. I smell a strange scent coming from what I believe must be the den's entrance. It is something that was not there when the outpost was under Belvenguard's control. Not when I resided in that hole. And it is most likely arising from something inside the den. The shadow dragon may be... I cannot tell what it is. I can only smell an off scent in this realm and the other. I believe I should know what the scent represents, but I was not long with the wild before I was tamed by man."*

Cyran hunted for the den's opening. Only a small portion of it was visible around a corner of the keep. *"There is nothing I can do about it either way. There are dragons everywhere in here."*

"I can draw her out. The shadow dragon. She must be in the den. Murgare would not allow all their dragons to leave the castle, but some will. And there are plenty of places out here where a forest dragon can hide."

Cyran turned for the outer gates. *"We need to return to Galvenstone. There's a chance we could still save some of my people."*

"It is your choice. But I do not know if this thing will still be present or in the same state when we return."

Cyran hesitated. *"Is this some kind of trick to try to kill me off?"*

Eidelmere groaned. *"I almost wish it were, but our souls are bonded. And although I can despise you, I cannot lie to you or do you harm. I have already explained this."*

"And what is stopping you?"

"It is the law of the dragon realm, and we dragons still uphold our oaths. Also, it is harmful to both bonded souls when one dies."

Cyran glanced at the den's entrance and crept around so he could visualize it more clearly. *"What could possibly be in there besides more dragons?"*

"I do not know. But it carries a very strange odor. It could be the result of bone and earth magic. Or a new lair of some kind. Dragon treasure or an artifact. I do not know why, but I believe it is of enough consequence that it could affect any counterattack we bring to the outpost."

Cyran gritted his teeth.

"If you do not wish to investigate, I will await your arrival," Eidelmere said.

"No." Cyran's fist closed around the hilt of The Flame in the Forest. *"If you can safely draw the shadow dragon out, I will try to sneak down there and have a look."*

The hooting of a forest dragon sounded from a distance. The

dragons on the walls grunted and groaned as they shifted and rose from sleeping postures. The mist dragon shrieked, and Cyran clamped his hands over his ears as he trembled. The ice dragon beside the keep stirred, flicking its tail and rising to its feet. The distant dragon call sounded again.

A roar erupted and vibrated the stones of the castle. Cyran pressed his back to the wall and slid down into a crouch. None of the three dragons on the battlements or the ice dragon on the keep had roared. Footsteps pounded and echoed, carrying up from the den. The head of a beast emerged from the opening, its black scales glistening under firelight. Its pupil within a blood-red eye narrowed as it flashed around. The shadow dragon growled and had to contort its wings and shoulders in order to slip from Nevergrace's den. Then its wings swung outward, the leather monstrosities flapped, and the beast lifted itself from the grounds of the Never. It circled the keep and landed on the keep's roof. Stone creaked and groaned beneath its massive weight, and the dragon roared again as it glanced around.

"If you plan to slip into the den, you best do so now," Eidelmere said.

"If you can somehow sense that the shadow dragon is returning to the den, you will *again make the hooting call of the forest dragon, or whatever sound you think will best grab its attention. And you will do so as loud as you can to try to draw that beast out of the Never."*

"Of course. But I cannot sense where she goes. I simply saw her on top of the keep. And I didn't see her on the walls prior."

Cyran's hands shook on the hilts of his swords as he hurried for the den. After he slipped through the shadows hugging the base of the walls, the den's opening loomed before him. A strange odor he'd never smelled before wafted up from below. The closest thing he could relate it to was something he'd experienced with horses, but he couldn't even recall what that something was.

He ducked as he darted into the den, slipping into its darkness. His footsteps sounded louder than they ever had before, although he stepped as lightly as possible.

This is a terrible idea.

Cyran glanced back to the entryway where guttering torchlight crawled inside in faint wisps. If the shadow dragon returned through that opening, he would be trapped down here with no way out. The rumble and roars of dragons resumed outside, and he turned and dashed down the incline. The walkway to the harnessing chamber led to his left, the passage to the stalls to his right. The off smell came from the direction of the stalls.

When he entered the passage, darkness engulfed him, and terror flailed its many-headed whips at his insides. He froze, recalling his encounters with the forest dragons down here. *Eidelmere...*

"I do not await you in the den." Eidelmere's voice echoed in Cyran's mind, and he jolted. *"And there should not be any more dragons down there, if that worry is why your fear has escalated."*

"But I cannot see." Cyran spun around. *"I will have to go for a torch, and that may signal the end of this venture."*

"You chose the sword, remember? I gave you a choice. Either to take it from the woods and wield it or to leave it all behind."

The Flame in the Forest. Cyran drew his blade, and its green glow flared, driving the darkness back and chewing at its margins. But the green hue couldn't contend with all the shadows, and its light fell pale upon the mangled gates of each stall. He peeked into the first stall—nothing more than straw and leaves piled into a dragon bed. He searched each stall as he went, leading with his sword as he crept into them. And because his light did not travel far, he had to walk the outer edges of each stall to make sure no treasure or artifact was hidden.

When he approached the last few stalls, he hadn't found

anything out of the ordinary. But near the end of the den, blackened stones had spilled out onto the walkway, and the last three
stalls had their walls torn out, which combined them into a
single enclosure. Cyran's breathing deepened, and his scalp
tingled. This was the bed of the beast—the Dragon Queen's
shadow dragon. Cyran envisioned where the dragon had
padded around in these past weeks, where it had lain and slum-
bered. The bed in this stall had raised edges composed of straw
and wood that were piled as high as his chest. He shuffled
forward. If only he could incapacitate or kill this evil dragon
somehow... Maybe he could leave a poison for it to ingest.

He peered over the edge of the bed and gasped, and the
sound of his voice rang off the walls. Inside the bed lay a nest of
eggs. Eggs the size of barrels. And scales as black as the shadow
dragon's armored each egg.

"*What is it?*" Eidelmere asked.

Cyran did not respond.

"*Your surprise is flooding our link in the other realm.*" Eidelmere's
tone carried a bitter anticipation that pierced his deep sadness.

Cyran glanced back toward the opening of the stall and then
in the direction of the den's entrance. He waited, listening.
Nothing sounded. He climbed over the side of the nest and
lowered himself until he stood amongst the eggs.

Nine eggs. One for each of the gods. Nine chances at birthing
beasts of pure evil, those Belvenguard had outlawed due to their
inherent danger. And if these eggs hatched, the north would
raise shadow dragons in Nevergrace. Terror lashed at him again.
Cyran did not know how long it took for a dragon to hatch, but if
Murgare maintained control of the outpost for long enough and
reared these creatures, the Dragon Queen could grow so
powerful that it would be impossible to drive her out of the
Never. Cyran didn't want to kill dragons. He especially did not
wish to participate in slaughtering baby ones still in their eggs,

but the risk to the outpost and all of Belvenguard was too great. These evil dragons would grow up to aid his enemies.

Cyran slashed an egg, his dragonsteel sword hewing through the outer scales and rending shell and membranes. A gelatinous yellow substance with black streaks spilled out as the egg was cloven in two. Most of the inner bulk oozed out and pooled over the straw before soaking through, leaving behind the curled fetus of a dragon the size of a melon. The fetus was black tinged, and rubbery scales ran the length of its back. It didn't move, didn't breathe.

Cyran struggled to hold back a rising tide of bile that climbed his throat. He steadied himself and hacked through the next egg and the next, spilling their foul contents. After eight eggs had been destroyed, he spun to face the last one, a smaller egg wedged under the rim of the nest's wall. He waded through the contents of the nest—straw soaked with dragon egg yolks and albumin. He loomed over the final egg and raised his sword over his head, poising himself to hew the last of the evil birthed in the den. But he stopped.

Now that the eggs didn't outnumber him so badly, this last smallest one—less than half the size of the others—didn't feel as threatening, and many of its scales were discolored. He mulled over its existence. It reminded him of Smoke, the runt of the litter, the smallest but the friendliest. Was there any chance he could raise such a dragon as his own? And could a dragon with wicked tendencies be trained for good? He ran a hand over the scales on the egg's surface, each one as lined and detailed as those on a dragon, reminiscent of the rings of a felled tree. Such markings must hold some significance or tell a story he could not comprehend.

His hand paused. Initially he'd thought this runt of an egg had a speckling of discolored scales amidst the black ones, but the other scales were actually a dark green... forest green.

"What is it?" Eidelmere's voice rang in Cyran's head again.

Cyran squatted and picked up the egg, able to carry it before him in his curled arms while still holding on to his sword. All the other eggs around him were sliced open but not destroyed. He double-checked, and he could not find a green scale on any of the others.

"The Dragon curse you, boy." Eidelmere's vitriol mounted. *"What do you keep from me?"*

Cyran set the egg down and hewed all the others into fragments, so hopefully no one would be able to tell that the smallest was missing. Then he hefted the intact egg again. A roar sounded from above, from near the den's entrance.

Cyran froze, almost dropping the egg and urinating in his leggings. Echoing footsteps mixed with the screech of claws scraping on stones. After experiencing another second of pure terror, Cyran attempted to scramble up the walls of the nest, his legs flailing and his chest pressed against the egg. He tore his way to the top, and there, the egg slipped from his arms and rolled over the lip.

Cyran gasped and lunged for the egg, but it was too late. The egg dropped and bounced off the side of the nest before striking the stone floor. It rolled off into the darkness. Cyran clambered down the nest and charged in the direction it had rolled. His green light washed across the egg, and he ran a hand over its scales.

Still intact.

After quickly probing around and not finding any cracks in the shell, he scooped up the egg and raced for the walkway. Another roar sounded, and his knees buckled. He would never make it out of the den.

"Make the call," he said to Eidelmere.

"You wish for me to help you, but you do not share in our bond and answer my questions."

"*Please!*"

Eidelmere did not respond.

"*I command you.*" He felt a rift of light around him and reached into it with his mind, grasping at the thread he knew contained Eidelmere's true name.

Faint hooting sounded outside and carried into the den. The steady thud of dragon footsteps slowed and then stopped. Outside, more dragons shrieked.

A long moment passed as Cyran stood on the walkway, holding his breath.

The hooting called out again. More dragons shrieked and shook the ceiling overhead as they lumbered about the bailey. Dirt rained down on Cyran's head. Wings beat the air, and dragons likely flew away to investigate.

The shadow dragon's footsteps then resumed, not traveling away but continuing down the incline.

Cyran leaned against the wall as he glanced around. He dashed along the walkway, decreasing the gap between him and the shadow dragon. He would never be able to slip into the harnessing chamber without the dragon seeing him from the rampway. When he reached the first stall, he ducked inside, sheathed his sword, and covered himself and the egg with straw, hoping to hide their smells.

The slow and steady scraping of claws on stone drew closer. The footsteps reached the lower landing, and they shifted and came toward the stalls. Cyran clamped his eyes shut and held his breath.

The snorting of a dragon sounded just outside the stall. Gauging by the character of its sniffing, the beast must have been turning its head about in the dark, probably having detected an unfamiliar scent or something else amiss. Cyran's heart thumped against his breastbone, sounding like the drums that boomed over Nevergrace at summer's end. Cold sweat trickled down his back.

The shadow dragon unleashed a roar, and the blast pierced Cyran's ears as the beast suddenly lurched toward the end of the den. Cyran clambered out of the straw with the egg and ran. He tore onto the lower landing as more deafening roars rang through the chambers, and he raced up the incline and burst out of the den before creeping along the walls as fast as he could manage. Two dragons remained in sight—the one guarding the keep, which now clung to the keep's walls and gazed out beyond the Never, and one on the outer wall. Archers spoke in hushed voices as some walked the battlements and others stood before the keep.

Cyran pressed himself against the curtain wall, sidling along as quietly as he could manage. Two soldiers neared, their torch-light and voices betraying them before Cyran could make them out. He ducked behind a round of wood with an axe buried into it but peeked out between the buried blade and its handle. He held his breath until the soldiers passed by. When he made it to the gates of the inner curtain, he slipped into the outer bailey before sprinting across the grounds and finding the entrance to the castle.

"I need you to come for me," Cyran said through whatever connection he maintained with Eidelmere as he kept an eye out for the sentry he'd seen when he'd entered. Now with the egg in his hands, he wished he'd killed the archer when he'd had the chance. "To the front gates."

Eidelmere did not answer.

Cyran could not see anyone in the mist hovering within the gateway, so he slinked his way through while hugging one wall. On the other side, moonlight outlined three soldiers who stood beyond the mist and surveyed the fields.

"Murgare will see me," the forest dragon finally replied in his

head. *"Meet me on the far side of the old oak. The few of my kind that are here search for a legion of dragons. Or an army of men. You are small enough they may not spot you."*

Cyran maintained his position against the stones of the castle and snuck away from the soldiers. After he placed what he hoped was enough distance between him and them, he ran blindly into the night.

37

JASLIN ORENDAIN

A PAGE CRACKLED UNDER JASLIN'S FINGERS AS SHE READ. THE story featured elven characters, including a king and queen of the city east of the lake. The queen had been the true ruler of the realm, but the king wielded more powerful magic. These elves did not wish to delve into the dragon realm—the only way to master and control such beasts—but others did. The tone of the story alluded to a tragic ending, where the hero might not realize his flaw, and because of that he would die. The crystal fragment in Jaslin's hand slipped and cut clean through the page and into the tip of her finger, drawing blood. It dripped in red splatters across the page.

"What was that?" Menoria asked.

Wolves howled off in the Evenmeres, pulling Jaslin's thoughts back to the real world as she sucked on her wound. "Wolves." *Little Smoke still waits for us to escape the keep.* Without even thinking about it, she started to hum, and the woods called to her, making her yearn to leave this place and slip into the forest. Her need to find whatever was out there was as strong as her need to find food.

"Are you injured?" Menoria stood from where she'd been sitting on a bed and approached Jaslin.

Jaslin shook her head as she glanced around. "Not badly." A guard leaned against the wall just beyond their doorway, and he looked in at them every so often. The ice dragon waited outside the keep. Fortunately, after their last incident, the dragon hadn't killed everyone inside the lower chamber by blasting them with its breath. But all of those suspected to be Jaslin and Menoria's accomplices had been sequestered with them in the lord's personal chamber on the top floor of the keep. There wasn't much of a chance of escaping from this level, which must have been the Dragon Queen's intention in placing them here.

"Just don't do anything else to draw suspicion." Emellefer— who had been linked to the would-be escapees by proximity— was lying on a cot. She rolled over. "Poor Ulba is dead."

"But little Renily must have gotten away." Brelle, who was sprawled across a rug on the floor, yawned. "The ice dragon didn't eat her or breathe on her. So maybe she's free and running about the woods with our wolves." Brelle pointed to the cot Emellefer rested on. "And you're lounging on the same bed where the lady of the Never was butchered."

"I sincerely hope that is not true." Emellefer pulled a pillow over her head but squirmed. "Even the north probably doesn't execute people in their beds. And if Renily isn't dead, she may be starving and terrified, hiding under a cart and hoping the dragons don't eat her next."

Menoria started sobbing, and Jaslin wrapped her arm around Menoria's shoulder and whispered, "We do not know that your mother is dead. The Dragon Queen may be holding her somewhere else."

"If you don't believe the lady was killed on that cot, how do you explain all the blood on the sheets when we arrived?" Brelle folded her arms over her thick chest and raised an eyebrow.

"The blood was closer to the pillow than a woman's waist, and the lady was too aged to be a fertile maiden. Blood was also plentiful on the new lord's bed."

Emellefer did not respond, but the piled sheets near their doorway drew Jaslin's attention. A spotting of red was still visible in their midst. Menoria sobbed harder.

"Leave Emellefer be." Dage sat in a corner with his head between his knees. "You are all lucky they did not butcher us inside the lower chamber."

"I think they need Menoria." Laren was lying on the floor against a wall. "*If* the lord and former lady are dead, there is no one more valuable than her."

Menoria settled her head into Jaslin's chest as she cried, the squires seeming oblivious to her plight.

"You are of value," Brelle said to Laren.

"Of course I am, scale squire." Laren sat up. "But I meant there would be no one else of more perceived value. At least not in the eyes of Belvenguard's nobles. If the Dragon Queen is holding us until she gets her queen back, and someone in our kingdom has the Murgare queen, I worry. The Murgare queen would be worth a lot as a prisoner. Her captors could interrogate her for information about our enemies, not to mention use the threat of her bodily injury to halt any attacks or brewing wars. I'm not sure anyone in their right mind would want to trade her for us or our tired old outpost."

"You're as pessimistic as a three-legged burro, tender of dragon shit." Brelle turned away from him.

"Stop arguing, please!" Emellefer threw her pillow at Brelle, and it bounced off the squire's head. Brelle didn't respond.

"Wait." Jaslin stood and glanced to the doorway to make sure the guard was not peeking inside. "Before Ezul was taken by the archer, he mentioned a tunnel that could be used by the lord during a siege. Only the nyren didn't know where this tunnel was."

Menoria wiped her tears aside and glanced around the room. "And you believe it could be hidden in the lord's chambers."

Jaslin nodded.

"Any such tunnel would have to lead underground to allow someone to pass out of the castle and into the forest unseen," Laren said. "So it would have to be on the ground floor or in the basement."

"Or the tunnel could simply run down through there but start somewhere else." Jaslin walked beside the walls, running her fingers along the stones and pressing against them. "Maybe there's a concealed stairway leading down from this chamber. It cannot hurt to look." She lifted a blue tapestry, hoping for a hidden passageway, but only less faded stone lay behind it. "Would you rather just lie here, waiting to die? I used to think of Cyran and his friends as brave warriors."

Laren grumbled.

Menoria walked the perimeter of the room in the opposite direction as Jaslin, feeling along the stones as she stifled her sobs. Brelle joined them. Laren kicked at the floor in a half attempt. Dage didn't even budge. They circled the room, and Jaslin stopped at the hearth. Only scorched stones and a few ashes sat below a grate. Jaslin ducked and peeked around inside the hearth, running a hand over its rear surface. Her palm came away covered in soot. As she turned to feel along one side, a deep hooting carried out in the night and echoed over the castle. Everyone stilled.

"A forest dragon?" Jaslin paced to the window and shoved it open, letting the night drift into the chamber. "There aren't any left in the Never. And a wild one wouldn't venture so close to man." The north's dragons shrieked and roared.

"Please, close the window." Emellefer covered her ears and writhed on the cot as all the others trembled and fell to their knees.

Jaslin clambered to her feet, shut the glass panes, and latched them. She noticed a line of what looked like fresh scratches on the stones beneath the window, and the panes did not rub against the stones there. Similar marks also covered the window's latch.

That is odd. And because they were at the top of the keep, the strangeness of the scratches lingered in her mind. Someone *outside* might have tampered with the window.

Another series of hoots rang out. The calls were too loud, too conspicuous, as if something were impersonating a forest dragon or wanted its presence to be known. Two dragons on the battlements beat their wings and rose. They flashed past the window and flew west into pale moonlight. Wolves howled in the forest.

"Did you see anything?" Brelle peeked over Jaslin's shoulder.

Jaslin shook her head. "Only two Murgare dragons flying away."

"Those two dragons that arrived the other night didn't do anything more than offer a quick chase for the Dragon Queen." Laren stood behind them. "And then they gave up their lives. Unless Belvenguard sends a legion, we have no hope."

"They will come," Menoria said. "It may just take time to plan and prepare."

The titanic shadow dragon emerged from the den and flapped its wings, creating gusts that battered their window. It rose into the air, circled the watchtower, then disappeared from sight. A moment later, the walls around them shuddered and groaned.

"The beast roosts on the keep." Brelle stared upward with wide eyes.

"Someone is running through the bailey." Jaslin pointed at a dark form that hunched over and darted through the shadows at the periphery of torchlight before disappearing into the den.

"Probably one of the north's archers," Laren said.

"It was no archer." Jaslin pressed her face to the window. "They had two swords strapped to their back."

"Then we are surely saved." Laren threw up his hands. "One lone person trying to sneak into an empty den. They will find no more forest dragons in there."

It was true—the forest dragons had been taken from the den and flown away, chased by the north. None had returned. Either Belvenguard had retrieved them, or the dragons and their riders were dead.

Several minutes later, the stones of the keep groaned again, and a roar erupted overhead, rattling the walls around them. The shadow dragon swooped down out of the sky and dived for the den. It landed, hunched over, and slipped through the enormous opening.

"They didn't make it," Menoria said. "Whoever went into the den will not survive."

"What are you doing, handmaid?" a woman's brazen voice said behind them.

Jaslin whirled around. The Dragon Queen stood in their doorway, her black armor and its wicked barbs instantly instilling fear. She walked across the room, and everyone scooted away as she passed.

"I was checking for an exit." Jaslin's tone was flat and even as she held up her soot-covered hand. What Jaslin wanted least of all was for the Dragon Queen to know someone was in the den. "Because you did not take Menoria and me up on our last bargain."

The Dragon Queen took an instant longer to answer than expected, as if she were weighing Jaslin's response. "Entertain yourself with your book, handmaid who isn't a handmaid but who also is not the young lady of the Never." The Dragon Queen nodded toward the blood-spattered pages Jaslin had been reading. "Belvenguard is not coming to save you." She grabbed Menoria by the wrist. "Former young lady of the Never, it is time to come with me. Alone."

Menoria's pupils dilated, and her lip trembled as she was pulled along. Her feet scuffed stone long after she disappeared around the doorway.

38

CYRAN ORENDAIN

THE OLD OAK LOOMED AHEAD, BACKDROPPED BY PALE MOONLIGHT suffusing the sky sea. Cyran heaved for breath as he ran toward the tree, glancing over his shoulders every few strides. The roars of the shadow dragon shook Cyran's bones, and his nerves thrummed with fear. Such a beast could not influence the Dragon Queen to kill more captives, could it? A sucking feeling pulled at his core. If its rage was so great it did influence the Dragon Queen, Cyran would be to blame, something he'd not considered prior.

He stepped around the tower of the oak's trunk, still hauling the scaled egg. But the field appeared empty. Moonlight splashed the grasses and stole through the canopy of the oak, speckling the ground. But there was nothing as large as a forest dragon waiting for him.

A sensation of cold fingers turning his stomach over played inside him. He'd been deceived by the morose old dragon after all. But he still felt Eidelmere's bitterness and sorrow lingering around him.

"Eidelmere," Cyran said in his head as well as in a sharp whisper. "Where are you?"

"I am here." Boughs shook overhead, and leaves and twigs rained around Cyran. A black mass detached from the tree and landed beside him with a thump. "The shadow dragon is angry, and it will eventually search this area. We must... What have you taken?" Eidelmere extended his neck and lowered his head. His nostrils huffed as he sniffed and studied Cyran. "The egg of a dragon. That is what I smelled. A rare find. Then we are even, and I owe you nothing more for tending to my wounds." The dragon's tail waved in the air, emphasizing the leaf bandage on its flattened end. "And so that is why the shadow dragon is so enraged. You stole an egg from her clutch. A crime punishable by death in our realm. She will want to roast you with her black fire."

"I destroyed all the others," Cyran blurted. "There were so many. Too many."

Eidelmere pulled back. "Destroyed dragon eggs?" The dragon fell silent for a few heartbeats, and fear of what the dragon might do scraped at Cyran's nerves. "The egg you hold is from a shadow dragon. It will hatch and grow into a sinister creature that will attempt to deceive you and manipulate you into committing ignoble deeds."

"I thought you said you couldn't lie to me."

"I cannot. It is the rule of the realm."

"But a shadow dragon can?"

"I've never known one of their kind, but that is what the forest dragons I have lived with believe. Shadow dragons are akin to marsh dragons in that regard—they do not adhere to the laws of our realm. You should destroy the egg, the last of her hatchlings that could have covered the walls of the Never and become the outpost's black gargoyles. Do it before the mother comes."

Cyran set the egg down and drew Kayom's sword. Its blade shone with green light. He took a deep breath and raised it over his head before pausing again. "This was by far the smallest of them. Less than half the size of the largest egg."

"Size does not correlate with wickedness. Do not let a soft spot in your heart overrun your wisdom."

Cyran groaned and lifted his sword again, but a vision of Smoke popped into his head, the smallest of all the wolves. Everyone at the Never had told him the wolf pup would be useless, the runt of the litter. But Cyran hadn't cared. Smoke was the friendliest of the pack, the only one that had bounded up and sniffed him when they had found his starving litter abandoned in the woods. Smoke had licked Cyran's hand as he wagged his fuzzy tail. King Igare might even overlook the fact that such dragons, and probably their eggs, were outlawed in Belvenguard if the south had the opportunity to possess one of the mightiest of the species, particularly if such a dragon could help them retake Nevergrace or help win a war against the north.

"This egg also has green scales." Cyran wasn't sure if he was a being a fool for hoping the egg could be part forest dragon. He pointed to the dark green scales and held the light of his sword close.

Eidelmere pressed his nose and then eye to the egg as he squinted. "And so it may, but my eyesight is poor and I cannot tell for sure. It is known that almost all types of dragons only breed with their own kind, but that law is also not infallible."

"The others all had pure black scales."

A murmur began and then abated in Eidelmere's throat as the dragon brooded on that. "It is also known that a single clutch of eggs can have multiple fathers. A single dragon cannot have multiple fathers, but one dragon from a clutch can have a different father than some of the others. Dragons are similar to wolves in that regard."

Cyran pondered that. He'd heard the same thing concerning

litters of dogs and wolves. Perhaps the same was true of some birds or reptiles.

"The shadow dragon may have carried a clutch from the north within her but then also bred with one of the forest dragons of the Never."

Cyran's mind wheeled and spun. "I will keep this egg." He sheathed his sword as the roars of the shadow dragon blasted from the castle, growing louder and rolling out over the fields. "It seems like it could be a gift and should not be wasted." Or was he foolishly being partial to a smaller creature?

"You cannot. This beast will still be driven by the evil tendencies of its stronger and more dominant—"

"I command you to leave it be. Do not force me to enter that rift of light again and grab your thread."

Eidelmere fell silent, but the rage seething within him throbbed the air around Cyran.

"But do not fear," Cyran said in an honest and not overly placating voice. "I will never do anything foolish with the egg or the hatchling, if it ever emerges. I will also not allow such a creature to bend me to its will. Consider me warned. *And* I will not bring it to Galvenstone." Cyran glanced around for a spot to hide the egg.

"I fear that you already play the fool."

The beating of colossal wings sounded in the night.

"We must flee this place." Eidelmere glanced over his bulk, but the oak obscured the outpost.

"We cannot leave this egg out here in the open. She will find it. And then all I have done will have been for naught."

"Then bury it, boy. And quickly. She will not be able to smell it if it lies beneath a pile of dirt."

Cyran knelt and scraped at the grasses and roots and soil, removing only a thin top layer. The beating wings carried away to the west. "Can you dig well with your talons?"

"Much better than you." Eidelmere tore into the ground near the base of the oak and piled fresh dirt into a mound, his talons plunging into the earth with each sweep. When he'd created a hole as deep as a man was tall, Cyran rolled the egg into it, and the egg dropped onto moist dirt without a sound. The forest dragon hurriedly covered the egg and tamped down the dirt. "Now, can we fly?"

Cyran slinked around the trunk of the oak and looked skyward. "She wheels over the outpost in enlarging circles."

"We will fly low and continue south until we are far from here. Then, if you still so desire, fool of a boy, we may continue west to Galvenstone and the Summerswept Keep."

A feeling of regret and doubt gnawed at Cyran's resolve. An egg of the enemy's did seem like something he might be able to use against them, if an opportunity arose. If he'd destroyed all the eggs, he could have removed the risk entirely, but he might have also lost a weapon of immense power. Alternatively, given the current condition of the Never, he could sell the egg, which would probably fetch enough coin to restore the entire castle to its previous splendor and beyond. Someone would pay a king's ransom for the egg of a shadow dragon.

Cyran stepped up to Eidelmere, and the dragon lowered his neck. Cyran swung into the mage's saddle, noting the wrinkled and cracked old scales around it. Eidelmere's scales were not as deep green as those of the younger forest dragons or the egg. He might not be fit for battle for much longer, and he would not be able to stand against the shadow dragon.

"To Castle Dashtok." Cyran placed his palms against the dragon's neck, and Eidelmere flapped slowly and as quietly as he could, rising only a horse's height from the ground before gliding along as he'd done in the canopy of the angoias. But the lightheartedness the forest had aroused in the dragon was gone, all of it replaced with resentment and despair.

The shadow dragon roared, and its cry boomed over the fields.

39

SIRRA BRACKENGLAVE

"IF OUR CAPTIVES ESCAPE, BELVENGUARD WILL CRUSH US." SIR Vladden gazed out over the battlements of the inner curtain near Sirra, staring southwest across the fields and along the scalloped margins of the Evenmeres. Dawn's light created long shadows across the land. "We cannot afford to send any dragons away. There are too many captives to watch over, and some of these captives are less than compliant."

Quarren hunched as she sat atop a crate, her staff lying across her lap. She watched the sun rise in the east. "*If* the young man you saw on that forest dragon's quarterdeck was the same man who went down in the woods when we took the outpost, then King Igare must know where we are."

Sirra nodded. She cupped her helm and held it against her breastplate and the sigil of the rampant shadow dragon. "This boy must have fled to Galvenstone and returned hoping to reclaim the keep. But he did not bring nearly enough dragons to accomplish his task. Why? Because King Igare must fear splitting his legions and leaving Galvenstone less fortified. He knows our armies would need to strike his capital city to win a war."

"Then he must be overly worried that at least some of our

legions have already been assembled and are waiting along the northern shores of the lake." Yenthor toyed with a huge mounted crossbow on the wall, absently swinging it around and aiming its loaded bolt. Zaldica inspected its cranking mechanism.

Vladden nodded. "Protecting Galvenstone is likely Igare's primary concern, but it is possible that he may not be worried about the fact that we have occupied this outpost." The dragonguard stared into the depths of the Evenmeres and the rising red and pale walls of the angoias. "Even if a primary assault arrives from across the lake and we could use our position here to flank him."

"I am beginning to suspect that Igare will never send us Queen Elra." Sirra paced along the walk. "And given my conversation with the Never's dragonguard, I worry she is not well. So we must twist Igare's arm."

Zaldica faced her. "With the hostages and the types of dragons we house at this castle, we could hold out against almost anything Igare sends at us. But how do you intend to twist the arm of a king?"

"I have been considering sending an ice dragon and its guard back to Castle Northsheeren to stand against whatever Oomaren is plotting," Sirra replied. "I fear he will not wait for the queen's return or honor Princess Kyelle's rights, and that he will use this interlude to instill himself on the throne." The warm wind stirred her hair as she walked, her plated boots punishing the stones beneath her feet. Down in the bailey, Shadowmar had fallen into a fitful rest after having scoured the fields and lands around the Never for most of the night. The dragonbolt that had impaled her cheek during the most recent incursion had been removed and the wound dressed, but her pain lingered. Shadowmar's rage still sheeted off her in waves. To lose every egg from a shadow dragon's clutch was beyond tragic. Sirra's roiling animosity over the loss of her king and abduction of her queen had settled a bit over the past days but churned anew now. Something more had to be done. "I must also deal with those in the Eastern Reach who use this moment of weakness without a king to cause uprisings. But I am bound to this keep. At least for now."

"Then what course shall we take?" Vladden paced behind her. "The south will see Oomaren's and the Eastern Reach's actions as the wicked north turning on itself and devouring one another."

"We must further weaken Galvenstone and *all* of Belvenguard," Sirra said. "Make them fear what is to come. Any infighting in Murgare will be short and decisive, and then our legions will rise. Then they will sail south."

"I do not see how we can weaken Belvenguard from where we stand." Quarren's long fingernails tapped against her staff. "Not with so few of us."

Sirra pursed her lips. "It is a difficult decision. I do not want to send any guard or dragons away." Sirra drew a parchment from a slit in her dragonsteel armor. She unfolded it and read aloud so that all those present could hear. "Mighty Dragon Queen. I commend you on your victory and conquering of a small outpost in the north of Belvenguard, as well as for taking action in response to my brother's recent murder. But along with my many praises of your abilities and achievements, I must also make it clear that the outpost you currently reside in is of no consequence to Murgare and our coming war. You have also taken a legion from Northsheeren without royal authorization. I will hold no grievances with you or Murgare's legion if you return to the north at once. We have a war to prepare for, not a simple skirmish. You must assist us and employ your status to help Northsheeren unite its banners as quickly as possible. I will grant you another fortnight to return to the castle, or you will be branded as one no longer compliant to the crown of Murgare." Sirra cleared her throat. "The letter is signed by our late king's brother, Oomaren."

"What Oomaren failed to mention was anything about our objectives here." Quarren tapped her staff on the stones repeatedly. "It is as if he wanted to belittle the reasons why we came, or to have us forget."

"That is my belief as well." Sirra lifted her blade from its fully sheathed position and lit the parchment on fire. The letter snapped as it burned, and a few black ashes drifted away on the wind.

"We are here to avenge his brother's soul," Vladden said, "which he may stand a better chance of accomplishing with his war, but we are also here to recover our queen."

Sirra nodded. "It seems that Oomaren does not want the queen returning to Northsheeren."

Zaldica cursed under her breath, and Yenthor joined her and added, "Bloody bastard."

"Then how shall you answer the summons of this false king, Dragon Queen?" Vladden's posture turned even more rigid than usual.

"That is what we are here to discuss." Sirra smirked. "Why we are waiting out here on the battlements."

A whoosh of wind and the rapid flutter of wings sounded behind them. Zaldica and Yenthor swung the crossbow around as the others lurched. A deep blue dragon a fraction of the size of an ice dragon swooped over the castle, its agility and speed making it hard to track. It landed on the merlons nearby, and its nearly unarmored guard dismounted. He strode over carrying a steel bolt.

"Dragon Queen?" The man removed a fur wrap that covered most of his face. His dark beard fell over his brigandine, and he indicated the message on the bolt while raising an eyebrow. "You asked for me?"

Sirra nodded as he approached, and she said, "Indeed I did. We require your assistance. You will no longer serve Murgare by reporting to Sir Trothen at Northsheeren. Or to Oomaren, if that is who sent you to watch over us."

A cloud passed over the guard's expression.

"Whatever Oomaren is paying you, I will double it, and I will also allow you to live." Sirra's hand clamped onto her sword's hilt, and down in the bailey, Shadowmar hissed, feeling Sirra's rising anger. "Because if you betray me now, Shadowmar and I will not stop hunting you until you are dead."

The guard swallowed and nodded. "Yes, of course, Dragon Queen. What would you have me do?"

"Belvenguard has always held a tentative position amongst the southern kingdoms." Sirra spoke so all those present could hear. "The Weltermores lie to their east, the Rorenlands to the south. If we can convince either of those kingdoms to turn against Belvenguard—or even persuade some of Belvenguard's many cities not to support Galvenstone—we could crush King Igare and his capital in an enclosing fist."

"An interesting proposition." Quarren's tawny hair streamed around her dark hood. "It will be difficult to turn either city or kingdom against Igare. They respect and fear the man and the power of Belvenguard and Galvenstone."

"But... But if we could turn even one." Vladden's tone brightened. "Then it will become more likely that others will follow. One city and then two and three and so on. One full kingdom and then the second. They will feel the weakening of Igare's grip, and more and more may unite against him."

"But how do we convince these cities and kingdoms who have been loyal to Igare for so long to do such a thing?" Yenthor asked.

"We spread word of Igare's actions." Sirra paced with her head low. "How he incited war by killing our king and abducting our queen. We tell the other lords and rulers what they need to hear. We let them know that war is already coming and there is nothing they can do to stop it. Igare chose this fate for them. Now they only have to make a choice. They can side with Igare and face the full onslaught of the north's legions of dragons and ships as we roll south like a black tide and cover all of Cimeren in our wake. Or they can side with us. The cities and houses shall not answer their king's call when he summons his banners. When he asks the Weltermores and Rorenlands for aid, his begging will fall on deaf ears."

"We will need to offer them something valuable as incentive," Vladden said. "Something more than fear of what will happen if they oppose us."

Sirra nodded. "We will offer lands and titles from the new kingdom we will forge to the lords who support us. And those who oppose us, we will strip their lands from them and give it to their enemies. There will be marriage pacts arranged between the mightiest of houses that support the north, and all of Cimeren will be united again. As it was in the past age when the elves ruled from Cimerenden. All will be united once Castle Dashtok and the Summerswept Keep fall."

"It is a fine plan," Quarren said. "The ears I have out in the world whisper that the Weltermores desire more freedoms of their own and wish to be further from Galvenstone's influence."

A moment of quiet contemplation followed.

"Mayhap we could even ask the Weltermores king if he'd be interested in wedding the former young lady of the Never," Quarren continued. "To align this outpost with the kingdom that may be more likely to turn. The kingdom that is much closer to Galvenstone. The Weltermores's biggest deterrent from extending west past the Scyne River is Nevergrace. And it seems

Igare is not trying hard enough to rescue Menoria. You, my Dragon Queen, may be able to persuade the young lady and convince her that a marriage pact is in her and her people's best interest."

"You heard the mage," Sirra said to the dragonguard of the storm dragon. "We require your mount, but you will stay here and assist us."

"But that is my dragon, milady," the guard said.

"It is no longer." Sirra gripped the hilt of her sword. "You are now one of the riders of an ice dragon. And your mage will stay with you. If she would be so kind as to offer her mount to Quarren for a time, Quarren will reciprocate the gesture." Sirra waved for the mage on the storm dragon to dismount. "But if we discover that Oomaren has become aware of what we are doing, the blame will fall upon both of you. Do you understand?"

The guard slowly nodded as the mage hesitantly climbed out of her saddle.

"As for Oomaren, he is in no position to make demands for the crown," Sirra said. "And thus he does not deserve an answer from us." She folded her arms across her chest. "Sir Vladden."

"Yes, Dragon Queen?" The guard stepped up.

"You are now the messenger who rides the storm dragon. Quarren is still your mage, if the dragon's current mage allows it. Strip your armor and mount the beast. You shall begin your campaign in the Weltermores cities. You are now a diplomat of the north and have full acting power to grant promises of titles and lands as you see fit. Allow Quarren to guide you as always, but it will be best if the lords and kings only see you, Sir Vladden." *Any mage's appearance could make others more anxious and fearful rather than trusting.* "You will become the face of the north. Make the Weltermores believe what I have come to believe is possible through our discussion. Then move through the cities and houses in southern Belvenguard and continue all the way to the western shores of Cimeren. After that, seek out the lords and king of the Rorenlands."

Sir Vladden nodded, and he dropped his helm and began stripping off his breastplate. Quarren approached the storm dragon with her palm and staff held before her. The storm dragon hissed and flicked its tongue, but it did not attempt to fly away.

Sirra helped Vladden remove his vambraces, and she said, "Fly high and swiftly as only the storm dragons can do."

40

CYRAN ORENDAIN

THE AUDIENCE HALL IN CASTLE DASHTOK WAS NEARLY EMPTY SAVE for its looming throne fashioned of dragon bones and gold and red dragon hides. Decorative dragon teeth created serrated borders all around it. A few silent and ever-present kingsknights stood like statues and lined the walls of the chamber.

"If King Igare is not here, we will find him in the trial chambers," Sir Paltere said and exited the audience hall, leading Cyran through the castle. They wound down staircases and traveled through hallways, proceeding deeper into the Summerswept Keep until the circular trial chamber stood before them. Voices carried through the barred doors. Soldiers stood on either side of each entryway, and Paltere approached them. "I need to see the king."

"I have orders not to allow *anyone* inside at this time." The soldier stood firm.

"I am Sir Paltere, dragonknight of Galvenstone, and I ask that you step aside." He placed his hand on his sword's hilt.

The soldier glanced to his comrade on the other side of the doorway, but that soldier only stared directly ahead, attempting to avoid being brought into the situation. The first soldier glanced back at Paltere and then stepped away from the entrance.

"Have them unbar this door." Sir Paltere pointed.

The guard knocked twice and then three times in quick succession. The creaking of hinges sounded, and one of the twin doors shuddered. It swung inward just enough that a kingsknight could peek his head out. "There is no admittance. You were told." The knight pulled his head back inside.

"I must speak with Igare." Paltere stepped forward, pressing his palm against the door to keep it open. "It pertains to Never-grace and the Dragon Queen."

The kingsknight's head appeared again, and the knight studied Paltere for a brief instant before quietly swinging the door open only enough for Paltere and Cyran to slip through. Inside, the king and his four councilmembers sat at the table in the center of the chamber. The multi-layered chandelier hung overhead, its hundreds of tapers casting bright light only in the middle of the room. The attendants sitting on the surrounding benches were far fewer than the previous time Cyran had visited this chamber with Kayom.

Kayom. Cyran's heart ached.

Paltere strode down the steps to the waist-high barricade separating the audience from the trial area. He sat in the first row, and Cyran took a seat beside him. The king and his councilmembers were listening to a man who was dressed in a shimmery and embroidered gold and black tunic.

"We cannot completely disrupt whatever is occurring," Paltere whispered. "Not in the middle of this nobleman's speech. I feel the need to, but we must wait until this supplicant from Somerlian is finished."

Two adolescent women sat on the bench seat beside Paltere, and they conversed quietly amongst themselves. The voluptuous Queen Hyceth sat on the other side of the women, toying with her curling brown locks. Cyran had first seen these three at the king's tourney in Galvenstone before he was a dragonsquire.

"Now, Nistene, Jaken would make a fine husband," the queen whispered. "The son of Riscott the Orator is as high a station as you will find in Galvenstone. And you should not withdraw now. Not unless this supplicant can persuade the king that he has a better offer."

"But Jaken doesn't find me attractive," Princess Nistene said as she rubbed at her bulbous nose, the feature making her nearly absent chin look even smaller. "I think his father is forcing him to court me."

"What makes you say that?" the queen asked.

"He's always looking at Vysoria."

"The conjuror's daughter?" The queen scoffed. "Her power and station are not comparable to yours."

Cyran absently toyed with the merchant's ring on his finger, feigning interest in the unassuming burro.

The man addressing the king spoke louder, discussing a topic similar to the women's. "The princess would make a fine wife for the first son of Lord Baronshire of Somerlian. And your daughter would not have to reside in some far corner of Belvenguard. She could live in the grandeur of one of the capital's closest cities."

Riscott stood and paced around the table. Igare stared into his folded hands, lost in some other world of more pressing thoughts.

"I cannot make any final decisions on the king's behalf," the orator said, "not when it comes to his family. But he cannot promise his daughter to the next lord of Somerlian. Not at this time. We have simply called you to Galvenstone to remind your lord of the old oaths. Oaths that were made and honored by your father's house in times past. Oaths to stand strong against Murgare and the north."

The supplicant bowed. "May the king speak, if he will?"

King Igare sighed as he stood from his chair. "It is not that I do not respect and cherish the friendship between myself and Lord Baronshire. It is that I cannot promise Princess Nistene to every lord in the kingdom in order to reaffirm old alliances. There are far too many fiefdoms and shires in Belvenguard. And my daughter is nearly betrothed to another."

The orator cast a furtive glance at the king, and a suppressed smirk played across Riscott's lips. A darkened expression and a frown fell across the faces of the king's clergyman and his nyren.

"To whom is she *nearly* betrothed, Your Grace?" the supplicant asked.

"I cannot say at this time, but since the matter has not been finalized, she could again become available for Lord Baronshire's first son."

It is the orator's son, Jaken.

"Please return to Lord Baronshire and share my deepest condolences for his brother," Igare said. "Remind him of the rising danger in the north and that if Galvenstone falls, so will Somerlian and then every city in Belvenguard. All the fiefdoms must call in their soldiers and any who are capable and willing to fight. The unwilling may be needed soon enough. Our bannermen must remain strong, now more than ever."

The supplicant bowed, his posture and tone carrying an edge of disappointment. "Very well, Your Grace." The man turned with his head held high and exited the inner circle, stepping past Cyran before walking directly out of the chamber.

Sir Paltere leapt to his feet and waved to grab the council's attention.

"We need to send envoys to the Weltermores and the Rorenlands." Igare slumped back into his seat. "I am sensing hesitation on the part of the lords of Belvenguard. And why?" He raised his hands over his head in frustration. "Do they not believe the north will send its legions?"

"I believe they fear the north and a war that will ravage all of Cimeren." Tiros, the nyren, sat comfortably in his red robes and chain belt, his fingers knitted together.

"They do not want to honor oaths that may cost them all their coin," Cartaya, the conjuror, said. "Oaths their deceased grandfathers once made."

"I believe in the Siren's book these men's sins would fall under that of greed and vanity," Lisain, the young man in the white robes of the clergy, said. "They all wish to be granted favors or rewarded with altered trade routes and ports. Or marriages. All to uphold their vows and responsibilities as lords of Belvenguard."

The king rubbed at his bare forehead, where his crown had once sat. He circled a finger in the air. "Bring in the next one."

"Your Grace," Sir Paltere said, and the council fell silent. Everyone inside the chamber turned to regard the dragonknight. "I have requested admittance to this chamber because another rider has returned from the errand at Nevergrace."

The king gestured for Paltere to step forward, and the dragonknight did so. Cyran followed him through a gap in the barrier wall.

"After the moon dragon returned, we believed the others to be long dead." Riscott's expression folded into one of skepticism and suspicion. "And now here stands the same squire who was the lone survivor of the initial attack at the outpost. Please, tell us what happened to Sir Kayom."

"Sir Kayom was—" Paltere began, but the orator cut him short.

"Allow the young dragonsquire to answer in his own words," Riscott said.

"He was unseated." Cyran stood as tall as he could with his

hands clasped behind his back. His voice began unevenly, but he cleared his throat and steadied himself. "The guard who rode the silver believed the moon dragon to be in danger, and he ordered his mage and mount to fly in and try to help them. Sir Kayom believed the moon dragon would not be seen and that we should all wait in the fields until the moon dragon's riders made their assessment of Nevergrace and returned. But the silver's guard disobeyed Sir Kayom's orders and swooped in. They were soon attacked. When we flew in to assist the silver, the moon dragon fled. Then the Dragon Queen arrived, and at first we merely spoke with her."

"Oh, indeed?" Riscott raised an eyebrow.

"His story is similar to Sir Niolo's." Tiros tugged at the curls of his beard.

The dragonguard on the moon dragon.

"Continue," Riscott said.

"The Dragon Queen demanded the return of the Murgare queen, but seeing that we did not bring her, the Dragon Queen attacked us and unseated Kayom and our mage."

The councilmembers studied him but remained quiet.

"And the three forest dragons we thought we may be able to regain are no longer at the outpost," Cyran added. "They are likely all dead."

"And how do you know this?" Riscott asked.

Cyran considered telling them about how he had entered the den and found the other stalls empty, but that story might bring up too many questions, questions about the dragon egg. "We swept over the Never, and while most of the dragons rose to attack us, there were no forest dragons in the sky or on the ground."

"They could have been locked in the den," Tiros said.

A minute of silence lingered as thoughts and wishes and desires—each councilmember attempting to hide theirs behind a curtain of feigned neutrality—seemed to mingle in the empty spaces above them.

"Surely, Sir Niolo reported back about their types of dragons and that the Dragon Queen was with them," Cyran said.

King Igare walked over and stood before Cyran, the king's posture growing rigid with determination. "And what do you plan to do to take the Never back?"

Cyran had to fight off a rising smile. "I humbly ask to be inducted into the dragonguard and to then lead an adequate number of dragons against the outpost. To take it back for Belvenguard and for all of those who have died at the Dragon Queen's hands."

Riscott scoffed. "You, squire, are not nearly broad or big enough to be one of the guard. Your mage would be an easy target and could be unseated even before you. And all that you say still rings strange in my ear. I find it odd that only you seem to survive the confrontations with the Dragon Queen. Do you remember us speaking of a traitor?"

Cyran nodded. "I recall the topic. And if it is true, I vow to hunt down whoever from Nevergrace turned on their own."

Tiros gestured to dismiss Riscott's interrogation, and the nyren said, "Sir Niolo returned long before you, squire. And during this interval, we have been weighing how to respond."

You have also been assessing the loyalties of other lords.

"The traitor who turned and gave away Nevergrace's secrets and weaknesses is already known." Cartaya pushed back her hood. Her strangely young face contrasted with her stark white hair.

Cyran's guts writhed. "Who was it?"

"Their identity will remain within the council," the conjuror replied. "For now. They fled the outpost and are hiding in the various villages along the Scyne Road. You will know of them when the time is right."

"And your evaluation of the situation at Nevergrace?" Igare addressed Lisain.

"In light of this new information, I will seek guidance from the Paladin and the Shield Maiden." The clergyman dipped his head and interlaced his fingers.

Riscott opened his mouth to speak, but the king silenced him with a raised hand. Igare faced Cyran, remaining silent for a moment and gathering his thoughts. "The problem with your request is that there are hundreds, if not thousands, of squires who yearn to become one of the guard. Such young men are plentiful, not only in Galvenstone but throughout Belvenguard. As well as in every city around the kingdoms. I trust you are skilled, but because dragonsquires are far more plentiful than dragons, we only induct the most adroit of all of you. And only when an opportunity arises. Even more difficult to find than dragons are dragonmages. As you may or may not know, these people are typically born in destitute living situations, and their abilities are unknown to everyone, except for maybe themselves. They are physically decrepit and are usually shackled by addiction and other unsavory habits. Their ripples of dragon blood, or their bond or whatever it is they carry, do not mingle well with that of their human blood. It makes them overly meek, and they often desire to spend most of their time daydreaming, or walking the dragon realm, as I've heard it explained."

"To summarize for the king," Riscott began, "if you can convince us you are worthy of the guard, and if you can find a mage hiding somewhere in the slums of the cities around Belvenguard, one who will not run away at their first opportunity, *then* we will find you a dragon to satiate your lust for vengeance and war."

"All I ask—" Cyran took a step closer to the king to stress his entreaty, and several kingsknights strode forth from their positions in the shadows. Paltere gripped Cyran's shoulder and pulled him back. Cyran met the king's gaze. "All I ask is to wear the armor and sigil of a dragonguard of Nevergrace, and for enough dragons to help me reclaim my home."

Cyran slipped Sir Kayom's sword from its sheath, and its green light glowed within the chamber. He angled the blade downward and pressed the back of his hand to his forehead. Sir Paltere stepped up alongside him, the dragonknight's chest swollen with pride, but his hand remained on Cyran's sword arm. The fast-approaching kingsknights who were drawing their swords slowed their advance.

"I already have Sir Kayom's dragon." Cyran's voice was cold and definitive. "And I am already a dragonmage."

Sir Paltere grinned.

41

CYRAN ORENDAIN

THE PLAINS BLURRED BENEATH EIDELMERE AS CYRAN WATCHED the sun rise in the east. The forest dragon's wings beat the air repeatedly and then settled as he glided along. A small village to the south disappeared in a flash, but the Scyne Road created a brown ribbon that lingered amidst green fields.

"This is a day for redemption," Eidelmere said in Cyran's head, the dragon's melancholy as thick as ever. *"A bittersweet day where I hope to avenge Morden and once again find my bed inside a den I resent but have called home for centuries."*

"This shall be that day, my friend." Cyran sat in Sir Kayom's saddle and patted the dragon's neck as the wind whipped at Cyran's hair. He still did not wear the armor of a dragonguard, as he had not been dubbed, but maybe if he could lead an assault to take back the Never, he would earn the title and his armor would be forged and emblazoned with the colors and sigil of Nevergrace. He gripped the handle of his lance, a lance as long as a typical dragonlance but not forged of dragonsteel, only of pine or oak. The weapon was probably carved with the intention of using it to train, or perhaps only for show rather than for battle against other dragonguard and the legions of the north. At least he'd been supplied with a dragonsteel shield, and he wore fresh leathers and a new suit of chainmail.

Cyran glanced over his left shoulder and then his right. At each side, two dragons soared along behind him, maintaining their wedge formation. Two silvers and two rose dragons created symmetry in their formation. And directly behind Eidelmere, a sun dragon and its guard led a colossal stone dragon with gray scales. The stone dragon's curled horns armored its head, and its four wings flapped in sweeping arcs as it tried to keep pace with the others. Such a behemoth could not fly fast or for long distances, its body more than twice the size of the sun dragon's. This beast was even larger than the Dragon Queen's shadow dragon. Six archers spanned a sloping quarterdeck atop the stone dragon's back, three on each side, their positions staggered, allowing them to sight enemies at different angles. A mounted trebuchet sat poised on the middle of the dragon's back, a stall for its throwing stones secured behind it. Three more dragonarchers rode in turrets beneath the enormous dragon from the rock mountains. It would not be long until their legion would have to stop and allow the stone dragon to rest again. The beast needed to catch its breath a good distance away from the Never so their legion would not be seen too soon, but they didn't want their last stop to be too far away either or the dragon might have to land and rest again soon after their arrival.

Cyran smiled as he faced the warm wind, its gentle hands tossing his hair and caressing his cheeks. *Seven dragons, including a stone dragon garrison.* The king still could not send too large of a legion or his best dragonknight, Sir Paltere, as he feared the Never was only a distraction for a war that would arrive when Galvenstone wasn't as heavily defended. But hopefully seven dragons, their guard, and all of their archers would be enough to face the Dragon Queen and her five dragons.

Three mountainous forms lying near the edge of the Evenmeres blurred by to the north.

"What are those?" Cyran pointed.

"Hills?" Vyk, the archer appointed to man the crossbow on Eidelmere's back, said. His voice cracked with bounding vigor, almost bordering on hysteria. With the promise of battle, some men grew quiet and reserved. Others roused and became enlivened. Vyk seemed to go well beyond the latter, and his demeanor had not changed during the entire voyage from Galvenstone.

"They do not look like grass, but they are green." Ineri's voice carried up from Eidelmere's turret. Then she coughed, a deep hacking sound that rattled her ribs. She'd been coughing regularly since Cyran had met her. Once he'd even seen a spotting of blood on her hand afterward, but she quickly wiped it away on a kerchief. The poor woman was supposedly one of the best dragonarchers in all of Belvenguard, but she was sickly—and not in the manner of a crippled dragonmage. Ineri was so thin and pale that it seemed likely even without battle, she might not live to see the next summer. But she was alive now and more than willing to join them, although quiet and in need of frequent rest.

Cyran fought off any doubts and worries. They would face the Dragon Queen, and he would bring the best archer in the kingdom before her shadow dragon.

"Whatever they are, they were not there on my past trips to and from Galvenstone," Cyran said. "Unless I passed this area in the dark." He veered Eidelmere north.

"Where do you go, guard, er, squire?" the guard on the closest rose dragon asked.

"To those mounds." Cyran pointed. "You may call a rest for the stone dragon. I will return shortly."

"We stay together," the guard on the silver at the edge of their formation said.

"Then do as you wish." Cyran hunched low against the back of Eidelmere's head and squinted as he shielded his eyes. The mounds drew closer. There were three of them. And they were scaled. They had wings that splayed across the ground.

Eidelmere braced with his wings as his running feet caught the ground, and he lurched to a halt. Cyran climbed down the stirrup ladder on Sir Kayom's saddle.

"Dead dragons." Vyk's voice thundered against the curtain of the Evenmeres.

Cyran strode up to the three mounds—carcasses of forest dragons. One had a bolt impaling its skull. On the other two, he found gaping wounds with seared flesh around the edges. The wounds were punctures but did not have sharp margins like those caused by a stabbing sword. These injuries were more akin to what Cyran expected if a lance had skewered both of them. But dragonlances did not cause burns.

Eidelmere's outrage, grief, and anger crescendoed in the other realm, and he roared the raspy roar of an old dragon. Cyran's heart melted in sympathy for his mount.

The stone dragon landed with a thumping of four massive feet, and its two sets of wings, which each spanned fields, slumped downward. The rose and silver dragons settled around the colossal beast, followed by the sun dragon.

"One of the cleanest shots I've ever seen." Ineri stood behind Cyran, eyeing the bolt buried into the one dragon's skull. She hacked a few times and spat blood into the grass. "I do not believe any archer could have made such a shot while in the air. Unless they are blessed with the luck of the Thief."

Cold fingers crept along the back of Cyran's neck. "And so you believe... what exactly?"

Ineri hacked and almost fell over as she circled the carcasses of the forest dragons. "That the beast was shot here on the ground. At close range."

"And these were dragons of the Never." Vyk spat in disgust as he stormed around the wing of a dead dragon, his cheeks flushing, his blond beard bursting from beneath the strap of his helm. "Dragons of Belvenguard."

Cyran inspected the puncture wounds again, this time examining them more closely. "But how would someone shoot the dragon at close range? Surely, one of the Never's forest dragons would have defended itself with breath and claw, or they would have simply flown away."

Ineri shrugged as she reached up and ran a hand along the quarterdeck on the back of the body with the bolt through its brain, the only dragon harnessed with a quarterdeck. "I've never seen wounds quite like those on the other corpses, either."

Cyran's attention settled on the lone crossbow up on the quarterdeck. Because the body was slumped over on its side, he could see that there was no turret beneath the dragon, crushed or otherwise. A forest dragon harnessed with a quarterdeck but not a turret seemed... odd. And a close-range attack could mean the dragon was shot by its own crossbow, but the dragon would have had to be looking directly back at its archer for that to be a possibility. Who could and would do such a thing? Suspects flashed through Cyran's mind. Tales of Murgare's people painted them as despicable and vile, but even they should not want to slaughter dragons they could have otherwise commandeered.

But the traitor the king's council mentioned seemed the most likely culprit. This person would have to be a dragonmage to fly the dragons out here though, and that would narrow the suspect or suspects down to the six mages of the Never, if any were still alive. Cyran had seen three of them die. And this person would likely need two other mages to control the other dragons, unless they traveled long distances back and forth for each dragon. A mage could also command the dragon to look back at the crossbow, but there were no mages Cyran knew who could climb the rope ladder of a quarterdeck. If that were the situation, another person would have had to assist the mage. Cyran couldn't convince himself that there were so many traitors living at the Never, but again, the alternative didn't make sense either—the Dragon Queen and the north should not kill dragons they could incorporate into their own legion.

Cyran sighed, arriving at a dead end in his theorizing, just as with the sealed letter he, Brelle, and Garmeen had received. One of the dragonguard of old probably would have surmised something more. He vowed to find the traitor of the Never after they reclaimed their outpost. Then maybe if he interrogated this person, the answers would become clear.

"The damn Dragon Queen supposedly carries a sword that burns with black fire." Vyk heaved for breath against his unrestrained anger. His fists clenched. When he passed close to Cyran, a whiff of smoldering alcohol followed him.

Was this archer intoxicated before battle?

"Then it is probably her work," Ineri added before coughing. "She may have sacrificed the Never's dragons so we could not recover them. But the injuries do not look like sword wounds."

"Why would these dragons let that loathsome queen get close enough to them?" Vyk asked. "They would know she could control them."

"There are so many legends about the Dragon Queen, none can know what is truth and what is myth." Ineri leaned against one of the dead dragons, her face paler than usual. "She may be able to bond with many, even from a distance. And then she can control them and bend them all to her will."

Visions of the Dragon Queen slaughtering all the dragons of Belvenguard, one by one, stormed through Cyran's thoughts.

"Then she will die!" Vyk shook a fist in the direction of the outpost. "It is time for us to end her reign at the Never."

"There are also legends of the Dragon Queen summoning

what was once called a *luënor* blade," Sir Jedsin, the guard on the gilded sun dragon, said as his mount stepped closer. "A blade brought over from the dragon realm. It is said to be a shard of the wielder's own soul laid bare. Usually in the form of a sword or lance. It kills by piercing or slicing through the souls of its victims. And if a soul is severed, the dead do not pass on."

Cyran's heart spiraled downward as sadness and despair bit into the slowly beating organ, and Eidelmere's emotions burned even hotter. Cyran looked over the dragons and ran a hand across each of their scales. If these creatures truly had their souls dismembered and those souls were forever lost from their realm, lost to the... nothingness, then there would be no forgiveness for their killer. No retribution too grave.

"There is nothing we can do here," Sir Jedsin said.

"Then it is time to take our revenge." Vyk scrambled up the rope ladder to Eidelmere's quarterdeck, as if he needed the blood of his enemies to feed his anger, or even to survive.

"And for you," Sir Jedsin addressed Cyran, "it is time to earn your armor."

42

SIRRA BRACKENGLAVE

"AND IF YOU COULD CHOOSE, WHAT WOULD YOUR FATE AS A LADY be?" Sirra asked the former young lady of the Never, whose identity she'd confirmed through questioning and sensing the truth in the dragon realm. Menoria sat across from her in a small bedchamber of the keep. The two of them were alone. Menoria's hands were clamped between her thighs to hide their trembling.

"I—I would not want to be sent away to become the lady of some lord I did not know or respect." Menoria stared at her lap, avoiding eye contact. Through title and station, this young woman should now hold the power to rule Nevergrace, but it was the other young woman, the one pretending to be her handmaid, who most interested Sirra.

"What if you were to marry the king of Belvenguard?"

"I... the king has already taken a queen."

"Yes. A hypothetical question, of course."

"I would obey my duties." She brushed her golden hair behind her ears. "For the Never. I would use my station to try to help the kingdom in whatever way I could."

"But you would prefer to stay here. If it were possible to have a lord or husband brought to the Never instead of you being sent away, would you accept this lord?"

Menoria pondered that as her eyes danced and worked through possibilities. "I would prefer to remain the lady of the Never over anything else."

The truth of the young woman's words flooded the dragon realm. Sirra sipped from a tankard, her drink another light mulled wine of the southlands. "Drink as much as you'd like." She nodded at the tankard beside Menoria.

Menoria flinched, as if she suspected Sirra was attempting to intoxicate her, to have her become the drunken fool and spill all her secrets.

"I will drink from your cup, if it is poison you fear," Sirra said.

Menoria shook her head, and she took a sip. "No. I do not believe you would use deception to kill me. You could have already had me executed by a multitude of other methods."

Sirra nodded.

"Did you have our nyren, old Ezul, put to death?" Menoria asked.

"We promised to execute a hostage every dawn and dusk until King Igare brought us our queen. And he has yet to do so."

"Then you intend to kill me next?"

"There are still others of lesser worth in your king's mind. You are my bargaining piece."

"How do you decide whom to execute?"

Sirra shrugged. "Tell me about your handmaid, this Jaslin?"

Menoria's faced paled. "Then you are considering killing her."

Sirra did not acknowledge the statement.

"She is not my handmaid." Menoria swallowed, and anxiety rode behind her eyes.

More truth.

"She is the sister of a dead dragonsquire and a farmhand," the young lady continued. "The farmhand died recently, but he was killed in a tragic accident in the woods. Not during your attack."

"I see. And do you know how she came by the artifact she carries?"

Menoria glanced up and, for an instant, met Sirra's gaze. "What artifact?"

"A fragment from a crystal decanter."

"That shard is an artifact? I believed it to be sentimental."

"If that is so, then this Jaslin has no inherent value to Nevergrace. She could be my next victim. At dusk this coming night."

Menoria's expression fell flat as she paled further. She glanced to the unshuttered window. Late morning sunlight leaned into the chamber. "The shard could be an artifact. I do not know how she acquired it."

"But Jaslin also attempts to resist more than any who are still alive."

"Supposedly, her brothers have told her she's always been that way."

The hiss of an ice dragon carried through the window. The fire dragon on the western watchtower trilled. Sirra paced to the window and feigned disinterest in her next question. "And which of the dragonsquires was her brother?"

"His name was Cyran. We've not seen him since you took over the castle."

"Oh, is that right?" She shook her head as if saddened. "And this Cyran, what did he look like?"

Menoria sipped at her drink as she stared out the window. "Shoulder-length brown hair. Tall but not nearly big enough to be a guard. Not much in terms of a beard. In fact, he hardly had any stubble. He'd just begun his second decade of life."

All truths. And I know this squire. Jaslin could become a more important hostage than Menoria for any coming attack.

Footsteps sounded outside the chamber. A pounding knock followed.

"Enter." Sirra studied the limited view of the battlements, the western watchtower with the fire dragon atop it, and the fields beyond.

"Dragon Queen." Zaldica burst into the room. "It is best we speak outside."

Sirra followed her archer out of the room, closing and locking the door behind her. As long as Menoria remained by herself, she would not try to escape.

"They are coming." Zaldica hurried down a stairway, waving Sirra on. "Our dragons spotted a legion flying this way. We do not know their numbers yet, but the estimate is that they have a few more dragons than we do. And one is so massive, it must be a stone dragon, if not a cave dragon from the dwarven mountains."

After descending many stairs, Sirra stepped onto the lower landing and marched for the doorless entryway of the keep. She trod onto the stone walk outside and gazed upward. "Where are the others?"

"Preparing the dragons."

"Good. Have them move the outpost's soldiers and knights into the dragons' den. *Quickly.* Keep the mist dragon at the den's entrance so none try to escape. Have her fog the area. For the more important hostages being kept above the ground floor, bar their chamber doors. Leave only three archers inside the keep. Have the other three guard and their dragons follow our planned counter. Now. *Go.*"

Zaldica raced away around the corner of the keep.

"Are you seeking battle here?" the fire dragon's mage asked

as he appeared, hobbling up the walk. Sir Kragnar, the fire drag-on's guard, strode just behind the mage but was swiftly gaining on him.

"I believe it would be best if we do not try to engage all these approaching dragons at once," Kragnar said as he stopped before Sirra. "With a fully armed stone or cave dragon, their number of archers will far exceed ours. And they appear to have a mixed group of other dragons, given their sizes. This legion was probably designed specifically to enhance their strengths and exploit our weaknesses."

"Do you not seek vengeance for our king?" Sirra tapped her lips.

Kragnar nodded. "I do, my Dragon Queen, but if we die here at this outpost, we will not avenge Restebarge."

Sirra watched the western skies. "It seems Igare will not return Elra no matter the danger to his legions or who he loses here at this outpost. My fear for our queen grows."

The clatter of men and women preparing for battle filled a gap in their conversation.

"What would you do in this situation, Sir Kragnar?" Sirra asked.

"I would send a message back to Northsheeren to inform them of the coming encounter and of your worries about the queen."

"We no longer have a storm dragon flying through the clouds, remember? And the new guard and mage of one of our ice dragons are not as adept as Sir Vladden and Quarren."

Kragnar's expression fell. "Then I shall mount Dorthrax."

"Do not fret, Sir Kragnar." Sirra slapped his pauldron. "Sir Vladden's work is now far more important to the north than anything we can do from this outpost."

Kragnar stared into the distance.

"Mount up, dragonguard of Murgare," Sirra said. "And follow the counterattack option we've laid out for you." Sirra turned and strode back into the shadows of the keep.

"And where will you be?"

"I will be waiting in the keep with one of our prisoners."

43

CYRAN ORENDAIN

EIDELMERE CLIMBED HIGHER IN THE SKY, RISING OVER THE OLD OAK and reaching a height even with Nevergrace's battlements before soaring forward, his rage seething and sheeting into the other realm.

"They will have seen the coming of our dragons by now," Ineri said from below. "Particularly the stone dragon. You cannot hide that beast behind a mountain. So, Vyk, there is no longer any need for stealth."

Vyk immediately cried out, bellowing a strange battle call, his mouth gaping, his teeth seeming like blunt-edged weapons waiting to be unleashed on their enemy.

The six other dragons swooped in behind them, and they all fanned out to surround the southern, western, and eastern walls of the Never. The north's dragons no longer sat on the battlements. Cyran couldn't see any of their heads in the baileys, either. A warning lanced through the back of his mind. The Dragon Queen had known they were coming long before now.

"Dragon Queen!" Sir Jedsin, the guard riding the sun dragon, belted, and his voice rumbled over the castle and echoed around the baileys. "We have come to reclaim what is ours. But we wish for you to depart our lands in peace. If you allow your remaining hostages to live and walk free, we will not attack."

The keep remained as quiet and empty as a graveyard during the witching hour. Cyran circled Eidelmere around and swooped in closer to the sun dragon and the outer wall.

A lithe figure clad in black armor with barbs and spikes like dragon horns strode from under a stone canopy atop the roof of the keep. The Dragon Queen kept a hand clasped on her sword's hilt and moved with absolute confidence. Massive black wings unfurled behind the keep, extending outward as if the keep itself were a shadow dragon ready to transform and take flight.

Cyran's blood surged with ice.

"Certainly by now you know why we are here, rider of the sun dragon." The Dragon Queen lifted a booted foot up onto the base of a crenellation and stood even with the sun dragon and Eidelmere. Her brown locks flowed out of her helm and visor and snapped in the wind. "We are not willing to release any living prisoners or leave this outpost until our queen is safely returned to us. And because you already know this, I assume you've finally brought her in this"—she swept her hand out beyond the keep, indicating Belvenguard's legion—"overwhelming gesture of peace."

Vyk raged behind Cyran, cursing and demanding her blood.

Sir Jedsin hesitated, and his voice cracked. "This is our final offer, or we will destroy you and whatever dragons you have brought with you."

"Then you will destroy your own outpost and kill all the residents of the Never in the process."

Cyran's eagerness for battle ebbed. Jaslin could still be inside the keep or somewhere else within the castle, as could his friends and so many others.

"I have a proposition." The Dragon Queen held out one of

her hands. This time she gripped a folded parchment. "Take this to Igare and have him decide how this day will unfold for the north and the south, and for all of Cimeren. I wish he would have come, but he must be hiding away in the Summerswept Keep where he feels safe and warm."

Anger spewed inside Cyran. It would not be safe for the king to be here, and Igare needed to ready and command the defenses at Galvenstone.

The Dragon Queen waited, but the sun dragon did not approach. Sir Jedsin kept his mount hovering out near the outer curtain. The Dragon Queen scoffed, faced Cyran, and said, "You, young man of the Never. You have returned yet again. And *you* ride without a mage. Perhaps you should be leading this incursion."

Cyran swallowed.

"And yet you do not even wear the armor of a guard, much less bear the weapons of a dragonknight," the Dragon Queen continued. "Take this message to Igare, and if he does not agree to my demands, then we may kill each other. I do not yearn to kill you now."

Cyran studied her for a minute. Was she attempting to trick him by drawing him closer? Her other dragons were not in sight, but by coming closer to grab a message, he would make himself more vulnerable to the shadow dragon. He glanced around, searching for other hiding wings. Only those of the shadow dragon were visible, extending from behind the keep.

"I do not know if she speaks the truth," Eidelmere said in Cyran's head, *"but if she has archers and dragons hidden around the castle, she could start this battle at any moment. I, however, no longer care. I yearn to devour her, and damn the consequences. I will even welcome death."*

"You cannot try to eat her," Cyran replied. *"Not yet. Those I love could still be inside, with blades held to their throats."*

"I have already lost all those I loved."

"I am truly sorry, my friend. When this is over, I will do all I can for you." After swallowing and taking a deep breath, Cyran urged Eidelmere over the empty baileys and toward the keep. The forest dragon flapped and hovered near the merlons of the keep before turning sideways and slowly drifting closer. Cyran kept his eye on the shadow dragon's wings. Or was that what the Dragon Queen wanted him to do? The obvious could be a distraction.

The Dragon Queen reached out farther. "I do not even have my sword drawn."

Cyran snatched the parchment from her, and Eidelmere swooped away. No dragons came screaming from their hiding places around the castle. No fire spewed at them. Eidelmere slowly flew back to the sun dragon as Cyran glanced at the message. It was sealed with black wax and stamped with the insignia of a rampant dragon.

"I will take this to Igare." Cyran held the parchment over his head.

The Dragon Queen nodded.

"Dragons of Belvenguard, follow me." Sir Jedsin turned and flew away from the battlements and didn't stop until he reached an area around the old oak. He lifted his visor and turned to Cyran. "We have a storm dragon that can take you."

"I thought only the north had storm dragons," Cyran said.

The guard cast him a quizzical look. "We would be at a severe disadvantage if we did not have some of our own." He motioned to his archers, and the two on the quarterdeck unfurled and waved red and gold flags of Galvenstone.

A minute or so later, a dark blue dragon with a mage and unarmored guard dropped from the sky and hovered with them.

"This young man will take the storm dragon to Galvenstone and return with the king's answer," Jedsin said to the storm dragon's riders while pointing at Cyran. Then he addressed Cyran. "You are unarmored, so the storm dragon can carry you as you are, and you know more about the Never than any of us. I would be of less assistance if the king must decide on a strategy to regain the outpost. You may also be able to offer tips that could lower the risk to the hostages, if it comes to that. Having a guard of Galvenstone make such decisions led to the downfall of the first scouting mission. Fly as fast as the storm dragon is able, and return here with the king's decision."

The guard on the storm dragon hesitantly nodded, and the storm dragon alighted in the field below. Cyran landed Eidelmere beside them and, after the guard had dismounted, climbed onto the storm dragon with its mage—a young woman with a scarred face and only one arm.

"I can take you to the keep straight away," the woman said. "Without having to go through the hassle of passing my bond with the dragon over to you."

Cyran nodded, not entirely sure what she was referring to or how the intricacies of bonding with dragons worked. The storm dragon flapped its wings, and Cyran was thrown back against his saddle as the creature leapt into the air and soared upward. They flew through gales of wind, rising into the clouds, and Cyran feared they might collide with the sky sea and be sucked into its depths.

Only storm dragons can fly where the air is so thin.

"You better bundle up," the mage said as she passed a roll of thick furs to him.

"Can a mage simply take over another's bond with their dragon?" Cyran slid the furs around his body.

"No. Only if the first mage dies, thus breaking the bond. Then another mage can try creating a new bond."

Like I did with Eidelmere.

"Though it doesn't always work a second time," the dragonmage continued. "An alternative that can sometimes be used is when a mage allows another to utilize their bond for a time. But the bond has to be willingly offered. Coercion or compelling a mage will not work. However, it is rumored that the Dragon Queen, or a mage as powerful as she, can break another mage's bond and forge a new one even if the first mage is still alive. And there are also dragon thieves who can sever and steal such bonds."

Dragon thieves? Conflicting ideas and thoughts shuffled around in Cyran's head before molding together. All this information seemed like things he probably needed to know.

They burst through a cloud bank into clear skies between the bank and the sky sea, which loomed in all its majesty overhead. The storm dragon leveled out, and for a moment the world seemed still and quiet, even peaceful.

Then the dragon rolled and plunged back into the clouds, a cold wet biting into Cyran's nose and cheeks before he tugged a fur up past his jaw and nestled into it. A white shroud whipped past as the storm dragon trilled and bolted onward. Cyran could not see more than a dragon's length ahead of them as the clouds raced by.

King Igare gripped the parchment, the seal of the rampant shadow dragon torn in two. Cyran wished he could sever a shadow dragon so easily. The king's eyes darted across the message, and everyone in the chamber remained quiet. Riscott, Tiros, Cartaya, and Lisain all studied Cyran now. He tried to pretend he didn't feel their judging and questioning eyes.

Memories of the letter he'd received in the tavern returned. Someone wanted to warn him about one of the king's councilmembers. They wanted to warn Sir Kayom as well, although

Cyran hadn't been able to learn much about the matter from Kayom before he was killed. Maybe if Dage had shared his letter and who might have sent it, they would be closer to understanding whom the warning referred to in addition to the clandestine face behind the messages. It could have been any one of these four who sent the letters, or even the king or Sir Paltere for all Cyran knew. The only facts Cyran held were that Dage's message had been sealed with red wax, supposedly indicating it was from Galvenstone, as had theirs, and they had received theirs in this city while Dage had been at the Never when his message was given to him by a servant of the previous lord.

King Igare huffed and crumpled up the letter in one fist. "I want to do everything I can to make sure any survivors at Nevergrace make it out of the outpost alive, but the Dragon Queen is making that an impossibility."

Cyran's heart swirled in a sea of emotion. *Jaslin. Emellefer. Garmeen. Laren. Brelle. Dage.* He could only offer the king a subtle nod.

"She demands the return of her queen, but..." Igare held a palm upward and shook his head. "If it weren't for that assassin, who was probably sent by one of their own battling for Murgare's throne, this would all be *much* easier."

Cyran's mind snapped away from the present and focused on a run of ideas tumbling through his head. The Dragon Queen wouldn't have sent the assassin to kill her own queen only to fly all the way over the Evenmeres on a risky venture none before had accomplished—except on storm dragons—only to demand her return. Unless she was truly trying to confuse both sides and was willing to undertake a lot of strain in order to do so.

But what were other, more likely, alternatives? He had to piece together possibilities from what little evidence he had, like one of the dragonguard of old. It had been Jaslin who first told him she read that in one of her stories.

The king's reasoning made the most sense, that some heir of the deceased dark king or contenting lord feared what the queen would say, and they wanted her silenced. Then this person could rise to power in Murgare. All Cyran knew was that the assassin had a missing tongue so he could not speak and he had a tattoo of a raven inside a triangle on his throat. The assassin also used sorcery—the bone and earth magic of a conjuror—and climbed walls and was hiding in the rafters when he was found.

Why would a man, even a tongueless one, kill the queen if it almost guaranteed his own death? It could be the temptation of riches. Or maybe Cyran couldn't fully comprehend the dark workings of the north. A slippery itch of suspicion bloomed inside him like a black vine and ensnared his bones as he glanced to each of the king's councilmembers.

Cartaya the conjuror studied him from beneath her mauve hood and white hair. Riscott wore his typical haughty smirk. Tiros stared without emotion, has hands folded on his red robes and chain belt. The quiet Lisain, the clergyman who seemed too young to even be wearing the white cloth, met his eye and offered an amiable if not forced grin.

Who else would benefit from the death of the Murgare queen? Cyran recalled the council discussing the possibility that a lord in the south might have sent the assassin. Perhaps, if this lord wished for a war between the north and Galvenstone, but such a war would likely involve the fiefdoms as well and would come crashing down on all of them. That left a lord or the king of the Rorenlands or the Weltermores. Maybe one of them desired to start a war between Belvenguard and Murgare, the two mightiest kingdoms. Or it was possible one of those king-doms hoped to crush the weakened victor of such a war, or to crush Belvenguard *during* the war, as Belvenguard lay between them and the north.

The last possibility was that the queen had herself killed. Was that absurd? If the north tortured and killed their prisoners, they might believe all others did as well. Then the queen might have wanted to kill herself before the long days of pain began.

The council was discussing the current matter quietly when Cyran caught Cartaya's eye again.

"Conjuror?" Cyran asked.

"Squire?" she replied. "I cannot call you 'guard' as you have not been inducted."

Cyran smiled as affably as he could manage. "When you cast the magic of bone and earth, do you need your voice to do so?"

Cartaya's eyebrows rose, and she cocked her head. "Conjurors do have to say the word of power associated with their... let's simply call it a 'spell' for simplicity. You have to know the true name of the spell. But it is much more than that—it is a feeling pulled from the lands we tread and the framework of our own bodies. I can try to teach you someday, but it takes decades to learn, and only a rare few are able to harness the power."

"But you need to at least utter this word? Not just think it?"

She nodded, her forehead wrinkling in confusion. "It can be very quiet though, so others do not hear it. Only the earth and its bones need to hear the name."

The other councilmembers fell silent and scrutinized him.

Then the tongueless assassin could not have been using magic to climb a wall and float amongst the rafters as they claimed. Not if he couldn't speak. From what Cyran knew of dragon magic, which was far rarer than bone and earth magic, it was very limited and did not have broad and encompassing capabilities such as floating up into the air or climbing walls like a spider.

Cyran looked at the councilmembers again. Someone here must have created the lie that the assassin used magic. Cartaya was the one who initially mentioned the kingsknights had already pulled the assassin from the rafters before she'd arrived.

It seemed likely that this intelligent conjuror would have thought of the discrepancy of needing to speak to use bone and earth magic and would have questioned such an allegation. She would not have been so dense as to use that as her lie if it were her doing. But maybe she was protecting someone else. *One of the four has become very unlikely.*

"But if we cannot give her Queen Elra, then the Dragon Queen is demanding to be granted more lands around Nevergrace and for the outpost to remain the property of Murgare." Igare rose and paced about the trial chamber. He flung the Dragon Queen's message into the hearth, where the flames caught it and crackled as they chewed at its fibers with wavering orange teeth. "We cannot give away our lands to such evil. She is also threatening the hostages and is still killing one every dawn and dusk."

"I wonder how many of them are still alive," Riscott said. "Maybe we should have the squire continue with the assault. If more die, they would have died anyway."

Those words felt like a kick to Cyran's gut.

"The longer we leave a legion—no matter how small—away from Galvenstone, the more we weaken ourselves here." Tiros twirled a finger in the curls of his hair. "I see no alternative but to take Nevergrace back by force. And if that is the case, it would be better to do so now rather than wait any longer. More hostages could die during the battle, but two die every day already."

The king looked to Cartaya, who was still watching Cyran as she strummed a lock of white hair, lost in thought. After a moment, she noticed the king's attention. "I see no other option than to reclaim our northernmost outpost by force. We cannot allow Murgare to hold it when their legions come sailing across the Lake on Fire. And clearly, we cannot give them the Never and more lands around it."

"The Thief and the Assassin are deceptive." Lisain's head was lowered over his folded hands. "But I have prayed to the Siren of the Sea and the Great Smith, and they have hinted that we follow the path of the Paladin and the Shield Maiden."

The king paced about for a few minutes in quiet contemplation before stopping and facing Cyran. "Then I am left with no alternative. I do not wish any harm to the captives of Nevergrace. They are an honorable and brave people whose history dates back to the last age." He swallowed, but boldness rang in his following words. "Do whatever you can to avoid causing harm to any of the captives. But you and the rest of the legion have my authority to take your outpost back, son of the Never."

44

CYRAN ORENDAIN

CYRAN STEPPED FROM THE STORM DRAGON'S SADDLE ONTO A FIELD south of Nevergrace. The stone, sun, rose, and silver dragons and their riders all awaited him, their anticipation of him speaking flooding from their demeanors.

Cyran faced them. "We go to war."

Vyk shook his fists in the air and yelled. The others either nodded or silently went to work tightening harnesses and preparing weapons.

Sir Jedsin approached Cyran and said, "Give me the king's orders exactly." Cyran quickly summarized all the king had said, and Jedsin addressed everyone. "We fly within the hour, before the Dragon Queen discovers that our messenger has returned. We will take them by surprise."

"I was starting to lose my thirst for blood." Vyk worked the mechanism on his crossbow, his long blond hair cascading from his helm and hanging to his backside. "And I didn't like the feeling."

"None of the captives are likely to still be alive anyway," Sir Jedsin said. "The north is probably only deceiving us by threatening to kill them. Expect Murgare to continue to try to trick and bait us. They will hope to use that massive black beast of theirs and the Dragon Queen to even the odds. The rest of them will swoop in from wherever they are hiding and will concentrate on one of us at a time, probably starting with the one they consider the most dangerous—the stone." He pointed to the stone dragon's guard. "Be ready. Our defense strategy is to not let them converge and attack only a single one of us. If they manage to do that, the advantage of our numbers will mean nothing. Our primary objective is to kill the shadow dragon. If we can drop that creature out of the sky, the others will also fall. Or they may even flee."

"But how do we kill that thing?" the stone dragon's guard asked.

"With a lot of lances and bolts." Sir Jedsin turned to address all of the legion. "You may be thinking we should strive to unseat the Dragon Queen, but that has never been done. And you shall not endanger yourselves and everyone else attempting such a feat. If you see an opportunity for a joust, pretend to aim for her, but mages"—he pointed to several of them—"veer your dragons so your guard can strike her mount instead. Preferably in some vital area."

"We could just fly in and ram the keep," one of the many archers of the stone dragon said. "We could put our beast's battering horns to good use here and kill every Murgare soldier still inside."

"Our dragon *could* topple the keep with a couple good blows, but that will kill any captives left inside as well," the stone's mage added. "It would be a great risk since we don't know if any captives are in there."

"It may be worth the sacrifice if the collapsing keep takes the Dragon Queen with it," Sir Jedsin said and then noticed Cyran, whose expression probably appeared wounded. "That was simply hyperbole. I was focusing on the thought of her dying."

Cyran nodded to dismiss any offense the guard's suggestion had caused, and he said, "But we cannot collapse the keep. Not with the possibility that there may still be people of the Never trapped inside. Even if there is only one such person left. And our attack should not turn the proud watchtowers of Nevergrace into rubble, either."

"More than one captive will likely die no matter how we approach this situation," Sir Jedsin said. "And more have died every day that we have waited. We will try using our dragons' other means, but we will not wait much longer before attacking the keep. And if it comes to it, we will have the stone dragon smash the keep to pieces."

Cyran swallowed a hard lump in his throat. Everyone else loaded up whatever supplies—bedrolls, food stuffs, pans—from where they had made camp and brought their possessions to their dragons. The storm dragon's guard and mage moved their mount, retreating behind the others, but they did not appear to be leaving quite yet.

"Then this is it," Vyk said. "The day of redemption. For the Never."

"You may see her as she is today," Cyran said. "Scorched, missing gates, unkempt baileys. Empty. But Nevergrace still stands her ground. She is proud and has stood watch over the Evenmeres and the unknown beyond for centuries." Others looked up from their crossbows and saddles. "Her people are few but proud. Her last dragon's heart is wounded, but he also remains proud. And determined."

Eidelmere's anger and sorrow parted amidst a flash of surprise.

Cyran continued, "We of the outpost know we are not Murgare's primary target, but we've stood watch, patiently, living with dignity and honor out in the eastern reaches of Belven-guard. Whatever lurks in the forest has watched her as well, and yet it does not dare challenge her or her people. But now the north has come knocking at her gates. With dragons and ice and fire. And yet she still stands. Her people have been taken prisoner. Most of her dragons slaughtered. The Dragon Queen resides in her bosom. Murgare beasts defile her den and wreak havoc upon her watchtowers, her walls, her keep. But she still stands. And today, we will throw down the dragons that have taken her. We will smite the Dragon Queen and release Belvenguard from the grip of the north. We will free the prisoners locked inside her. We may bring fire and bolt and lance. Wings and dragonsteel. And yet even if we shall fall, she will still stand."

Cyran walked over to Eidelmere, who lowered his head without a sound or word. Silence drifted over the field south of the old oak like a warm breeze, and Cyran climbed into Sir Kayom's saddle, taking up his seat and unsheathing his sword. The dragonsteel blade burned with green light, the light of a forest dragon. The light of Nevergrace.

"Now, we take her back!" Cyran brandished his sword and pointed north.

Vyk screamed, veins bounding in his temples and neck as others cheered. Ineri quietly strapped herself into the turret below before hacking. The stone dragon's four enormous wings rose and dipped, and the beast lifted into the sky. The legion spread out and swept over the broken crown of the oak where the last silver had flown into it. They soared north, hoping to arrive before Murgare saw them and had time to mount their dragons.

Once they reached the Never, they fanned out around three of its walls again, and Sir Jedsin flew to the forefront. "A mighty speech, dragon rider," he said to Cyran with a rueful grin, "but now we have to wait and see if this bloody bitch will listen or if we will have to smash the Never into the earth."

Cyran's stomach clenched, but he remained silent. The watchtowers, keep, and baileys appeared empty again, with no sign of dragons at all. Only the smell of smoke lingered over the area. "Why is there still smoke?"

"It is nothing more than dissipating mist dragon breath." Jedsin pointed to the fog around the archway and walls, which was less dense than it had been on Cyran's previous visits.

But now it *smelled* like smoke. Cyran didn't recall the mist smelling before. And there was a thicker patch of it back somewhere around the den.

"Dragon Queen," Jedsin said as his mighty sun dragon drifted back and forth just beyond the southern wall of the outpost. "We have taken your message to King Igare. Your queen cannot be returned to you. Her crimes against our people and many others have made her a prisoner who cannot be released. You may go now in peace, if you leave your prisoners and vow to never return to these lands."

The murmur of the wind in the distant pines was the only voice to answer them.

"And so we wait," Jedsin said. "For a few minutes." He swung his mount around and swept over the land beyond the southern wall but appeared afraid of the north side of the keep, where the shadow dragon had been hidden. And he did not pass over the battlements.

"Are they still here?" Cyran asked Eidelmere, only through their connection in the dragon realm.

"I cannot tell," the dragon replied. *"Something is blanketing this place, and I cannot smell a thing other than smoke and burned wood and stone."*

Cyran attempted to still his hands. Heartbeats passed like hours as the forest and the distant wall of angoias watched and waited. Their dragons hovered and released shrill cries. Archers slowly swiveled their crossbows to aim at different points of interest.

"Then we are forced to ram the keep down and kill the Murgare guard and the Dragon Queen while they are inside it." Jedsin motioned to the stone dragon. "Prepare the trebuchet and gain momentum. Archers, keep your bolts trained on the sides of the keep where that beast will emerge. Mages, have your dragons heat up the north's soldiers if they run for their mounts or anything else."

The stone dragon drifted away, its wings beating in a slow and steady rhythm. As the dragon circled back to the oak to return at its swiftest speeds, two men prepared the trebuchet on its back by cocking the catapult's arm into launching position and loading its sling. Vyk growled, his breaths coming in raspy bursts. The other dragons hovered. Lances creaked in their mounts.

"What if she is not even here?" Cyran asked. "We would destroy the keep for nothing, and Murgare would laugh at our folly."

"And where else could she be hiding her beasts besides in the den or behind the keep?" Jedsin shook his head. "The forest is too dense for dragons of their size. And the angoias are too far away. I will not allow you to land and walk about in there, so do not even consider that option. You would compromise our legion by taking our number of dragons down to six."

Cyran swung around in his saddle, studying their surroundings before looking up. A matting of clouds clung to the lower reaches of the sky. "What about up there?"

Jedsin scoffed. "Only a storm dragon can fly that high and remain there, where the air is so thin, for any length of time."

Cyran lidded his eyes in defeat. "But what if some of my people are still inside the keep?"

"I do not hear anyone screaming for us to stop. There are

windows. Surely we'd be able to hear someone, if they wanted to talk to us."

"Maybe they are not being allowed to scream."

"Then we once again fall back to either waiting for the captives to be put to death, or we risk reclaiming the outpost, even though we will cause some damage in the process. I hope to kill the Dragon Queen *before* she is prepared and mounts that beast of hers. At a minimum, shaking the keep a little and making the north think it's going to fall down around them will strike fear into their hearts. It could make them listen to us once they realize we can and will destroy them."

Cyran groaned and squeezed the hilt of Sir Kayom's sword. *Tamar. What do I do now? Jaslin, are you in there?*

The stone dragon swung about and began beating its pairs of wings faster and faster. The beast lowered its head, aligning its neck with its body. The gargantuan curled horns on the sides of its head seemed to grow larger and more threatening.

Sir Jedsin veered his sun dragon aside as the stone dragon soared faster and faster. The two silver and two rose dragons flew in close to the stone dragon to escort it over the castle's walls. The escorting dragons breathed rivers of silver fire and red light—to blind their adversaries—as they passed over the outer bailey.

Damn this situation, and damn the Dragon Queen.

The rose and silvers flanked the larger beast at different heights, their archers swinging outward and preparing to loose bolts at any targets that appeared. Cyran sat paralyzed, only able to watch.

The stone dragon rammed into the upper keep, and a deafening crack blasted over the Never's walls. Stone fissured. The archers and riders of the stone dragon were flung forward against their restraints as the dragon was slammed to a halt. Its wings beat out of sync for a few flaps until it righted itself. The wall of the keep collapsed inward. Stones crumbled and toppled, and the entire keep shifted and leaned. Muffled screams carried out from within the keep.

"Loose the trebuchet!" Jedsin cried.

The two soldiers manning the ballista released its throwing arm, and its huge counterweight plunged downward. The arm whipped forward, and a boulder was hurled from its sling. The boulder sailed and smashed into the top edge of the keep, crushing merlons before being deflected and smashing into the canopy the Dragon Queen had strode out from prior. The small shelter collapsed with a crash, leaving a pile of rubble atop the roof of the keep.

"Pray to the Paladin that the Dragon Queen was still under that." Jedsin glanced about, anticipating the arrival of the shadow dragon. He shouted at the keep so those inside could hopefully hear him. "That was only the first blow. We will continue battering the keep until it is—"

A massive shadow fell over the castle and grew in an instant to encompass all of the Never. A skirling wind pierced Cyran's ears. When he looked up, the shadow dragon had long dropped from the clouds and sky above, and the beast pounded into the stone dragon's back, the black dragon biting and clawing at the archers and ballista on its enemy.

Fuck.

Archers screamed, and bolts launched with wild trajectories. The shadow dragon latched its teeth around the base of one of the stone dragon's wings. The shadow dragon jerked its head and tore the wing clean off, sending the stone dragon into an erratic weave and then a downward spiral.

Archers shrieked and wailed as the shadow dragon ripped them from the stone dragon's quarterdeck and flung them away. A volley of men rained upon the Never's walls and bailey. The trebuchet splintered and fell from the quarterdeck as logs and sticks.

"Converge on the shadow dragon!" Sir Jedsin barked, and the others, many of whom were stunned by the swiftness and ferocity of the attack, regained their senses.

"Take the shot if you have one!" Cyran said to his archers as he urged Eidelmere toward the carnage.

"Currently, I risk hitting the stone dragon or its men," Ineri said. Vyk bellowed in anger.

The smell of smoke lingered. It was not dispersed mist from a dragon's breath. It carried a strong scent of burnt pine and oak, and it was thicker than it had been during Cyran's previous visits. Then he knew. The shadow dragon's surprise attack was a distraction for the rest of their legion. Its savage ambush drew attention and would aid the remainder of the north's dragons by allowing them to burst from hiding and arrive unnoticed. The lingering smoke was from the forest, where their dragons must have burned trees to create pockets for each of them to lie flat and hide.

As Cyran's comrades raced toward the shadow dragon, Cyran swung Eidelmere around. A fire and two ice dragons had already surfaced from the canopy of the forest and swooped toward them, about to take Belvenguard's legion unaware.

45

SIRRA BRACKENGLAVE

THE SUN DRAGON'S GUARD FINISHED MAKING HIS DEMANDS FROM beyond the walls of the castle.

"The windows are still all barred and shuttered, but we don't have enough men to watch all the prisoners and keep them quiet," Yenthor said to Sirra.

"Bar every chamber with people inside." Sirra pointed to the rooms housing prisoners as she strode along the hallway, and Yenthor and Zaldica and two other archers who had remained behind continued wedging beams against doorways. "We do not have to keep them quiet any longer. And these men will probably not destroy their own keep with that dragon. Not if there are captives inside. When you are done here, meet me on the roof." She paced to an empty bedchamber in the upper keep and furtively glanced out the window that had been partially shuttered. The stone dragon wheeled away from the keep.

They may indeed try to destroy their own outpost.

Sirra strode out of the chamber and entered the bedchamber where Menoria was being kept.

"Then Belvenguard has answered your demands?" The

young lady scratched at one of her forearms and did not stop scratching.

Sirra shook her helmed head. "They never intended to. The Murgare queen must be dead, and it is time for the north to answer."

Menoria gasped. "Then what will become of the people of the Never?"

"That will be decided by your dragon riders outside this keep." Sirra weighed taking this young lady with her as a hostage versus taking her friend, Jaslin. Most people only saw power where it was displayed and reassured by others. Menoria was of more value to Belvenguard. Thus, she should stay and, in essence, defend her keep by remaining inside it. "Stay where you are, and all will be safe."

Menoria nodded, her face pale and grave.

"We will settle our dispute this day." Sirra turned and exited, barring the door behind her. She hurried past the furiously working archers for the stairway and ascended to the uppermost story.

A crack exploded through the keep, and the walls boomed and shook. The stone fist of the Never's foundations quaked, and a wall not far away buckled and collapsed. The keep teetered, and Sirra braced herself against another wall.

And so they are *willing.* "Shadowmar, dive," Sirra said into the depths of the dragon realm, her voice and connection with her mount extending far beyond what any other dragonmage could achieve. She raced for the roof, climbing higher, but she stopped just shy of opening the door, her senses tingling.

Aylión. She saw the stone canopy over the roof collapsing, and she hesitated. The whistling of a massive projectile sounded just before stone exploded against stone. The keep bucked again. The canopy collapsed just beyond the doorway, and rubble pounded against the door's planks.

Sirra descended a flight and flung open the door to a soldiers' chamber, striding for the balcony. She stepped outside and ascended the outer stairs she had used before to reach the roof. When her head rose above the crenellations, she saw the remnants of the canopy piled high in the center of the roof. Shadowmar's screeches and growls rang over the castle. After Sirra climbed onto the summit of the mound of rubble, Shadowmar had torn a wing from the stone dragon, and the two of them crashed into the inner bailey. Five of the other dragons flew toward her mount, and in the dragon realm, she heard their crossbow's triggers snap.

"Shield yourself," Sirra said in her mind.

Shadowmar seized the flailing stone dragon at the base of its skull with her teeth and reared back, pulling the stone dragon up and exposing its underside. A volley of dragonbolts thudded into the stone dragon's neck and underside of its chest. Gasps sounded, and curses flew. The stone dragon wailed as its head whipped around before falling still. Shadowmar leapt into the air and flew toward the roof.

The fire and ice dragons took flight and soared toward the unsuspecting legion. And the mist dragon launched out of a pit of fog in the den and came at them from below.

46

JASLIN ORENDAIN

THE SHOUTING OF A MAN AROSE OUTSIDE THE KEEP, BUT THE window in the lord's room had been boarded shut. Jaslin peeked through the gaps but could only see a slit of the outside, which overlooked the west watchtower. Inside the keep but likely a story below their chamber, someone shouted to the Murgare archer guarding their doorway. The archer replied and then glanced into their room.

Something is finally happening. Once the archer turned his back to their chamber, Jaslin crept toward the doorway.

"What are you doing?" Emellefer whispered in a frightened tone. Brelle glanced up as Jaslin passed by her, and the squire stared, likely sensing Jaslin was about to attempt something. Laren nudged Dage, and they both sat up.

A thunderous crack sounded, and the keep bucked and swayed beneath Jaslin's feet, throwing her toward the archer who had just stumbled to his knee and shouted in surprise. Jaslin collided with the archer's back and grabbed the hilt of the broadsword at his waist, ripping it from its sheath. The archer whipped around, striking her on the temple with his elbow as he grasped the crosspiece of his sword in one hand. Their eyes locked as Jaslin tried to tear the sword from his grip, but he gritted his teeth and clamped onto his weapon with a strength much greater than hers.

The archer cast her a devious grin as he raised the crossbow in his other hand. It was too large of a weapon to hold steady with only one hand on the trigger handle, but because she was so close, he wouldn't have to maintain much control to impale her. Jaslin considered releasing the sword and jumping out of the way, or grabbing for the crossbow. But either way, he could cut her down.

The crossbow rose and pointed at her chest. Brelle leapt in between them and seized the crossbow, leveraging it with both of her hands and twisting it farther upward. Laren struck the archer with an open palm to the chin, and the archer's head snapped back. Brelle kept pushing on the crossbow and angled the bolt straight upward before the archer's wrist started to give. She continued to force the end of the weapon up and away from her, and the crossbow swung toward the archer and pointed directly at his face. His wrist popped, and he bellowed in pain but managed to jerk his sword away from Jaslin.

The crossbow twanged. The bolt buried into the bottom of the archer's chin. His eyes turned glassy, and he toppled over. Footsteps sounded out on the stairs.

"Quick, drag him inside." Jaslin tugged on the archer's feet.

Laren and Brelle grabbed hold just as Dage seized the man below the arms, and they carried him into their chamber. Jaslin quickly but quietly shut the door. The footsteps continued up the stairs and onto the landing.

Another bang erupted somewhere above them. Stones crashed, and the keep shuddered. Jaslin cracked the door open and peeked out. There was no one there. She pulled the door open farther and stepped out. More footsteps sounded below, racing up the stairway. As Brelle was about to step out, Jaslin flung the door closed again, trapping herself out in the hall. She ran and hid behind a sitting chair.

A man and woman archer stepped onto the landing. "Bar that door." The woman pointed at their chamber. She and the man hefted a beam leaning against the wall, and the man held it in place as the woman used a maul to quickly drive one long nail through the beam and into the door. The beam extended beyond the margins of the door and to either side of the doorway. The beam held the door—whose frame only allowed it to open inward—closed by overlapping the stones of its frame. After the two archers had finished, they rushed up the stairway to the roof.

Jaslin waited a moment and hurried back to their door. Someone inside shook the handle and banged on the oak planks.

"They've left," Jaslin said, "but they nailed the door closed."

"You have to get us out of here," Brelle shouted.

Jaslin glanced around. She dashed through the open doorway of a chamber across the hall. The shutters on this chamber's window were open. Dragons swooped around outside the keep. Jaslin trembled as she darted to the hearth and grabbed an iron poker. She hurried back to the lord's room and wedged the poker between the beam and the door, levering the beam. She heaved and used all her weight to bounce against the poker. After a dozen attempts, the nail slid out of the door a finger's width.

"Yank the door open." Jaslin kept prying at the beam. Dragons shrieked outside, and men yelled. The keep shuddered, and the floor leaned and sloped farther to one side. The door pulled open a crack and slammed the beam against the stones on either side of its frame. "Keep doing it."

After several minutes of trying, the nail slipped farther and farther out of the wood, and with one mighty jerk from those inside, the nail popped free. The beam crashed onto the floor. Jaslin glanced around and strained to listen. No footsteps sounded over the clamor outside.

Brelle stepped up to the doorway, but Jaslin held up her hand and said, "Get the poker from the hearth. There will probably be others we will need to free."

Brelle disappeared for a moment as Dage and Laren stepped into the hallway.

Once Brelle reappeared, she was still empty-handed. "They must have taken the poker from the lord's chambers."

Jaslin cursed and motioned to the stairs. "We have to get out of the keep. The whole thing could collapse. But if there are any others from Nevergrace who are still alive, we must free them as well."

Emellefer did not exit the lord's chamber, and Jaslin ducked back inside. Emellefer huddled on the cot, rocking with her head in her hands.

"Emellefer, we have to get out of here." Jaslin grabbed her wrist.

"Leave me be." Emellefer scooted away and cowered. "You're going to get us all killed!"

"The keep is collapsing." Laren raced back into the chamber and pulled Emellefer up as she punched at his chest.

"Leave me," she said. "I don't want to be executed."

Brelle took one of Emellefer's arms and wrapped it around her shoulder so she and Laren could both carry Emellefer between them. Brelle said, "You're going to die if you stay here."

The two squires hauled Emellefer out and down the stairs, following the others. On the next lower floor, three chamber doors were barred. Jaslin gave Dage her poker, and he and Brelle levered the beams loose with a few tugs. A dozen more people of Nevergrace rushed out, most of them women and children.

"To the next level." Jaslin led them down another flight of

stairs and opened more chambers, repeating the process with the third and second levels of the keep while gathering more iron pokers and tools to pry the beams off the doors. Menoria stepped out of one of the bedchambers, dazed and trembling. Jaslin hugged her and pulled her along. "I thought you had been killed."

Menoria barely managed a brief nod. When they finally reached the ground floor, they had amassed roughly fifty women and children, as well as a few men.

Two archers standing at the open doorway leading out of the keep turned to face them. The archers' eyes widened as they raised their crossbows. "Stop!"

Brelle hurled a poker at the archer on the right, and it struck the man's crossbow as he loosed. The bolt flew wide and hit the side wall. The other archer's crossbow twanged, and his bolt impaled the old blacksmith running beside Jaslin. The blacksmith collapsed with a bolt in his throat.

The others they had freed swarmed the archers as one archer tried to pull his sword, but Brelle, Dage, and Laren tackled him and finished him with his own blade. They did the same with his comrade before taking up the archers' crossbows and swords. The mass of people ran for the entrance.

"Wait!" Jaslin shouted, but most of the people did not stop. "There is still the chamber we were initially kept in." She ran past the throne room to a barred double doorway, her heart thudding chaotically. Strained voices rumbled inside the chamber.

She gripped the beam holding the doors closed and dug her fingernails into the wood, tearing and pulling. Brelle ran up beside her, as did Dage and Laren, and they pried the beam free. Wood fell and clattered on stone, and the doors swung inward. Three score of women and children, and a few knights and soldiers, ran out the doorway with wild eyes and sunken cheeks.

These were not the same people who had been in there with Jaslin. Those had mostly been soldiers.

The few men took up battle cries, and their footsteps thundered through the lower keep as the keep banged and thudded. The people they had just freed bolted out of the keep and into the courtyard. Jaslin followed the squires through the archway, and sunlight blinded her for a moment as dark forms swooped and shrieked overhead. The freed people of the Never darted about in different directions, some wailing in fear, others shouting for weapons as dragons danced and dived around the castle. Someone grabbed Jaslin's arm.

"Jaslin." Renily, the little redheaded girl, was hiding between a pile of straw and the wall of the keep.

Jaslin scooped her up and hugged her. "We must flee the outpost. Now."

"No. Not yet." Renily pointed to a cloud of fog hovering before the entrance to the den. "They took most of our soldiers and knights and put them down there. One of their dragons went in there too."

Jaslin stared at the swirling mist as possible outcomes swarmed in her mind. She shouted for Brelle, who stopped and turned. Laren and Dage did as well. Jaslin said, "We have to go into the den and free the others." She set Renily back behind the straw pile and ran for the fog, unsure if anyone was coming with her.

47

CYRAN ORENDAIN

"THEY'RE COMING FROM BEHIND US!" CYRAN YELLED AND BANKED Eidelmere away from the rest of his legion, attempting to lead the fast-approaching Murgare dragons away from his companions. Vyk screamed, and bolts from the Murgare dragons whistled as the projectiles sailed through the area where Eidelmere had just been. If they hadn't turned around and seen the other dragons coming, Eidelmere would have been dead.

The three attacking dragons released shrill battle cries, and the fire dragon dived with teeth and claws extended, its guard's lance angled for Cyran. Cyran ducked low, and Eidelmere dipped over the far side of the battlement. The fire dragon roared as it flapped frantically, attempting to ascend. The beast skimmed the wall with its wings and belly as its archers shouted and reloaded. Eidelmere swooped upward, and a bolt from one of Cyran's archers whizzed past his shoulder.

"Hit the bastard!" Vyk said just before his bolt impaled the fire dragon's neck with a thud. The beast roared and thrashed about as fire burst from its jaws. It whipped its wings wildly.

The two ice dragons veered off and swooped down at the rest

of Belvenguard's legion. Eidelmere's turret crossbow sprang, and another bolt sailed in a blur of steel and glinting sunlight. The bolt struck one of the ice dragons in the chest just under its rising wing, behind the shoulder. In the heart. A perfect shot while Eidelmere was twisting and rising and the ice dragons were speeding along.

The ice dragon tilted, and its opposite wing and shoulder clipped the side of the keep. The keep's weakened walls shuddered and fissured, but the impact stopped the dragon's flight abruptly and sent the beast spinning away in a maelstrom of wings and legs and neck. It crashed into the outer curtain with a bang.

"Ineri!" Vyk roared and pumped his fist.

A pale dragon with black wings burst from some hiding spot in the fog below and streaked upward. It took one of the rose dragons by surprise, biting into the rose dragon's neck. The lance on the attacking dragon impaled the bottom of the rose dragon's jaw, and the steel tip of the weapon poked out through the top of the dragon's skull. The rose dragon's eyes rolled back into its head. Its tail twitched with one final jerk, and the mist dragon tossed the rose aside, letting it plummet downward.

Cyran's nerves lurched at the sight, and he swung Eidelmere after the fleeing fire dragon, realigning his lance with every rise and fall the air currents put them through. The shadow dragon flew away from the dead stone dragon and its shattered quarterdeck and trebuchet, and the shadow dragon streaked for the roof of the keep.

More bolts flew from Murgare's dragons, the attackers concentrating their projectiles on only one of Belvenguard's dragons at a time. At least three bolts struck one of the silver dragons over its chest and flanks, and the silver shrieked before careening through the sky and crashing into a field. The impact hurled a cloud of dirt into the air.

People rushed from the open gates of the keep and swarmed the courtyard and bailey. They darted around, seeking cover while yelling and pointing to the sky.

Some of the people of Nevergrace are *still alive!*

The mist dragon shrieked as it buzzed over the escapees, and people collapsed or fled in terror.

Eidelmere hurtled toward the injured fire dragon, but their adversary flew faster and increased the gap between them before reaching the fray and taking the sun dragon by surprise. The fire dragon's guard skewered the sun dragon's flank with his lance, and the sun dragon wailed.

Eidelmere closed on the fire dragon as it slowed for its joust, and Cyran dipped Eidelmere, bringing his mount under his target. Cyran released his wooden lance, worried he might destroy it and not do much damage, and unsheathed The Flame in the Forest, holding it high. He yelled as they sailed under the fire dragon's belly, and his blade cleaved through the base of the fire dragon's turret and through the dragonsteel armor of the archer above—Murgare's archers all seemed to be wearing the coveted armor. As they screamed past, the turret split in two, and the body of the archer dropped from the sky. Ineri and Vyk loosed bolts. Their crossbows thrummed as Eidelmere's momentum carried them beyond the battle.

Cyran wheeled them about. The fire, ice, and mist dragons swarmed around the sun, silver, and rose dragons. Bolts flew between them, and teeth and claws flashed. The ice dragon raked pale claws along the silver dragon's neck, and rubies of blood spilled from gashes between scales and dripped from the sky. The mist dragon spewed fog before it and used its breath as cover to swoop in at different angles. When the dragon emerged from its cover, its archers loosed while Cyran's companions had to realign and aim. One bolt pierced the remaining silver dragon's scales. The rose dragon used its blinding breath of starlight in a manner similar to how the mist dragon used its breath.

Simple fog and light are the most powerful breaths when dragons fight dragons, as ice and fire are useless.

Cyran flew Eidelmere into the carnage.

48

SIRRA BRACKENGLAVE

SHADOWMAR SWUNG ABOUT AND LEANED HER NECK OVER THE decimated roof of the keep as her massive feet touched down. The keep rumbled under her weight. Sirra climbed into her saddle. Yenthor and Zaldica came running over the rubble. Yenthor leaped for the rope ladder and scaled up to the quarter-deck as Zaldica climbed into the turret. Sirra had left three of her own archers to guard the keep and its prisoners. Not enough to watch everyone inside, but more than she and her legion could spare.

Sirra grabbed her lance and pivoted it about as Shadowmar swung around the keep and launched back toward the attacking legion, what remained of them. The lone forest dragon had sailed past the fray but now hurtled back toward the others.

The dragonknight, Cyran. He could potentially be the most dangerous of the Belvenguard legion.

She veered Shadowmar to cut off the forest dragon's attack, but when the young rider saw Shadowmar's trajectory, he angled away. Still, Shadowmar was much faster and more agile. Sirra swooped between the melee in the sky and the forest dragon before drawing Shadowmar to a halt and hovering. The forest dragon pulled up short and swung to the side. The young man studied Sirra and stopped his dragon's flight.

"Your sister still lives," Sirra said as Shadowmar hissed and heaved smoke through her nostrils. Her breath created plumes of smog that looked like writhing horns. "She is in the keep."

Cyran's face—he wore no armor or helm of the guard—fell flat as he glanced down at the chaos of people storming about the bailey.

A flash of surprise hit Sirra. *They have escaped.*

"How do you know of my sister?" Cyran asked.

"She was the sharpest thorn in my side during our entire occupation of the Never." Sirra felt the poised archers behind and below her, their bolts hunting for targets on the forest dragon. "You can still call off your attack, and your sister may live."

"I cannot do that, Dragon Queen," Cyran said. "We cannot risk the ongoing sacrifices, and the king cannot return your queen."

But this was not your decision. You would not have wanted to risk your people. "Then we will all die over this place you call home. And will you believe it was all worth it? To have abducted and killed our king and queen to start a war that will swallow all of Cimeren and wrap it in dragon fire?"

"I simply want to reclaim my castle and have my sister live."

"Then you are going about this in all the wrong ways. No one but Shadowmar and me will survive this incursion."

Cyran did not answer, and Shadowmar slowly drifted closer, her nostrils twitching as if catching the scent of something interesting.

"One cannot help which side of the Evenmeres one is born on, but there is always the opportunity to realize misfortune," Sirra said. "You, a dragonknight, would be rewarded with the armor and shield and lance of your station and would not be forced to play a part for a king before receiving what you have earned. You would not fly a tired old forest dragon either. No offense to you, my friend"—she addressed Eidelmere directly—"but you have seen too many summers and should no longer be forced to carry riders into battle. And while you have probably served the outpost well for your days, your days are numbered. You should be returned to the woods of your home. To die in peace. And you, Cyran, could be riding the second most powerful dragon in the north."

"Do you honestly believe I would turn on my friends and family for armor and a dragon?"

She shook her head. "I do not. But I hoped you would so you could seek the truth. *And* for the opportunity to reform the dragonknights of old—a legion of those who fought side by side for justice and righteousness."

"What truths do you speak of?" Cyran flexed his hand on his lance and shield, his surprise and agitation seeping through his anger.

"The truth of the matter between the north and south. Of who was responsible for the so-called planting and cultivation of the Evenmeres. The truth about who destroyed old Cimerenden and the ancient kingdom of the elves."

"I'd rather focus on what each of us chooses to do with the present than some ancient past." His hair whipped in the wind. The forest dragon snarled.

"Oh, but it concerns the present. All of it. And the present is not always what it seems, especially to those who are blind."

Cyran laid a palm on his dragon's neck, possibly for his own reassurance or to reassure his mount. The tumult of bolts launching and dragons roaring and clashing played on behind Sirra, but her primary objective was to sway this man—the one who held a power almost no others did. Her guard could handle themselves.

"And of all the many types of people still living in Cimeren, I was one of the very few to have been there that day five hundred and three years ago," Sirra continued.

"You will not sway me with lies and promises of power. Leave my home. Even if you leave it as it is now, many lives may still be saved."

Shadowmar's nostrils twitched again, and rage spilled through her as she roared and spewed her wrath—her black fire —at the forest dragon.

"Shadowmar, stop!"

The forest dragon swooped up and shielded its riders with its wings before settling and hovering overhead. Cyran and his archers appeared more confused than wounded.

"I thought it was ignoble for one dragon to breathe at another," Cyran said. "That shows the true character of your mount."

Shadowmar's rancor roiled and seethed, and Sirra felt the object of her mount's fury like a bolt of lightning. Outrage and anger overflowed within Sirra. "Her wrath is attributed to your true character, dragonknight. She knows your scent. And not from prior encounters in the sky. She smelled it in the den of Nevergrace."

The young dragonknight paled, but he regained his composure. "I am technically still a squire of the Never. And I often had to go into the den."

Sirra lifted her spiked visor and glared at him with a knowing smirk. "She smelled your scent all over her nest and butchered eggs. You were the one who snuck in and hacked them to pieces."

Cyran did not answer for a minute. "Yes. I did it to stop the birth of a host of evil."

"Then you have been deeply deceived."

Shadowmar's malice stewed as she beat her wings and

hissed. *"This one must die,"* the dragon said in her mind. Shadowmar rarely ever spoke, even to Sirra.

"Not yet," Sirra replied to her mount, although her own rage heated her core and face. "We must be wise about this and control our anger. At least for the moment. If he joins us, he could help change the slowly spiraling fate of Cimeren and the north. But if he does not join us, we will kill him. And I will let you do the honors."

Shadowmar roared in frustration and fury, her cry blasting across the fields and the Never.

"You could have at least stolen the eggs instead of destroying *all* of them," Sirra said to Cyran after the roar had faded and the young man's ears might have stopped ringing. "The eggs of a shadow dragon are rare and barely seen each decade, and only then if the situation and environment is right. That clutch could have bought you your own kingdom, and if you would have raised them as your own, you could have taken a throne from anyone." She stopped, unleashing *desirité*, hoping to find out if he'd deceived them at all.

But Cyran did not answer.

Sirra suppressed a curse of frustration. The dragon realm could not detect a lie if no words were uttered. Only words could distort its many threads.

49

CYRAN ORENDAIN

"*She is trying to distract you,*" Eidelmere said in Cyran's head, "*and it is working.*"

"No," Cyran replied. "*I am distracting her. Think how much damage she could be doing to our comrades if she were in that fray.*"

Behind the shadow dragon, an ice and mist and wounded fire dragon swooped and wheeled about as lances flashed and bolts flew between them and the surviving rose, silver, and sun dragons. The rose dragon breathed a flash of red light, blinding its adversaries in a manner similar to direct sunlight.

And the Dragon Queen doesn't know I saved an egg.

"*But you are not considering her lies, are you?*" Eidelmere asked.

"*Of course not.*" But the temptation of forming a group of honorable dragonknights and guard, like those in the old legends who worked for good and came from a more just time, swirled in his thoughts. But none of this was true. She was trying to sway him, to lure him away from his comrades and make him question everything. Such were the stories of good and evil. And the Dragon Queen's lies sounded like so many tales Jaslin had read and often used to tell Cyran about when they were children—how an evil conjuror type attempted to draw a hero away from his good king by tempting him with coin or power beyond reckoning. Cyran had even briefly considered the possibility that this woman might not be as evil as he'd been led to believe, but that was always part of their trickery, breaking down the first barrier. *"It would be best if we could put a lance or dragonbolt through her breastplate."*

"Indeed." Eidelmere flapped higher, keeping an advantageous position over the much stronger shadow dragon.

"If we could kill or unseat her—the ultimate evil leading this legion—the skirmish at Nevergrace would be over."

"Then decide." Eidelmere turned and floated in the wind.

"Fly at her." Cyran gripped his lance tighter. *"We will take her by surprise. That is our and the Never's only hope."*

"Your lance is wood. It will never work. It would be best to have the archers shoot her down."

"It will probably take more than two dragonbolts to bring that beast down, and I don't think it will give us time to shoot more than that. It already wants to kill me."

"Are you ready, then?" Eidelmere asked.

"Is there any other option that will allow you to leave Nevergrace in peace?" Cyran called out to the Dragon Queen.

"If I have either Queen Elra or you. Those are the only two options for peace."

Cyran's hand nearly slipped from his lance's grip. The Murgare legion would all leave the Never and stop the killing if he went with them? "I thought you desired more lands for the north."

Sirra scoffed. "And why do you believe that?"

Because of your message to Igare. But you don't think I would have read it or known its contents. "She is nothing but lies, Eidelmere. If I go with her, they may just kill the rest of the legion, and then me."

The flurry of fighting dragons rolled closer to them as lances flashed and darted about and dragons circled away to charge each other. Crossbows thrummed and reloaded. Bolts screamed across the sky.

"Your companions arrive," Cyran said.

For an instant, the Dragon Queen glanced over her shoulder. *"Dive!"* Cyran commanded Eidelmere.

"I hope you know what you're doing." Eidelmere collapsed his wings, and they plunged downward straight at the flying fortress of a dragon.

"Of course I do not." Cyran angled his lance. "But it is all I have the power to do."

The shadow dragon roared and reared up, trying to meet their sudden attack. Her tail flashed, and a barbed stinger at its tip dripped black liquid. The Dragon Queen glanced back and slammed her visor closed, gripping her lance and bracing against her shield. But she and her dragon did not start accelerating before Eidelmere was upon them.

Vyk screamed a battle cry.

Eidelmere streaked in, and Cyran angled his lance, adjusting for every movement, knowing when and where his mount would move. He had no middleman, no dragonmage, and what Sir Paltere had taught him came flashing back.

Cyran's lance rushed downward. He knew the Dragon Queen would do as Sir Paltere had shown him—deflect the blow. At the last instant, Cyran had Eidelmere dip lower, and he realigned his lance just before the movement, taking a new position and angle of attack only a sword's length from his target.

The Dragon Queen braced and angled her shield to deflect the blow, but Cyran anticipated it and struck her shield full on.

His lance shattered into splinters, the blow throwing him back. Her lance nearly pierced his neck, but he did not fight the force of his impact, instead allowing that force to bow him back farther. The tip of her weapon grazed his hair and scalp.

The Dragon Queen grunted under the impact of his blow.

Her body snapped back at the waist, and she was bent backward over her saddle and the dragon's neck. But she uttered a quick word and seemed to take on new strength. And she remained seated.

No! Cyran sailed past the shadow dragon, and his shoulder throbbed where the base of his shattered lance had smashed into him. Two bolts flew. Vyk's bolt punctured the shadow dragon's shoulder, and Ineri's impaled the beast's chest. But neither bolt sank deep enough through those scales to pierce her heart.

The roaring shadow dragon swung around, pursued Eidelmere, and snapped out, but the forest dragon contorted himself and dodged the other dragon's teeth. The dragons collided, and their talons latched onto each other's as they struggled, their jaws lunging for each other's necks. The shadow dragon bent Eidelmere's feet backward, and her black talons raked his flesh. Some of the old forest dragon's scales on his underbelly ripped off and fell. Eidelmere slipped free of the shadow dragon's grip and dropped backward into a plummeting dive. Cyran did not bring him up or slow him as the shadow dragon shrieked and used her teeth and talons to tug at the bolts lodged in her chest.

"I cannot outrun or contend with that beast," Eidelmere said.

"Neither can I contend with its rider." Once they had created a gap between them and the shadow dragon, Eidelmere's wings flared, and Cyran banked his mount around, headed for the base of the keep to hide. They skimmed over screaming people and the body of the stone dragon. Its titanic lance drew Cyran's attention, but such a weapon would be too heavy for Eidelmere. "We need another lance. One made of dragonsteel."

Cyran glanced back. The shadow dragon circled the keep as she tore a bolt from her flesh and dropped it into the mass of people in the bailey. Cyran searched about the castle's grounds.

The body of the dead rose dragon lay below the carnage in the air, but it was too close. If he went for it, he would not have enough time before the shadow dragon or another was upon him. However, the dead silver dragon's body had fallen out in the fields just beyond the Never.

They swooped over the battlements and dived.

50

JASLIN ORENDAIN

JASLIN COUNTED THE DRAGONS SWIRLING IN THE SKY AS SHE rushed for the den, wondering if there could still be a Murgare dragon waiting in the mist and darkness ahead. Men, women, and children tore past her, crying and wailing as they attempted to hide or find weapons. Smoldering fires of silver and gold and more typical fires of red and orange spotted the bailey as Jaslin fought her way through the madness. She had seen one ice dragon fall from the sky. The other ice dragon, a fire and a mist dragon, and the massive black shadow dragon were still all battling overhead. She glanced at the clouded entrance to the den.

What else could be waiting for her? She had accounted for the five dragons that had attacked Nevergrace.

"They're in there." Renily stepped out from behind the pile of straw and pointed at the den. "Lots of people."

Jaslin clenched a hearth poker in her hand and yanked a torch out of a sconce on the wall as Brelle and Laren trailed her. Jaslin lit the torch on a smoldering pile of straw and approached the fog before the den. Dragons hissed and circled above, the beasts sometimes diving with talons extended. Jaslin hunched and kept her head low. The mist dragon shrieked, and most of the people around her collapsed. Jaslin clamped her wrists over her ears and dropped to her knees. She trembled for a minute before her sheer terror slowly faded and she could think clearly again. Nearby, Menoria lay in the bailey and had curled up into a ball. Jaslin crawled over to her and covered her with her body.

"You are all right, lady." Jaslin rubbed Menoria's shoulder, and Menoria's trembling waned. "Come, wait for me behind that cart." She pointed with her poker. "Soon, we will flee this place together."

"Where are you going?" Menoria grabbed her wrist. "Don't leave me."

"Renily said there are others in the den."

"The mist dragon will have eaten them by now. They were fodder, nothing more."

"I have to make sure before we abandon them." Jaslin glanced back. Brelle and Laren continued to hurry toward her through the throng of people in the bailey, most of whom were still lying on the ground. Dage was not far behind them. Jaslin prayed they would continue to follow her into the den.

Jaslin hunched over and darted for the fog. She slipped into its depths. The mist was so thick that the light from her torch could barely pierce it. She couldn't see more than an arm's length in front of her, and she raised her poker, leading with the implement.

When the mist began to thin and she emerged from its last tendrils, the walls of the den surrounded her. All of the stones were scorched black. She stood on the rampway that led into the bowels of the earth, and she slowly tread forward, her hands shaking, which caused her torchlight to waver and jump across the stone around her. The walls boomed and shook from some impact on the battlements above.

She was alone, and the smell of dragon thickened the air. She'd never been down here, as no one other than the mages and the dragonguard and squires were allowed. It was too dangerous. But now she walked the lowest halls in Nevergrace like some of the people she'd read about in her stories.

She neared the end of the rampway and arrived at a junction. Cyran had mentioned this to her. To the left lay the harnessing chamber. The stalls were to the right.

Where would any captives be held?

Either chamber could potentially still be guarded by some other dragon. No, she'd counted them in the sky... But if there wasn't a dragon down here, wouldn't any prisoners have escaped already? Her rioting nerves told her she could not be certain of anything. She paused, and her hands shook. The air down here was musty and carried a weight of its own, wrapping around her like black wool.

Then she realized with the fog outside and the darkness in these depths, the mist dragon could have left its post at times and any captives down here would never know. It would take a very courageous or mad man to tempt passing through the mist without knowing if something was still lurking in there.

A scuff of stone sounded behind her, and she whirled around and gasped. Two shadowy figures stumbled down the walk.

"Where are you going?" Laren said, and Jaslin's racing pulse ebbed a tad.

"I'm trying to help free other captives," she replied.

"Slow your pace," Brelle said in a harsh whisper. "If there's something down here, I want to see it before it sees us."

"I didn't know you were coming." Jaslin waited until the two of them reached her, and then Dage emerged from the fog, carrying a torch that burned silver.

"We should try the harnessing chamber first," Laren said. "It will be easier to find people in there. It's not nearly as long as the stall chamber."

All four of them crept forward into a darkness that pounced at their light, attempting to smother it with ethereal black hands. They couldn't see more than a couple paces, and the scorched flagstones seemed to be leading them to a pile of burned bodies, or to a feeding chamber for dragons. The walls boomed again, and dirt rained from the ceiling. Jaslin tried to ignore the possibility that tons of stone could come crashing down upon them.

"I'll search the perimeter." Dage's voice rang out, making Jaslin jump as the sound echoed around the domed ceiling and ran along the walls.

The squire walked beyond an evenly spaced ring of columns, his now distant torchlight helping to pierce the darkness. But his firelight disappeared behind the columns at times and cast long shadows in their direction.

"I should've brought a bloody torch." Laren turned a slow circle, holding out his poker. "But the torches down here are usually lit, and I never needed one before."

"Well, if there's anyone still alive down here, they will have already heard Dage." Brelle cupped her hands to her mouth and said, "Come out. We are squires of the Never." Her voice echoed and returned to them several times, growing more and more hollow with each pass.

No one answered.

"I'd sure love to see Cyran and Garmeen again." Laren stepped away from Jaslin, headed for the far wall.

"There's something over here!" Dage cried, and Jaslin lurched again.

Laren vanished into the shadows, leaving only scuffing foot-steps in his wake as he angled toward Dage. "There's still a lot of tack in here," Laren said.

"No," Dage replied. "This is glinting. Like piles of metal."

Jaslin followed Laren's footsteps, and when they neared the far wall, a heap of metal awaited them—piles of armor and swords and spears. Green and gray caparisons for destriers and warhorses. Brigandines and shields.

"Our soldiers' arms," Laren said.

"As well as our knights'," Brelle added. "But all this is of little use without the legions of Nevergrace. Or its horses."

A sick feeling stirred in Jaslin's chest and tormented her heart. "There are still the stalls." She stepped forward, dropped her poker, which clattered on the stone floor, and pulled a broadsword from the pile of weapons. Then she turned and headed for the exit.

The other's footfalls sounded behind her. A minute later, she recrossed the junction and headed through a much higher arch-way. The smell of fetid rot and the stink of urine and worse hung thick. Jaslin stifled a gag as she held her torch high and her sword close.

Rustling sounded in the darkness ahead, and then a groan. Jaslin threw herself against the wall and peered at the first stall. The twin reflections of eyes gazed back at her. Dozens of them. Maybe even hundreds. The walls quaked, and Jaslin gasped. A moment later, the stone around them settled again.

"Who is there?" Jaslin asked as Brelle stepped closer to a mangled gate.

Something in the darkness shrieked, and something else muttered.

"We're here to set you free," Brelle said. "Are you from Nevergrace?"

Torchlight fell across fear-riddled and dirt-streaked faces. There were many men and a few women in the stall. Most held up hands to shield themselves from the torchlight, as if flame were as bright as the sun. One short man stepped forward and shaded his eyes as he whispered, "But the black-winged beast guards the entrance. How did you slip past it?"

"It is gone," Jaslin replied. "A battle is raging in the skies over Nevergrace, and the dragon is fighting up there."

The man's eyes gaped, and a smile slowly tugged at his lips. He laughed quietly, and then louder and louder still. Other voices rang in the darkness of the long chamber and amplified as more and more began to speak and cheer. Some cried.

"There are weapons, too!" Jaslin shouted over the rising din. "In the harnessing chamber. Follow me."

She turned to lead the people from the stall. Dozens emerged, and they continued to pour out in droves, likely having wedged themselves into a space where they felt safe—protected by stone. The sound of hundreds of more shuffling feet carried from farther down the hall.

There are so many.

Dage waited ahead, and he, Jaslin, Brelle, and Laren led the captives to the harnessing chamber and its piles of weapons and armor. Men and a few women—there were no children down here—took up swords and spears and shields. Jaslin pulled torches from the walls, lit them, and passed them out. When she finished, the entire harnessing chamber was filled with soldiers and knights of the Never.

Jaslin pushed her way through the masses, attempting to ignore their stench. "Move forward through the middle of the chamber," Jaslin shouted. "Grab your weapons and exit along the periphery. Do so as quickly as you are able. We will fill the baileys and man the battlements. And we will fight. The Never shall not fall again."

The walls boomed and quaked, and a few columns creaked.

"Let's hope we can get them all armed before the den collapses on us," Brelle said.

Jaslin turned and followed the flow of the masses. She circled around and out of the chamber with the squires. When they stepped onto the rampway, the cry of dragons rang outside.

Scores of men waited behind them, and most fell to their knees.

"It is the cry of the black-winged beast!" A man grabbed at his ears and trembled. "It trapped us in here and screamed at us until we were nearly deaf. It paralyzed us all with fear."

"It has left the entrance," Jaslin said. "We just passed through its mist unscathed."

"But it could have come back." Another soldier stepped forward, his helm and shield glistening under firelight. "No one can see through its fog."

"Or another dragon may have taken its place," a man wearing the breastplate of a knight added. "One mighty breath of fire or ice blasted through the den's entrance would fill these passages. We'd soon find ourselves in the hottest inferno or the worst blizzard man has ever seen. We could all die in an instant."

More dragon wails sounded, some carrying pain, others rage.

"Then we march on and face whatever awaits us." Jaslin brandished her sword, hoping to instill courage, but the petrified soldiers didn't budge. "I will go first." As she turned, she noticed a blossoming look of shock and embarrassment lighting up the knight's eyes. Soldiers muttered behind her. Others shouted. But she paid them no mind as she marched defiantly up the incline. If the mist dragon had returned, it would shriek and then eat her. If there was a victorious fire dragon waiting at the top, they would all be roasted alive.

Jaslin dropped her torch as she entered the fog. Firelight would not aid her in the mist, and once outside and beyond its margins, she would no longer need it. She held a hand before her, feeling around like a person struck blind. But she kept her sword arm cocked and ready to strike.

The beating of wings thrashed somewhere beyond. Crossbows loosed, their metal arms thrumming. Steel clashed.

Jaslin stepped into the light.

The bailey opened before her, the chaos of the dashing people no better than when she'd left them. Menoria waited in the shadow of a wall nearby, her eyes wide as she stared at the sky.

Jaslin ran over and grabbed the young lady of the Never by the wrist and said, "It is time to flee this place." Menoria slowly nodded, her face pale.

A boom shook the entire castle as a dragon was flung into the keep. Menoria screamed. Stone exploded outward, showering the bailey and striking and killing people who ran about. The keep teetered and groaned, and the top half slid and rumbled. The moving stones paused for a breath, and Menoria pulled Jaslin away and tugged her along before one wall of the keep gave way and sank inward. The keep toppled over and smashed into the inner and outer curtains, hurling stones beyond the curtains and out into the Evenmeres.

Jaslin paused and heaved for breath as shock gripped her, and she could only stare at the destruction. Menoria stood like a statue in the bailey, her eyes gaping.

"Thank you," Jaslin said between gasps for breath, but Menoria did not respond.

A din erupted behind them, and when Jaslin looked back, rows upon rows of soldiers and knights erupted from the den, shouting and brandishing spears and swords as they circled the baileys. Scores ran for the stairways leading to the battlements and the mounted crossbows there. There were hundreds of men.

One old man shuffled past them, his white beard stained, his robes tattered. The chain at his waist clinked as he moved.

"Ezul!" Jaslin ran to him and hugged him. The nyren tensed and stumbled back, holding his arms out in surprise, unable to respond audibly or physically.

51

SIRRA BRACKENGLAVE

S~IRRA'S ARM AND SHOULDER THROBBED WITH PAIN, BUT SHE HAD~ called upon the *dramlavola*—strength and vigor and the healing ability of the dragon realm. Her pain didn't abate completely, but it faded to only a slight annoyance. Shadowmar's anger flared as she clawed at the bolts buried in her scales.

"We will end this now," Sirra said in the dragon realm as she wheeled Shadowmar around, their souls and minds fused. She glanced around at the maelstrom of fighting dragons, so unlike her planned attacks and what they trained for—battles utilizing form and beauty. The forest dragon was no longer in the fray. It was not up in the sky above her either. She scoured the castle and its grounds before buzzing over screaming people and winging around the keep. She spotted the forest dragon in the distance, in a field. And it was on the ground. *Is it gravely wounded?*

"We should take down the sun dragon," Yenthor said. "It is the next strongest. And when it falls, their legion will be finished."

As they neared, Sirra could make out Cyran grabbing for the

lance mounted on the dead silver dragon's saddle, and she realized what he meant to do. She dived with Shadowmar, streaking for the forest dragon with her lance and her mount's talons extended.

"Not even the silver?" Yenthor's voice was nearly drowned out in a rush of wind. "Still the forest dragon?"

A blow struck Shadowmar across the flank, and the massive dragon wheeled to the side, having been clipped by what must have been the sun dragon's talons. The attacking dragon's lance was too far overhead. As the sun dragon blew past, its archers loosed their bolts. The silver and rose dragon followed it, all converging on Shadowmar as Sirra's dragon dipped below most of the sailing projectiles. But one bolt punched a hole through the leathery portion of Shadowmar's wing—always the largest target but one that dealt the least amount of damage to any dragon.

Shadowmar hissed and whipped around, pursuing the sun dragon as the rose and silver pursued her. Sirra's three companions chased all of them. The sun dragon reached the side of the keep and wheeled around abruptly, hoping to trap Sirra between it and its two approaching companions. But Shadowmar kept coming. Sirra angled her lance at the sun dragon's rider, and Shadowmar crashed into the dragon. Lances smashed into shields. Sirra deflected the guard's blow, but the sun's rider flew away with a cry. Shadowmar gripped onto the dragon's neck with her talons and squeezed, and Shadowmar's barbed tail lunged forward and impaled the sun dragon in its throat. The sun dragon began twitching and then started convulsing as Shadowmar spun about in a circle and hurled the dying creature into the keep.

Stone exploded, catapulting outward. The golden body of the sun dragon burst through a wall and disappeared into the keep. The keep teetered and sagged, the top half moving against the bottom half. Then the top leaned to one side and collapsed, crashing and flinging its stones into the baileys and fields beyond the castle walls.

A few people carrying arms burst from the den and yelled as they ran haphazardly through the bailey. More people soon followed them, masses of people crying in outrage.

Their knights and soldiers are now escaping. Sirra's heart turned hard and brittle.

The rose and silver dragons that pursued Sirra halted abruptly, and the fire, ice, and mist dragons flew at them from behind. Shadowmar whipped around in a tight circle and dived for the forest dragon. Cyran was mounting the silver's lance onto his saddle, but he glanced up as Shadowmar screamed closer. He jumped into his saddle as his archers loosed two bolts. The bolts tore through the air, and Shadowmar had to weave about to avoid them. The forest dragon lurched and ducked behind a pile of stones. If the young man's mount could not get into the air before Shadowmar arrived, any potential tilt would be finished before it began.

Sirra pulled up just before swinging around the mound of rubble in the field. "Cyran," she said, and the young man's head peeked over a stone. "I see the potential in you, and I do not want it to be wasted. There are so few of us. And to find you when you are young, when we could still accomplish so much, is a rare opportunity. But this is your last chance to hear me out. I will not let this absurd battle carry on any longer."

"If you allow my dragon to get into the air, I will hear you out," he replied.

Sirra chuckled. "I will not grant you that option. But can you not see it? We could join forces rather than fight each other. And you could become one of the most powerful dragon riders in all of Cimeren. *We* could decide how the north and south should behave and what the laws of the kingdoms should be. You could attain that power. The rest of the world is not like us. They will never understand. They cannot see the things we see—or that you will once you experience the dragon realm in full. Do not throw this away." She held out a hand, an offer to hoist him onto Shadowmar as she drifted lower.

The forest dragon burst upward, and two dragonbolts screamed toward her. One perfectly aimed bolt tracked straight for her shield. A shield would never stop such a heavy dragon-steel projectile traveling at such velocity. Sirra reacted with the swiftness of the still humming *dramlavola* and flung herself from her saddle, only gripping onto its cantle and her dragon's scales. Her shield exploded into shards of dragonsteel that flew over Shadowmar as the dragon hissed and took the other bolt in her neck.

"I do not desire power," Cyran said as his dragon climbed into the sky and swooped away.

Sirra suppressed a rising tide of fury as she pulled herself into her saddle. Her fingers flexed, yearning to summon a shard of her soul as a weapon—the *luënor* blade. *No, there is no need to take his soul.* She gripped her lance and soared after him, chasing his dragon over the castle and to the Evenmeres. The forest dragon raced away, heading for the wall of angoias. They had fled Shadowmar once before by that method and assumed it would work again.

"If you flee into the angoias, your legion will fall," Sirra shouted after Cyran. "And your outpost will fall with them."

The forest dragon wheeled around and sailed straight back at her. Cyran's new dragonlance flashed in the sunlight and was already poised for the joust, as if he had only intended to place enough distance between them to run a tilt.

Then our first tilt has left him with a false hope and conviction in his abilities. She would use that inexperience and overconfidence against him now. Let him believe it all until it was too late. Her thoughts spun rapidly. *To use* aylión *and see his movements before they occur? Or* opthlléitl *and make him fall just before we collide...*

52

CYRAN ORENDAIN

CYRAN STRUGGLED WITH UNFASTENING THE LANCE ON THE DEAD dragon. The massive black beast and its Dragon Queen flew about, hunting for him. She had recently been shaken, and now she was likely burning with anger and the desire for revenge.

The shadow dragon dived for him, and his hands trembled as he worked at the latches for the lance's mount. A cry rang out as the sun dragon and the others of his legion flew into and engaged the shadow dragon. Cyran ripped the lance free, and with Vyk's help, hauled it to Eidelmere's saddle.

The shadow dragon flung the sun dragon into the keep. Stone cracked and rumbled as one wall sank in and another wall exploded. Cyran couldn't move for a second, his mind reeling. A hand grabbed him and pulled him behind Eidelmere. The keep shuddered and pitched over at half its height, crashing into the battlements and hurling stones in Cyran and Eidelmere's direction.

"Best do whatever you need to in a hurry." Vyk's voice bordered on the edge of madness as he ran for the ladder to the quarterdeck. "She's coming back this way."

Cyran jerked as the shadow dragon flew toward them. He

leapt into his saddle. Vyk and Ineri launched two bolts, but their target avoided both. Eidelmere scrambled behind a mound of freshly fallen stones, and the Dragon Queen stopped her descent and called Cyran's name. Cyran peeked over the stones as he slid the lance's handle into the bracket and arret hook on his saddle, and he clamped the weapon in place. The Dragon Queen spoke of allegiances and of combining the power of the dragonmages and guard, but he was only half listening.

"If you allow my dragon to get into the air, I will hear you out," he replied as he bought time for his archers to reload more bolts.

The Dragon Queen continued her wheedling until Ineri hacked and sputtered and said, "I am ready."

"Leap into the air," Cyran said only to Eidelmere as he imagined what they would do, and the dragon mimicked his vision. They rose over the fallen stones, and Vyk's and Ineri's crossbow ropes thumped, launching two bolts. Ineri's bolt screamed straight for the Dragon Queen as Eidelmere ascended in a flurry of beating wings.

The Dragon Queen dived from her saddle with lightning-like quickness and agility, and at almost the same instant, her shield exploded into flying fragments. Vyk's bolt impaled her dragon's neck, and the black dragon hissed in outrage.

"I do not desire power," Cyran said as they flew away, angling over the forest. In the castle, hundreds of armed and armored men poured from the den. Hope surged inside Cyran like a rising tide. He needed to put more distance between Eidelmere and the shadow dragon in order to turn around, gain enough momentum, and face the Dragon Queen for another joust. Sir Jedsin had ordered everyone not to joust with the Dragon Queen, but that beast of hers had already taken a few bolts and didn't seem overly fazed. If Cyran could unseat and kill the Dragon Queen, then the shadow dragon would leave Nevergrace and the battle. And Cyran had done well in his first tilt against the Dragon Queen—even better than her—and, at that time, he'd only wielded a wooden lance.

The pines and oaks blurred beneath Eidelmere as they sailed along, skimming over the canopy. The wall of angoias towered ahead. The Dragon Queen shouted something as Cyran swung Eidelmere around to face her. This time, she had no shield to protect her. Her armor and her body would splinter like wood.

"Fly as fast as you ever have," Cyran said to Eidelmere. His sense of duty, not only to his king and the crown, but to his outpost and home, throbbed inside his heart. And he wore that feeling like a sigil on his breast.

Vyk bellowed behind him. The wind tore at their hair and ears, the breath of the Evenmeres swooping over Eidelmere as the dragon extended and streamlined his form. Threads of wind seemed to turn visible and appeared as gusts of white fog against Eidelmere's scales. The shadow dragon paused for a moment in surprise before starting to beat its wings faster and faster. Their adversary angled to the north and flew close to the wall of angoias, as if to use the trees as a tilt barrier—although both dragons would be on the same side of that wall. Then the shadow dragon veered to face them.

"Take her down, boy!" Vyk roared, no doubts lingering in his tone. Ineri hacked.

Eidelmere sped along with the angoias to their left. The shadow dragon bore closer but rose to a higher level, forcing Eidelmere to try to meet the beast by climbing. The forest dragon was not as nimble or swift in making the adjustments. Cyran maneuvered his lance around as he anticipated where he would have Eidelmere positioned for the attack, but a hint of worry and doubt broke through his frozen determination. The Dragon Queen knew what she was doing, and she was using the angoias and her experience and dragon for some plot. In the prior tilt, when Cyran had performed better than her, he'd taken her by surprise. But she was no fool. With him now wielding a dragonsteel lance and her without a shield, she must have assumed he would believe that to be a huge weakness for her. And she would probably attempt to use that assumption against him.

As the shadow dragon roared toward them, the Dragon Queen raised her visor and stared directly at Cyran. Cyran's nerves frayed. The angoias blurred beside them, and the pines swam just beneath their dragons' feet. The Dragon Queen shouted a word, and Cyran's lance arm trembled. "*Opthlléitl*." Immediately afterward, a few booming words rumbled from her lips. "*Vördelth mrac ell duenvíe.*"

Her voice blasted and echoed around Cyran, hitting him like a blow to his soul. His insides wrenched and writhed, but his body did not break. Vyk screamed in pain. Ineri released a gasp. Only Eidelmere appeared mostly unfazed.

But the Dragon Queen sat straighter and leaned back in her saddle, her face falling slack as they raced closer.

She muttered another word that carried through the threads around Cyran. *Aylión.* Cyran winced, feeling its power wrap around him. The substance of the realm of light tugged at his mind.

Cyran shook his head. The threads were pulling at his thoughts, attempting to determine all his choices and potential actions and which one he would follow. He fought against their might, severing almost all of their grasping ends. But one remained, and it foresaw how he hoped to attack her.

She knows.

The last few angoias marking the diminishing gap between their dragons flashed by, and Cyran dipped Eidelmere as he'd intended. He fed the last grasping thread of the Dragon Queen's only that thought, but he instead twisted his dragon to the side in an instant.

The Dragon Queen's visor snapped closed as she dipped her lance.

Cyran swung Eidelmere higher, tipping the dragon into a vertical position with one wing pointed at the sky and the other at the trees below.

The Dragon Queen's weapon clashed with Cyran's shield, releasing a metallic bang, but he turned the blow aside, deflecting most of its force. Still, the impact blasted through his hand and arm and up into his shoulder, cracking something and throwing him back in his saddle while whipping his head and neck forward.

As Cyran's lance bore down on the Dragon Queen, she twisted and turned, angling her shoulder. But he used what he knew of the *omercón* and followed the path of her movement. The force of his blow first smashed but then gave way, skipping off her armor.

The Dragon Queen flew aside and into the air, spinning and falling.

She vanished into the canopy below.

Eidelmere swooped up as he banked and wheeled about. Two bolts sailed from the forest dragon. Two more bolts came streaking toward Cyran. One tore through Eidelmere's wing, the other whizzing just over Vyk's head and narrowly missing the forest dragon's tail.

Vyk's bolt struck the shadow dragon in the upper leg, and Ineri's buried into its eye, which the beast lidded the instant before. Still, the bolt sank deep, only its fletching protruding as black fluid burst and sprayed. The shadow dragon shrieked and twirled about as it rose and flapped. The beast careened away along the line of angoias, wobbling in its flight like a wounded raven.

"Bring that beast down!" Vyk said.

Eidelmere flew after the shadow dragon, but the beast glanced back and then soared higher, rising straight up into the sky.

"I cannot fly as high as a shadow dragon," Eidelmere said, and Cyran reluctantly let them drift back down. He watched the protruding end of the bolt sticking out from the beast's eyelid until the shadow dragon disappeared into the clouds.

Eidelmere veered away from the angoias, and soon, they soared over the Never. At least a thousand soldiers and knights manned the walls and cheered as they whipped past. The upper half of the keep had toppled, but the twin watchtowers stood proud. The red fire dragon lay dead in the outer bailey, at least a half-dozen bolts sticking out of its hide. The ice and mist dragons had already fled, headed for the lake, only small spots on the horizon. A silver dragon and a rose dragon circled the outpost.

Cyran imagined the distant peel of bells. Galvenstone's watchtowers would sight the absconding dragons and raise the alarm. Then the legions of Castle Dashtok might bring down the ice and mist dragons before they fled back to the north.

53

CYRAN ORENDAIN

Bonfires burned in the baileys as twilight settled over the outpost, these fires bestowing feelings of hope and joy. Music filled the air, although the scorched stones and walls, piled rubble, and the half keep cast a somber air over Nevergrace. But there were so many survivors—far more than anyone expected.

Cyran's shoulder throbbed with sharp pains as he paced away from Eidelmere, who lay against a wall, grumbled, and closed his eyes. The dragon's anger had abated, which allowed for a new surge of grief. Cyran turned back and raised a hand in hopes of comforting the beast.

"*Go.*" Eidelmere snapped inside his head. "*Leave me be. I have not had time to mourn, and I must do so. Alone.*"

"We are not so different, my friend. I will find you soon."

"*I would be much happier if it were not too soon,*" Eidelmere grumbled.

Cyran nodded and faced the bailey, hoping to find many specific people, but Jaslin's name emerged at the top of his list. *My little sister, who I left behind...* His sister, whom he'd quarreled with when they last spoke. And he'd broken Tamar's final gift to her. His heart ached and burned.

"I appreciate your commitment in searching for the Dragon Queen's body." The guard who had been riding the surviving rose dragon paced away from his mount and approached Cyran. "We will continue scouting over the forest at first light. If the Dragon Queen lives, we will hunt her down." The dragonguard halted and looked Cyran over before grabbing the wrist and elbow of Cyran's wounded arm. He bent Cyran's arm to ninety degrees at the elbow, and Cyran winced in pain. The guard squeezed Cyran's wrist and gave it a swift jerk of a movement, pulling it away from his body. A pop sounded in Cyran's shoulder, and Cyran almost yelled in pain, but, instead, he grunted in surprise. The pain he'd been experiencing lessened immediately. "We call it the Sir Bleedstrom technique. Your shoulder was dislocated. It happens to most of the guard at some point or another." The guard patted his arm lightly. "But we're not overly worried about the Dragon Queen surviving her fall. And if the legends about the old woods have any truth to them, whatever lurks out there should have otherwise finished her. Good work."

Cyran nodded, and his worries trailed away as he imagined the creatures he'd encountered in there. For the moment, they seemed like a blessing. "I couldn't see anything through the canopy, but she is likely dead."

"You may go join your people." The rose's guard gestured over his shoulder.

Cyran's heart lightened, and he approached Vyk, who had already passed out with a tankard in his burly hand. Foam seeped over his knuckles, his wild beard and long hair hiding most of his face. Ineri sat beside him, her knees huddled to her chest as she sipped her drink.

"Nevergrace, nor I, could not have done any of what we did without you." Cyran bowed to Ineri, who waved him away and hacked a few times. "Have you seen the nyrens about your... cough?"

She nodded. "I've been through many different kinds of treatments. Nothing makes it go away."

"Well, now the king of Belvenguard and the entire kingdom are indebted to you. I will request that the king's best nyrens see you."

Ineri smiled and hummed along with the music playing in the courtyard.

"Cyran!" Brelle came running toward him and threw her arms around his neck, nearly knocking him over. "What in all the bloodiest hells took you so long? We were trapped in that damn keep forever."

Laren and Dage followed her, Laren's boyish grin now a full smile.

"Well, will you look at our very own dragonguard." Laren crossed his forearms and bumped fists with Cyran. "A damn sight." Laren hugged him and smacked his back, sending shooting pains through his shoulder.

"I'm glad you came back." Dage bowed his head, and Cyran hugged him, but the huge squire remained stiff and tense.

"Where is Garmeen?" Cyran glanced around.

"He's..." Brelle let the thought trail away.

"What happened?" The rising warmth drained from Cyran's cheeks.

"We haven't seen him since the outpost was taken," Brelle said. "I think he must have been one of those who died in the initial attack."

Garmeen. Sadness burrowed through Cyran's burgeoning shield of happiness. Garmeen had been the quiet leader of Nevergrace's dragonsquires long before Cyran was sent to join them. Garmeen probably also saved Cyran's life when that flaming silhouette of a man and ball of light outside the Evenmeres drew Cyran in against his will. Garmeen had risked his own life to come and grab Cyran and pull him away.

"Maybe he escaped from the den with the others and hasn't been able to find you yet," Cyran finally muttered, although he didn't believe it himself.

"We've been searching through the survivors." Melancholy choked Laren's words.

"But there are so many people of the Never who are still alive." Brelle swung out an arm and spun around, although she wobbled and accidentally hit Dage. "So many more than we ever thought."

Laren forced a grin. "The Dragon Queen must have been hoping to trade us for her queen after all. She must have thought we were actually worth something."

"It was probably hard for her to tell that you were made a dragonsquire so you could shovel dragon shit while the rest of us were being trained to become one of the guard," Brelle said. Then she faced Cyran. "From what we've seen of the survivors, it looks like most who were killed died during the initial raid and takeover."

"But I was told that the north was executing one of our people every dawn and dusk." Cyran glanced around.

"We were told the same." Brelle shrugged. "But most of those who disappeared are still alive. Even old Ezul. Maybe the threat was only a trick to hurry the king's response."

"Except for Ulba." Dage shook his head. "She was killed when we tried to escape. Bitten in half by a dragon."

Cyran winced, and his voice turned tense. He could barely speak the following names. "And J-Jaslin? And Emellefer?"

"Both are alive and somewhere around here." Brelle waved at the masses in the baileys.

Cyran released a long sigh of relief, and the weight of an entire dragon lifted from his shoulders.

"And your little sister showed her true qualities." Laren gulped from a tankard.

Cyran's stomach clenched. *What did she do?*

"She made all the dragonguard and knights and soldiers, and even Brelle and Dage here, look a bit craven." Laren wiped foam from his lips with the back of his hand.

Dage punched Laren on the shoulder and said, "I just didn't want to get any more old ladies killed."

Cyran's worry and elation twined inside him. "What did she do?"

"She led a resistance against the Dragon Queen." Brelle tossed aside a tankard and belched. "Made me proud. She concocted some plans to escape, although most of them failed. But she did not give up. It was your sister who released us from a barred chamber when Galvenstone's legion finally showed up. It was Jaslin who led us into the den and freed all the soldiers and knights of Nevergrace."

Cyran's heart stilled as he glanced around in wonder. "Jaslin?"

Brelle nodded. "If I see her, I'll make sure to send her your way."

Cyran studied the three dragonsquires, but none of their faces betrayed any hint of jest. *Jaslin?* Cyran's eyes settled on Dage, and memories and worries and questions came storming back to him.

"Dage, certainly now you can tell us what that letter you received was about," Cyran said. "The letter sealed in red wax. I learned that Sir Kayom received one as well, and there was a discrepancy concerning his presence at Dashtok when we first arrived there."

Dage grumbled until Brelle elbowed him and said, "You better tell us now. After all this."

Dage glanced around. "It wasn't even important. More strange than anything. All it said was that if I was called to the guard, it would be in my best interest not to answer the call.

Whoever wrote it suggested I should avoid the guard like a plague, or something along those lines. It made me angry is all it did. And that's why I didn't bother telling any of you about it, because it was only a half-witted jape."

Thoughts whirled in Cyran's head. Who would want to warn him and his companions about someone in the king's council, warn Sir Kayom, deceive them about Sir Kayom's arrival at Dashtok, and also, initially, try to convince Dage not to join the guard? Cyran couldn't answer the question with a face. But, also, what was this person's intent and objective? Cyran gritted his teeth. He could not readily answer that question with the few facts he had either.

A howl carried out just beyond the walls of the castle, breaking Cyran's contemplations.

Cyran turned. "Smoke?"

Three wolves came bounding through a rent in the outer curtain, the smallest and darkest one racing for Cyran. Cyran knelt, and the wolf barreled into him, leading with a wet nose and tongue, licking away a few tears that dribbled down Cyran's cheeks. Cyran hugged the wolf around the neck and patted his head. When he turned back to his friends, Emellefer stood beside Brelle and stared at him in wonder. Cyran's heart leapt. Emellefer's eyes smoldered as she stepped forward, but Renily darted past her, her red braids bouncing. The little girl carried a lute.

"Cyran, play!" Renily said as she ran up to him and held out the instrument.

Cyran took the lute and rubbed the girl's head. "I hardly feel prepared to play after everything that has happened."

"Please!" Renily hopped up and down. "It will feel so much more like the old Never if you do."

Cyran flexed his fingers, and his eyes met Emellefer's before he nodded. He cleared his throat and strummed a few chords.

Soldiers and servants and women and men and children gathered in clusters around him.

He sang softly at first, a lament to all the fallen and to Sir Kayom and Sir Ymar. Everyone fell silent, and the music from the courtyard faded to a murmur. Cyran's voice grew louder and bolder as he praised the guard of Nevergrace as well as the servants and workers of the fields who kept the stones and the soldiers strong. His lyrics brought a flash of sword and shining lance and dragon but returned to the outpost and its vigilant watch, a watch only able to be maintained through its people. He sang of horse and bow and woods and of fathers and mothers and sons and daughters, of love and loss and joy and heartache. He sang the ballad of the people of Nevergrace.

When he lowered the lute, all eyes were fixated on him, most of them moist with emotion. Tears trickled down Emellefer's cheeks as she lifted a hand to her heart. Then the crowd parted. Two young women—the young lady of the Never and Jaslin—strode through the mass of people.

Cyran's eyes burned as he ran to Jaslin.

But Menoria held out a box, stopping him before he reached his sister, and the young lady of the Never said, "For you. For returning to free us and reclaim our outpost."

Cyran laid a hand on the box as he eyed Jaslin, attempting to force a look that would tell her he was sorry for how he'd left her, sorry for how he'd broken her crystal decanter and scolded her. He'd only done it to protect her, but none of it protected her from the real danger that befell Nevergrace.

"Are you going to open it?" Brelle asked.

Cyran snapped back to the present and ran a hand over the top of the box before cracking its lid open. A silver pendant lay within. Upon the face of the pendant was the image of a keep and twin watchtowers crafted out of platinum, and these structures were backdropped by angoia trunks made of ruby.

Menoria slipped the pendant out of the box and dangled it from its silver chain. She motioned, and Cyran bowed. After she slipped the chain over his head and he rose, the pendant settled against his chest and resembled a sigil. The sigil of Nevergrace.

"To always remember where you came from," Menoria said.

Cyran tensed his jaw to fight off a rush of emotion. "I would never forget, but thank you." He stepped before Jaslin, swept her into his arms, and lifted her up.

She hugged him back. "I am glad to see you, too, Brother. I was so scared you had…"

He set her down. "I was worried about you. And I regret how our last talk ended. I am so sorry for—"

"Just play something light and happy." Jaslin grabbed his hand holding the lute. "For everyone. We need it."

Cyran nodded and gathered his thoughts and memories. "For you, heroine of the Never." He strummed bold and ringing chords and sang of ancient days when a maiden of a shining city held back a storm of evil.

When he finished, Brelle shouted, "She said happy, you fool."

Cyran lowered his head in embarrassment and strummed a light and joyous tune of drinking and dancing on summer's end.

54

CYRAN ORENDAIN

THE TWIN WATCHTOWERS OF NEVERGRACE LOOMED IN THE NIGHT to the east and west, and soldiers once again stood guard on either side of the road leading into the Evenmeres. A legion of sun and rose and silver and moon and sapphire and ruby and ember dragons landed outside Nevergrace, stirring the moon-frosted grasses while rumbling to each other. Cyran stood on the battlements, watching as dragonguard, mages, and nobles dismounted under torchlight and approached the open gates of the outpost in regiments.

"My king." Menoria bowed as King Igare led his men through the archway. Jaslin stood just behind the young lady of the Never. "I did not expect you to journey all the way to Nevergrace."

"The north will not immediately strike back." Igare took her hand and kissed it. "Not this time. Not after such a stinging defeat—the loss of their Dragon Queen. And I have all the watch at Galvenstone on duty for these days. Our storm dragons will be here in no time if anything is sighted."

Menoria rose. "I apologize for the state of the Never and the keep. We are still removing the debris and must do so before we can mend anything. And the watchtowers do not have a chamber large enough for us to dine in. I fear you may have to accompany us in the throne room of the keep."

Igare waved off her concerns. "I stayed in much worse before I was ever crowned and lived in Dashtok. And the fact the Never still stands at all is a blessing."

"A blessing of the Siren and the Great Smith and the six righteous gods," Lisain said from behind the king.

And of the Dragon.

"As long as the keep does not come crashing down on our heads, it will be well enough for me," Igare said.

"Our builders have confirmed the stability of the remaining lower half of the keep." Menoria turned and, with Jaslin at her side, led the king and his entourage through the bailey.

Cyran followed along beside a line of hundreds of archers and guard members as the king entered the castle, the smells of roasting meat and fired breads wafting out into the courtyard. Servants brought out flagons and tankards in addition to plates loaded with dark rolls and haunches of meat for the new arrivals.

Cyran paused. Something had sprouted in the packed dirt of the Never's grounds. He stooped and plucked it. A flower had unfurled, one with petals as pale blue as glacial ice. He twirled the stem between his fingers, making the petals spin and blur.

"It is a glacial rose." Sir Paltere, in his red and gold dragon-steel armor, stepped through the ranks and approached Cyran as he whistled a tune of longing. He held his helm between his arm and his side. "It grows only in soil that has been watered by blood and fired by the breath of dragons."

Cyran studied the rose, and his gaze was drawn across the grounds as he wondered about all the recent events. Other buds had pushed their way through the dirt as well.

"It is said that before the angoias dominated the Evenmeres, there was only pine and oak and maple." Paltere scrutinized the flower. "And some say the angoias are simply glacial roses that have been allowed to thrive away from the shears of men. Others say the angoias stemmed from those roses that were cursed."

Cyran ran a hand over the petals, the merchant ring on his finger dragging against them. Did the blood of his people live inside this flower?

"And how was the jousting in this recent affair?" Paltere asked with a grin.

"I remembered what you told me." Cyran shrugged, unsure about displaying too much emotion. "And I believe it saved my life."

"How so?"

Cyran quickly recounted his battle with the Dragon Queen, as best as he could recall.

Paltere stared with wonder. "The Dragon Queen, unseated." He shook his head. "And you heard her utter a few words before she appeared surprised?"

"Opth little, I think. And aye lion, maybe? Although at the moment, I felt I understood them. The first came before she said some other words in a voice that shook the sky."

"*Opthlléitl* and *aylión*." Paltere brushed his hair from his face and studied Cyran closer. "Words from the dragon realm. Those whose power even I cannot evoke. There are few who can."

A fist of wonder opened in Cyran's chest. "And what is their magic?"

"I do not fully comprehend it all, but the first grants the use of the dragon's voice. It can break the strongest warrior's will. The latter unleashes an ability to see different paths extending out of the present and into the next moment." Paltere gripped his chin for a moment as he stared at the ground. "And you say you did not feel their effects?"

"No, I did not say that. I heard the power of the first carry through her voice, and it shook and frightened me."

"But it did not make you fall."

Cyran shook his head. "And with the second command, I felt... something like threads grasping at my mind. But I broke most of them and tried deceiving the last."

"Then no wonder the Dragon Queen was surprised," Paltere said. "Even though you are skilled with the blade and lance when upon the horse, the only reason she probably lost to you on dragonback may be because she'd grown too accustomed to seeing things before they happened. She may have been doing that for centuries. But when that strategy suddenly didn't work for her, she was likely too surprised to adapt quickly. You only had to adapt in similar ways to what you've always known." He swallowed and met Cyran's gaze. "Only those who can wield the magic of the dragon realm are immune to its effects."

"But I have no knowledge or control over anything other than the single thread of my dragon."

Paltere rubbed his gloved hands against one another. "Then this is something we must discuss further. Any potential ability must be investigated. We'll find someone to help you. But there is no one here who can answer any questions regarding the magic of the other realm, and tonight is not the night for it." He paused and pointed to both of Cyran's shoulders. "You now carry two swords?"

Cyran unsheathed Sir Kayom's blade, and its dragonsteel glowed green.

"The blade of a dragonguard of Nevergrace," Paltere said. "You are worthy of it." He bit his lip and glanced at the keep. "I must go and take a seat at the table." He nodded to Cyran and departed for the keep, whistling his tune where he'd left off.

Cyran wandered over and found Laren, Brelle, and Dage sitting outside the squire house with many other squires. Smoke thumped his tail in the dirt where he sat, and Cyran scratched his ears while twirling the glacial rose and gazing into its petals.

"And so the now poor and famished Never has to feed all the king's men before we feed our own scrawny arses," Brelle said.

As Cyran turned to sit, Jaslin's voice called out, "Cyran, your presence is requested in the throne room." His little sister stood in the distance and waved for him to follow her.

"You've won the favor of the king and thus a timelier meal." Brelle threw a stick she'd been picking her teeth with at Cyran.

Cyran shrugged and followed Jaslin through the crowds and into the charred archway of the keep with its bright firelight. She led him to where all the remaining tables of the keep had been set up and ran the length of the throne room, and she showed him to an open seat beside hers and Menoria's. The king and his council were not far away. Cyran sat and passed the glacial rose under the table to Jaslin as he whispered, "I want to give you something. To remember Tamar."

Jaslin accepted the gift and leaned back so she could quickly glance under the table at the flower. Her eyes misted over. Cyran squeezed her leg.

Emellefer set a plate brimming with rolls and a fillet of venison before Cyran and furtively ran a hand across his shoulders before hurrying away. Cyran watched her go, and she glanced back and winked. Other than for a few words of casual greeting here and there, he'd not had time to speak with Emellefer since returning, not with everything else that had to be done around the castle.

"Ah, and so the dragonsquire of the hour joins us." Riscott set down his cup and motioned to Cyran, offering him a soft applause.

"We owe you a great deal." Igare stood and addressed the tables while indicating Cyran. "This here is a simple squire who had the audacity to lead a legion against the Dragon Queen of

Murgare. And so he is not such a simple squire after all, but rather a commander of dragons."

"The war is only about to begin." Tiros nibbled on a haunch of pig. "We should take the offensive and not sit and wait for our enemies to come to our door."

"The north is broken, and they will be fighting amongst themselves more than anything." Cartaya ran a finger through her long white hair as she sipped her drink.

"Murgare is far too powerful and, up until recently, has grown stronger every day." Igare slammed his tankard down, and dark liquid sloshed over the edge and ran onto the table. "We cannot grow too comfortable or arrogant. Yes, celebrate a grand victory here, but do not think anything between Belvenguard and Murgare is over. We *had* to take Restebarge and Elra from them, or there would have been no hope of standing against their rising power and numbers. But make no mistake, if Murgare is not weakened to the point of collapse, which it most definitely is *not*, we are all in grave danger. We could all become their slaves, as in the years after Cimerenden was destroyed with dragon fire and the north ruled the five kingdoms. After overthrowing the shining city—when the old kingdom was dismantled—Murgare tricked all the surviving strongholds. They claimed rights to all the lands and used dragons to enforce their will. They ruled with wings and with dragonsteel and an iron fist. Only it came to be that the Evenmeres, which they cultivated, grew and created a barrier between us, and our ancestors were able to free themselves of Murgare's tyranny by raising and harnessing their own dragons. They found dragonmages in their own people, and they built their legions. The north has sought their former power ever since. And they will not rest until they have enslaved every last one of us and their darkness reigns over the five kingdoms."

A solemn hush fell over the throne room as everyone

stopped eating and watched Igare, who now paced along the length of the table.

"And now the Rorenlands are not heeding my call to raise their banners." Igare's boots slapped the stones beneath him. "A new man has named himself king of the Rorenlands and does not acknowledge the rule of Belvenguard and Galvenstone. Nor does he honor the old oaths. I fear that the people of the Rorenlands do not understand the dire nature of what we face here in Belvenguard."

Wisps of anger and feelings of doubt streamed through Cyran's gut. Was the southern kingdom simply not listening to the call of their allies when need had arisen? Or were the Rorenlands turning against Belvenguard? But surely, if Belvenguard were to fall, the more distant kingdoms would soon follow.

"And I fear the Weltermores are following the Rorenlands's lead." Igare downed his tankard and flung it aside. "I still have not heard from the messengers I sent east. It seems as if they were abducted or are not being allowed to return with word of what resulted from their diplomacy."

Riscott raised his drink. "And, Your Grace—"

"I am still getting there." Igare glared at his orator. "All must be laid on the table now. Even our banners in southern Belvenguard are not answering my summons. We've heard nothing from beyond Dallow and Somerlian. Silverbow, Lynden, Progtown, Trasten, and so many others seem to be taking their time, weighing their responses when the time for action and standing firm is at hand." He glanced around at the several dozen people at the tables. "I fear that if the north wages war soon, Belvenguard will fall. And all the rest of the kingdoms will fall with us."

Silence lingered for a couple minutes, and Menoria trembled beside Cyran. Jaslin sat as still as death. The rising anger inside Cyran mounted and swirled and mixed with sadness and regret. People of their *own* kingdom were also to blame for not standing united? Cyran's sense of duty—which Jaslin had noted many times, and not always in a positive light—and loyalty tugged at the fibers of his soul. Did other men not feel these same threads?

"Then mayhap it is more imperative that we strike on offensive." Tiros tugged at the curls of his white beard. "Bring war to the north instead of letting war unfold on our lands. We have dragons of all types. We have strategists among the nyrens who have studied the Dragon Wars and who know how to use our strengths against Murgare's weaknesses."

"Or maybe we should send emissaries of higher station to our former allies and remind them of their oaths and of what Murgare does to those they conquer," Riscott said.

"We should reclaim the Rorenlands and the Weltermores." Lisain sat with his head down and his hands folded against his chest. "The Paladin has shown himself to me, and I see his will."

"I side with Tiros." Cartaya pushed her hood back, revealing her face again, which made her look like she could be in the mid second decade of her life, although her beauty and youth seemed somehow unnatural. "Do not allow the amassing north to sail across the Lake on Fire. Strike them on their own shores."

Igare held up his hands. "Enough. We decided to bring up the matter with the lord of Nevergrace, who unfortunately is no longer among us, and so the young lady Menoria now bears the responsibility of a lord." He gave Menoria a sympathetic nod. "Until we can find another to rule this outpost. Now, milady, you are aware. But tonight, we will discuss nothing more of these matters. Emissaries have already been dispatched to the Weltermores, the Rorenlands, the southern cities, and even to Murgare. We will soon have peace." The king rotated to address everyone who was seated. "Now, there is one last pressing matter. I have a ceremony to perform."

"But we should also discuss the traitor," Riscott said.

Igare huffed and lowered his head. "And so we must."

"Any traitor must be punished appropriately, but catching this man should be the least of our concerns at the moment," Cartaya said. "What can one man do to further harm Belvenguard that the north cannot?"

"We do not have the time or resources to sweep all the lands and villages between Nevergrace and Galvenstone hunting for a traitor," Tiros said. "The enemy the traitor served is our primary worry. Defense before vengeance."

"Who is the traitor?" Cyran asked, and everyone turned to regard him. "Before, in Galvenstone, you mentioned that you know who this person is."

Igare nodded. "His identity was discovered by some of Cartaya's watchers, and her magic. He was a man of Nevergrace. A dragonsquire."

Cyran's heart teetered on a cliff. *No. A dragonsquire?* "Who is it?" Visions of Laren and Dage and then other squires he hadn't seen since his return bombarded his thoughts.

Riscott leaned back in his chair, a sly smirk playing across his lips. "A man known as Garmeen."

Cyran lurched as he glanced at Jaslin, who reached under the table and gripped his hand. *Garmeen is dead.*

"And from what we could gather in the midst of everything happening at Nevergrace, it seems he was a squire of Sir Kayom's," Riscott said. "The leader of the dragonsquires at the outpost. At least before he fled. All we know is that he funneled the north information about the Never and its defenses."

No. Garmeen would never do that. But no one had seen his body. They only assumed he must have died in the initial attack. It was possible that he fled the outpost just prior, because he knew what was coming. But how would he even make contact with Murgare? The entire accusation didn't make sense. If Garmeen's actions and betrayals had truly led to the attack on

Nevergrace—all the destruction, torment, imprisonment, and death—he would be the evilest person Cyran had ever known, playing the part of a friend and comrade to so many only to assist in their suffering and deaths. If that was all true, then perhaps Garmeen was also the writer of the cryptic letters the squires and Kayom received. Maybe Garmeen had been attempting to keep the other squires distracted with something, so they wouldn't notice him... or maybe he'd been trying to influence them.

"I'll search for the accused traitor," Cyran said.

"But you would have known him." Riscott smoothed his steel gray goatee. "We do not typically send a previous comrade after a traitor. There is the potential that too many emotions may become involved, including sympathy and forgiveness."

"Garmeen already broke my heart once, when I thought him dead," Cyran said, and Jaslin's hand pulled away from his. "He will not break it again. I have a dragon that I could use to aid me in my search, if the king would allow me to keep the creature."

Igare studied Cyran for a moment and nodded. "You must help defend the wounded and vulnerable Never, but you may make outings to the villages all along the northern border. Start by working your way west from this outpost and, if need be, then travel to the east." Igare walked over to Cyran and paused. "But your search will come later. There is a ceremony you and I must attend first."

Igare reached out and grabbed Cyran by the arm, helping to hoist him up.

55

PRAVON THE DRAGON THIEF

PRAVON SIPPED AT SPICED WINE AS HE SAT AT A GREASY TABLE beside Aneen, whose ale foamed over her tankard. Bawdy music from a few bards in the corner of the tavern rambled on, and the bards swayed as much as any of the drunken patrons. Kridmore sat under torchlight at a nearby table, throwing cards face down before two other patrons. One of the men sneered and grabbed a tankard, downing its contents.

"Been getting a lot of those runs," the patron said to Kridmore, and Pravon shivered. If this man had any inkling that he would be impaled with a lance if he angered the dragon assassin...

The other patron at Kridmore's table grumbled and made some comment as he slid a few coins into a pile in the middle of all three of them.

"Have you been thinking about it?" Aneen whispered under the gales of laughter and blasts of heated conversation.

"The outpost?" Pravon asked. "And what happened afterward?"

Aneen nodded as she stared into the depths of her ale. "But not only our targets and what they meant. All the rest of it."

Pravon drank. "Our employer wanted those two lords killed, but they could have also wanted us to do more."

"And that was why we had free rein to do anything else we liked."

"And all three of us chose to take dragons." Pravon studied her—feminine cheeks and chin, long red hair, toned figure. She also carried a haughty air about her. "It is all that is on my mind."

"You are a dragon thief, and you have experience in one of the rarest of professions. I would guess there are fewer than a dozen of us in all the five kingdoms of the north and south."

Pravon nodded. "Our employer must have put us together for some design."

Aneen swallowed and wiped at the foam on her lips with the back of her hand. "He must have known that even if one of us had doubts, with two dragon thieves and another who yearns to kill such beasts—be it for pride or arrogance or namesake or some other shady longing—at least one of us would seek out the dragons at the outpost."

"Then the others or other would have a hard time resisting the temptation. It is already in our blood, what we have always been generously compensated for."

"I once stole a marsh dragon from the pits of Tablu." Aneen cast him a wicked grin. "Didn't have to take any work for a full year. I did, but I didn't *have* to. I could have just lounged by the sea under the sun of the Rorenlands."

Pravon stared at Kridmore's back, and his vision blurred. "My greatest feat was slipping a lake dragon from its den."

"Underwater?" Aneen's eyes widened.

Pravon nodded.

"I am impressed." Aneen ran a hand along his arm, her roughened fingers showing a hint of tenderness as she massaged his flesh.

Pravon studied her, trying to concentrate in spite of the tingling that her touch sent radiating across his skin. "That would mean our employer *wanted* us to steal those forest dragons. He laid them at our feet. And he *wanted* Kridmore to kill them all."

"I grow weary of wondering and waiting. Maybe we should retire to our room... and a single bed." Aneen's eyebrow arched, and something stirred in Pravon's loins. It had been a long time since an attractive woman had desired him. He'd found whores useful every now and again, but their fake desire left his stomach unsettled after the event. "He holds something over you, doesn't he?"

"Who? Our employer?"

Pravon nodded.

Aneen looked away. "He must have something on all of us to keep us here waiting for his next request. Otherwise, after the first village, you would have never seen me again."

"Me as well."

Aneen looked back at him, her eyes searching his face. Her expression softened, as if she'd found some truth there amidst a lifetime of lies and treachery.

"I told you I grow tired of pondering these same questions." She rose and pushed her bench back from the table. "I will be in the room if you care to join me." She downed the contents of her tankard and slammed it down on the table.

The man Kridmore was gambling with stood up and grabbed Kridmore's cloak, twisting it into a ball in his fist. "I told you, I wouldn't take no more cheating."

Kridmore's hand moved under his cloak.

Pravon leapt to his feet and rushed over, grabbing the patron's hand and twisting it free of Kridmore's cloak as Pravon said, "I will buy you another drink, my friend."

"Friend?" The patron looked Pravon up and down and wiped

at his crooked nose with his palm. He sniffed and smeared grease across his cheeks. "I ain't never seen you before, and this man is stealing all my coin."

Pravon flashed a friendly smile as he hesitantly tried to guide Kridmore away. His palm, where he pressed it against Kridmore's shoulder, heated up as if he touched flame, and he realized he'd never come close to touching the man before. He had never wanted to. Pravon jerked his hand away, and Kridmore turned to eye him, his shovel chin and ivory teeth catching the torchlight.

"Best not to touch me, my friend." Kridmore's voice carried an obvious threat.

"I thought it best if you did not kill a man in this small village," Pravon whispered. "It would draw... scrutiny and make it difficult for us to hide."

"These people would never see me kill him." Kridmore rubbed his fingers together and uttered a quick word before turning to the patron who had grabbed him. "If you can quaff the remainder of your drink without need of a respite, I will repay you whatever you believe I owe you."

The patron's piggish eyes narrowed, but he grabbed the flagon he'd been filling his tankard from and started chugging. The bulge in the middle of his throat jumped up and down several times before he gasped and froze. The flagon fell from his hand and clattered onto the table. Foam erupted from his mouth like a geyser and sprayed across the way, striking the patrons at another table. The man's eyes gaped. He collapsed and hit the floor before seizing uncontrollably.

Kridmore scooped the coin on the table together as only a couple nearby patrons who had been hit by the spray turned to gawk and point. The other patron who had been at the table with Kridmore studied the assassin and slowly got up and backed away.

"Let me have my fun," Kridmore snapped at Pravon. "I am no fool."

Reflections of flame flickered in Kridmore's shadowed eyes as his gaze bore into Pravon, and Pravon's throat started to squeeze shut.

"Let's keep our trio from killing each other," Aneen said as she settled a hand on Pravon's back. She eased Pravon away, and the strangling sensation vanished.

When they turned for their table, they found a man sitting there—another man in a cloak. He was older and thinner than Pravon.

Our employer. Or at least our contact.

"Please, sit," the man they had last seen when he'd ridden in on a storm dragon said. "I know you've been waiting, but this next stage has taken some time to come to fruition. You three will find that you will enjoy each other's company much more when you are working."

Pravon stared, but all he could make out beneath the man's hood was a sharp and pointed chin with a dimple.

"Sit, I said." Their contact spoke in a commanding voice as he gestured.

Pravon sat, followed by Aneen and Kridmore.

"We killed the forest dragons," Kridmore said.

Their contact flashed a smile filled with yellow and crooked teeth. "Whatever else you did during your last undertaking was left up to each of you. Now"—he paused and used two fingers to wipe at the corners of his lips—"certain emissaries have been sent to the other kingdoms. Even to Murgare. To cities in the south."

"Who are these emissaries?" Aneen asked. "And who are they working for?"

Their employer smiled again but did not answer her question. "Your next errand is to find these emissaries at their meeting spots." He passed across a letter sealed with red wax and the rampant dragon of Belvenguard. "Their audiences will include court officials and nobles. You need to remove certain emissaries before any of their negotiations get too far along."

Kridmore snatched the letter, broke its seal, and unfolded the message. He grunted as he eyed it and then spread the parchment out on the table before them. They all studied an inexact map of Cimeren with marked locations and a few scrawled notes under each point of interest. After a minute, Kridmore folded the parchment up and slid it into his cloak.

"Do you understand?" Their contact looked at each of them in turn, his tone carrying a threat and a reminder of what he held over each of them.

Aneen nodded.

"We must travel as far north as Breather's Pass?" Disbelief swirled inside Pravon.

"Do not fear." Their contact nodded at Kridmore. "He has been to the pass before."

Pravon faced the assassin and asked, "To the Valley of the Smoke Breathers?"

Kridmore smirked. "Well, I didn't visit the valley at the time he was referring to. At that time, I was simply playing the dragonmage of a rose dragon. We only flew to the pass. So I could make my dragonguard accidentally skewer the Murgare king."

A snap of confusion sparked inside Pravon, and a heartbeat later, his doubts and worries swelled. He studied Kridmore for a minute, but the assassin didn't clarify anything.

"Any other questions?" their contact asked.

"Will we have to use the trails to cross through the Evenmeres?" Pravon's fear revealed itself in his shaky words.

Kridmore cast him a side glance. "Do not worry yourself over that either, my friend. I consider those woods one of my homes."

56

CYRAN ORENDAIN

A BATH LAY BESIDE CYRAN, ITS DARK LIQUID ROILING WITH HEAT AS bubbles rose to its surface and popped. He stood on bare stone in nothing but a thin undergarment. Another bath of water waited behind him and carried floating chunks of ice.

Firelight danced inside the western watchtower's lowest chamber, a chamber below ground level. Three blacksmiths worked over yellow and white-hot flames, pumping bellows and making their forges roar. Hammers chimed against anvils in regular intervals, creating a song all their own. A song of steel and scale. Dragonsteel was being forged.

"You have been summoned before the king of Belvenguard to uphold your duty to the realm," Riscott read from an unrolled parchment. King Igare stood before Cyran with a harsh look, and Jaslin and Menoria, his squire friends, Emellefer, and Paltere all bore witness. "From this man, his mind will lose distraction. His thoughts and abilities will sharpen and become the ethereal lance of Belvenguard. He will enter the lost realm at will. And he will dance with the dragons."

Cartaya stepped away from a forge, holding a glowing brand,

her mauve cloak covering her face again. She slowly approached Cyran.

"From flesh we shall make the mage," Riscott continued as Cartaya advanced, holding out the glowing brand of a rampant dragon with its tail curled around it and forming a circle. Cyran focused on the sigil, and he could barely breathe. "For he has been granted the will of the dragon. The ability to reside in the lost realm. And for the crown, he must uphold justice and protect the innocent and the weak. To protect the throne and all it stands for."

Cartaya stepped behind Cyran, and he was no longer able to watch her.

"This flesh is now one of the mages whose soul twines with the mightiest of beasts." Riscott's voice rose and echoed around the firelit and shadowy chamber.

A burning sting struck Cyran on the back, and the sizzle of metal searing flesh sounded. He attempted not to wince as the brand sank into the back of his shoulder, the rank smell of burning skin billowing around him and wrinkling his nostrils. The brand was torn away with a hiss, and Igare stepped up to him and looked him in each eye. The king shoved at Cyran's chest, and the back of Cyran's heels hit the lip around one of the baths. He toppled over like a falling log, slapping into ice cold water with a splash. His arms and then body and head plunged into the frigid cold, and he strained against the reflex to gasp and suck in water.

And there he waited for nearly a half minute, only the charred flesh on his back finding relief. Two strong hands gripped him by the arms and jerked him out. Icy water ran in rivers through his hair and down his trembling body as he clutched his hands together and fought off the instinct to hunch and attempt to retain body heat.

Cartaya draped a cloak over his shoulders and stepped back.

"Dunked in water from the Valley of the Smoke Breathers," King Igare said. "Beginning this day, and all days forth, you are a mage of dragons. Rider of scale and tamer for the guard. Freighter of archers. Master of flight. Will you uphold these duties?"

"I will uphold all duties of the dragonmage." Cyran's voice was strong and rigid.

A line of dragonguard in red and gold armor marched up behind the king, brandishing swords whose blades flamed with orange fire.

"From the line of Sir Bleedstrom, before the end of the age of Cimerenden and the Dragon Wars," Riscott continued, "the guard summons you before them now. From this man, let his skin shed its weakness and take on iron and dragon scale. His blood shall become fire. His bones will harden to ice and stone. His lance arm will find no equal."

Those of the guard stepped up to either side of Cyran and crossed swords in the air, forming a canopy over his head and creating a path between him and the king. The flames on the guard members' blades snapped and flared. The air grew hot.

King Igare walked through the tunnel with the fiery roof. "You, Cyran Orendain, as others have born witness to your skills and abilities, are called to duty and for honor. For Belvenguard and the throne." The king raised both of his hands and placed his palms on Cyran's chest. A rush of sliding steel sounded as blades separated and fell toward Cyran, forming a line on either side of him, the tips of the closest blades lying on his shoulders. All the other blades pointed at him. The king shoved him over.

Cyran plunged into the bubbling dark liquid where heat swept over him like liquid flame. Everything was red before his eyes snapped shut and he sank.

Blood...

His skin burned as he yelled in his silent world. Two of the guard yanked him out in an instant, and others flung buckets of cold water on him, his skin screaming and feeling the flying water like icy slaps from a waterfall in the north. Blood drained off him in rivers and diluted on the floor.

Some of the guard toweled him off and began dressing him in leather leggings and a tunic. Other guard members approached the blacksmiths and stood at attention. The blacksmiths used tongs to dunk red-hot metal in buckets of water. Plumes of white steam billowed into the air.

"The guard began after the dragons were tamed," Igare said as he paced before Cyran. "To provide protection for the mage and for the archers. To be the first eyes upon the field of battle in the sky. The guard has seen wars rage for decades. They witnessed the fall of Cimerenden. The guard was there for the rise of Belvenguard and the five kingdoms. When Cimeren was split in two by the Evenmeres, the guard rode the skies above us. The guard has walked among men and flown with dragons since the day men entered the lost realm. And the guard will still be here long after each of us has passed."

Bated silence blanketed the chamber and turned the roar of the forges into a background murmur.

"Tempered in the blood of dragons, from this day forward, you shall be one of the guard," Igare said in a resonate voice.

The guard members who stood near the smiths were handed sheets of metal, and they approached Cyran with hardened stares. They clamped the green and gray dragonsteel armor of the Never around his shins and thighs.

"Protector of mage and scale," the king continued. "Leader of archers. Master of shield and lance."

The guard members placed a breastplate across Cyran's chest and jerked its leather straps tight against his back. Vyk and Ineri stood side by side among the watchers, and Vyk supported Ineri as she fell into a fit of coughing.

"Green for the forest dragon and the Evenmeres." Igare stared deep into Cyran's eyes. "Gray for the stones of Nevergrace. Will you, Cyran Orendain, uphold all the duties of the dragonguard?"

"I will."

The guard members armored Cyran's arms and hands. When they finished, they settled a helm over his head and closed its visor.

"Then from this moment forth, you are one of the legion," the king said. "One of the chosen few. A protector of the dragon and the mage and the throne. A protector of Belvenguard itself. When you walk and ride and fly, it will be for your kingdom."

Paltere stepped forward, holding a wooden chest. Two of the guard pressed Cyran down and forced him to kneel on the stones. Single sword hilts stuck out from both ends of the box Paltere carried.

"Take up the swords of the guard and leave the squire behind," Paltere said.

Cyran reached out and grasped each hilt. He drew them from the box in one fluid motion. Two dragonsteel blades slid outward with a whisper of steel on wood. One glowed red from the scales of a rose dragon, the other gold in the hue of a sun dragon. The box collapsed on itself.

"Bathed in ice and tempered in the blood of dragons, it has been done." Igare's words boomed inside the chamber. "Arise, *dragonknight*! First of the outpost. One of the rare of Belvenguard and the five kingdoms. For you are now Sir Cyran, dragonknight of Nevergrace."

Cyran raised the two swords and pressed the back of one of his gauntleted fists against his forehead, angling the blade downward. He held his other palm against his belt, blade up, and both blades overlapped and created a halo of red and gold. Two of the guard lifted something longer than a dragon's head from the center of the forge area between the smiths. They carried it forward. A dragonlance. It glowed with a greenish hue. The guard held the weapon by its shaft and offered the handle to Cyran. Paltere slipped sheaths over the swords Cyran held and took the blades from him. Others of the guard approached carrying a massive shield.

"*Mörenth toi boménth bi droth su llith.* Till the end of days we soar," the king and those of the guard all chanted. "*Mörenth toi boménth bi nomth su praëm.* Till the end of nights we reign. *Röith moirten íli. Ílith ëmdrien tiu gládthe.* You honor me. My soul sees yours."

Cyran grasped the shield and the hilt of the lance, and everyone in the chamber broke into deafening applause. He peered through his visor at those watching. Menoria wore a determined look as she eyed him. Brelle and Laren grinned like fools. Dage scowled. Emellefer was entranced. If only Tamar had survived to see this day, what all his sacrifices and help had allowed Cyran to become.

And Jaslin, who toyed with a crystal shard in her hand, stared directly through Cyran's visor, a look of awe and wonder and worry and doubt all swirling in her eyes.

~

Thank You! And for the good of the realm, Please Read!

Through Blood and Dragons and *The Forged and The Fallen* series have been brewing in my thoughts and dreams for decades. It is the epic fantasy I've always wanted to create but which took life and blood and tears and lack of sleep to turn into reality. For years, I couldn't tempt myself to tread the same waters as such legendary fantasy writers, not without some spin or idea to add to the traditional fantasies I love most.

Now, with all that I am, I want to thank you, reader, for taking a chance on an unknown. For taking the time and risking your imagination on *Through Blood and Dragons.* Without readers, books and most stories would be lost, and without your support, I could not continue to write and dream.

Please, if you enjoyed *Through Blood and Dragons,* consider rating or quickly reviewing it on **AMAZON**. Every single review is important and aids me in practicing my art and standing out among millions of other books by encouraging other readers to take a chance while also showing Amazon the book is worth promoting. A review is the single most powerful thing a reader can do for an author—if not for Cimeren, Cyran and his friends, and the unfolding story I've only just begun (although I've drafted and outlined so much more). Reviews make all the difference in the digital book world where each year hundreds of thousands of authors spar for your attention and a place in your heart.

Creating this world and its characters and connecting with readers through story is an incredible feeling and the reason why I write. As weird as it may sound—I want to get out of bed each day to continue this dream, and I would be honored if you could help guide me along the path of honing my craft and making this dream come true.

My vow and oath to you, reader, is that I will always continue to treat my skills like a blade and continue to sharpen them, and I will not stop looking for stories to bring into our world.

Röith moirten íli. Ílith Ëmdrien tiu gládthe. You honor me. My soul sees yours.

. . .

A fan of all those who still dare to read and tread the worlds of imagination,

Ryan

R.M. Schultz

Review and/or Rate Here: ***Through Blood and Dragons***

RECEIVE A FREE THE FORGED AND THE FALLEN PREQUEL!

Receive a free *The Forged and The Fallen* prequel novella by joining the Sky Sea Council!

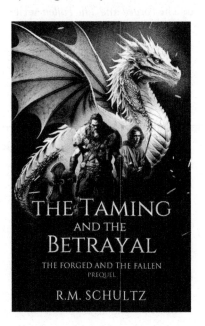

Forged in blood. Fallen in death

The shining city of Cimerenden has reigned over the continent for thousands of years. But one man envisions a future where the dragon is tamed and used for war.

In the Valley of the Smoke Breathers, a spark ignites. The Dragon Wars arise, and Cimerenden is poised to fall.

Dragons swarm the skies.

The Dragon Queen rides.

The shining city burns.

The Taming and The Betrayal is a prequel novella set hundreds of years before the events in *Through Blood and Dragons*—book one in *The Forged and The Fallen* series.

Grab your FREE novella here!

www.rmschultzauthor.com

(Or type the info above into your phone or browser as the Kindle sometimes has its quirks. Or scan the QR code below.)

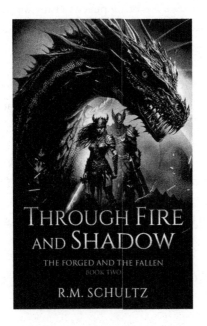

THROUGH FIRE AND SHADOW

THE FORGED AND THE FALLEN
BOOK TWO

R.M. SCHULTZ

Kingdoms burn. Heroes soar.

At the decimated outpost of Nevergrace, Cyran Orendain and his companions stand watch. They search for the Dragon

Queen's remains while awaiting the full onslaught of Murgare's retaliation. But some of their own turn against them, and a village is ravaged by whatever lurks in the woods.

With the young lady of the Never by her side, Cyran's sister Jaslin arrives at the king's city of Galvenstone to answer a summons. She will find the answers to the queen's murder and the darkness lurking beneath the streets, no matter what—or who—stands in her way.

Meanwhile, Pravon the dragon thief follows the unpredictable dragon assassin across the lands of Cimeren, hunting down emissaries who seek to bring peace to the kingdoms. For only one path can stop the coming war, and they will ensure this path is never found.

Only those at Nevergrace sense the coming dangers—that which stalks the far side of the Lake on Fire and that which prowls within the forest.

The growing shadows will consume all of the kingdoms and cover the lands in blood and dragon fire.

The second book in *The Forged and The Fallen* series is now available for pre-order.

CLICK HERE to continue the story and reserve your copy at the lowest price it will ever be!

Pre-ordering helps solidify a series by showing an author how much demand there is. It also allows an author adequate time to write to the best of their ability.

ACKNOWLEDGMENTS

I wish to thank the following people for all their help and sacrifices in turning this story into a book.

To Matt Schultz for reading and editing the first sorry version of every book I write and making the story shine.

To Jason Weersma for cheering me on from the beginning.

To Laura Josephsen for the most detailed questions and concerns I'd ever consider.

To each and every reader in the Sky Sea Council and the Small Council. Without your support and insight and reviews, I couldn't have come this far.

GLOSSARY

Cimeren (SIM-er-en): The largest continent consisting of the five major kingdoms.

The Elder Tongue

Luënor (lu-EH-nor): An ethereal weapon summoned from the soul.

Mëris (MEH-ris): A dragonmage—one of those who can walk in the dragon realm and form a bond with a dragon.

Neblír (neb-LEER): The dragon realm.

Omercón (oh-mer-CONE): A hand-to-hand combat maneuver opposite of a parry—to meet the force of a blow—the *omercón* is to follow the force.

Sïosaires (sy-O-sair-es): The title bestowed upon a dragon or human who has shared a bond with the other species but the other has died, severing that bond.

Names

Aneen (a-NEEN): Female dragon thief in Pravon's party.

Brelle (brel): Female dragonsquire companion of Cyran's.

Cartaya (car-TY-yah): A conjuror who wields bone and earth magic. A member of King Igare's council.

Cyran (KY-ran): Young male point-of-view character from Nevergrace.

Dage (dayj): Hulking dragonsquire companion of Cyran's.

Eidelmere (EE-del-meer): Sir Kayom's forest dragon.

Emellefer (em-EL-lah-fer): Young serving lady of Nevergrace.

Garmeen (gar-MEEN): Eldest of and the leader of the dragonsquires of Nevergrace.

Igare (EYE-gair): King of Belvenguard. Resides primarily in the Summerswept Keep of Castle Dashtok in the capital city of Galvenstone.

Ineri (in-AIR-ee): Female dragonarcher of Belvenguard. Sickly.

Jaslin (JAS-lin): Cyran's younger sister.

Kayom (KAY-ohm): Genturion of the dragonguard at Nevergrace.

Kridmore (KRID-more): Dragon thief companion of Pravon's.

Laren (LAH-ren): Young male dragonsquire companion of Cyran's.

Glossary

Lisain (lis-AYN): A clergyman of the nine gods. A member of King Igare's council.

Menoria (men-OR-ee-ah): The young lady of Nevergrace.

Nyren (NY-ren): A faction of scholars and healers trained to recall everything they have read or learned.

Paltere (pal-TEER): One of the very few dragonknights of Belvenguard.

Pravon (PRAY-vohn): Dragon thief point-of-view character.

Quarren (QUAR-ren): Dragonmage for Vladden.

Riscott (ris-cott): King Igare's orator. A member of the king's council.

Restebarge (REST-ah-barj): The Murgare king.

Shadowmar (SHA-doh-mar): Sirra's shadow dragon.

Sirra (SEER-ah): Female dragonknight from Murgare. The Dragon Queen.

Tamar (tah-MAR): Cyran's brother.

Tiros (TY-rohs): King Igare's nyren. A member of the king's council.

Vladden (VLAD-den): Dragonguard of Murgare.

Vyk (vike): Male dragonarcher from Belvenguard.

Yenthor (YEN-thor): Male dragonarcher from Murgare.

Ymar (YA-mar): The master-at-arms and dragonsquire trainer at Nevergrace.

Zaldica (ZAL-dih-kah): Female dragonarcher from Murgare.

World of Cimeren

Belvenguard (BEL-ven-gard): The largest of the southern kingdoms. King Igare rules over Belvenguard.

Darynbroad (DAHR-in-broad): The small northern kingdom of the dwarves.

Dashtok (DASH-tock): King Igare's castle in the city of Galvenstone.

Evenmeres (EE-ven-meers): A massive forest the size of a kingdom that, along with the Lake on Fire, divides Cimeren into northern and southern halves.

Galvenstone (GAL-ven-stone): The capital city of Belvenguard wherein lies Castle Dashtok and the Summerswept Keep.

Lake on Fire: A lake the size of a kingdom that, along with the Evemeres, divides Cimeren into northern and southern halves. The lake was termed the Lake of Glass in the past age.

Marshlands: A borderlands between the Lake on Fire and the Evenmeres.

Murgare (MOOR-gair): A sprawling kingdom that makes up almost all of the north.

Nevergrace (NEH-ver-grace): Also known as 'the Never.' A castle and outpost that lies along the northeastern margins of Belvenguard and against the Evenmeres's border. Cyran's home.

Northsheeren (north-SHEER-en): The primary castle of Murgare and where Murgare's king typically resides.

Rorenlands (ROAR-en-lands): A kingdom in the far south.

Summerswept Keep: The keep associated with Castle Dashtok in the city of Galvenstone. Where King Igare typically resides.

Valley of the Smoke Breathers: An icy wasteland in the far north where the brotherhood of the Smoke Breathers began and where they tamed the first dragon.

Weltermores (WELT-er-mores): A small kingdom in the south that lies to the east of Belvenguard.

Terms

Dragonarcher: A crossbowman or woman who mans a mounted crossbow on a dragon's quarterdeck or in its turret.

Dragonguard: The armed and armored warrior who is seated just behind a dragon's head and wields a dragonlance and shield. Their primary purpose is to offer commands to the crew on the dragon and to defend their dragonmage.

Dragonmage: One of the *mëris* who rides behind a dragonguard. Their soul is twined with their dragon's, and they guide and navigate the dragon.

Dragonknight: One of the rare few of the *mëris* who is not crippled by the dragon realm and can act as both dragonmage and dragonguard.

Dragonsquire: A squire to a member of the dragonguard.

Dragonsteel: Steel forged with the scales of any type of dragon. Such steel has an array of colors and properties based on the types of scales used.

Genturion: The commander of the dragonguard at each city and outpost.

Quarterdeck: A wooden platform strapped to a dragon's back by cinches and harnesses. The quarterdeck can carry one or more mounted and heavy crossbows for use by a dragonarcher.

Turret: A platform hanging below a dragon's belly and legs that houses a mounted and heavy crossbow for use by a dragonarcher.

ABOUT THE AUTHOR

After reading Tolkien, R.M. Schultz wrote his first 100,000-word fantasy novel as a freshman in high school. When he's not saving animals, he has continued writing across genres for over two decades but always includes fantasy elements. R.M. Schultz founded and heads the North Seattle Science Fiction and Fantasy Writers' Group and has published over a dozen novels.

Someday, he hopes to be knighted by George R.R. Martin.

www.rmschultzauthor.com

ISBN-13: 9798397889940

Published by Sky Sea and Sword Publishing

www.rmschultzauthor.com

Printed in Great Britain
by Amazon

24757381R00301